MW00491980

THE BOWIE BRIDE

BOOK TWO OF THE MACKINTOSHES AND MCLARENS

SUZAN TISDALE

TARGE & THISTLE, INC.

Cover art by: Wicked Smart Designs

Copyright 2017 by Suzan Tisdale

All rights reserved. No part of this publication may be reproduced, distributed, or transmitted in any form or by any means, including photocopying, recording, or other electronic or mechanical methods, without the prior written permission of the author and publisher, except in the case of brief quotations embodied in critical reviews and certain other noncommercial uses permitted by copyright law.

This is a work of fiction. Any resemblence to persons alive or dead, events, or locales is completely coincidental.

ISBN: 9781943244225

ALSO BY SUZAN TISDALE

The Clan MacDougall Series

Laiden's Daughter

Findley's Lass

Wee William's Woman

McKenna's Honor

The Clan Graham Series

Rowan's Lady

Frederick's Queen

The Mackintoshes and McLarens Series

Ian's Rose

The Bowie Bride

Rodrick the Bold

Brogan's Promise

The Clan McDunnah Series

A Murmur of Providence

A Whisper of Fate

A Breath of Promise

For Barb Batlan-Massabrook, for your unfaltering belief in indie authors, your never-ending support, and for simply being one hell of a great lady! Also, thank you for helping with the pretty, yet difficult, Gaelic.

For Anne Alba. I love you more.

For the SSA: You know who you are. Thanks for helping pick out names for characters, and for your love and encouragement.

For Virgina Smith and Sheryl Koffman: I am YOUR biggest fan.

ACKNOWLEDGMENTS

There are a few people I need to acknowledge for their never-ending encouragement and support.

Lynda Cox, and the other readers who provided pictures and information, I thank you for helping with the bandogge!

Kathryn Le Veque & Tanya Anne Crosby, I thank you for being my inner circle.

GP Ching, Tara Cromer, and Laurie Larsen: I'm glad you're my tribe.

PROLOGUE

*A*lec Bowie has decided to marry.

'Twas all the idiot Dougall's idea. 'Marry someone from Ian Mackintosh's clan," he said. "'Twould unite us in peace," he said.

If I did no' ken any better, I'd swear Alec was no' a true Bowie. Peace. 'Tis all he talks about. 'Tis what he be speakin' of today.

"Lay down yer weapons and pick up the plow," *he tells us. Standin' atop the wall, lookin' down at us as if we were the idiots.* "Let us become a prosperous clan through farmin', through weavin' and whisky makin'. Let us leave the old ways behind. Let us leave a legacy to our children that does no' include reivin', stealin', or killin'. Let us be more than we are. Let us become a clan that people do no' fear because we might take their purses or stab them in the back—but fear us as warriors, as a fightin' force to be reckoned with. But only in times of war. Let them ken us as allies, no' thieves.

"I realize peace is no' as excitin' as warrin' or reivin'. But excitement can be found in the simple knowledge that ye do no' have to be lookin' over yer shoulder fer people seekin' revenge. There can be excitement in layin' down yer head at night, knowin' ye put in an *honest* day's work. In knowin' ye're buildin' somethin' bigger, somethin' better than any of us has ever known before. In knowin' ye be leavin' yer children a better life."

Peace. Bah! The Bowies ken nothing of peace, and why should we? Have we no' survived for more than a century as we are? I see how the men, no' all, but most, look up to him. They believe all that he says. They believe peace be a better road than the life we've been livin'.

What fools they are! I expected more from Alec than this. How can he allow Dougall to lead him down this treacherous path?

To hell with peace, I say. To hell with it.

Chances are that no one in their right minds will agree to a marriage betwixt our clans. I can only hope that the people of the Mackintosh and McLaren clan will see the folly of this offer and refuse it.

Alec can no' marry. I have plans for him.

I am no' worried though. If there be a woman amongst Ian Mackintosh's clan foolish enough to marry Alec, she will no' live long enough to regret her decision. I'll see to it.

I'll kill Alec's bride.

CHAPTER 1

*P*eace was tenuous at best.

Alec Bowie was loathe to admit it. Of course, he was loathe to admit many things of late.

Two months had passed since his brother had been killed. It had been a painful, horrible death. Had Ian Mackintosh's piercing blade not been enough for Rutger, then the horse that trampled him into the earth had finished the job. Even though his brother had been mad with greed for gold and power, Alec still missed him. Besides their endless lines of cousins, Rutger was the last living kin he had.

Now he was dead. Laid to rest in the family plot without much ceremony, near the loch not far from the Bowie keep. In death, as it had been in life, Rutger was placed between his parents. While their parents loved their sons without question, they often used them as weapons against the other. Parents and son were probably all three burning in hell. Alec couldn't be certain, of course.

He had begged his brother on numerous occasions to take the opportunity to bring peace to their clan. To change the tide and bring the outside world in. But Rutger refused.

Too entrenched in the past, too afraid to take chances, too greedy and obstinate, he had left it up to Alec to give the clan what they needed most: a future.

A far different future.

A life without thieving, without terrorizing neighboring clans, a life without crime or prices on their heads.

And now he was their chief.

He'd never held any designs on the chiefdom of any clan, let alone this rag-tag one filled with criminals, horse thieves, and ne'er-do-wells. How the bloody hell was he supposed to turn these people into farmers? Weavers? Whisky-makers?

Mayhap 'twas folly. Mayhap 'twould all be for naught. But he had to — at the very least — *try*.

And that was what he was doing this day. *Trying.*

Trying to find a wife while trying not to wring his cousin Dougall's neck.

The man was mad. Daft. Delusional.

But he had a point. One more thing Alec was loathe to admit.

In order to bring ever-lasting peace to his clan, alliances must be made, friendships nurtured and cultivated, much like the seeds of barley he had planted a sennight after his brother's death.

So here he sat in Ian Mackintosh's tent, looking out at the McLaren and Mackintosh people. The tent, while quite large, was filled to bursting with curious people.

His fingers rested gingerly on a dirk he had hidden at his waist. The blood of generations of murderous men and thieves ran through his veins. 'Twas hard to let one's guard down when one was used to an entirely different way of interacting with people.

To his left were his men, Dougall and Kyth Bowie. Tall, strong men, with the same dark hair and eyes as he. Ruthless they were, when the need arose.

To his right sat Ian Mackintosh, laird and chief of clan McLaren. Ian was one of those handsome men, with blonde hair and blue eyes and enough self-confidence for fifty men, that women swooned over. He admired Ian a great deal. Not only did he possess an inordinate sense of honor, of justice, of right versus wrong; he was one of the few people Alec could call *friend*. Hell, he was the only person outside his clan he could refer to as such.

Next to Ian sat his brothers, Brogan and Frederick Mackintosh. Ginger-haired men whose skills on the battlefield were legendary. And for good reason. Either of them could kill a man with their bare hands, or so their enemies claimed. At the far end of the table sat a man he'd met just this morning, but had heard much about. Roderick the Bold. Roderick was neither a McLaren nor a Mackintosh by blood, but he considered himself a member of their clan all the same. Alec was as yet uncertain what to make of the odd fellow, but decided 'twould be best to watch his back whenever the man was near.

The long table faced out toward the crowd. He had the odd sensation that left him feeling as though he were some mysterious creature on display. He supposed, mayhap, 'twas because people were not used to seeing a Bowie unless he was trying to steal their purse or cattle, raid their lands, or behave in some other immoral manner.

Ian leaned in and whispered, "Are ye *certain* ye wish to do this?" for what seemed the hundredth time.

Alec gave a curt nod, which belied what he was truly thinking. *Bloody hell, no! I do no' wish to do this, but I must.*

With a sigh of resignation, Ian said, "Verra well, let us get started. But we must hurry, I do no' wish to leave Rose fer long."

Rose Mackintosh. Alec liked that woman verra much. Strong, blunt, and quite pretty. She was a week past when she should have delivered Ian's babe into the world.

Babes and wives. They would be the downfall of human civilization. Eventually.

While Ian fawned all over his lovely wife, worried and fretted over the life of their babe, Alec felt confident that he would never suffer such indignities. He was not here to find a love match. Nay, he simply needed to marry a McLaren lass in order to ensure peace betwixt their clans. That was why he was so bloody angry with Dougall. This had all been his idea — the bastard.

But again, Alec had to admit there was wisdom in the plan. No matter how ugly or deplorable the idea of marriage was to Alec

Bowie, he had to find a wife. Hopefully, she'd be a quiet, biddable lass, who would understand the importance of peace.

She must also understand, unequivocally, that he had no wish, need, or desire for a *happy* home life. Nay, theirs was a matter of business not a matter of the heart, and that was how he intended for it to remain for all the rest of his days.

That was if he could find someone brave enough amongst this crowd. With his luck — and he knew 'twas God-awful luck he possessed — he'd be married off to some mousey wench with missing teeth and moles scattered across her face. He shuddered at the thought. But again, he was not here to find a love match. Just a woman willing to wed him, bed him until she got with child, then leave him the bloody hell alone.

Outside, 'twas a clear, bright afternoon. A stark contrast to how Alec was feeling to his very core: doomed. They might as well have been taking him to the gallows, such was his inevitable fate. For marriage was like that; you lost your freedom and your mind. That was if you weren't careful and diligent.

Ian stood then, raising his hands to hush the murmurs of the crowd. When silence fell, he spoke. "I have called ye here today to discuss the matter of peace betwixt our clan and the Bowies."

Riotous laughter broke out amongst Ian's people. It set Alec's nerves on edge. This was not going to go well, not well at all. More images of a mole-covered wench flashed before his eyes. With his awful luck, she'd most likely be missing a limb as well.

A loud voice rang out above the laughter. "What do the Bowies ken of peace?"

Another cried, "Ye can no' trust a Bowie as far as ye can pick one up!"

"Aye! All they ken is stealin' and reivin'."

Ian raised his hands once again and called for quiet. "I ken we be unused to the idea of a peaceful Clan Bowie," he began. "But they have a new laird. A laird who risked his own life to save Rose's."

That point hit home. Heads nodded as people murmured in agreement. 'Twas Alec's only saving grace, that; saving Rose Mackintosh's life. Rescuing her and bringing her back to her people. Of course, he couldn't have done that without help from the lass named Leona.

Upon thinking of her, he searched the crowd surreptitiously, but saw no sign of her. Earlier that morn he had asked Ian how the lass faired. But they'd been interrupted and Ian had not been able to answer.

No matter. The lass was far too intelligent, far too beautiful, to settle on the likes of him.

Ian speaking to his people pulled Alec back to the here and now. "I want peace with the Bowies as much as they want it with us. I have spent time gettin' to know Alec Bowie and a few of his men." He cast a glance at Dougall and Kyth before turning back to the crowd. "I find them to be honest and genuine in their pursuits."

More murmurs from the crowd as they all stared at the three Bowies with curious and doubtful eyes.

"After a long mornin' of discussin' just how this peace can be everlastin' and ensured, we have come to the conclusion that a marriage is the best approach."

Stunned and uncertain silence filled the air. 'Twas as if the world froze in that instant.

Ian took a breath before going on. "This marriage would need to be betwixt Alec Bowie and a lass with McLaren blood." He let the words sink into the minds of his people for a moment. "The only true lass who qualifies is me niece, Ada Mackintosh. But since she be only a year old, that will no' work. So," he took another deep breath and rested his palms on the table, "we will be willin' to accept *any* lass from our clan, no matter her bloodline. Any lass of marriageable age."

The deafening silence stretched on and on.

Alec looked out at the crowd of slack-jawed, stunned individuals. Their expressions said it all: not only was the Bowie mad, but their laird was as well.

Before Ian could speak again, someone in the far back of the tent stood up.

"I will do it."

He could not see her face clearly, for she was in shadow. But he felt quite certain he recognized her soft, sweet voice.

"I will marry the Bowie."

Bloody hell, 'twas Leona Macdowall.

"FER THE SAKE OF CHRIST, LEONA! SIT DOWN!" INGERAME MACDOWALL yanked hard on his daughter's arm, pulling her back onto the wood bench.

A loud, collective gasp broke through the crowd after she volunteered to marry the Bowie. Yanking her arm from her father's grasp, she stood again and stepped away from him. This time, her voice was louder, more resolute. "I said I will marry the Bowie."

One moment they were gasping in stunned surprise, the next, they were all laughing at her. Not a one of them made any attempt to cover their feelings on the matter. Used to the taunts and ridicule, she ignored them. Or at least tried to.

"Bah!" A man's voice laughed loudly. "Leona Odd-Eyes, marryin' the Bowie!"

"'Tis no less than he deserves!" came another voice.

"Or she!"

Doing her best to ignore them, she scampered away from her father before he could pull her back again. Out of the shadows and into the light, she looked directly at Alec Bowie.

'Twas an odd expression his face held. She couldn't tell if he was shocked or horrified. 'Twas probably a blend of each.

Ingerame shot to his feet. "Fer the sake of Christ, Leona!"

Her father was always taking the lord's name in vane, so she ignored him.

"No one wants to marry ye!" he said as he made his way toward her.

The crowd laughed at his declaration.

"No one with a right mind, anyway!" someone nasty replied.

"Mayhap that's why she be volunteerin', because we all ken the Bowies ain't in their right minds!"

More guffaws at her expense. It hurt, oh it truly did. No matter how hard she tried to ignore them, their words always stung like a slap to her face.

Her father was pulling on her arm again, cursing at her, as was his way. "Yer mum should have let me drown ye when ye were a bairn!"

From the dais, Ian's voice boomed out over the crowd. "That is enough!"

The moment Ingerame began making his way toward his daughter, Dougall and Kyth started making their way through the crowd. Alec was on his feet, his insides a blend of relief and astonishment, unable to utter even something incoherent.

Unsheathing their swords, Dougall and Kyth pressed the tips of the cool blades against Ingerame's neck. "We'll thank ye kindly to remove yer hands from our laird's betrothed." Dougall said with a most menacing tone. It made Leona's knees knock.

Ingerame swallowed twice in an attempt to dislodge the knot of fear from his throat. "Ye can no' be serious?" he stammered. "Yer laird does no' want *her*."

Her. He'd said the word with such distaste, he made it sound as if she were a pox-riddled, diseased whore. That was his way, when it came to Leona. He despised her. Hated her. Passionately.

"Aye, we are." Dougall glowered at the man intently.

"But she be bedeviled," Ingerame argued, as if it were both true and would bring clarity to the situation. "Just look at her eyes."

Dougall had seen her eyes before. Didn't give a rat's arse about them. He'd liked this young lass from the moment he first met her. She'd taken a hellish beating from Rutger Bowie not long ago. He'd witnessed it with his own eyes. 'Twas her sense of loyalty to her mistress, Rose Mackintosh, that impressed him most of all. No matter what Rutger said or did to her, she refused to divulge where Rose was or who had her. You had to admire a woman like that.

Besides, she'd volunteered and Alec would undoubtedly accept her. So as far as he was concerned, 'twas as good as if the marriage contract had already been signed and the ink dried.

"I'll no' tell ye again," Dougall warned. "Take yer hands off our laird's betrothed."

"Ingerame," Ian called to him. "I think ye best listen."

Stupefied, Ingerame let go of his daughter's arm. Leona let loose the breath she'd been holding. There'd a bruise on her arm by morning but she'd not let him see her discomfort.

Alec finally managed to find his voice. "Lass," he said as he stepped around the table. "I would like to speak to ye. *Privately.*"

Leona swallowed hard, willed her nerves to settle, and gave a curt nod of agreement. With great tenderness, he took her by the elbow and led her out of the tent.

Ingerame was fit to be tied. "Ian, ye can no' allow this!"

"I would think ye'd be glad to be rid of her, Ingerame." Ian's words dripped with sarcasm that barely hid his anger.

ALEC LED HER AWAY FROM THE TENT, TOWARD THE ARMORY. HIS MIND was beset with questions, most of them concerning the lass's mental state. No one in their right mind would marry a Bowie.

Past the armory, near the tall, massive wall, he came to a stop. He had to admit, she was a pretty woman. He knew what lay under that god-awful apron she wore to cover her ample bosom. Oh, he hadn't seen them free and bouncing over his head, but he knew they were there. Had seen just a hint of their majesty when she'd dressed like a common bar wench in order to help affect Rose's escape less than two months ago.

Gold hair, the color of honey, shone brilliantly in the afternoon sunlight. Her skin he knew to be softly kissed by the sun, even though it was currently a dark crimson. He was much relieved to see she had healed from the beating she had endured at the hands of his brother.

"Lass," he began. The scratchiness of his voice surprised him. Odd that. "Lass, are ye sure ye want to do this? To marry *me*? After all me brother did to ye?" Although it hadn't been Alec who had beaten her so badly, he still felt a good measure of guilt for what had been done to her.

She thought it a very odd question considering she was the one labeled witch, daughter of the devil, or the devil's whore, depending of course, on who you asked. "Aye," she murmured. "I ken ye be nothin' like yer brother."

If she could lay aside the past, then he should try to do the same. He swallowed once, then again. "Why?"

Oh, she imagined it could take a fortnight to answer that question. *Why? Because I do no' want to spend the rest of me life under me father's thumb. Because I do no' want to spend the rest of me life alone, never married, never touched. Besides, I like how warm yer hand feels right now, holdin' me elbow. And ye're no' runnin' away in disgust or fear. That has to mean somethin'.*

Instead, she answered with the only believable reason she could think of. "We both want the same things, m'laird. Peace."

Alec doubted that was her sole reason for volunteering.

"M'laird? If ye were no' truly serious about findin' a wife here, I will no' hold it against ye. And if ye do no' want me, I will understand." Pain flashed behind those odd eyes of hers before she stared at her feet.

She was giving him an out. 'Twas as plain as the delightful freckles on her slender nose. Inexplicably, his stomach turned to knots. He didn't like what he saw in her eyes in that brief moment before she looked away. He also did not like how it made him feel when he saw it.

All in all, she was a good choice. They were not complete strangers and he admired the determination and quiet strength he had seen in her months ago. And her skin was free of moles; she had all of her teeth and limbs.

"I was indeed quite serious about findin' a wife," he said. With his fingertips, he gently lifted her chin so he could look into her eyes. Aye, they were odd. One was a deep, olive green. The other was the palest blue. The color of ice when it forms on the loch in winter.

"Me eyes," she whispered after he had stared for such a long while. "They unsettle ye."

Cocking his head to one side, he said, "Nay, they do no' unsettle me. They intrigue me."

From her bewildered expression, she either didn't believe him or thought him completely insane. He couldn't tell.

Suddenly, he felt the overwhelming urge to kiss her. Odd that, for he was rarely beset by such urges. At least not toward innocent maidens. But put a bar wench or whore in his path? 'Twas an all together different story then.

Instead of kissing her and terrifying her in the process, he felt it best to list all of his bad qualities. If she were going to be his wife, 'twas best they start off as honestly as possible. Besides, once she knew what a cad and scoundrel he was, she would change her mind.

"I be no' an easy man to live with," he said. "I am verra set in me ways. I work verra hard and expect others to work the same. I prefer late nights to early morns. I like order in my life and despise chaos. I drink far too much than is probably necessary or wise." If that didn't get her to change her mind, what he was about to say next surely would. A lass as pretty as she deserved far better than what he could offer. "I never wanted to be chief, but I accept that responsibility wholly and with great respect. This marriage, if ye agree to it, will never be a love match. 'Tis simply the best way I ken how to obtain peace fer me clan."

She was quiet for the longest time. Her eyes searched his, looking for, he supposed, any sign of deceit or treachery. "Are ye tryin' to talk me out of marryin' ye?"

He could be brutally honest or skirt the truth. He chose the latter. "I merely be tryin' to warn ye what ye would be gettin' yerself in fer, with me as a husband."

12

Leona could certainly appreciate his straightforwardness. Mayhap she too, should be just as honest.

"I prefer morns over late nights, m'laird. I am used to solitude, so I do no' expect ye to entertain me all the day long. I sometimes get weepy when I've gone too long without sleep, but I will try to manage that out of respect fer ye. I prefer cider over strong drink but I'll nay keep ye from enjoyin' somethin' stronger." She took in a deep, steadying breath.

Her father abhorred the sight of her most days. People, people she didn't even know, believed the lies he told. Mayhap she should let Alec know about that before he agreed.

"Me father is convinced I be a witch, because of me eyes, ye ken. A witch or the devil's spawn, he be never really sure. But I swear to ye, I be neither."

My, but those brown eyes of his were captivating. Before she could lose herself in them, she mustered the courage to go on. "I too, like order. And I am no' afraid of hard work. As fer a love match betwixt us? I do no' expect that of ye either. I've gone the whole of my life without bein' loved, so I be accustomed to such. I will be happy to have a marriage with mutual respect, mayhap even friendship. I'll nay ask ye fer more."

'Twas as honest as she could be. Not since her mother died had she felt loved, save for the friendship she had with Rose Mackintosh. The whole of her life had been a cold, desolate plane of existence. She knew 'twas folly to ever expect anything more than that. However, if she and Alec did marry and she were blessed with children? Aye, that cold, isolated life would be no more.

Never loved? 'Twas it an exaggeration or the cold hard truth?

He'd been loved and adored by both his parents. 'Twas each other they despised. But their children? They loved their children without condition.

Though he had only met Ingerame Macdowall once before today,

Alec knew he was a callous, hard man, and a fool. He treated his only child abhorrently.

A warm sensation, wholly odd in its entirety, spread from his stomach to his chest. He was not a man who sported tender feelings. Those had been drilled out of him by his father over many years. *Never trust a woman. They may be soft and pretty, but they all lie,* he had told Alec more times than he could count.

'Tis nothing more than compassion. It showed he had a heart in that he did care for others, nothing more. He cared for his people, therefore it would make sense that he could care for this woman.

Clearing his throat, he gave the lass a warm smile. "We be in agreement then, aye? We shall go into this marriage fully aware of what the other expects."

She gave a slow nod of affirmation. "Aye m'laird," she said.

"I shall have Ian draw up the marriage contract," He informed her, with an inclination of his head.

"Wait!" she said before he had a chance to leave.

With a knitted brow, he paused.

"I would like a contract betwixt the two of us. Just ye and me." Where she found the courage to voice her desire for such a thing, she did not know. She could only hope he would not take offense.

"What kind of contract?" he asked, most curious.

Clearing her throat, she lifted her chin. "Promises, betwixt ye and me," she stammered out.

"What kind of promises?"

Swallowing again, she wiped her sweaty palms on her apron. "I would like yer promise that ye'll never beat me."

The idea appalled him to his marrow. "I would never—"

She went on before he could finish. "And yer promise that I can have as many bairns as I want."

Flummoxed, he tried to respond to that request but she kept going.

"And if ye ever tire of me, ye'll no' just toss me out. Ye'll take me to a convent."

"A convent?" The idea appalled him just as much as the idea of beating her.

"And ye'll never lock me away anywhere dark. And if ye take a mistress, ye'll no' flaunt her in front of me. Ye shall be discreet about it."

He could bear no more. Raising a palm, he was able to stop her long list of demands. "Lass!" He didn't mean for his tone to sound so sharp. She took a timid step back. "Lass," he started again in a softer tone. "Draw up whatever contract ye wish. I will gladly sign it, if it means to set yer heart and worries at ease."

Relief fell over her. He could see it in the sparkle of her eyes and the way her shoulders relaxed.

"Thank ye, m'laird," she said with a curtsey.

"We'll be married soon. I think 'twill be good fer ye to call me Alec."

"Very well, Alec. If ye have any promises ye'd like me to make ye, please, let me ken."

He could think of many things he'd like from her, but none of them appropriate to put to voice at the moment.

"I have no dowry, m'laird - Alec," she explained. "I fear I'd be comin' into this marriage with no' more than the clothes on me back."

His thoughts immediately turned lascivious. If he had his way, there would be little need of clothing most of the time. The thought was unsettling, to think he could have such strong feelings of lust and desire for this young woman – a woman he barely knew. "Do no' fash yourself over it, Leona," he told her. "I care no' of dowries, only peace."

Relieved to hear it, she smiled up at him. 'Twas a warm smile, quite beautiful.

Before he could fall to the urge to kiss those pink lips, Ian found them out. "Leona, me wife needs ye."

She smiled again, a bit brighter. Brighter even than she had smiled at him. Why that irked him, he hadn't a clear idea. 'Twas just a smile. Why should he have such a strong need for her to smile at him that way?

As they stepped away, it suddenly dawned on his addlepated mind that he was going to marry. Leona Macdowall was going to be his wife.

CHAPTER 2

 pon hearing the news of Leona's betrothal to Alec Bowie, Rose immediately sent her husband to fetch the girl. What she did not tell her husband was that her pains had begun early that morn. If she did not get a respite from his hovering — no matter how well intended — she was going to kill him in his sleep. Or, mayhap, 'twas just the birthing pains making her want to put a pillow over his head. Either way, 'twas for his own safety she sent him to find her.

Bedamned if he didn't return in less than a quarter of an hour.

"Ian, would ye mind if I spoke to Leona alone?" she asked, using her sweetest voice, her brightest smile.

"I'd prefer no' to leave yer side, Rose," he said. His smile was a blend of worry and joy, if such a thing were even possible.

"Husband," she said as affectionately as she could, considering the sharp pain twisting in her womb. "Leona does no' have a mother. She is betrothed now, so this is the type of conversation we should have alone. Amongst women."

He paled visibly when he realized what she was saying. He kissed the tip of her nose. "I shall be right outside the door."

Blast it. "Mayhap ye could find me some berries while ye're out?" she asked sweetly. "I have a strong hankerin' fer berries."

"Verra well," he said. "I shall return shortly."

She knew better. For days now, she'd been in collusion with every woman in the clan. They knew that if Ian appeared with anything she might have a 'hankering' for, the food would mysteriously be unavailable and he'd have to go from one woman to the next in search of it. 'Twould take him at least a good hour before he found the berries and returned. 'Twould be a much welcome respite.

Her smile faded as soon as he stepped out the door. "I love him, I truly do, but he hovers like flies over a rotten apple," she blurted out as she bent over, holding her back.

Leona rushed to her side. "When did yer pains start?"

"Early this morn," she replied with a wince.

"Shall I fetch Angrabraid?"

Rose gave a rapid shake of her head. "I want to speak to ye first."

Leona helped her to sit on the edge of the bed and joined her. "I already ken how a man and woman join, Rose. Are ye sure I should no' fetch Angrabraid now?" The last thing Leona wanted was for Rose to give birth before their healer arrived.

Ignoring Leona's concerns, Rose said, "We have plenty of time before the babe arrives. I need to talk to ye first." Taking in a deep, cleansing breath, she went on to say, "There be a difference between joinin' with a man and *joinin'* with a man."

Leona wasn't sure what the difference was, other than the inflection in her tone.

"Are ye sure ye want to marry Alec Bowie?" Rose asked.

"Aye, I am."

Rose ran a hand across her belly as she looked into the embers of the fire. "Why did ye volunteer?"

Just why her motive for volunteering was so important, Leona couldn't understand. "Many reasons, I suppose."

"Are ye worried this is yer last chance at ever havin' a husband?" Rose asked, hitting the mark on her first attempt.

Leona nodded as she fought back tears of guilt. "Do ye think that is wrong of me? Do ye think me desperate?" She certainly felt that way.

"Mayhap no' desperate so much as naive? Marriage can be wonderful when a man and woman care for one another. It can be hell on earth if they do no'."

Leona'd already thought about that. "I like him well enough," she admitted. "And he *is* quite handsome. And he was awfully kind to me when we were helpin' ye escape from his brother."

Those things were all true. Alec had been as much of a gentleman as any man could be. More so even than her own father or his laborers or even her own clansmen. It had been he who carried her out of the cold, dark dungeon that day. She'd been badly beaten, covered in bruises, and as cold as ice. To this day, she marveled at how such a tall, powerful man could be as gentle as he had been.

And not once during the entire ordeal had he or his men made any off-color remarks or jests regarding her eyes. And just a little while ago, he told her he found them *intriguing*. She could only hope he meant it in a good way and not bad.

"He was kind to me as well," Rose admitted. "He certainly does no' behave like the other Bowie men I've kent in me life."

Alec Bowie was unlike any man Leona had ever known. Save fer Ian, Brogan, and Rodrick the Bold. But there was something different about Alec. He was handsome, to be certain. But there was a gentleness to him. She'd witnessed it with her own eyes, and felt it as well, when he carried her across his lap, all the way to Rowan Graham's keep. All the while, he had whispered words of encouragement to her. *Ye'll be right as rain soon enough lass. Me brother be dead, lass. He'll never harm ye again.*

There was little she remembered of those few days, but what she could remember, left her with nothing but warm feelings toward the man.

"I think we will get along well enough," Leona offered.

Rose shifted her weight, trying to gain a more comfortable position on the bed. "What of yer father? What of a dowry?"

The urge to laugh was inescapable. "I do no' care what me father thinks. I am of an age where I can make such a decision. As fer the dowry? There is none, but Alec said he did no' care." They had been discussing that very thing when Ian had come for her.

Another pain shot through Rose's abdomen. This one was much stronger than the last.

"I think I should get Angrabraid now," Leona said as she shot to her feet. She'd never seen a woman give birth before. The thought of being alone with Rose was frightening.

Rose grabbed her arm to stop her. "Aggie has already gone to fetch her. Do no' tell Ian, fer I do no' want him to worry."

Even in pain Rose worried over her husband's feelings. Leona thought it a most beautiful sentiment, to love a man so deeply that you put his feelings above your own pain. But Alec had already warned her that their marriage was nothing more than an agreement for peace betwixt two clans. Lying to her heart, she believed that would be enough. An amicable friendship between he and she would be enough.

"I'll no' tell him, I promise."

~

Very little went on inside his clan that Ian Mackintosh did not know about. Especially when it came to his wife. He knew about the conspiracy betwixt Rose and the clanswomen, had discovered it on the very first day of its inception. Loving his wife the way he did, he could not hold it against her. He knew he hovered and worried too much, but he had come close to losing both of them not long ago. It stood to reason he'd worry.

He also knew her pains had started that morn. He wasn't a simpleton. But if pretending he didn't know brought her at least a small amount of comfort, then he would feign ignorance.

The last thing he wanted for his wife to struggle through *anything*. Least of all with bringing his child into this world. There had been far too many struggles these last months. He'd fall on his own sword before he added to them.

So he pretended he didn't know. Pretended he couldn't see her face contort and twist whenever a pain hit. 'Twas one of the most difficult things he'd ever done.

So when he saw Angrabraid crossing the yard with his sister-by-law, Aggie, in tow, he pretended he hadn't seen them.

Pretended his insides weren't a jumbled knot of worry and dread.

Pretended he could get through the next hours of his life with his sanity still in tact. All because he loved her.

ALEC WAS JUST MAKING HIS WAY ACROSS THE YARD WHEN BROGAN Mackintosh and Rodrick the Bold approached him. Brogan, he liked and admired. But he had only just met Rodrick, a man with cold-as-ice eyes and a countenance to match.

"We would like a wee moment of yer time," Rodrick said, blocking his path. "We want to talk to ye."

Alec studied him closely for a moment. Why the man was glaring at him, he could not rightly say. "By talk, do ye mean where we actually converse? Or the kind of talkin' where ye pierce me heart with yer sword?"

Brogan chuckled and said, "Converse."

Rodrick looked as though he were pondering the latter option.

"Verra well," Alec said as he braced his feet apart and rested his fingertips on his hips. "What would ye like to discuss?"

"Leona," Brogan replied.

Alec should have known.

"She be a right bonny lass," Rodrick said. "With a good heart and carin' spirit."

They'd gain no argument on that from him.

"We just want to make certain ye understand she be quite special to us," Brogan said.

"And we'd no' want to see her hurt. In any fashion. By any man." Rodrick's warning was as sincere as it was clear.

Alec could appreciate their concern. 'Twas not as if the Bowies were known for being kind or generous people. "I can assure ye that when Leona becomes me wife, she shall be well cared fer as well as protected."

"Aye, that, I do no' doubt," Brogan said. "But there are many ways a man can hurt his wife. Besides the obvious."

So 'twas her heart they worried over. He was beginning to learn the Mackintosh men cared for their women in ways he'd never thought to. The poor bastards. He was tempted to explain the danger of worrying over a woman's tender heart, but knew 'twould fall on deaf ears. "I will guard her heart as well," he told them. *But I'll guard me own first.*

"See that ye do," Rodrick warned. "Fer if we learn ye have hurt her in anyway, we'll no' think twice of burnin' yer keep to the ground. With ye still in it."

'Twas not a boast, Alec knew. He wondered if this man had wanted Leona for himself? If he did, 'tis his own fault for not speaking for her sooner.

"Ye have me word," Alec said. With a slight inclination of his head, he left them standing in the yard. If he hadn't seen Dougall watching from up ahead, he might have worried Rodrick would plunge a dirk into his back.

OH, WHY OH WHY DID ROSE INSIST ON LEONA BEING PRESENT FOR THE birth of her first child? There was barely enough room in the little cottage for Rose, Angrabraid and Aggie, let alone Leona.

She considered Rose her only true friend. She was also her only living relative aside from her father. A fact they both had only recently been made aware of. Their mothers had been cousins, which did much to explain why she and Rose looked so much alike.

Because of that, Leona boldly agreed to be there for the momentous occasion. But each time Rose winced in agony, Leona's resolve to remain grew thin.

Eying a bucket warming near the hearth, Leona told the ladies in the room, "I'll fetch more water."

"We have plenty of water," Angrabraid told her as she placed straw on the mattress near Rose's...nether regions.

Flummoxed, embarrassed, wishing for all the world she could flee this cottage, run far away so she wouldn't have to hear her friends cries of agony. "Sheets? Do ye need sheets?"

Angrabraid pinned her in place with a furious glare. "What Rose needs is fer ye to hold her hand and encourage her."

Oh, why oh why had she agreed to do that? Why had she made the promise to *never leave Rose's side* when her pains started? *Because ye're an eejit.*

Shoring up her courage, Leona left the small corner and went to stand beside her friend. *Ye can do this,* she told herself. *Ye have endured much worse. Birthin' babes is the most natural thing in the world. Besides, it could be ye lyin' in this bed a year from now.* That single thought comforted her. A year from now she would be the one cursing her husband to the devil for getting her with child. 'Twould only make sense to watch, observe, and learn.

"Ye be doin' well," Aggie told Rose. "'Twill no' be long, and ye'll be holdin' yer bairn in yer arms."

Leona had come to adore Aggie Mackintosh, Leona's sister-by-law, almost as much as she adored Rose. She had met her for the first time when she arrived at Rowan Graham's keep. It had been Aggie and Rose who had taken care of her those first days. It had been they who fussed over her, tending to her every need, along with Lady Arline, Rowan's wife.

For the whole of her life Leona had lived without a single person to call friend. Now, she could count the three women as such. But Rose? Rose was her dearest and closest friend. There was naught she wouldn't do for her.

Rose and Aggie were as close as sisters, probably more so. They had each survived hell on earth. Leona was certain she did not know everything the two women had gone through. But she knew enough.

Even with the long scar that ran down her face, Aggie was a beautiful woman, inside and out. There was something about her, a quiet inner beauty that made one ignore the scar. She also had a way of making Leona feel quite at ease.

Wanting very much to be as strong and determined as her friends, she decided the best course of action would be to simply mimic whatever Aggie said or did. The woman had two children of her own. Certainly she knew what she was doing.

Sweat dripped off the tip of Rose's nose, soaked through her chemise and the bedding. With each pain, her face contorted and twisted, and at times, she shook from the intensity.

Her friend's suffering was difficult to watch. But Leona was not about to leave her side.

As his wife fought to give birth to their child, Ian paced outside their cottage. Brogan and Frederick each sat on old tree stumps and watched.

Brogan understood his brother's worry and could not hold it against him. Anything could happen. Though he'd lost his wife to the wasting disease before he even had the opportunity to get her with child, he understood Ian's worry.

Frederick understood as well, but the circumstances here were far different than when his wife, Aggie, brought their daughter into the world. Aggie had been poisoned and nearly died. To this day, she could not remember anything about the birth, for she'd been far too ill. But she had survived.

"If Rose be half as strong as me Aggie," Frederick said as he stood up, "then she will be fine. Try no' to fret so, brother."

Ian cast him a wary glance but said nothing. Instead, he continued with his fretful pacing. His only thoughts were of his wife.

'Twas a miracle she'd even gotten with child. Three babes she had lost with her first husband. All before she reached the end of her third month. But somehow, the seed he and she had tried so hard *not* to plant, planted itself and grew.

Now, his sweet wife lay within their cottage, fighting to bring their child into this world.

He loved her beyond reason and she him. Silently he prayed God would not hold any of his sins — and there were many — against his wife or his babe.

If anything happens to me wife...

OH, THE THINGS LEONA LEARNED OVER THE NEXT HOURS!

For instance, she did not know it possible for a woman as tiny and wee as Rose, nor as sweetly dispositioned, to know so many curse words. All of which she either screamed or whispered, depending on the intensity of the birthing pain. *Poor Ian,* she mused. Surely Rose did not truly wish to gut him with his own sword. Or to cut his manly parts off with a rusty dirk.

Nor did she realize just how painful bringing a babe into the world could be. Hence the cursing and swearing.

Nor did she realize a woman's body could open as wide as Rose's did when her babe's head popped through. She hadn't meant to look, but Angrabraid had needed her help, to turn the babe's head around in the right direction. "If the head be facin' up instead of down, he could breathe in the fluid. So we must turn the head," Angrabraid explained.

Neither was she prepared for all the things she saw next. The babe, not fully born yet with only its head sticking out, squalling at the top of its lungs. Or all the pushing, crying, and blood that came afterward.

But all those things paled in comparison to the inordinate sense of awe, utter joy, and longing that came when Angrabraid handed the child to *her* to hold until she could tie off the cord.

'Twas the first time in her life she'd ever held a babe. Och, he was beautiful! Even though he was covered in blood and goo. His little hands balled into fists, his face contorted as he cried and cried and cried.

Damn it all, but she couldn't help but cry along with him.

All too soon for her liking, Aggie wrapped the babe in a swaddling cloth and handed him to his mother.

Her arms felt empty, sadly empty.

But the relief and joy in Rose's eyes, the blissful glee of holding her child for the first time? 'Twas enough to make a grown woman want to cry a puddle of happy tears. And long for a babe of her very own.

FIT TO BE TIED AND UNABLE TO WAIT A MOMENT LONGER, IAN Mackintosh, upon hearing the sound of his babe crying for the first time, burst into the hut. For a brief moment, Leona would have sworn he was going to keel over.

He took one look at his babe before focusing on his wife. Leona watched as he let loose a sigh of relief, his shoulders sagged, and his eyes grew damp. He went to his wife then and knelt beside her.

"I have never been so worried in all me life," he admitted.

Rose smiled up at him as she held her babe close. "Even more terrifyin' than the night I was stolen away?" she asked, only half serious.

He kissed the tip of her nose. "I be no' certain. Mayhap both events were equally terrifyin'."

"Yer wife and bairn be well, m'laird," Angrabraid told him.

With a gentle finger, Ian drew the blanket away from his child's face. Rose smiled up at him. "Ian, I would like ye to meet yer son."

His son.

'Twas a boy.

Aggie took Leona by the arm and led her to a corner of the room so that Rose and Ian could have this moment together.

SUDDENLY, IAN MACKINTOSH WAS BESET WITH AN OVERWHELMING sense of relief, awe, and love, all of which turned his eyes damp. Until this very moment, he hadn't realized how much he wanted it. Ian

Mackintosh, the rake, the breaker of hearts, the womanizer, overcome with such intense feelings. Who would have thought it even possible? He certainly hadn't. Not until he held his son in his arms for the first time.

Of course his days of breaking hearts were over the day he met Rose for the first time. But now? Now he was quite certain his life would never be the same. As he looked down at his wee son, swaddled in a Mackintosh plaid, he knew his life was irrevocably changed.

CHAPTER 3

*L*eona Macdowall had never thought to be married. Therefore, she'd never given any thought to weddings. Oh, perhaps a fleeting thought here and there, whenever she was on one of her longs walks and allowed herself a moment or two of girlish daydreaming. Daydreams in which her eyes were each of the same color. What color never mattered, only that they matched.

And daydreams of a life filled with friends and a family that loved her. A home where she felt safe. Safe from harsh words and harsh hands. A home where she could be herself without worrying others would think her daft, or worse yet, bedeviled.

There had been daydreams too, of a husband who adored her, thought her pretty and witty and smart. Her imaginary, faceless husband had all the good qualities she found in both Ian and Brogan Mackintosh. Kind, considerate, and oh, so very much in love with their wives. Aye, Brogan's wife was long since dead, but to this very day, he loved her. What a woman she must have been to have a man still pining for her more than four years after her death. What a love the two of them must have shared.

But on this day of days, her wedding day — a scant fortnight after agreeing to marry the Bowie Chief — dressed in the beautiful buttercup yellow gown Rose had made for her, the last thing she wanted to do was daydream.

Nay, she was going into this marriage with her eyes wide open and her heart protectively shut. This was not a love match. 'Twould and could never be *that*.

"Leona!" 'Twas Rose's voice breaking through her machinations. And she sounded exasperated. "Are ye no' listenin' to a word I am sayin'?"

Feeling duly chastised, she apologized. "I fear me stomach is in knots," she admitted.

Rose rolled her eyes. "I said, a messenger just brought this."

In her hands was the rolled parchment, the private contract between she and Alec. With more trepidation than eagerness, she took the scroll from Rose's dainty hand. Had he agreed to all her requests? Had he made changes or offered any requests of his own?

Careful not to sully her gown, she lifted the hem and stepped away for as much privacy as she could garner in these small confines. Taking a deep breath, she untied the string and tossed it onto the small table.

He had neither changed nor added a thing. Every request was just as she had originally written it. And there, at the bottom of the parchment, was Alec Bowie's signature.

I, Alec Bowie, do promise and swear to:

> *Never beat my wife, Leona MacDowall*
>
> *To allow my wife to have as many children as she wishes*
>
> *At least twice a year I will allow her to return to her clan for visits of at least one week*
>
> *If ever I take a mistress, I will be discreet*
>
> *I will never turn her away from our marital bed*
>
> *I will never take her against her will*
>
> *I will never, no matter how angry I might be, ever lock her away in any small, dark space, no matter her transgressions.*

For some odd reason, her heart pitter-pattered against her breast.

He'd agreed to every single one of her terms. That could only mean he was a man with a kind and tender heart. Her spirits were much improved. When Ian came to take her to the large tent where they would hold the ceremony, she left with a bright, beaming smile and a skip in her step.

LEONA'S BREATH WAS STOLEN AWAY THE MOMENT SHE SAW ALEC BOWIE standing at the altar. Resplendent and regal in his dark blue silk tunic, black leather trews, and the Bowie plaid — dark blue, green and black — draped over his shoulder. Black leather boots fit snugly around his well-muscled calves. The hilt of his sword had been polished, the candlelight glinting off it. He was a living, breathing wall of hard muscle that reeked of power and virility.

His dark hair was pulled away from his face, held at the nape of his neck with a leather thong, giving her a clear view of his more than handsome face, with its square jaw, straight nose, and full lips. She sent a silent prayer up to God that any children she bore him would look just like him.

SHE WAS BEAUTIFUL. GOD'S TEETH, BUT SHE WAS.

Strikingly so.

Her honey-gold hair — with tiny little flowers tucked here and there — hung in waves, cascading down her back, all the way to her waist. The dress, made of silk, clung to every wonderful curve. The silver belt showed off her tiny waist. For once, she did not wear an apron. Instead the bodice showed all too well the swell of her breasts.

In her hands she carried a small bouquet of flowers whose names he couldn't recollect. Were she not so stunning, he might have been able to think more clearly.

'Tis dangerous ground upon which ye trod, he warned his pounding heart. *She is to be yer wife. Nothing more.*

Cursing his traitorous heart, he forced his smile away, and chose an air of indifference. He would not allow himself to have any kind of tender regard toward this woman who was to be his wife. 'Twould be his downfall if he succumbed to such feelings. Nay, he needed to be firm and indefatigable when it came to her. No matter how gloriously beautiful he found her to be.

He could appreciate her beauty, even her body and her mind. But that was as far as he was willing to go.

"Do ye, Alec Bowie, take this woman, Leona Macdowall, to be yer wife? To have her and hold her and cherish her all the rest of yer days?"

He was so lost in his own thoughts – thoughts of later when he would divest her of that yellow gown and take his pleasure with her – he hadn't heard the priest ask the question. Dougall, his best man, had to elbow him in the ribs to remind him where he was.

"I do," Alec answered firmly.

"And do ye, Leona MacDowall, take this man, Alec Bowie, as yer husband? To have him and hold him and cherish him all the rest of yer days?"

"I do," she answered before the priest had even finished the question. Apparently his betrothed and soon-to-be wife was not as distracted as he.

He made more promises that day, promises he would never be able to recall. 'Twas all necessary, of course, according to the law and the church, for him to make these promises. All of this, the wedding, the marriage contract, the celebration that would be held afterward, was nothing more than a means to an end.

He was doing it for peace. Peace for his clan. To cement a future for them that did not involve reiving, horse thieving, or any other criminal activity.

The fact that Leona was voluptuous and beautiful was merely a bonus.

~

EVERY WORD OF HER VOWS WOULD BE FOREVER BURNED INTO HER memory. Every moment, every look Alec gave her, every breath she took. She would never forget any of it. Not ever.

The more she thought on it, the more she began to believe he was an extraordinary man with an extraordinarily kind and generous heart. He had, after all, signed their private agreement. Only a decent man would have done such. Only a man with a generous and caring heart would have agreed to her terms.

With their oaths taken and promises made, the priest gave Alec permission to kiss his bride.

Oh, how she hoped she would not make a mess of this first...

He gave her no time to think any further on the matter. He had her chin cupped in his hand, his lips pressed to hers, before the priest could even finish speaking.

His lips were warm, oh so very warm. His callused hand felt as soft as silk against her skin. Tiny fissures of excitement and wonder tickled at her spine, her toes, her stomach.

There was no way to think clearly, no way to think at all. All she could do was feel his lips against hers, his fingers touching her chin, his other hand at the small of her back, pulling her in closer.

Then, 'twas done. Just like that, he stopped, smiled down at her and turned away. She stood there with lips parted, her eyes wide as trenchers. That kiss, that sweet blissful kiss, was but a promise of things to come.

The crowd behind her cheered. Well, mostly 'twas Rose and Ian and Brogan doing the cheering. The rest of her people were not so summarily thrilled about the union. She did not care.

She was now the Bowie bride.

CHAPTER 4

*W*ith the ceremony long over and a feast that would most assuredly last until dawn, the only thing Alec could think of was getting his new wife back to their tent.

She was a quiet thing, this wee sprite. Occasionally, he caught her glimpsing at him out of the corner of her eye. She barely touched her food or her wine. Hardly said two words to him during the celebration.

That was fine with him. He didn't want a talkative wife, one who would burn his ears off with inane questions or stories or what have you. Nay, quiet was good.

The large tent was filled with McLarens and Mackintoshes. The only people he'd brung were Gylys, Kyth, and Dougall. The three men stood unfalteringly behind him the entire day, and now through the evening. While he knew each of them agreed with this union, they were not quite as trusting of these people as he.

Lively music, laughter, and chatter filled the space, making it nearly impossible to hear himself think. Some people had taken to the dance floor earlier. All in all it was a festive affair.

Few people, however, came to congratulate the couple. Alec believed 'twas Dougall, Gylys, and Kyth who kept any well-wishers away. Who could blame them? They didn't exactly reflect the countenance of friendly men, what with their scowls and piercing glares and all the swords, dirks, and *sgian dubhs* affixed to their persons.

Leona's father had walked by the table earlier. He said not a word. Instead, he glowered angrily at his daughter, before casting a look akin to pity at Alec. That was it. No congratulations, no *please treat me daughter well,* no nothing. Just clear, unadulterated anger. Alec despised the man.

Dougall leaned in to whisper something into Alec's ear. He could barely hear him. Finally, he stood, excused himself to his wife as well and Ian and Rose, so that he and Dougall could go outside to talk. Gylys and Kyth stayed behind to watch over their new mistress.

Stars dotted the inky night sky. A cool breeze drew in from the east, lifting plaids and firelight the same.

"I want to have a word with ye," Dougall said. "Since yer da be dead, and really no one else to rely on at times like these, it falls to me."

Alec could not begin to guess exactly what his cousin referred to.

"I have been married fer twelve years now, ye ken?" Dougall said with a most serious expression. "I do no' pretend to know what kind of experience ye've had with the opposite sex."

Alec rolled his eyes and crossed arms over chest. "Dougall, I have been with plenty of women. I do no' need ye to speak to me like a lad on the cusp of manhood."

Nonplussed, Dougall gave a slow shake of his head. "I ken ye know *how* to join with a woman, ye eejit. That be no' what I am speakin' of. There be a tremendous difference between a whore and yer wife."

Alec waited for him to expand on that. And he waited. Exasperated, he said, "And yer point?"

"What do ye mean, *and yer point?* That *is* the point."

Alec looked at him with a blank expression. He knew his cousin meant well, but really. Did the man think him a fool?

"There be also a difference with beddin' a whore and beddin' yer wife."

Of course there was.

"I like the lass. She has a strong character. So go easy with her."

He was almost afraid to ask the question. "Go easy with her?"

"Aye," Dougall replied with a comfortable smile.

As if it made all the sense in the world.

When Dougall realized his cousin and laird sincerely did not understand his meaning, he thrust his hands onto his hips. "What I be sayin' is, ye can no' go at her like a ruttin' bull. She be a fine lady. Be kind to her. She'll likely be quite terrified of what will happen tonight."

"Good, lord, man! Do ye think me so ignorant? So cruel?"

"Nay," he replied. "I think ye be that inexperienced with women of no more refinement than an Edinburgh whore. Ye may have bed a fair number of wenches and whores. But again, there be a grand difference between a whore and a wife."

Wanting to be done with the topic, Alec gave him a firm pat on his shoulder. "Rest easy, cousin. I will no' go at me wee wife like a ruttin' bull. I shall show her every care and mercy."

AFTER RETURNING TO THE CELEBRATION, ALEC TOOK THE TIME TO study his wife more closely. Seldom did she look anywhere but her lap, her hands, or the occasional furtive glance toward him. Was she, as Dougall suggested, nervous about consummating their marriage? Mayhap. And seldom did she look him in the eyes.

Another hour passed by, the revelry growing louder as the people partook of ale, wine and whisky. If they were to leave at dawn as he planned, they would need rest. He remembered the journey he'd taken with Leona that spring, back to his keep to rescue Rose. The lass had no experience riding so they had kept what he considered a reasonable pace.

But he needed to return to his lands, to his people, as soon as possible. There was still much work to be done.

Leaning in, he whispered, "I think it be time we retire, lass."

She sat as still as a stone for a long moment. He began to wonder if she'd even heard him. Finally, she gave a curt nod, stuffed her eating knife into the leather pouch that sat on the table next to her, and began to push away from the table.

All three of his men stepped forward to offer assistance. Though quite chivalrous, 'twas highly unnecessary. He could bloody well help his wife, thank you kindly. The glare he shot them said as much.

"Good night, Ian. Rose. We thank ye kindly for the lovely feast," Leona said, to which Alec added, "Aye, we do thank ye."

Ian smiled at the two of them, while Rose winked at Leona. "'Twas our pleasure," she said.

Taking Leona's hand, Alec placed it in the crook of his arm. She was trembling. He hoped 'twas not out of fear.

The revelry quieted somewhat as they made their way through the rows of tables. Dougall led the way, whilst Kyth and Gylys brought up the rear.

There were no bawdy jests asking him if he knew what he was doing. No whistles. No tawdry calls to offer assistance. He'd been to weddings before and all those things seemed to be customary.

Mayhap 'twas because he was the Bowie, the chief of a clan that had, until very recently, been their sworn enemies. Mayhap 'twas the fear instilled by his men. Who could know?

As soon as they stepped out into the dark night, the party-goers returned to the festivities. The music picked up again, the laughter and noise went back to nearly deafening levels.

"Ian said they have prepared a tent for us," Alec said.

In a barely audible whisper, she replied, "Aye, 'tis this way."

THE TENT SAT NEAR THE WOOD WALL, SEVERAL FEET AWAY FROM THE armory. Away from the little huts and tents where the McLarens lived. Alec was thankful for the attempt at privacy.

With her hand still in the crook of his arm, for reasons he could not explain, he felt an odd need arise. Not in his groin, but in his gut.

To protect her, to make her feel safe. Gently, he placed his free hand on top of hers.

Whether her sharp intake of breath was born out of fear or excitement or trepidation, he couldn't be certain. He felt her fingers tremble, but she made no attempt to pull away. 'Twas a good sign, or at least he hoped.

Once they reached the tent, Dougall opened the flap, stuck his head inside, undoubtedly to look for any would-be assassins. Always on guard, that one.

Apparently no one awaited them inside, for he stepped away, holding the flap open. "Good night to ye, mistress," Dougall said as Alec led her through.

Really, his men were behaving as if she were the queen of Scotia. Alec gave an inward roll of his eyes as he followed his wife inside.

'Twas by no means palatial, but it would serve its purpose. A nice sized bed sat at the far wall, flanked on either side with small tables. Candles were lit, bathing the tent in warm light.

A low fire had been set in the brazier that stood in the center of the space. A small table held a bottle of wine and two cups. There was even a vase of fresh flowers next to the wine.

All in all, the attempt to make this tent presentable was successful.

Leona stood between the wall and the bed, her eyes firmly planted on her slippered feet.

"Will yer men be standin' out there all night?" she asked, her voice still but a whisper.

"Nay," he lied. They would be acting as sentries all the night long. 'Twas their way, these Bowie men. Oh, they would not stand so close that they could hear everything that might — or might not — be taking place. But they would be close enough to make sure their laird and his new wife were well guarded.

"Would ye like wine?" he asked, holding up the flagon.

A slight shake of her head was her only answer.

He let out a long, slow breath. Dougall was right, the bloody bastard. His wife was nervous. Probably frightened out of her mind. He thought back to that ridiculous contract she had sent him earlier that morn. *I'll never take ye against yer will.* Of course he wouldn't. No matter how hard he ached, no matter how badly he wanted to see her hair tumbling around her shoulders, no matter…

Reining in his lust, he stepped closer to her. "Lass, if ye do no' wish to consummate our marriage this night, if ye wish to wait until we ken each other better, I will no' argue against it."

He thought he was being quite honorable, border-line chivalrous, offering her an out, trying to set her mind at ease.

For the first time since he'd kissed her at the altar hours ago, she looked at him, straight into his eyes. If he didn't know any better, he would swear she was angry.

"M'laird, I think ye should have thought about joinin' with me before ye proposed."

"But I did no' propose. Ye volunteered," he pointed out as politely as he could.

"Then ye should have thought about it before we took our vows."

Aye, she was angry, but for what reason, he could not begin to guess.

"If ye find the thought of joinin' with me," she paused briefly, searching for the right word, "*repulsive!*" she said, as if she'd just found a king's ransom worth of gold. "If ye find the thought of joinin' with me so repulsive, then mayhap ye should find the priest and ask fer an annulment."

He tried to interject but she was speaking so rapidly, 'twas impossible.

"The only boon I ask is that when ye set me aside and ask fer an annulment, ye'll send me to the convent at St. Agnes'."

Was she insane? He dare not ask that question.

"Lass, I do no' find the thought of joinin' with ye repulsive. In fact, I find the notion quite pleasin'." He'd been thinking about this night for weeks. Often to the point of needing to jump into the cold loch in order to cool his ardor.

She stood in stunned silence.

"I do no' want an annulment and I be no' settin' ye aside." He took one step closer. "And ye bloody well are no' goin' to a convent."

Perish the thought! That beautiful face, those glorious curves? In a convent?

Her mouth formed into a little 'o'. Seductive, and yet she had no idea 'twas so.

"So ye *do* want to join with me?" she asked for clarity's sake.

"Aye, I do. I was merely bein' kind, lettin' ye ken we could wait if it was what *ye* wished."

She studied him closely for a time. "Nay, I do no' wish to wait."

His relief was palpable. Save for the rising need in his groin. There was no relief there, but soon…

She grabbed her pouch from the bed and riffled through it. "Because me mother died long ago, I could no' go to her fer advice on joinin'. So I went to the women of me clan."

She pulled a hand sewn leather-bound book from the pouch and began to riffle through it. "Now, accordin' to the women, I can no' get with child unless I find me woman's release. I do no' quite understand what *that* is. Do ye?"

He was so taken aback by her sudden shift in mood, her asking the women folk for advice, he was at a loss for words. "Do I what?" he stammered to ask.

"Do ye ken what that be? A woman's release?"

All he could do was nod his dumbfounded noggin.

She nodded back and said, "Good," then immediately returned to her book. Using her index finger, she ran down the uneven parchment page until she found what she was looking for. "Now, accordin' to Rose, if ye're doin' things the right way, I am supposed to find my release before ye find yers. And if yer exceptionally good at it, I might find it twice. Though I really do no' understand what any of this means."

Flabbergasted, he could only stand there like a fool whilst *she* gave *him* instructions on the act of loving.

"Some of the women folk, they talked about tongues. Quite frequently actually. Apparently, there is a good measure of pleasure to be found usin' yer tongue, though again, I fear I do no' understand completely."

"Ye took notes?" he asked. He was as curious as he was dumbfounded.

"Aye," she answered distractedly. "'Twas all quite fascinatin', ye ken?" She turned back to the book.

Like a lion going in for the kill, he was on her in a heartbeat. Unable to bear waiting, or listening to her go on and on about releases and tongues and heaven knows what else because frankly, he'd stopped listening.

Tenderly, he lifted her chin with his knuckles, drawing her attention away from the tome. Without permission, he pressed his lips to hers. He'd fully intended for it to be a chaste kiss, like the one he'd given her at the altar. But in a matter of a few rapid heartbeats, it turned from chaste to something quite passionate. Moments later, he heard the book fall to the floor.

～

JUST WHY HIS FINGERS TREMBLED WHEN HE UNTIED THE LACES OF HER dress, he could not say. Anticipation? Desire? He'd felt such things with other women in the past. But now? With Leona? Nay, 'twas an entirely different experience.

What was it about this woman, *her*, that made him quake with a need that burned so hot he felt it to the bottoms of his feet, to the tips of his fingers? Why *her*?

She was not the most beautiful woman he'd ever seen. Nay, he'd travelled the world, had spent time in Italy and France where the women were cut from far different cloth than Leona. They wore their beauty without restraint, without demurring.

He'd also known more educated, refined and elegant women. Women who he had paid handsomely for their time to sate his lust.

But this woman, who stood on trembling legs, whose breath was ragged, who was clumsily returning each of his kisses? She was nothing like them. Mayhap that was it. She was the first woman who had ever come to him willingly without the request for a bag of coin.

And she was a virgin. No hands had ever roamed her body as his were now doing. No other man's lips had kissed the soft, tender flesh of her neck. Of this, he had no doubt. Not even the most practiced and seasoned whore could feign such innocence blended with fear of the unknown.

But there was so much more than her inexperience and chastity that fueled the fire of eager lust making him as hard as granite. He knew this young woman, or at least a little part of her. She was brave, this bonny lass with the odd eyes and hair softer than any silk he'd ever touched.

He slipped the sleeves down over her shoulders, past her arms, and heard it swoosh as it fell to the floor. With other women, he had not bothered to explore their bodies. Nay, 'twas a simple act, a simple deed, meant only to slake his need.

But with Leona, he took his time, inch by slow inch, his fingers hooked under the fabric of her chemise. He caressed her leisurely, enjoying the softness of her skin as he drew the chemise over her shoulders, down her arms, to her waist. It landed on top of her dress, leaving her completely exposed to him. For him. *Only* him.

With other women, he'd never had to hold back. 'Twas always but a business transaction. He would plunge into them, find his release, and be gone within the hour.

But that was not what he wanted or needed with his wife. Inexplicably, he needed this to last. The realization unsettled him, made his fingers tremble, his pulse pound in his veins.

He pulled away then, fear seizing his heart. He watched as she slowly opened her eyes, her brow furrowed with confusion, her breaths ragged, her eyes filled with questions. Candlelight glanced off her dewy skin that was, at the moment, covered in gooseflesh.

"Have I done somethin' wrong?" she asked with a good deal of trepidation.

His voice was lodged behind the knot in his throat. 'Twas next to impossible to form words. "Nay," he whispered. Before she could speak again, he closed his mouth over hers.

She melted. In his arms. Never had any woman *melted* against him, not like this.

All at once, he didn't know if he should feel proud or afraid. Proud that he was making her feel all these new and exciting sensations, or afraid he would end up losing his heart to her.

Pushing the fear away and replacing it with steely-eyed determination, he decided these odd feelings pounding in his heart were nothing more than the anticipation of taking his wife's maidenhead. Wasn't that it? And what if he ended up *liking* his wife? Would that be so bad? He didn't suppose so. Nay, liking his wife was a perfectly acceptable emotion. He could like her, admire her, and even desire her. That did not mean she would ever have his heart.

OH, HIS LIPS! THE KISS! HOT AND EXCITING SENSATIONS CRAWLED through her veins, from her lips to her toes. This was not the same, tender kiss he'd give her at the altar. Nay, this was a kiss born of desire, passion, and need. Almost ravenously, he claimed her mouth with his. When he tickled her lips with the tip of his tongue, she parted her lips to ask a question, but the question fell away, along with any strength she had left in her legs.

Their tongues danced together, his sliding around hers as his hands found the small of her back, her buttocks, drawing her in closer.

There was no need to ask if he was enjoying the kiss. She could feel his hard, swollen member as it pressed against her belly.

With her dress and chemise puddled on the floor, he pulled away, leaving her cold and feeling … empty. When she finally found the courage to ask if she'd done something wrong, tears threatening behind her eyes, for a moment, she wanted to grab her clothes and flee the tent. But then he claimed her mouth once again.

His fingers felt hot against her chilled skin. They no longer felt calloused, but rather, soft as silk as they explored her shoulders, her arms, her waist. She prayed he'd not notice the scars on the small of her back, for she had no desire to explain how she'd come by them.

A moment later, he was scooping her off the floor and laying her on the small bed, his lips never leaving hers until she was prone. Then those magnificent lips left heated trails across her cheeks, down her neck, and back up again.

Rose had never mentioned anything about how this would *feel*. Nay, she'd spoken only in generalities. Positions, things that could be done with the tongue and hands. But never once had she mentioned how Leona would *feel*. Of how her womb would fill with an achy need, a need so intense she thought she'd go mad from it.

That need only intensified when he pulled the tunic over his head, leaving his chest bare. She could only marvel at it and stare in awe at its magnificence. When he began to loosen his sword belt, she closed her eyes tightly. He'd be naked in a thrice and no matter how bravely she went into this marriage, she hadn't the courage to look *there*.

She wasn't certain, but she thought she heard him chuckle, right before he climbed into the bed. It creaked and groaned under his weight. Or were those odd noises coming from her?

She'd just opened her eyes when his hands began another exploration. This time, he did not trace them down her shoulders. Instead, he cupped her cheek as he pressed his lips to hers once again. As her tongue danced eagerly with his, his fingertips trailed away down her neck, feeling as light as the wings of a butterfly. 'Twas difficult to breathe, to think, as her skin felt afire wherever his fingers roamed.

When he cupped her breast in his hand, 'twas shocking in both its intimacy and sheer unadulterated delight. Nay, no one had mentioned this. 'Twas probably a good thing, or she might have fainted from fright.

She lay there, stiff and uncertain, with no clear idea about what she should be doing. 'Twas nearly impossible not to sigh, not to suck in deep breaths, not to tremble.

She wanted to touch him. Wanted to trail her fingers across his chest, his back, but was uncertain if 'twas appropriate.

"Lass, are ye well?" he asked softly, stopping the tender caresses and kisses.

"Aye!" she blurted out.

His silence begged for further explanation. Moments passed before she added, "I be no' certain what I am to do." She felt her face grow warm with embarrassment.

He chuckled lightly. "Well, what would ye *like* to do?"

Keeping her eyes closed tightly, she replied, "Be it acceptable fer me to touch ye?"

"Aye, lass," he chuckled again. "Perfectly acceptable."

She let loose the breath she had been holding.

"Lass, I ask that ye make me a promise."

Nodding her head rapidly, she agreed. "What promise?"

"To always be honest with me."

Slowly, she opened her eyes and looked into his. "Aye, I can do that."

He met her answer with a warm smile. "At all times, in all circumstances. But especially when we be lovin'. I never want to do anything that ye do no' wish fer me to do."

His request made her heart beat even faster. In that small instant, she knew without a doubt that he would never hurt her. There was something magnificent in knowing that and feeling ... safe. For the first time since her mother died, she felt *safe*.

Feeling safe lead to the ability to enjoy, albeit slightly fearfully, all these new sensations flooding throughout her body. Sensations she had never felt before. Odd and exciting all at once. Sensations she wanted very much to explore and understand.

HER PROMISE MADE, HE WENT BACK TO KISSING HER. TENDERLY, sweetly, slowly. As he plied her with those sweet kisses, she eagerly touched his shoulders with her fingertips. Feeling more brazen, she trailed them over and down his back. When he sucked in a deep breath, she was prepared to stop, until she realized he sounded much like herself and took his response to mean he enjoyed her touch.

His skin was soft, yet hard. Goose-fleshed, yet hot.

As she trailed her fingers up his back, he moved his downward, along her side. Gently, his palm glided down her thigh, her calf, and back up again. Cupping her breast, he smiled when she gave a low moan of pleasure.

"God's teeth," he whispered, low and deep against her neck. "Ye are beautiful."

Beautiful? Her heart skipped several beats. No man had ever said that before. A few of the womenfolk here had told her she was *just as beautiful as Rose.* But 'twas always a comparison *to* Rose, never Leona on her own merits. Which often left her to wonder, if she didn't look so much like the woman everyone adored, would they still think the same?

She knew not what to say, how to respond to his sweet words. Oh, how she wanted to let the tears fall, to thank him, to tell him something intelligent or sweet in return. But when he took the tip of her breast into his mouth, her mind went completely and utterly blank.

'Twas a most peculiar yet thrilling, sensation, his tongue circling the taught peak. Drawing in a deep breath, she held it for a long moment before expelling it in a soft, low hiss.

He caressed her stomach before slowly gliding his hands downward. When he reached the apex of her legs, his gentle touch nearly sent her flying from the bed. Alec let out a slight chuckle. "Wheesht, lass," he whispered against her breast. "Relax. I believe ye will find it most enjoyable."

Good lord, she screamed silently. Enjoyable? 'Twas beyond that, beyond anything she could have imagined. With deft fingers at the apex of her legs, his mouth on her breast, she was soon discovering just what a *woman's release* was.

UNTIL THIS NIGHT, HE NEVER THOUGHT HE COULD FIND SUCH PLEASURE with a woman. It went beyond the physical delight, to something he was unable to name, to describe. Listening to her soft sighs, her gentle moans, he dared open his eyes to watch as she found her release for the first time. Aye, there was pleasure to be found there, to know 'twas he who was showing her the way to the age-old delight to be found betwixt man and woman.

Unable to hold back any longer, he did not wait for her to catch her breath.

Joining with her husband was nothing at all as she had imagined. It went well beyond exciting and thrilling to something she could neither put a name to or describe in any manner that would make sense.

Alec had been patient, kind, and generous in all regards. And aye, he made certain she found her release before he found his own. Not once, not twice, but *three* times.

All the while, he whispered words of encouragement, tender words, remarking on her beauty, the softness of her skin, how intoxicating he found her scent to be. It had been impossible for her to return his compliments, to form words had been impossible. The only thing she had managed to say was his name. Repeatedly.

After they found their release together, Alex collapsed on top of her, his breath ragged, sounding as if he'd just run all the way from Edinburgh. His hair, damp with sweat, clung to his forehead and neck.

Leona was not in any better a state. She lay there, out of breath, stunned, happy, confused, elated. Nay, neither Rose or the other women had mentioned any of *this,* of how magnificent it all would be.

After a long while, Alec rolled onto his back, his breaths slowing to a more tolerable pace. Instinctively, she knew he had enjoyed himself, but she had a need to hear him say as much. Before she could put the question to voice, he was slipping his arm under her waist and drawing her to his side. With a happy sigh, she rested her head against his chest as she rested a palm against his stomach.

They lay there in silence, with Leona listening to his heart pound. A thousand questions and a thousand things she wanted to say tumbled about in her mind. Had she the courage, she would have asked, *"Did ye enjoy that as much as I?" "Did I truly please ye?" "Will ye keep me?"*

A long while passed before she realized he had fallen asleep. 'Twas probably a good thing, for if she had been brave enough or had possessed the energy to speak, she might have spoiled the mood entirely. *No matter,* she told herself. *Ye can always ask him next time. Mayhap in the morn.*

CHAPTER 5

'Twas just past dawn when Alec woke. It took only a moment to remember where he was and who he was with. And only another moment before he was fully awake and hard as granite with need.

Now, on the one hand, she had eagerly participated in their love-making the night before. He was her husband, she his wife. 'Twas perfectly natural and acceptable for him to want to take her again. And again. And yet again.

But on the other hand, his heart warned against it. 'Twas a dangerous road he was on, lusting after a wife. Such things as desire could only lead to his utter ruin. It had happened to his father, and his father before him. They'd given their hearts to women, only to have them destroyed.

So as much as he ached with need and desire, he refused to act on either. But God's teeth, she was beautiful. Lying next to him, naked under the blankets, her hair falling around her like honey spilled from the jar. The sound of her soft breaths, so much different from the ragged breathing last night. Her lashes kissing her cheeks. She was a sight to behold.

Cursing under his breath, he swung his legs over the edge of the bed. She was dangerous, this seductive, beautiful lass. More dangerous than an asp, or a horde of sword-wielding Highland warriors.

Taking deep breaths, he raked a hand through his hair, stood and hurried to dress. The sooner he got his wife to the Bowie keep, the better.

~

When Alec woke Leona just after dawn, it took only a moment to get her bearings, to remember where she was.

"Ye need to dress, lass. 'Tis time to leave."

Leave? Nay, she wanted to stay and sleep a few more hours, and have him love her again, as they'd done last night. She'd almost put her objection to words, when he patted her bottom. "We have a long journey ahead. Come now."

Begrudgingly, she pulled the blankets up to cover her chest, sat up, and swiped the sleep from her eyes. "Do we have to leave so soon?" she asked, wishing she could crawl back under the covers.

"Can we no' stay another day?" She tried to manage a come hither look but apparently failed.

"I have many pressing duties back at my keep," he said as he left her side. Standing at the entrance of the tent, he stared at her for a long moment. "I do no' like to be kept waiting." Giving her a curt nod, he left the tent.

Was that a word of warning? He had mentioned he preferred late nights over early mornings. Mayhap he was just grumpy.

Deciding it best not to test the limit of her husband's patience on only their second day of marriage, she hurried through her morning ministrations, rummaged through her trunk for her dark green wool gown, and dressed quickly. She slipped the apron over her dress, twined her hair into a long braid, shoved her feet into boots and packed up her comb and nightdress.

She didn't believe she had taken too long to ready herself. But when she stepped out into the morning sun and saw her husband waiting by his horse, she began to wonder. His face bore the oddest expression. "I hurried," she said as calmly as she could.

She wondered if she would always find him so handsome? His broad shoulders appeared as though they were trying to escape the confines of his dark blue tunic. She felt her face grow warm while she took her slow perusal. Black leather trews were stretched tightly over his thighs. Thighs she knew to be dusted with dark hair. Hair that had tickled her skin to the point of madness only hours earlier.

"Lass," he called to her, disturbing the lustful images bombarding her mind. "We must no' tarry."

Swallowing back her embarrassment, she asked, "May I say goodbye to Rose?"

He rolled his eyes and let out a quick breath. He supposed they should thank their hosts for the wedding, the ceremony, and the use of the tent.

"Verra well, but we must be quick about it."

When she smiled at him, as she was doing right now, it set his nerves on edge. Not because 'twasn't a beautiful, brilliant smile. 'Twas because it *was*. And it unsettled him when he realized the effect it had upon his groin, his mind, as well as his heart. Aye, she was a dangerous woman, his wife.

Cursing his ardor as well as his heart, he handed the reins to his horse off to Kyth and went to say thank you and goodbye to their hosts.

WHAT SHOULD HAVE TAKEN ONLY A MOMENT OR TWO, ENDED UP TAKING nearly an hour. 'Twas a teary-eyed goodbye shared betwixt his wife and her cousin. He could live to be a thousand years old and would never understand women.

"I shall miss ye terribly," Leona cried as she and Rose hugged each other tightly. "And wee John as well!"

The babe chose then to begin wailing. Alec had absolutely no experience with babes, bairns, or weans. Aye, he had a few nephews, but they were older and he'd missed their births and early years. Nay, they were older and far more quiet.

The sound grated on his ears, setting his teeth on edge. But then something utterly unexpected happened when his wife picked the babe up from his cradle and held him in her arms.

"Wheest, now, laddie," she cooed as tears streamed down her cheeks.

If he weren't so terrified of losing his heart to the beautiful woman he'd married, he might well have enjoyed watching her with the babe. And she was beautiful. Too damned beautiful.

"Aunt Leona and Uncle Alec will be back before ye ken it. We'll visit often, I promise."

The babe quieted as she rocked him gently. God's teeth, that smile! 'Twas enough to make him daft with need and desire.

"I can no' wait to see ye with a babe of yer own," Rose told her. "Ye'll be a verra good mum."

Taking note that her husband was standing at the entrance, impatiently tapping his toe, Leona handed the babe to his mother. "Ye take good care of yer mum and da," she whispered against the crown of the babe's head.

Swiping away tears, she steeled her resolve. "Ian, I shall be ferever in yer debt."

Good lord, this was going to take ferever!

Another half hour to say goodbye to Brogan, Rodrick and Angrabraid before they were finally able to leave. At this rate, they would not be home for a week.

LEONA FELT HALF DEAD. EVERY MUSCLE IN HER BODY ACHED, INCLUDING the very tender one betwixt her legs. Alec had loved her for hours last night. 'Twas a wonder she could sit a horse at all.

Kyth rode to her right, Gylys to her left. Her husband was ahead, while Dougall brought up the rear. Surrounded by men, even if one was her husband, offered little in the way of comfort. Unless, of course, they were set upon by thieves or murderers. But as for companionship or someone to talk to, to answer the multitude of questions bouncing around in her skull, they were as useful as the teats on a boar.

Her husband was — for reasons he didn't explain — hell-bent on returning to the keep. The daydreamer in her wanted to believe he was eager to return home so he could introduce her to his clan, so proud he was of his choice in a bride. It also wanted her to believe his clan would welcome her with open arms, glad and thankful their laird had chosen *her* above all others.

Of course she knew there were no 'others'. She was the only one brave enough – or insane enough – to volunteer for the position of Alec Bowie's wife. She wouldn't know for certain which for at least another month or two, she reckoned.

Pounding across the land after all she had shared with her husband last night was not an easy feat. There had been a few times already where she came close to falling asleep in her saddle. But just as she would nod off, a shooting spark of pain would twist in her back and shoot down to her knees and betimes, to her toes.

Mayhap it was a good idea to hurry to the Bowie keep. Before she fell from her horse and broke her neck.

'TWAS VERY LATE IN THE AFTERNOON AS KYTH AND GYLYS WATCHED their mistress doze off once again. They were fully prepared to catch her should she begin to list to either side of her saddle. Neither of them could understand why Alec was in such a hurry to return home, but 'twas not their place to question their lord. They'd let Dougall do that. And he did.

Their friend and fellow warrior went around them to speak with Alec. They watched with great interest at what played out before them.

"Alec," Dougall said as he glanced at the horizon.

"What do ye need?"

"How fares yer wife?"

"Well, I suppose. Why do ye ask?"

"Mayhap ye should turn around and see fer yerself why I ask."

Alec slowed his horse down a bit and twisted in his saddle. His brow drew into a hard line, his lips pursed together. He had just taken in a deep breath to call out to Leona, to inquire why she was asleep in her saddle, when Dougall stopped him with a hand to his forearm.

"Wheest!" Dougall whispered harshly.

Alec gave him a look of warning.

Dougall rolled his eyes. "The lass is in a good deal of pain, Alec. Mayhap we should no press so hard."

"What do ye mean she is in pain?"

"Ye've never bed a virgin, have ye?" Dougall asked, looking ashamed by his laird.

"No' that it is any of yer business, but nay, I have no'."

Dougall let his head drop as he shook it. "I can no believe I have to explain this to ye."

"Explain what?" Alec asked as he tried to keep an eye on his wife.

Dougall looked thoroughly disgusted. "Alec, when a woman loses her maidenhead, it can be quite painful. Not only durin' the act, but fer hours if no' days after. I can no' believe ye did no' ken that."

Alec's expression turned from confused to horrified in an instant. He had thought 'twas an old wive's tale. Had not for a moment given any thought to his wife's comfort. "But she did no' say anythin'," he all but whispered.

"Because she does no' want ye to think ill of her," Dougall explained.

Alec sighed, a long, frustrated sigh. A moment later, he was hauling his sleeping wife from her horse to his lap.

Startled, she opened her sleepy eyes, which were filled with astonishment. "What are ye doin'? What be the matter?" she asked as she looked around to gain her bearings.

"Ye were sleepin' in yer saddle," he said pointedly.

Her mouth formed that little 'o' shape. The one that sent his low burning desire for her into a fullblown blaze. Frustrated with his growing inability to quash the desires or thoughts, he pressed her head against his chest. "Sleep."

His command was born more out of a need to quell his lust than for her comfort.

"I be sorry, Alec," she murmured against his chest.

"Ye did no' fall asleep in yer saddle the first time ye made this trek with me," he said more to himself than to her.

She yawned as she snuggled into his chest and wrapped her arms around his waist. "In my defense, I hadn't been so deliciously ravaged the night before on that journey."

Alec went stone cold silent.

"Did I say that out loud?" she whispered.

"Aye, ye did lass." He could imagine those pink lips of hers forming that delicate 'o' again.

"I did no' mean — that is to say—" she couldn't quite form into words what she was thinking. She settled on, "I did no' get much sleep last night."

Alec chuckled as a tinge of pride crept into his soul. "So ye found our lovin' delicious?" he whispered against the top of her head.

"Mayhap I should return to me own horse," she replied.

Though he couldn't see her face, he could well imagine it now bore a pink blush. "Dougall says ye be in pain."

He felt her grow tense and gave her a gentle squeeze of reassurance. "I apologize fer no' takin' that into consideration."

She lifted her head to look at him. "I do no' want ye to think me weak, Alec. Because I am no'."

"I do no' think ye weak, lass," he said as he pressed her head against his chest again.

She sighed contentedly and he found he rather enjoyed that sound. And the way she felt against his chest. "I have no' slept in two nights, ye ken."

"Two nights?" he asked. "We were only married yesterday. What, pray tell, kept ye up the night before?"

She was quiet and still for so long, he thought she had finally succumbed to exhaustion. "I could no' sleep the night before our weddin'," she answered softly.

"Nay?" he asked. There was no doubt she'd come to their bed with her maidenhead still intact, and without an ounce of experience in how to love a man. Still, jealously reared its ugly head, for reasons he neither liked nor understood. "Who kept ye up the night before?"

"Ye did," she replied in a whisper.

That made not a lick of sense. "But I was no' with ye that night."

She giggled ever so softly against his tunic. "I mean me thoughts were on ye that night. So much so that I could no' sleep."

Oh.

Inexplicably, he had the need to know what the thoughts of him entailed. "Were they *delicious* thoughts?" he asked with a chuckle.

Oh, they eventually turned to that. But she was not about to admit it, lest he think her a lowly born woman or a whore.

"Lass, ye can tell me. I'll think no' less of ye." He sealed his promise with a kiss to the top of her head. He inhaled her scent. Lilac soap, the outdoors, and all woman.

"I worried ye'd no' come, that ye had changed yer mind."

That was not the answer he had anticipated. It made his gut lurch, his hair stand on end, and his ire rise. "Ye think so little of me? Ye think I be the kind of man who does no' keep his word?"

Sensing his distress, she sat up once again. "Nay, that is why I quit worryin' about *that*. I kent ye would keep yer word."

Much relieved, he gave her a curt nod. "I *always* keep me word."

"I ken ye do, Alec." She placed a warm palm affectionately against his cheek. "I did no' mean to hurt yer feelins. But I did promise to always be honest with ye."

"My feelins?" he asked, insulted to his bones. "Ye did no' hurt my feelins. Ye insulted me integrity."

Tears pooled in her eyes at his harsh rebuke. "I did no' mean to do that either. I was only tryin' to be honest with ye."

Her sincerity was genuine, as were the tears welling in her eyes. One escaped, trailing down her pretty cheek.

Guilt. He was beset by it. She had not intended to insult him, she was only sharing with him her fears and worries. He knew nothing of being a husband, but decided it best to put his worries over losing his heart aside, at least for the moment. "I did no' mean to bark at ye," he said. "Please, do no' cry."

Gently this time, he pulled her against him. "Ye should rest."

"I do no' wish fer ye to think me weak or mean of heart, Alec," she said as she wiped her tears against his tunic.

Nay, he'd never think her weak or mean spirited. Dangerous? Aye, she was that. Dangerous in that he could end up a besotted fool, easily giving his heart to her, to be wielded as a weapon against his male pride. Isn't that what his mother had done to his father? Nay, he would not think ill of her spirit or her heart. But he would tread as cautiously as he would were he sneaking into Stirling Castle to kidnap the king. Exceedingly cautious.

LEONA SLEPT FOR A SOLID HOUR, HER BODY LIMP AND PEACEFUL AGAINST his chest. When they stopped to make camp, she groused something unintelligible as Alec helped her to her feet. Sleepily, she offered him her thanks as he set her on the ground. "I feel better now," she lied. "Are we stopping for only a moment?"

He had to laugh. She was far from well rested. "We be makin' camp fer the night, lass."

She looked positively gleeful, in a sleepy sort of way, to hear it. "Shall I prepare ye a meal, Alec?" she asked, through droopy eyes and a wide yawn. She was still clinging to the saddle with both hands.

Dougall was unable to resist his own chuckle at the sight of his very tired mistress. To Alec, he said, "We'll put up yer tent. Ye keep her from keelin' over."

Alec agreed with a nod. "Nay, lass. We have the basket Rose gave us."

That brought forth another gleeful, sleepy smile.

After helping her into the woods to relieve her bladder, he brought her back to the camp. Dougall and Gylys were erecting the tent whilst Kyth was building a fire.

Leona sat on the ground, her skirts spilling out all around her. Seeing her settled, he went to tend to the horses. After rubbing them down with handfuls of grass, he tethered them together for the night.

When he returned, the tent was erected, the fire blazing, and his wife was fast asleep. In one hand, she had a half eaten leg of chicken. In the other, a nearly full mug of ale.

She was sitting strait up. Asleep. He thought it both comical and angelic all at once. Mayhap he *had* loved her too much last night. He should feel ashamed, but he didn't. Nay, instead, he took pride in it.

With a smile, he took the chicken from her hand and put it betwixt his teeth. "I just need to close me eyes fer a moment. I will be fine, really," she protested, though not vociferously.

He handed the ale to Kyth, then scooped his wife into his arms. With the chicken leg still in his mouth, he took her into the tent. 'Twas impossible for him to stand to his full height once inside. With care, he laid her on the pallet and drew up the furs.

"Really, Alec, I can walk on me own two feet," she murmured against the pillow.

He chuckled softly, patted her cheek, and left her to sleep.

CHAPTER 6

$\mathcal{A}$s much as he wanted to wake her when he finally returned to the tent later that night, he dared not. The poor girl needed her rest.

Her beauty bordered on celestial, which made sleep nearly impossible. His thoughts kept returning to the night before and the loving they had shared. It had been a wondrous and terrifying experience. One he looked forward to experiencing again, and hopefully soon.

When he woke the next morn, she was facing him with her eyes open. A most peculiar expression adorned her face. Her head rested on her hands, her golden hair all mussed, and her lips were curved into a warm smile, as if she were happy to see him.

"Good morn, lass," he said, his voice still scratchy with sleep.

"Good morn, Alec." She sounded most content.

They watched each other for a time before Alec asked, "Did ye sleep well?"

She nodded.

"Are ye warm?"

Another nod of affirmation.

"Be there somethin' ye need?" he asked, her silence and the manner in which she stared at him making him begin to wonder.

She drew her bottom lip in betwixt her teeth. "Are ye certain I can always be honest with ye, no matter the subject?"

"Aye," he said, growing wary and suspicious.

"Ye be absolutely certain?"

"Aye, lass. What is it ye wish to speak about?"

She bit her bottom lip again, choosing her words very carefully. "I be no' sore today."

It took a long moment for her meaning to register. As he smiled wryly at her, "That is good to ken, lass." He pretended not to know her meaning.

"Well, if ye wanted to, that is if ye're no' too tired, we could, well, we *could.*"

"*Could* what?" he asked, toying with her. He knew exactly to what she was referring.

"Ye ken," she said, her face turning a wonderful shade of pink.

Still feigning ignorance, he said, "No, I fear I do no'. Why do ye no' just *show* me what it is ye want."

Oh, I couldn't possibly... could I?

But she did.

WHO KNEW THAT A GOOD NIGHT'S REST AND A GOOD MORNING'S LOVING could leave a person feeling so … alive? She felt wholly different this morn, far different than yesterday. More mature, older, and wiser. She hadn't expected to feel so changed after marriage, but she was.

Refreshed and filled near to bursting with vigor, Leona tended to her morning ablutions, shook out her green dress and slipped it over her chemise. She hadn't realized she was humming cheerfully. As she slipped the wide, long apron over her dress, she heard Alec's warm, low voice.

"Why do ye wear the apron?"

He was still lying on the pallet, the furs pulled down to his waist, exposing that wide, muscular chest. Propped on one elbow, his brow furrowed, he watched her with a half-smile.

Her mind had wandered away, as it oft did of late, especially when either of them were without clothing.

"Why do ye wear the apron?" he asked again, jolting her out of her reverie.

She thought about what the most appropriate response would be.

"Tell me true," he prompted. "Ye wear it all the time, even when ye're no' cookin' or cleanin'." He felt certain he knew the answer, but wanted to hear it in her own words.

Tell him true? She took a deep breath and looked him squarely in the eye. "Men do no' like women with a big bosom."

He choked back his laughter but was unable to hide his astonishment. "Who in the bloody hell told ye that?"

Her face burned red, her eyes grew wide. "Does it matter who told me? 'Tis the truth, is it no'?"

He patted the pallet, asking her to sit. "Lass, I ken we've no' been married long, but have I ever once givin' ye the idea that I did no' care fer yer breasts?"

She bit her bottom lip as she thought on it. Nay, he had not said or done anything to lead her to believe such. If anything, he always looked at them with something akin to reverence.

"I do no' ken who told ye such a thing, but it be no' true," he said as he looped a bit of her honey-colored hair around his finger. 'Twas nearly impossible for him to resist touching her silky tresses. "I happen to hold yer breasts in verra high esteem."

Her cheeks grew darker. "Ye do seem to be fond of them when we're lovin'."

Chuckling, he gave her a slow nod. "I am quite fond of them."

"Even though they be verra big?"

Her embarrassment deepened endearingly. "I am quite fond of all of ye," he said. "Ye never have to cover or hide yerself. Least of all from me."

"But men often stare oddly at me when I do no' cover meself."

"I'll kill any man who stares *oddly* at ye," he told her. Jealousy could be an ugly thing, but in this case, he felt it quite appropriate.

~

THEY BROKE THEIR FAST OVER BANNOCKS AND DRIED BEEF AND WERE soon on their way. Although she was quite excited about starting her new life amongst the Bowie people, she was also filled with a good deal of trepidation. Would they accept her as one of their own? Would they be as kind as Alec and his men? Oh, how she prayed they would be.

Alec wanted peace for his clan. Leona too, desired peace, but an altogether different kind. She wanted peace of mind and heart. But most of all, she wanted a home. A home to call her very own. Filled to the rafters with love and laughter.

It hadn't been until she had come to live with Ian and Rose that she realized what had been missing in her life. She had known a cold void existed, but how to fill it? She'd never been able to figure it out, at least not completely.

She knew she wanted friends, friends who would not judge her or listen to the lies her father told. And a husband. Oh, how she had longed for a husband who would give her many bairns.

Home encompassed all those things. Home was where one felt at peace, safe, and content. Those were the things that had been missing in her life.

In addition to a home, she wanted very much to make Alec proud of her. Never did she want him to come to regret his decision to marry her. Completely prepared to do everything and anything she must in order to achieve that end, she looked forward to this new beginning.

They rode for several hours, stopping only long enough to rest their horses or tend to nature's call. The men rarely spoke, which was fine with her, for it gave her time to think. To gather her thoughts and to plan on how she would behave as mistress of the Bowie keep.

Today, she did not fall asleep in her saddle. Her eagerness to see her new home from a different perspective, propelled her forward.

Alec called for a stop again. This time, they rested near a meandering stream. He helped her down, for which she thanked him. She could not help but notice his hands lingered at her waist a bit longer than was necessary. Not that she minded. Nay, she rather liked how tiny his large hands made her waist feel.

Kyth spread a blanket out in the tall summer grass. Dougall brought the basket of food Rose had sent with them.

"Thank ye, Kyth," Leona told him, offering him a bright smile. "Ye are far too kind."

He looked as though she'd just slapped him, but she was in too good a mood, too happy to take notice.

Sitting as elegantly and as ladylike as she could, she looked out at the land before her. 'Twas beautiful, with the tall grass, the stream, the azure sky. Birds fluttered overhead, calling out to one another. Their horses nibbled at the grass next to the babbling brook.

All in all 'twas as serene and peaceful a day as she could ever remember having.

Gylys handed her a mug of cool ale, for which she thanked him kindly. "Ye're a good man, Gylys. Such a gentleman. I thank ye."

Mindlessly, she took the hunk of cheese Dougall offered, along with a handful of berries. "Och, Dougall, I be famished! Ye're such a good, kind man. I thank ye."

'Twas then she noticed them staring at her. They were appalled by something, but what, she did no' ken. "Have I something on me face?" she asked, as she began to wipe at her face to dislodge whatever the offending thing might be.

Alec chuckled as he sat down beside her. "Ye have to quit insultin' me men, lass."

Insulting his men? "Surely ye jest," she said.

He gave a slow shake of his head. "In the past few moments, ye've called them good and kind. Ye even called Gylys a gentleman."

Dougall cleared his throat. "Pardon, me mistress, but we would all thank ye kindly to no' be sayin' such things about us. It be insultin'."

Her eyes grew wide right before understanding set in. These were Bowies. Thieves, murderers, and God only knew what else. They took pride in the reputations they'd incurred over the years.

"Verra well, Dougall. Should anyone ask how ye behaved on this journey, I shall tell them ye were unkind and rude."

He smiled at her. He actually smiled. Proudly.

"And if anyone should ask of Gylys? Why, I shall tell them he was just as rude, makin' me sit on the prickly grass. Very *un*-gentlemanly."

Gylys' eyes lit up, his shoulders righted with such pride and relief 'twas almost laughable.

"As fer Kyth? He made me to suffer with drinkin' from the stream. A rude lout if ever there was one."

He was just as proud as his companions.

"And what of our laird?" Kyth asked. "What will ye say about him?"

Leona turned to stare into her husband's eyes. What would the opposite of generous, handsome, kind, passionate, tender, or sweet be?

Taking in a deep breath, she said, "I shall tell them he was the most ruthless, meanest, and biggest bloody bastard of them all."

~

LEONA COULD NOT TELL IF HE WAS HUNGRY OR ANGRY. LONG MOMENTS stretched by as they ate in silence. Suddenly, he declared *she* needed to make use of a tree. "But I really—" He gave her no time to argue.

Hauling her to her feet, he pulled her away from the stream, and headed for a small thicket, a good distance from his men.

More than half an hour later, they emerged from that thicket, looking quite blissfully happy. Dougall and the others had repacked the food and were waiting by the horses. Each of them dared not look at their laird, elst he would see their knowing grins.

Alec picked bits of twigs and leaves from his wife's hair as they strode toward their mounts. Dougall cast him a knowing smile, which he answered with a furious glare that warned his cousin to be silent.

CHAPTER 7

*L*eona had been to this castle only once before, when she was helping Rose Mackintosh escape from it. Back then, she'd been far too worried about getting out alive to pay attention to any of its finer qualities.

If there were any 'finer qualities' to this keep, she was hard pressed to find them.

Twilight had fallen and it only leant to the ominous air and presence. Dark and unpromising, three towers stood high and menacing, each five stories tall. They were positioned on the north, east, and west sides, with the main keep — three stories high — in the middle. The structure was surrounded by a thick, massive stone wall, manned by even thicker, massive men.

Silently, she prayed her husband was unable to sense her trepidation. If she'd been on her own mount, she might have been tempted to flee.

Oh, she searched for something positive to say. Searched and searched until her head throbbed. Finally, she settled on complimenting her husband on how safe the keep appeared.

"I doubt anyone will try to lay siege, aye?"

He took her compliment with a great measure of pride. It even caused him to smile. She found she rather liked his smile, for it made his eyes twinkle.

The drawbridge creaked and groaned as it was lowered across the moat. Alec gave her a slight hug as he clicked his tongue and encouraged his horse to proceed forward.

Once through the main wall, they spilled out onto a large yard. Men came out from seemingly nowhere to take their horses. Alec slid down first, then helped Leona. Sharp needles of pain pricked at the soles of her feet, but she said nothing.

They swept through the second wall and into a wide yard. A tall man with light brown hair, came rushing around the northern corner of the keep. Leona thought he looked apprehensive, quite worried about something. Ready to do battle, dressed from head to toe in padded vestments, mail, and armor. In one hand he carried a large stick, with a loop of rope at one end. In his other, a steel studded targe.

"M'laird!" he called out as he approached.

"Seamus," Alec said curiously.

Before Alec could ask the man anything, he started shaking his head. Beside himself, he stammered, "He's out, m'laird."

Alec sucked in a deep breath. His men unsheathed their swords, taking stances as if to prepare for battle.

Just who *he* was, Leona hadn't a clue. But he must be a terrifying madman to spark such a response from Alec and his men, and to have Seamus dressed for war. Seeking out her husband for safety, she clung to his arm, terror seizing her heart. "Alec? What be the matter?"

"'Tis the beast, m'lady," Seamus answered. "She be yer lady, right m'laird?" he asked Alec as an afterthought.

"Aye, Seamus, she be my lady and yer mistress." That was as far as introductions would proceed. "How long has he been out?"

"More than an hour m'laird. Chased every man to the walls."

Alec raked a hand through his hair. Dougall, Kyth, and Gylys were making a wide circle around their laird and his lady.

The beast? She envisioned a tall, hulking man with a bald head, fangs for teeth, and hands the size of buckets. What on earth was Alec doing with someone so terrifying in his keep? Was he a prisoner who had escaped the dungeons? More fear raced up and down her spine.

Just as she was about to inquire as to why her husband was holding such a dangerous man, she heard each of her champions gasp. Their attention was on something to the east.

Leona followed their gaze. Coming toward them was a massive bandogge. With his square jaw, long legs and giant feet, he was by far the biggest dog she'd ever seen. He was covered in black, bristly hair, save for a patch of white around his right eye.

Dougall held out an arm in front of Leona. "Do. Not. Move," he warned her, his words clipped, jarring.

Relief washed over her. A dog she could handle, but not the murderous man she had conjured in her mind.

Slowly, Dougall took Leona's hand. "Just step away from our laird, m'lady. 'Tis him he wants."

Upon seeing his laird, the dog began racing across the yard.

"Alec be the only one he likes or listens to," Dougall whispered, as he carefully drew his mistress away, one tiny step at a time.

The dog ran to his master, stood on his hind legs with his paws on his chest, where he summarily greeted him with a wagging tail and slobbery kisses.

"Och, ye big beasty!" Alec exclaimed as he petted the dog's back and head.

Relief surged through her. Alec had the matter completely under control. Mayhap the men were over-reacting. Her shoulders relaxed, her face softening.

Until the dog turned to face her. Normally, she was not at all frightened by dogs, until Dougall began behaving as if her life were in great peril. The dog licked his chops once, then again, and began to saunter toward her.

All at once, she was frozen in place and came dangerously close to losing control of her bladder.

Dougall was fully prepared to plunge his sword into the dog's heart, to protect his lady. Alec immediately withdrew his own sword, apparently ready to do the same.

But the dog did not attack, nor growl, or present an aggressive stare or stance. Nay, instead, he sniffed her hand, then licked it. Before she realized it, he was bestowing much dog-like affection on her. Slobbery kisses, whimpers, and the like.

"Och!" she said playfully. "Ye're no beast, are ye?" she squished his face betwixt her hands and kissed his nose. "Nay, ye're just a puppy. A big old, slobbery wittle puppy."

Alec and his men stood dumbfounded. The bandogge liked no one, save for his master. But he was licking and slobbering all over Leona, as if the woman had raised him from a pup.

'TWAS BEYOND ASTONISHING. 'TWAS BLOODY UNBELIEVABLE. THE bandogge was licking his wife's face. She was kissing *it* in return. And speaking in irritatingly sickening sweet voice. As if the massive dog were a wee bairn, and not a beast trained to protect the keep. A beast trained to answer only unto him. A beast who could tear a man from limb to limb at Alec's command.

"That be a good wee puppy," Leona cooed affectionately.

His wife had broken his blood-thirsty hound.

Broken him.

"And what is yer name, ye handsome puppy?" she asked, as if she expected the damned animal to answer.

Seamus stuttered a response. "We call him Satan, lass."

Alec could only watch, stunned mute, as he tried to wrap his mind around the fact that his bandogge, *his* dog, was not ripping out his wife's heart. Nay, he was nuzzling his nose against her face, licking her, with his tail wagging gleefully.

"Satan?" Leona repeated. Looking to Alec, she said, "Certainly, he jests?"

"What did ye do to me dog?" Alec asked Seamus.

"N-nothin', m'laird, I swear it. He damned near took a chunk out of Fergus's arse no' more than an hour ago."

Tempting fate or the gods, Kyth took a step forward, stunned with the miraculous change in Satan's countenance since last he'd seen him. He was but three steps away when the dog turned and snarled at him. A low, guttural growl that turns a man's blood to ice.

"Satan!" Leona called his name as she stomped her foot. "Be nice!"

BE NICE?

Was his wife mad? Insane? Tetched?

"He is a bandogge, fer the sake of Christ! Not a puppy!" Alec stomped toward his wife and grabbed the dog's collar. "He's a vicious, blood-thirsty animal, meant to protect me, my family, and my keep."

Leona did not know what she'd done to elicit such an angry response from her husband. "Was he supposed to bite me?" she asked before casting a loving smile toward the dog.

"Of course he was supposed to bite ye!" Alec ground out. "He is a bloody bandogge!"

"Really, Alec, I do no' ken why ye're shoutin' at me. I did nothin' to yer dog." She attempted to point out the folly of his argument. "The fault is no' with me, but with yer dog. Och! But please, do no' yell at him. He be just a puppy. Ye can yell at me."

A distinct throbbing began in his temple, right behind his left eye. Closing his eyes, he counted to ten, took another cleansing breath and opened his eyes.

His wife stood before him, her hands clasped in front of her, eyes diverted to the ground, and looking as though she was bracing herself for his wrath. She was perfectly willing to subject herself to his tirade so he wouldn't yell at Satan. As if he would do either.

To the dog, he said, "Satan, go with Seamus." The dog did as he was bid, happily padding toward the not so assured Seamus.

"I be terribly sorry, Alec," she murmured softly.

It dawned on him that his dog was behaving much like himself. A simpering fool when it came to Leona. 'Twas irksome. Irritating. Terrifying.

Alec held out his hand to his wife and said, "Come with me."

He took note of the tremble in her fingers, the way she swallowed repeatedly, either swallowing back tears or retorts.

With her hand in his, he led her up the steps and into the keep. He paused just inside the foyer. "Lass, I need ye to understand that Satan *is* a guard dog. He is no' a puppy, nor a lapdog. I can no' have anyone treatin' him as such."

She apologized again, her voice but a whisper.

"Ye must understand that I can no' have ye treatin' him as if he were a kitten."

"Of course no', Alec," she murmured.

"Good. As long as ye understand."

She said nothing but he could not help but think there was much she *did* want to say. The last thing he wanted to do was to argue with his wife. Nay, what he truly wished was to take her to their chamber and join with her. Pushing those lustful and lascivious thoughts aside for the time being, he led her into the keep.

AT SUCH A LATE HOUR, THE KEEP WAS DARK, SAVE FOR A FEW LIT torches. The flames skittered about in the drafty castle, casting everything in the eery glow of dancing shadows. She expected to hear a banshee's cry at any moment.

They stood in the gathering room, which was completely devoid of anything she might have considered 'homey'. The walls and floors were bare. Not even a carpet or handful of rushes spread out to stave off the cold seeping through the stone floors.

Two massive fireplaces, both empty, flanked either side of the long, narrow room. Even the dais was empty. The only place to sit was at the one table in the center of the room, surrounded on two sides by wooden benches. The three massive chandeliers drawn completely up, almost to the ceiling, were also bare. The only decoration was the Bowie crest that hung over one of the massive fireplaces.

'Twas a far cry from the opulence she remembered from her last and only visit.

72

The entire space screamed of desolation. 'Twas enough to bring tears to her eyes.

'Twas not so intolerably late that the people were all abed. At least she didn't think so. "Where is everyone?" she asked as she crossed the room.

"Everyone?" Alec asked. "What do ye mean?"

Leona peered into the hearth. There had not been a fire set in it for quite some time. "Yer people," she replied.

Alec shrugged one indifferent shoulder. "In their cottages, I reckon. The unmarried warriors all sleep in the armory."

Her lips turned to that that delicate 'o' again. "And the unmarried women?" she asked, trying to gain a clearer image of how things worked here.

"There be no' many, lass. But of those we do have, they share cottages."

"But who lives *here*. In the castle?"

He thought it an odd question. "We do," he replied, studying her closely.

Just then, Gylys and Kyth stepped into the room. "We'll put yer bags above stairs," Gylys said. They did not wait for a response before bounding up the stairs and out of sight.

"The five of us?" She nearly squawked the question.

"Nay, just ye and me."

Seeing her flash of distress — or disapproval, he wasn't sure which — Alec came to stand just inches from her. "Be there a problem?"

"Nay," she said breathlessly. 'Twas impossible to think when he was staring at her like that. She was beginning to recognize *that* look. The one that said he was secretly divesting her of her clothing and desiring nothing more than to love her wickedly and without abandon.

"There are no servants?" she asked him, tearing her eyes away from his.

He was disappointed in her question. Had she married him hoping for a life of luxury? Of being waited on hand and foot? "No," he finally replied.

Something close to fear flashed behind those odd eyes of hers. "Does that displease ye?"

"Nay, I am merely trying to gain a sense of how everything works." She swallowed once, then again, and began to fidget with the strings of her pouch.

Alec's brow drew inward as he tried to gain a sense of what she was truly thinking. "How everything works is that 'twill be just ye and me livin' here. After me brother's death, I gave my people the option of remaining here to work or not."

"And they chose the 'or not'," she said.

"Aye. I gave each of them a bit of land to work in exchange fer workin' in the bigger fields."

Clarity finally settled in. He could see it in her eyes. "There were too many bad memories here fer too many people." 'Twas not a question, more a statement.

Alec nodded.

"So they live away from the keep, but work here during the day," she said, proud she had figured it out.

She had figured incorrectly. "Nay, lass. They neither live nor work here."

Taking in a deep breath, she untied her cloak. "Then I am responsible for the entirety of the keep? "

'TWAS A FRIGHTENING PROSPECT, RUNNING THE ENTIRE KEEP WITHOUT anyone's help. But Leona would not let that be a deterrence. Nay, on the morrow, she would wake bright and early and begin her duties as mistress of the keep.

"I am no' afraid of hard work, Alec," she told him as he led her up the stairs. "I will have the keep in tip-top condition in no time."

Gylys and Kyth appeared from the shadows, empty-handed. "It be as ye asked, Alec," Kyth said as they walked by. Again, they did not wait for a response before bounding back down the stairs.

"What is wrong with it as it is?" he asked as he pulled a lit torch from the wall.

She paused before answering. "It be a fine keep," she replied. "Just a wee bit … cold."

With that, he could not argue. 'Twas a drafty place on temperate days. Down right bone chilling when the rains came.

"I should like to at least lay down some rushes," she told him as they reached the top of the stairs.

He saw no harm in rushes and told her so. "But I do no' want ye fillin' the rooms to burstin', with things we do no' need."

In her own mind, she added, *As yer brother Rutger did.*

"I do no' want ye turnin' the keep into a woman's boudoir or makin' it look like Stirling Castle."

His mood had changed drastically in such a short amount of time. "I have never been to Stirlin' Castle, m'laird," she told him. "So I do no' think ye need to worry in that regard."

"I think ye understand my meanin', lass," he said in a firm, irritated tone. "This be a keep, no' a cottage or a home."

"Might I ask why ye be so opposed to it bein' a home?" she dared ask.

Apparently, she could ask but he was not about to answer. He studied her closely for a long moment and she began to grow uneasy under his scrutiny.

Wanting very much to change the subject, she asked, "On the morrow, could ye show me the kitchens?"

"Why?" he asked, turning left.

"If ye do no' want to starve, I'll need to ken where to cook yer meals," she giggled.

"Cook?" he asked perplexed. "We eat with the men in the armory."

Leona came to an abrupt halt. Alec turned to face her. A look of horror had spread across her pretty face.

"Y-ye expect me to eat in the armory with yer men?"

"Ye look as though ye swallowed a bug," Alec said. "Do no' fash yerself over it. Seamus be a right good cook."

"But-"she stammered for the right words. "But I like to cook."

75

"Then ye can help Seamus," he said. With the matter settled, he turned again to lead her to their bedchamber.

Apparently the matter was not settled. She would not budge. "But Alec, I want to cook *here*. In our home."

Home. There was that bloody word again. It made the hairs on the nape of his neck stand at full attention. "I have no desire for a *home*," he told her through gritted teeth. "'Tis a keep. 'Tis a fortress meant to house warriors and its people during times of war. Nothin' more than that."

She was positively crestfallen. "And after we have children?" she asked. "Do ye wish them to eat in the armory with the men? What if we have daughters?"

In truth, he hadn't given that much thought. Her distress was plainly evident. Her odd eyes were filled with it.

Did he in truth want his children, more specifically his daughters, to dine daily with his hard, crusty men? Did he sincerely wish for his children to hear their tales of whoring and warring and thieving? Nay, he supposed that might not be the best environment in which to raise daughters. Nor was it the proper place for his wife.

"Verra well," he acquiesced. "Ye may cook fer us." But that would be the extent of her turning his keep into a bloody happy home.

Her shoulders fell, as if he'd just removed a great weight from them. Flinging herself against his chest, she said, "Thank ye, Alec!"

That god-awful sensation of warmth that bordered on joy crept up through his stomach.

ONCE ABOVE STAIRS, HE LED HER DOWN A DIMLY LIT CORRIDOR AND paused at the third door on the left. "This is me bedchamber," he said as he lifted the latch and opened it.

"Will it be mine as well?" she asked with a raised brow. "Or should ye like me to sleep elsewhere?"

Alec smiled warmly at her. "Nay, lass. I should not like ye to sleep elsewhere."

Returning his smile, she said nothing as she walked inside. After a quick perusal, she said, "Ye have changed things since last I was here," she remarked.

Aye, he had made a few small changes in preparation for her arrival. Before, it had been a simple room, with a hearth, a small bed with one table next to it. Gone was the small bed that barely held him, let alone a wife. He'd replaced it with a large, four poster, complete with canopy, fresh linens and furs. He'd also added extra pillows. 'Twas primarily Dougall's idea, but one he that, at the time, he could not argue with.

Opposite the bed was the hearth. In the corner, he'd acquired two empty trunks in which his wife could store her clothes and things. He'd also added a small table and two chairs which he had placed under the two, fur-covered windows. Next to the hearth now, was a pitcher and basin and clean washing and drying cloths that sat on a small, round table. Just who had thought to have fresh water in the pitcher, he was uncertain. More likely than not, Dougall had seen to the preparations ahead of time. He had also procured a dressing screen, which now sat in the far corner of the room, near the bed.

"Be it to yer likin'?" he asked hopefully.

"Aye," she said with an agreeable nod. "'Tis verra nice."

He hadn't realized her approval was important until he heard her voice it. Ignoring the sense of pride he felt, he set about lighting a few candles. Leona removed her cloak and hung it on a peg near the door. "Ye can wash up there," he said, inclining his head toward the pitcher and basin that now sat next to the hearth.

Leona washed up as he worked to build the fire. Suddenly, he began to grow nervous. 'Twas not as if this were their wedding night. Mayhap 'twas not nervousness he felt, but excited anticipation. Joining with his wife was something he'd quickly grown quite fond of. Out of the corner of his eye, he watched as she scooped soap from the jar and lathered her face and hands.

He saw her shiver as she rinsed with the cold water. Tiny droplets formed on her long lashes and dripped off the tip of her delicate nose.

When he realized just how much he was enjoying the vision of such a simple act, he tore his eyes away and focused on the fire.

He said not a word as she stepped away from the basin and toward the bed. Taking in a deep, steadying breath, he went to the basin and washed his face and hands. The cold water did little to cool the blazing desire that was growing.

Leona was standing near the bed with her back to him, untying the laces of her dress. His need to be with her overtook his good senses. In a few short steps, he was behind her, offering her nothing but husbandly assistance.

With fingers that all but trembled, he untied the bit of leather and began slowly unloosening her braid. Why he so craved to feel the silky locks against his skin, he didn't rightly know. Nor did he understand it. But the need was strong.

When he placed a tender kiss along her neck, she quit working at her laces. A slight moan escaped as she tilted her head to give him better access.

Once the hair was free, as he thought it ought to be at all times, he swept it away and trailed more kisses across her long, slender neck. She smelled of earth and outdoors and fresh soap. 'Twas as intoxicating a scent as he'd ever experienced.

When he kissed her tender flesh, taking delight in the way she breathed in deeply, he began to divest her of her clothing. First her dress, then her chemise. They pooled on the floor at her feet.

He pulled her in closer, and allowed his hands free-reign to go wherever they pleased. Up and down and back up again, until he cupped a breast in each hand.

"Would ye like to climb into bed?" she asked, her voice scratchy and breathless.

"Soon," he whispered against her ear.

God's teeth, but her skin is soft! He thought to himself. Leaving her breasts, he drew his hands up to her shoulders, caressing, touching, exploring, his desire growing and blazing.

Pushing her hair over one shoulder, he let his hands glide down her back, to her firm buttocks and back up again.

But something did not feel quite right when he drew his hands up again, along the small of her back. Something was wrong, odd, uneven.

He looked down, took a slight step back, and stared.

Several scars criss-crossed along her back.

He had felt them on their first night together, but at the time, he'd thought they were wrinkles left from the tight dress she had worn. That, and he was so consumed with lust that he didn't take the time to study every square inch of her body.

Anger boiled rapidly at the sight. Deep anger toward whoever had left those scars there. "Who did this to ye?" he asked, his voice deep, filled with a quiet fury, barely kept in check.

She was frozen in place. Silence filled and stretched the room.

"I asked, who did this to ye?"

Finally, she moved, stepping out of the pool of clothes at her feet. Without looking back at him, she grabbed her chemise and held it to her chest. "What does it matter? It happened a long time ago."

She was struggling to slip back into her chemise, when he took her by the shoulders and turned her to face him. "I do no' care if it happened a week ago, a year ago, or ten years ago. I want to know who did this to ye."

With her eyes glued to the floor, she asked, "Why? Do they make ye ill to look upon? Do they make ye no' want me any more?"

With his fingertips, he lifted her chin. "Look at me."

It took a long moment before she dared to.

"No, they do not make me ill to look upon," he told her. "And neither do they make me no' want ye. I simply want to know *who* did this and *why*."

Those beautiful, odd eyes of hers grew damp. "It happened a long time ago."

"I do no' care. Tell me." There was a deep, burning need to know, to have the man's name so he could someday do to him what he had done to Alec's beautiful wife.

Leona took in a deep breath and let it out slowly. "'Tis a long story."

"I have all night."

~

ALEC TOOK THE CHEMISE FROM HER HANDS AND HELPED HER INTO IT. She thought it awfully kind when he sat her upon the bed and drew a fur around her shoulders. With the patience of Job, he sat beside her, with one arm around her shoulder as she told him the story.

"'Twas summertime; I had just turned five and ten. Da was working fer the McNairs, helping to add on to their keep, fer they had far outgrown it. We had been there for several weeks and all seemed to be goin' quite well. Until the laird came to see him. Och, he was mighty angry. Ye see, there had been a change in the plans. Not a grand or humungous change, but a change nonetheless. Well, da, he had taken to drink after me mum died and he hadn't quite put it down completely, ye ken." She took a steadying breath, thankful that Alec kept quiet and simply listened.

"The laird, he was fit to be tied. Da was workin' off the original plans, no' the new ones, the ones that had added private garderobes to each of the rooms. Little closets, ye ken, where a body could *go* privately without the need of a chamber pot or havin' to go out of doors in the dead of winter.

"Da blamed me. He told the laird 'twas all *my* fault. That I must have mixed up the plans or lost them. Now, keep in mind, I never *touched* his plans or anythin' else like that. I only helped keep the ledgers of expenses. Still, he was no' quite brave enough to admit the truth, to say he'd been drinkin' and no' payin' attention."

"And the laird, he believed yer da?"

Leona shrugged. "Nay, I do no' think he did. Still, 'twas such an expensive mistake. One that required them tearin' down everything they'd already built and startin' anew. I believe the laird thought he could get me da to admit to it, but the laird was sorely mistaken."

"What happened?" Alec asked, his jaw flexing back and forth, his eyes glaring at a similar imaginary spot on the wall to the one Leona was fixed on.

"Well, the laird declared I should be beaten fer me mistake."

Alec swallowed hard before asking, "And still, yer da did no' admit to anythin'?"

"Nay, he did no'." She wiped away an errant tear. She had never told another living soul what had happened that ugly, terrifying day. There had been no need to, for Alec was the only person ever to see her without clothing. "So 'twas ordered I be taken to the center court-yard to make a public display of what happens when ye cost the laird so much coin."

Silence fell between them for a long while before she went on. "I was taken to the courtyard. They forced me to me knees and tied me hands to a long beam. The back of me dress was torn open."

Alec let a long, deep breath pass through his nostrils. 'Twas all he could do not to order his horse and head out to kill the men responsible.

"Then the laird gave me da the whip."

Stunned, he spun his head to look at her. His voice was lodged in his throat, the fury building and building.

"I think the laird truly believed that if me da had to inflict the punishment upon his own daughter, he would finally admit he was at fault. But instead, he took the whip. *'Ten lashes,'* the laird ordered. Only da did no' stop at ten. He kept goin. Finally, the laird and two men pulled him away. I think if they had no', he would have kept goin' until I was dead."

Never in his life had Alec felt the kind of rage he did in that moment. Blind fury all but consumed him. He got to his feet and began pacing back and forth. Leona watched from the bed, her eyes filled with uncertainty.

"'Tis a good thing I had not learned of this when we were still at the McLaren keep," he told her. "For I would certainly have killed the man who calls himself yer father."

Leona, surprised by his statement, sat silently for a long

moment as he paced. Her husband, a man she barely knew, was openly upset by an event that had taken place nearly ten years ago. Dare she believe Alec had some tender feelings toward her? Feelings that made him want to act as her champion?

"Why would a man abuse his daughter so?" he asked, stopping to glower into the flames.

"I was a disappointment."

He spun to look at her. "Disappointment?"

"Aye," she replied. "I was no' a boy. And after me, mum could no' have any more children. And then there be me eyes."

He threw his hands in the air. "Yer eyes? There be nothin' wrong with yer eyes, Leona. They work, do they no'? Are ye able to see out of them?" His words were clipped, his tone firm and resolute.

Tilting her head to one side, she studied him curiously. "Aye, I see well."

"Then there be nothing wrong with them."

He stated it so plainly, so honestly, and with such conviction that even *she* began to believe him. If they did not bother Alec, why should they bother her? Or anyone else for that matter? Certainly, that had to mean something. Unwilling yet to believe he might hold a tender regard for her, she decided mayhap 'twas his honor. Aye, he came from a long line of thieves and such, but could not a thief have a line he would not cross, such as beating a woman?

'Twas Leona who finally broke the silence lingering betwixt them. "So where does this leave us, Alec?"

His anger slowly subsided, his scowl replaced with something far softer. "Us?" he asked. "We are fine, lass. We are fine."

LEONA WOKE BEFORE DAWN, EAGER TO BEGIN HER DAY. ALEC SLEPT soundly beside her, exhausted, she supposed, from all their loving the night before. Aye, she took a good deal of pride in the fact that she'd left him spent and exhausted. After disclosing the truth about her scars, something between them had changed. Alec had made love to her with such fervor and passion, wholly different than what they had shared before. 'Twas as if he were branding her his and his alone with each kiss, each touch.

Slipping from the bed, she searched through her trunk and found her brown dress and apron. Tip-toeing out of the room, with her clothes in one hand and her slippers in the other, she left her husband to sleep.

The halls were dark, save for one lonely lit torch Alec had left outside their room the night before. She dressed in the hallway by torchlight. She hated dark spaces with a passion. Especially small dark places. Grabbing the torch, she lifted the hem of her dress, and cautiously made her way below stairs.

Below stairs was no better than above, no lighter, no brighter. She went about lighting whatever torches she could find to help ward off the bleakness. They didn't help much.

With her aversion to dark places, she quickly set about lighting fires in each of the massive hearths. Thankfully, there was a good supply of wood standing in the boxes at each fireplace.

Once that task was complete, she grabbed another torch and went in search of the kitchens. Determined to impress her husband with something other than the skills she was developing in their marital bed, she was going to make him a grand meal this morn. In her mind's eye, she saw him feasting on more than her breasts.

Nay, he would feast on warm bread, ham, eggs, sausage, jams and all manner of delectable delights.

The kitchens were as she imagined them to be. Just behind the main keep. Oh, they looked positively grand in their immense size. With her heart skipping happily in her chest, she stepped inside.

There were tall, wide windows on three walls. Another door straight ahead led to the back yard.

Not one, but three large tables took up the center of the room. The walls were banked with massive counters. Pots and pans hung from heavy wrought-iron hooks and racks overhead. Two immense fire-places sat side by side, each with pothooks.

Wooden platters, bowls, spoons were stacked neatly under tables.

All manner of instruments, more than she'd seen, were tucked neatly here and there. 'Twas heaven on earth! Bright and cheery and clean, save for the dust that had accumulated on everything.

No worry, she assured her happy heart. It might take a few days, but she'd have everything sparkling clean very soon.

Gleefully, she set her torch in the wall and donned her apron. Amongst the linens on the center table, she found a drying cloth that could serve as a kerchief. Quickly, she braided her hair, then wrapped the cloth about her head.

Empty and dusty buckets sat on the cold hearth and under the shelves at the back door. She grabbed two, swung open the back door, and went in search of the well.

To her right was a long, narrow chicken coup, ahead, the well. The chickens were still and quiet. Until she walked past and one of them squawked at her in protest. "Lay abouts," she whispered at the coop with a giggle.

Happily, she swung the empty buckets as she skipped to the well. She was much relieved to see a block and tackle with winch, to hoist up full buckets of water.

She lowered the bucket down, the crank squeaking and groaning in the early morn. She hoped she would not wake anyone, but there was no way around it.

In short order, she had two buckets of clear water to haul back to the kitchens. Much heavier now, there was no skipping of feet or swinging of buckets. But her heart was still light and happy.

Setting the buckets on the table with a thud, she wiped her brow with her apron. Next, she started a fire in one hearth. Once it was blazing, she set the buckets on the hearth to warm and went to retrieve more buckets of the icy cold water.

Soon, she had six buckets warming. She took a moment to catch her breath and wipe the sweat from her brow. Still, she was quite happy, quite eager to begin preparing a meal fit for her laird, her husband.

With a light heart and humming a lively tune, she all but skipped to the larder. The images of sizzling ham, warm bread dripping with butter and jam, brought a smile to her face.

It took a few yanks before the door opened. 'Twas eerily dark inside, so she fetched a candle from the table, lit it, and went back to the larder.

What she saw inside made her heart plummet.

'Twas bare.

There was nothing on the shelves save for an empty jar, a few empty egg baskets, and dust-covered salvers.

There was no ham. No cheese, no bread, no dried fruits, no butter, no jams. Nothing.

'Twas enough to bring tears to a grown woman's eyes. Enough to make her curse under her breath.

Of course the larder would be empty. Why wouldn't it be? There were no servants living within. No cook, no maids, no one for whom meals needed to be prepared on a daily basis. Her husband was used to eating in the armory with his men. Why would he even have so much as a nugget of cheese or a few bannocks?

Unwilling to be disheartened, she left the larder. Placing the candle on the table, she looked about the large space. Everything a body to could ask for with which to prepare a meal, but not a morsel of anything to prepare. How ironic.

Determination set in. Eggs. She could at the very least make a few hardboiled eggs to break their fast. Hopefully, her husband would be willing to replenish the empty larder.

Hardboiled eggs.

Alec looked at the bounty before him. Nothing but hardboiled eggs.

"I ken now, why there are no rats within the keep," Leona said as she placed three eggs on the table before him. "There be no' a morsel of food anywhere within."

His choices were few. He could pretend to be perfectly content with hardboiled eggs, thank his wife for her trouble, then hie off to the armory where he could eat sizzling slices of ham, eggs, and bannocks.

But he could not just leave her here with nothing more than hardboiled eggs for each meal. 'Twould be wholly unkind.

"There be a village about an hour's ride from here. Let us say we eat our eggs, then go to purchase supplies for our bare larder?"

The smile that lit her face? As if he'd just presented her with a ruby encrusted necklace. "Oh, thank ye Alec!" she exclaimed. Jumping from her seat, she wrapped her arms around his neck. "I wanted verra much to prepare ye a good meal this morn."

He patted her arm, enjoying her display of affection. "'Tis just a trip to the village, lass."

"Oh, but Alec, 'tis so much more than that. Ye're used to eatin' with yer men. Ye're no' used to havin' a wife to sup with. Ye could have gone to eat with yer men and left me here to fend fer meself."

"Och! The thought never entered me mind," he lied.

She hugged him once more before stepping away.

CHAPTER 8

The village of Kinbrea lay to the south and west of the Bowie keep. An hour by horse or more than two by wagon. 'Twas primarily a fishing village that stretched out along the coastline.

Alec drove the team of four and wagon down a grassy, winding path. Today, Kyth and Gylys acted as outriders, on the off chance any trouble arose. Dougall was spending the day with his wife and bairns. In his place was Patrick Fitzgerald who, if you stood him next to any Bowie, you would know right away that he belonged. The lad was in his early twenties, a distant relative of Alec's stable master, who had come to live with them several years ago, after the death of his parents.

As they drew nearer the town, Leona knitted her brow. "What is that smell?"

"'Tis the ocean, lass. Carried in on the morn's breeze."

Her eyes grew wide. "I did no' realize we were that close to the ocean." Her smile widened. "Is it yers?"

"The village or the ocean?" he teased.

"The village," she giggled.

"Nay, this stretch of land belongs to the MacLeods. They be the only clan who does no' wish to see the Bowie clan obliterated and wiped from the face of the earth."

"So they be our allies?" she asked hopefully. Oh, she knew the Bowie clan's reputation quite well and had made peace with it the day she married Alec.

"In so much as they leave us be and we leave them be."

Her thoughts fell to the wayside when they crested the hill. There, at the bottom, stretching along the seashore was the village. 'Twas breathtakingly beautiful from this vantage point. And beyond that, the ocean.

As far as the eye could see, blue water crested into waves and foam, like little clouds sent to the earth from the heavens above. Waves that crashed against an outcropping of large, jagged rocks or lapped against the sandy beach. Her toes all but itched to be near it, to touch it with her own fingers and toes.

"I never thought to see the ocean," she murmured with awe.

Alec studied her closely for a moment. To him, 'twas just another ocean, but to his wife? He took note of her wide eyes, brimming with tears of what he assumed were awe. When he searched his mind for how he might have felt when he saw this place for the first time, he came up blank. It had always been a part of his life, from as far back as he could remember. He could not ever remember feeling the sense of awe or wonder he was now witnessing in his wife. 'Twas as common as the trees across from the keep, or a bowl, or a hearth. 'Twas always there; therefore it did not seem quite as special as it ought.

"If ye like, I shall take ye down to the beach later, if there be time."

Pulling her eyes away from the ocean, she smiled that bright, beaming smile he was growing so fond of. "Och! Alec! I would very much like to dip a toe into it! Just to say that I have."

He returned her smile as she gave his hand a gentle squeeze.

Moments later, she was digging into her pouch where she retrieved her eye patch and settled it over her blue eye.

When Alec saw what she had done, he pulled the wagon to a stop. "What on earth are ye doin'?" he asked.

Facing him, she said, "Coverin' me bad eye."

"Take it off," he said through gritted teeth. Just why she felt it necessary to hide either of her eyes, he cared not. It made him angry.

"But Alec," she replied, her voice holding just a hint of trepidation.

His jaw set firmly, he said, "Ye do no' have a 'bad eye'," he ground out. "Take it off."

Reluctantly, she untied the patch, but did not immediately return it to her pouch. Instead, she rubbed it betwixt her fingers as she stared at her toes. "Ye do no' understand."

No, no he didn't. And he didn't care to. As far as he was concerned, her eyes were as intriguing as they were beautiful. "I'll no' allow ye to hide yerself from anyone, lass. Ye do no' need to be ashamed of yer eyes. Or your breasts. Or anything else."

She tried to explain that it wasn't necessarily shame, but a technique she had used over the years, simply to avoid the stares and taunts whispered at her back. "I cover me eye to avoid the ridicule. Ye could no' understand that, fer ye have no' lived the whole of yer life bein' called a witch or the devil's wife."

Nay, he had not been called either of those things. But he had been called much worse.

Gylys and Kyth rode up to the wagon. "Be there a problem, Alec?" Gylys asked.

"Nay. Go ahead. We'll no' tarry long," Alec said.

With a shrug, the two men left and made their way down the hillside.

When they were out of earshot, Alec turned to look at his lovely wife. His wife who was doing her best not to shed the tears clinging to her lashes.

"Leona, I ken ye've gone the whole of yer life facin' ridicule over yer eyes. I understand how that hurts. I am, after all, a Bowie. 'Tis no' as if people welcomed me with open arms."

When she looked up at him with those damp lashes surrounding eyes that had brought her nothing but pain, it stole his breath. "'Tis different fer ye, Alec. Ye're a man, and brave, and ye do no' let what others say about ye wound ye. I pretend the taunts do no' hurt, but they do."

With the pads of his thumbs, he wiped the tears from her cheeks. He did not want to have these tender feelings toward her, but she made it nearly impossible to avoid. Resisting the urge to pull her into his lap and make promises he could not keep, he chose, instead, to share a secret. A secret his parents and brothers had taken to their graves.

"When I was a lad, all of nine summers, me da wanted me to foster with a strong clan. None would have me, simply because of me last name." To this day, he could remember the dejected feeling.

"I thought ye fostered with the McGregors?"

"Aye," he nodded. "I did. But we had to lie. For five long years, I was known as Alec Mackenzie. I had to use me mother's family name."

Understanding settled in. "I did no' ken that."

"No one did, save fer me parents and me brother."

"That could no' have been easy fer ye, as a little boy," she whispered.

He pushed the old ache aside. "Nay, 'twas no' easy," he said. Mayhap, someday, he might tell her the rest of it. Of how, when other families came to visit their sons once a year, he was the only boy without a family. He'd made up stories of how his parents were off working for the king of Scotland, hence their reasons for not attending the yearly celebration.

"Now, let us go to the village," he said, clicking his tongue and snapping the reins. The wagon jolted forward at the pull of the team. "And ye'll be goin' in with yer head held high, lass. Ye be the Bowie bride. That alone will get ye more whispers and insults than if ye had *three* eyes and a second head."

THEY LEFT THE EMPTY WAGON ON THE EDGE OF THE VILLAGE. AFTER helping his wife down, Alec placed her hand in the crook of his arm before setting off down the narrow street. Gylys and Kyth followed close behind, while Patrick stayed with the horses.

Merchants and fishmongers called out as they passed by. A group of laughing children ran through the booths, weaving in and out, without a care in the world. Leona wished she could possess such a carefree attitude.

"We'll walk through once, to see what is being offered this day," Alec told her. "Do ye have a list of things ye need?"

"Aye, I do. 'Tis in me pouch," she said, patting the pouch at her waist with her free hand. "We'll need flour, salt, honey, spices, meats, and cheeses. As well as fruits, nuts—"

As she ticked things off the list, Alec only half listened. Ever watchful, ever on guard, he was scanning the crowd, looking for any sign of trouble. Whether it be from enemies or something as simple as a pick-pocket. Silently, he wondered if there would ever come a time in his life when he would not have to worry about anyone wanting to seek revenge for things his brother, or those lairds before him, had done to them.

"But ye've no' told me how much I can spend," Leona remarked. "Have ye a budget? Mayhap upon our return, ye could show me the books."

Distracted, he hadn't heard her.

"Alec?" she whispered his name. "Be there somethin' wrong?"

"Nay, lass," he replied, only hearing half of what she said. "Come, let us visit the miller."

So much for walking through the booths and stalls first.

THEY SPENT THE REST OF THE DAY WITH LEONA GOING FROM ONE merchant stall to the next. Alec soon realized his wife was careful and shrewd with her coin. He stood back, watching her haggle over the price of flour with one of the millers.

"I hear yer flour be the finest north of Edinburgh," she told him.

"Aye, 'tis, m'lady!" He all but beamed with pride.

Leona poked a finger into the sample he had on display. A heaping mound of flour set in a pewter dish. "'Tis well ground," she said. "I reckon I'll no' have to spend time digging out any big pieces of shaft."

Proudly, the man replied, "Of course no', m'lady! I take great pride in me work. Ye'll be makin' the best of breads this side of anywhere, of that, ye can be certain."

They haggled over price. In the end, Leona won over the man with her compliments, as well as pointing out she could get the flour cheaper from a miller three stalls down.

"Och! He does no' ground it as fine as me," the miller declared. "Ye'll be spendin' a good deal of time picking through it."

"Possibly," Leona said. "But it might be worth the coin I save."

Eventually, the miller acquiesced and sold her the flour at a discounted price. Alec felt quite proud of her and more than slightly relieved. She would not be one to simply pay whatever price was asked for anything. 'Twas good to know she was thrifty in her spending.

And so the story repeated, from one stall to the next. Although she had haggled down the price with every merchant, she somehow managed to make each feel as though he had gotten the better end of the bargain.

As Alec and the miller loaded her bags of flour into the wagon, Leona set off back down the street. Though she was never one to long for silk gowns, she did pause briefly to look at the fine wools and silks the milliner had on display. A dark green wool caught her attention. 'Twas nearly as soft as the silks. Deciding 'twas too early in her marriage to ask for such a fine fabric, she left it without even inquiring as to the price.

The streets were growing more crowded, the air more alive with chatter and bartering. Thus far, not one person had given her a second glance, nor had she heard anyone discussing her odd eyes as she walked by.

A few spaces away from the milliners sat a jewelers. All manner of fine necklaces, rings, and bracelets were on display. Just as she never longed for silk gowns, she also never longed to adorn herself with rubies or emeralds or other such baubles.

But as she walked past, something did catch her eye. 'Twas a very fine kilt broach, crafted out of silver. Intricately carved to resemble a dragon with tiny garnets for eyes.

"'Tis a fine piece, aye?" the man behind the counter asked.

"Aye, 'tis verra fine," Leona replied, unable to keep from staring at the brooch.

"Be ye lookin' fer something fer yer father?" he asked.

Leona gave a slight shake. "Nay, me husband," she said with a smile. She wondered if she'd ever not smile when she thought of him. Looking away from the brooch, she finally noticed the jeweler. Mayhap a bit older than Alec, with light brown hair and blue eyes. Not nearly as tall nor nearly as handsome.

"Do ye make custom pieces?"

"Aye, I do," he said, returning her smile.

"Can ye craft a brooch like this one, but instead of a dragon, it be a raven?" She had seen a crest over the mantle in the gathering room just that morning. Set against a deep, blood red background, was the image of a raven, with bright red eyes. In its mouth was a ribbon with the Bowie motto *Conquer With Might*.

"Aye, that can be done," he told her. "Mayhap with emerald eyes?"

"Nay, with garnets," she told him.

Before they could settle on a price or when such a piece could be made, she heard Alec's voice behind her. "Come away, Leona," he said.

Smiling proudly, she turned around. For some reason, he did not look nearly as happy to see her as she was to see him. He was scowling something fierce.

HE TOOK HER ARM AND LED HER AWAY. "I TURN ME BACK FER A MOMENT and ye're off spendin' me money on baubles?" he asked through gritted teeth. Aye, she had saved money on the things they needed. But to spend money on useless baubles? Married less than a sennight and already she was looking at expensive jewels. It angered him no end.

"Nay!" she argued.

He cut her off before she could explain. "We'll no' be spendin' money on emerald and ruby necklaces, or rings, or other such nonsense. Ye can get such ideas as that out of yer mind at once."

"But I was no' lookin' fer meself!" she told him as he stomped furiously down the street, dragging her behind him. "And please, slow down!"

Stopping abruptly, towering over her, he glared angrily. "No' lookin' fer yerself?" he asked incredulously. "Mayhap ye were lookin' fer bracelets fer Dougall? Or Kyth? Or me bandogge?"

She gave him a roll of her eyes. "Of course no'. Do no' be ridiculous."

"Then what, pray tell, were ye doin'?"

TRULY, SHE WISHED HE'D STOP GLARING AT HER. SHE DID NOT WANT TO sound like a besotted bride — even if that were the truth. "I was merely *lookin'*. I was no' preparin' to spend our hard earned coin on anything impractical." 'Twas not a lie, but neither was it the entire truth.

"But ye *were* lookin', aye? And how much, pray tell, would ye have spent had I no' come along when I did?"

Just why he was so confoundedly angry, she didn't know. Nor did she care. To stand in the crowded street and shout at her as if he'd caught her stealing, why, 'twas just insulting. She had been looking for a gift for *him*, the ungrateful cur. It rankled, it truly did.

"Will ye please stop shoutin' at me?" she asked as politely as she could, considering how angry she was with him.

"I am no' yellin'!" he seethed as he continued to glower at her.

Leona quirked a brow. "Then why be everyone starin' at ye?"

Her question stopped him at once. Glancing around, he saw that people were in fact staring at them. It made him all the more angry.

Leaning down, he whispered. "Ye will *no'* be spendin' me coin on frivolous things."

"I did no' intend to," she told him through gritted teeth. "And I shan't ever spend *yer* coin on anythin' of which *ye* do no' approve." *But I shall spend mine on whatever I wish. If I had any.*

"Good," he said with a curt nod. "As long as we understand one another."

Oh, she understood him all right. He was a thick-headed, stubborn man who easily jumped to conclusions. She decided then and there not to speak to him again for the remainder of the day. Better silence, than to tell him what she was truly thinking.

Though they hadn't actually settled their argument, they had at least come to a momentary peace accord. Newly married, the last thing Leona wanted was for her husband to think she was greedy, or worse yet, not frugal with a coin.

For a long while, they walked together in silence, each lost in their own thoughts and concerns. Soon, Alec's stomach began to growl quite loudly.

"Are ye hungry, lass?" he asked. His tone was calm, not nearly as venomous as it had been earlier.

She offered him an indifferent shrug. "I could eat a bit, I suppose." In truth, she was quite hungry, but she wasn't about to let him know.

With his hand on the small of her back, he led the way through the crowds until they found someone selling meat pies.

Of course there were only two left, such was his luck. He purchased both, giving one to her, keeping the other for himself.

Leading them away from the merchants, he found a grassy spot in which to eat their pies. He gave his to Leona while he removed his plaid and spread it on the ground. As he was settling in beside her, he realized she was staring at something.

He followed her gaze. It was locked on a woman holding a bairn. Next to her stood a lad of mayhap six. Urchins. Beggars. The woman looked gaunt, tired. The lad was no better, with dark circles under his eyes. The lad was staring at them, or more specifically, at their meat pies.

Absentmindedly, she gave Alec his food as she stood.

"What are ye doin'?" he asked.

Leona waved away his question as she headed toward the woman and her son.

~

"GOOD DAY TO YE." LEONA ADDRESSED HER GREETING TO THE WOMAN, but her eyes were on the lad. Alec sat in dumbfounded silence and listened.

"We have an extra meat pie, if ye'd like it," she told the lad. Holding out the offered meal, she smiled brightly at him. "Mayhap ye could share this with yer mum?"

The boy knotted his brow, his eyes expressing a weariness that should never be seen in eyes so young.

"Thank ye, kindly, mistress," the woman said. Even her voice sounded tired.

The boy looked first to his mother before reticently taking Leona's offering.

Leona uttered not a word as she patted the boy's head and returned to sit next to her stunned husband.

"Why on earth did ye do that?" Alec asked.

"Can ye no' see they be starvin'?"

As if that were something one did not see every day. Of course they were starving. They were poor. "So ye thought it a good idea to give yer food to them?"

Finally, she looked up at him. Tears dampened her lashes. "Aye, I thought it be a verra good idea."

What she did not tell him was that she knew what it was like to be poor and hungry. There had been a stretch of time in her young life, after the death of her mother, when she had been both things. 'Twas sometimes difficult to bury those memories.

"Did ye ever stop to ask yerself *why* they be poor? Mayhap she be a whore and her children are a result?"

"Or mayhap she be a widow with no way to earn a livin'?" she whispered. "And even if she is a whore, that be no reason to make her children suffer."

His face softened, as did his tone. "Nay lass, her children should not suffer."

SHE HAD TAKEN HIS BEWILDERMENT AS ANGER. IN TRUTH, HE WAS anything but angry. Surprised, aye, but also proud. He was learning much about his wife this day. A haggler when it came to dealing with merchants. But a soft-spot in her heart for those who were far less fortunate than they.

With a heavy sigh, he pushed himself to his feet. Without uttering a word, he walked toward the little family. "Here," he said, as he handed his own pie to the woman. As yet, she hadn't taken a bite of the pie Leona had given her. He'd watched as she tore off little bits to feed to the bairn in her arms as she encouraged her son to take his fill.

Surprise lit the woman's face; her eyes grew misty with thanks. "Thank ye kindly, m'laird," she whispered as she took the offering. "God bless ye and yer wife."

Silently, he turned away to head back to Leona. She was on her feet, tears streaming down her face. When he reached her, she flung herself into his arms. "Och, Alec!" she exclaimed.

"Do no' make my gesture more than 'twas," he told her.

"'Twas a verra kind thing ye did, Alec," she murmured against his chest. "Verra kind."

Still, she did seem exceedingly happy and quite pleased with him. Why her opinion of him mattered, he could not rightly say, and that irked him. 'Twas nearly as irksome as giving away their midday meal to a bunch of urchins when he was so bloody hungry. Aye, it had been the right thing to do.

Patting her back, he said, "Come, let us away this place before ye decide to give away our wagon of goods to them."

She giggled then. 'Twas a sweet, melodious sound that tickled at his heart. "I'd no' give away our wagon of goods, ye daft man."

He was not so certain she wouldn't.

STILL HUNGRY, THEY RETURNED TO THE MERCHANT STALLS AND SETTLED on bread, cheese and apples. Though he would not have been upset had she given the poor woman and her children this meal as well, he needed to eat.

Instead of returning to the clearing, he guided her toward the beach. Holding their meal in one hand, he helped her over the uneven terrain – through the grassy knoll and over large rocks – until finally they reached their destination. Not once did she let go of his hand, nor did she take her wide-open eyes off the sea.

Breathlessly, she held tight as she exclaimed, "Och! 'Tis beautiful!"

So they stood along the rocky coast. While Leona took in the sight before her, Alec took in the sight of *her*. She was in awe of the ocean, the gently lapping waves, the seagulls as they dove into the sea for their own meal. He was in awe of her.

She very much resembled Rose Mackintosh, who none would ever deny was a beautiful woman. But there was something *more* about Leona. Aye, she had odd colored eyes that did not match. Hair the color of honey kissed by the sun. And a bosom to shame Aphrodite and Venus. But she was so much more than that. Intriguing, delightfully honest when it came to their loving. Yet, there was more. Just what that *more* was, he could not as yet identify or put to words. She simply was.

Kindhearted to a fault — especially when it came to the poor, as he'd only just recently discovered. She was also kind to his men. Seemed to care about them really, which was an oddity in and of itself. For no one, save for another Bowie, actually cared for a Bowie.

Leona was a giving soul, as he was quickly learning. Giving of her food as well as her kindheartedness. As yet, he was not certain if this was a fault he should correct or something to be cherished. Odd, he found it, yet charming.

He sat on the sandy beach and began to eat his meal. "Sit, Leona," he said. "Ye should eat."

Instead of sitting next to him, she handed him her bread and cheese, but kept the apple. Quietly, she took a few steps toward the water, while eating her apple.

Alec watched her closely while he ate his own meager meal.

He knew she had secrets, secrets she did not wish to share with him. Suddenly, he found himself wanting to know what those secrets were. He had an inkling they were not the kind of secrets or memories anyone would want to share. Dark, deeply dark and closely held secrets that he knew, instinctively, brought her a good measure of pain. But she kept the pain hidden, deep in a place she'd not allow him to see.

Did he truly wish to know them? Did he truly desire discovery? And what could he, of all people, do to help ease those painful memories away?

He began to feel silly for allowing himself to wonder, to feel anything more than friendly compassion toward her. *'Tis a dangerous, treacherous road, ye fool.* Was that his own voice he heard in the recesses of his mind, or his father's? Either way, he would heed its warning.

Having lost track of the time to those treacherous thoughts, he also lost track of his wife. While his mind had meandered, so had she. No longer at his side, she was now heading barefoot into the waves.

"Leona! Take care!" he shouted. "It be awfully—"

His words were cut off by her delightful scream. "Cold!"

He knew the water would be frigid, but apparently his wife did not care.

"I be *in* the ocean, Alec!" she called out to him as the waves washed over her feet and ankles. "'Tis cold, but I care no'!"

Like a child discovering something for the first time. Gleeful, happy, and excited, much like he had been the first time he had joined with her. Odd that he should compare the two things.

A large wave rolled in, crashing over her legs, her knees, which he could easily see, for she had lifted her skirts to mid thigh. Damnation, if his loins did not begin to ache at the sight of her!

"Mayhap—" his voice caught on a lump in his throat. Clearing it away, he tried again. "Mayhap ye should get out now, before ye soak yerself clear through to yer bones." He went to her then, with his hand held out.

"'Twould be worth the soakin'," she said with that bright, beautiful smile that somehow managed to slice through his protective wall.

Deep down, he wanted nothing more than to relish the moment, to make it stretch for an eternity. Then he heard that word of warning, admonishing him for such tender-hearted thoughts. Pushing them aside, he said, "Come, lass, 'tis time to leave."

She let out a heavy sigh. "Only if ye promise to bring me here again?"

'Twas a request, not a demand. One he found, no matter how much his logical mind wanted to deny it, his heart could not.

"Aye, I shall bring ye here again."

Traitorous heart.

WITH THE WAGON LOADED, AND THE PROMISE OF MORE DELIVERIES TO come on the morrow, Alec helped his wife into her seat, climbed up, and grabbed the reins. He was angry with himself for making a promise to bring her back to the ocean again. Nay, not *that* specifically. Nay, he was angry for the softening of his heart. Angry with himself for behaving like a lad who had just discovered lasses weren't nearly as irritating as previously believed.

Leona, as happy as a lamb frolicking in the spring grass, grabbed his arm and hugged it. "Och, Alec!" she said happily. "'Twas a grand day, was it no'? No' one person remarked on me eyes!"

Guilt fell over him for being so gruff with her. "I told ye none would, did I no'?" he replied.

"Aye, ye did," she said as she squeezed his arm more tightly. "I thank ye, Alec."

"Fer what?"

Taking in a deep breath, she let it out slowly, as if she could never be more content. "Fer such a grand day. Fer bein' so kind, fer yer generosity, and fer lettin' me dip my feet into the ocean. Fer everythin'."

The words, spoken from her heart, took the wind out of his sails. Bloody hell if he didn't want to say *thank you for a good day as well.*

"Remember, a Bowie is never kind nor generous," he said in an amused tone.

Leona laughed at his jest. "Then I thank ye fer being the meanest, most terrifyin' bloody bastard I have ever laid eyes to."

Why that warmed his heart, he was uncertain, but it had. It had also made his groin ache with desire. The desire to toss her into the back of the wagon and have his way with her then and there.

Instead, he snapped the reins and clicked his tongue at the horses.

CHAPTER 9

For the remainder of their trek back to the keep, Alec sat in amused silence, while listening to his wife chatter on. "I can no' ever remember a day such as this, where no one teased or taunted me. 'Twas quite remarkable," she told him. "Quite remarkable indeed. Do ye like rabbit stew, Alec? I make a verra fine rabbit stew. I doubt I will have time to make it today, fer the day will be nearly over by the time we get back to the keep. But on the morrow? On the morrow I shall make ye a fine rabbit stew."

He was growing used to her asking a question and not waiting for an answer. How odd he found the fact that he liked the sound of her voice. Odder still that it did not grate on his nerves. 'Twas unsettling when he realized he found her charming. He wondered if the rest of his clan would deem her charming as well.

"Leona, on the morrow, I should like to introduce ye to our clan."

"On the morrow?" she exclaimed. If he didn't know better, he'd say she was terrified by the prospect. "But I have no gifts fer them."

Instinct told him not to ask to what she was referring, but he felt compelled to do it anyway. "Gifts?"

"Aye," she replied, sounding quite distressed. "As their new mistress, I should present them with gifts. Such as a jar of jam or cheese or bread or the like."

Alec could not quite understand her distress. "Lass, where do ye get these notions?"

She cast him a look that said she questioned his level of intelligence. "'Tis the way it be done, Alec. Before I came to live with the McLarens, Da worked fer the McCalpins. When their son wed and brought his wife back to their lands, she presented each of the clanspeople with a gift. Each family was given a basket with bread, jam, and honey. 'Tis how it be done."

He too had witnessed a similar situation years ago, but never gave it much thought. He had assumed the laird's new wife was simply trying to buy the affection of her new clan. He had also been witness to the clansmen giving their mistress gifts. "But we be Bowies, lass. We do no' necessarily follow such traditions."

Her mouth curved into that delicious 'o' as she thought on it for a moment. Damn, but it made his groin ache with desire whenever she did that.

"But Alec, I thought ye wanted to change from yer old ways?"

He did not want to admit she had a point. "Aye, but we needn't change everythin' all at once. 'Tis enough fer me that my men have laid down their weapons and picked up plows."

She looked deflated. "But I want to make a good impression when I meet them fer the first time."

He could not contain his chuckle. "Ye will make a good impression, lass. Fer ye were brave enough to marry *me*."

HE SHOULD HAVE KNOWN SHE WOULD NOT LEAVE THE MATTER ALONE. As soon as they returned to the keep, she was in the kitchens. Alec grabbed a few men from the armory to help offload the goods from the wagon. With a good deal of pride, his wife politely directed the men to where the items should be placed.

Remembering Bowie men were not keen on compliments, Alec

could see her doing her best to hold back any thanks or kind words. More than once she began to say "thank ye," but stopped herself. His men neither noticed nor cared.

As soon as everything was where she wanted it, she pulled two large bowls from under the table.

The hour was growing late and he hoped she was preparing a fine meal for them. "What be ye preparin'?" he asked hopefully.

"Bread," she replied as she took one of the bowls to the larder.

"But we bought bread," he said. As if needing evidence, he held up a loaf of dark bread. "See?"

"Och!" she said with a smile. "I ken we bought bread. But I also need to get some goin', so 'twill rise proper. Do no fash yerself over it, Alec. I shall also fix ye somethin' to eat. Just give me a little while to do so."

His stomach was growling. "But I've no' had anything today but a few hard boiled eggs, a hunk of bread and cheese."

"And an apple. Do no' ferget the apple."

He rolled his eyes.

"Same as I," she reminded him as she set the bowl of flour on the table. "Mayhap ye could help me?" she asked. "Can ye grab the wheel of cheese from the larder?"

Without realizing what was happening, Alec was preparing his own meal while his wife kneaded bread.

THOUGH SHE'D BEEN UP HALF THE NIGHT PREPARING LOAF AFTER LOAF of bread, Leona still arose before dawn. Leaving Alec to sleep, she quietly slipped out of their bedchamber, and once again dressed in the dimly lit corridor.

The sun was just beginning to kiss the morning sky as she made her way out of the keep and into the kitchens. She reckoned she was the only one awake at this early hour and remained as quiet as possible.

Once inside the kitchen, she lit candles and set about lighting the fires in both hearths. She made a mental note to ask Alec to help her replenish her supply of wood, for it would soon be depleted.

Once the fires were set to her liking, she removed the cloths that covered the loaves of bread taking up nearly every empty table and space in the large room. While the first batch of bread baked, she made herself a cup of warm cider.

It felt good to be in this room, knowing she was preparing gifts for the clanspeople she would meet later this day. She found peace here, as well as a purpose. She couldn't remember ever feeling so at ease anywhere in her life. Silently, she prayed for the peace to be everlasting and that Alec's people would, at the very least, be polite if not accepting. *"Let them no' hate me. And let them no' care about me eyes."*

After finishing her cider, she washed and dried her cup and set it back upon the open shelf above the sink. Spotting a bit of flour on the floor, she grabbed her broom and swept it out the door.

By the time she finished those tasks, the first round of bread was done. With great care, she removed the bread and set it upon one of the larger tables to cool. With another dozen loaves set to bake, she realized she should make a list of all the things she wished to do over the next few days. Oh, she had the list fully memorized. But writing it all down was one more way to keep her mind from worrying about Alec's people.

With no ink to be found in the kitchen, she returned to the keep. With a lighted torch, she set off in search of Alec's private study.

'Twas one bare room after another. Just like the grand gathering room; empty. If anyone by chance were to enter this first floor of the keep they would undoubtedly get the impression it had been abandoned.

With each vacant room, her excitement dwindled. Mayhap her husband did not think he had the need for a private room in which to work. She had no desire to return to her bedchamber in order to retrieve her own supply of ink. Only because she did not want to wake her husband just yet. He had told her once he preferred late nights to early mornings.

Finally, at the end of a long corridor, she found what she was looking for. Though it could hardly be called a study. One heavy table that held a few scrolls, one lonely candlestick, along with quill and ink. Two hard chairs sat on either side of the table. Two more chairs sat in front of the hearth.

Nothing adorned the walls. No books, no tapestries, nothing at all that would lend any warmth to the large space. There were three tall windows covered with furs, and that was it.

Was this a glimpse into her husband's heart? Was it too, desolate and barren? No, she could not believe that. Not after all the kindness he had shown her. And especially not after the tender and gentle ways in which he loved her physically.

But why must his home be so dark and dreary? There had to be a reason. Mayhap he had removed anything that might remind him of his brother. 'Twas entirely possible, and 'twas the only thing that made a lick of sense. She thought the prospect a sad one. Thus far, Alec had not discussed his brother. Mayhap 'twas all too painful.

Doubtful she could solve that mystery this morning, she grabbed the ink and returned to her kitchen.

By the time Alec came below stairs, she had baked four dozen loaves of bread, made out her list, and prepared him a lovely meal.

Alec stood in the doorway of the kitchen for a long moment. Gone was the frustration he had felt when waking up to an empty bed again.

Leona was standing at the counter, her back to him. Sunlight streamed in through the open window. A long, honey-blonde braid hung down the back of her dark green dress. She was humming a tune he did not recognize.

The smell of ham sizzling in the brazier, the warm scent of fresh baked bread, and the sound of his wife's happy tune was like nothing he'd ever imagined he would desire before. Yet …

When she turned to place trenchers on the table, she was momentarily startled at his presence. "Och! I did no' see ye there," she said. Right before she gave him a brilliant smile.

'Twas an honest, genuine smile. One that said she was glad to see him. A smile that said a thousand things at once without her uttering a word. It terrified him to his marrow simply because of the way that smile made him *feel*.

Content. Happy. Adored. Glad to have a wife such as she. Glad that she was here.

Nay, he did not want to feel anything of the sort for it made him a weak, besotted fool.

And he most certainly did not want to return her smile, but 'twas impossible not to. 'Twas akin to trying to hold back a raging river with his booted foot.

"How did ye sleep?" she asked as she returned to her task at hand. "I hope ye be hungry. Ye'll find more than a few hard boiled-eggs this morn."

Whenever Alec was near, she grew nervous and excited at the same time. Especially when he smiled, as he was doing now.

Those feelings often led to her prattling on about one thing or another. "I made ye ham, eggs, sausage, and bread. There also be berry jam and apples. But if that be no' what ye want, I can prepare ye somethin' else." She would have prepared him anything he wanted, just to have his smile.

"Nay," he said. "That will do."

'Twas then he noticed the dozens upon dozens loaves of bread. "What be this?"

Leona smiled proudly. "Bread. I told ye I did no' want to meet yer people without some sort of gift. Bread was the easiest thing fer me to make."

He frowned. "And I told ye 'twas no' necessary."

She could not understand why he seemed upset. 'Twas a simple gift. "But—"

Alec stopped her with a raised hand. "Our people will respect ye, Leona, simply because ye are me wife."

'Twasn't only their respect she wanted. Growing more uncomfortable under his glare, she looked at her boots. He could not possibly understand the importance of it all. "But I want them to like me."

BEFORE HE COULD SAY ANYTHING TO REASSURE HER, KYTH AND GYLYS appeared at the back door. Leona let them in.

"I told ye 'twas fresh baked bread I smelled," Kyth said triumphantly as he crossed the threshold. "And ham as well!"

Gylys rolled his eyes at his friend. "Ye're actin' like a cat about to get a bowl of fresh cream, ye lout. Our lady does no' want to feed us as well as her husband."

At seeing all the bread on the table, Kyth whistled. "Is the entire clan coming to break their fast?"

Leona smiled wanly. "Nay," she said. "Alec is takin' me to meet the clan this morn. I wanted to give each family a small token of my thanks and esteem."

"Thanks?" Kyth asked, genuinely puzzled.

"Fer what be ye thankin' them?" Gylys asked, sounding just as confused as his friend.

Tears welled in her eyes. Those tears apparently had the same affect on his men as they did Alec. A sudden pang of guilt stabbed at his gut.

"Och! M'lady, do no' fash yerself over it!" Gylys offered. "They'll be right thankful fer the gesture."

Kyth chuckled. "Though I fear none are used to people *givin'* things to them."

"Aye, they be more accustomed to takin' what they want," Gylys told her.

Aye, she knew what he said was true, but that did not mean she would not make the attempt to show them her sincerity.

~

WITHIN THE HOUR LEONA AND ALEC WERE READY TO SET OUT TO MEET their people. With Gylys and Kyth acting both as guard and basket carriers, they set out to introduce Leona to their people.

Over the drawbridge and down a narrow path lined with ancient trees, the party spilled out into a clearing. Dotting the land were numerous huts and cottages, many of which had only recently been built.

Each home, while slightly different in appearance, possessed the same patch of earth for gardens. A few had barns — either separate from or attached to their cottages — in which to house any livestock. Flowers grew around many of the cottages.

Smoke billowed out of countless chimneys. Running happily throughout the glen were dozens of children, all playing together. Squeals and giggles rang out in the crisp morning air.

Home. This be what I always wanted, Leona thought to herself. Her stomach tightened with glee; her mood was instantly lifted. Certainly happy children bespoke of happy homes, which in turn meant Alec's people would welcome her with open arms.

Catching sight of their laird, the children all stopped their frolicking and rushed to greet him.

"Alec!" A young lad called out as he raced toward them. Leona estimated him to be around eleven years of age and there was no mistaking he or any of the children who followed behind him were Bowies. They all sported the same dark hair as their laird.

"Good morn, to ye, Wills," Alec said. His smile was warm and affectionate. It made Leona's heart swell with pride and hope. If he could be this kind to these children, it only made sense he would be a good father to their own.

"Be that our new mistress?" Wills asked with a raised brow.

"She be verra pretty," one of the younger girls spoke out.

Leona felt her cheeks grow warm at the compliment.

Alec raised his hands to call for quiet. "Aye, this be yer new mistress, me wife, Leona."

"What be wrong with her eyes?" A little boy asked.

Leona felt her heart fall. *So it begins,* she mused.

"Not a bloody thing," Alec told the boy. His tone was firm, yet kind.

The children all seemed to shrug in unison. Apparently if their laird was unbothered by her odd colored eyes, then neither would they.

"What have ye in the baskets?" another inquisitive child asked.

"We've come to introduce ye all to yer new mistress," Alec told them. "She brings ye gifts of bread."

Dozens of perplexed and curious eyes turned to stare at their new mistress.

"And before ye can ask why," Alec began, "'tis because she be a good woman."

That was all the explanation any of them needed. Leona wondered if the parents would be as inclined as their children to accept Alec's word on any given matter.

Excited, the children fell into place around Alec as he led the way down the path. Two little girls, mayhap no more than five years in age, wriggled their way through to stand on either side of Alec. Each of them slipped a tiny hand into his. The vision of her husband walking hand-in-hand with these children, tugged and pulled at her heart. Oh, she could not wait to give him children of his own. How desperately she wanted to see him walking along, holding the hands of *their* children.

Leona was summarily pushed to the rear of the group, but she did not mind. She caught a few of the children staring at her, but she saw no malice in those bright, young eyes. Only curiosity.

Alec knocked on the door of the first cottage. A very pretty young woman, with a babe on one hip and a wean clinging to her blue wool skirts opened the door. She wore her dark hair in a long braid, draped over one shoulder.

"Alec!" she exclaimed happily. Realizing their laird was not alone, she stared curiously out at the throng of children. A moment passed before she called to her husband. "Fergus! Alec be here!"

Moments later, a young man appeared at the door. "Alec," he said before catching sight of his entourage. "I see ye brought company," he jested.

Alec offered him a warm smile. He turned to take his wife's arm, but she was not standing next to him. Turning around, he extended his arm to her. With a good deal of trepidation, she stepped forward.

"Fergus, Maisie," Alec began. "I would like to introduce ye to me wife, yer new mistress, Leona."

While Fergus welcomed her with a kind smile, the same could not be said of his wife. "'Tis a pleasure, m'lady," Fergus said with a slight bow. Maisie remained mute.

"I brought ye a gift," Leona said. Reaching into her basket, she pulled out a small loaf of bread and offered it to Maisie.

"Why?" Maisie asked. Her tone was sharp and quite unkind. "I ken how to make me own bread." She stared at the bread as if Leona were trying to hand her a pile of warm horse dung.

"'Tis a gift," Alec explained.

While that explanation might have satisfied the children, it meant very little to Maisie. "But I can make me own bread, Alec."

"I ken that," he told her.

Still holding the bread, Leona made an attempt to explain herself. "Where I come from, the mistress often brings gifts to her people. I did no' mean to offend. 'Tis simply a gift."

Maisie quirked a dubious brow. Before she could utter an unkind response, Fergus took the bread. "Thank ye, m'lady." He sounded just as confused as his wife, but was not appalled or offended by Leona's gesture.

Leona stood nervously and in silence while Alec and Fergus chatted for a while longer. Maisie continued to glare at her new mistress.

Leona tried to convince herself that the rest of Alec's people would not appear nearly as offended as this young woman. Wanting nothing more than to be kind, Leona offered her a compliment. "Ye have verra beautiful children."

Maisie responded with a very unladylike and derisive snort.

"And a very beautiful home," Leona tried again.

Maisie turned her gaze away, choosing instead to look at something other than Leona.

Gratefully, they were soon saying goodbye and heading toward the next cottage. She was introduced to another young couple. Their response was much the same as before. The young woman was insulted by Leona's gift, but her husband was much kinder about it all.

And so it went, one cottage after another, with similar and equally disheartening results. By the time they reached the tenth cottage, Leona was on the verge of tears.

Nay, she told herself. *Ye be Alec's wife, the mistress of the keep and its people. Ye'll no' cry, at least no' in front of anyone. 'Twill simply take time fer them to get to know ye.*

THE CHILDREN GRADUALLY LOST INTEREST OR WERE CALLED INTO THEIR homes by their parents. 'Twas long after the nooning hour when Alec knocked upon the door of an older looking cottage. This time, he did not wait for anyone to come to the door; instead, he opened it and stepped inside.

"This be Melvin's cottage," Kyth explained as they followed Alec in.

'Twas a bit unkempt, but by no means filthy. A small table holding a few dirty pots and bowls sat in the center of the small space. In the far corner of the room was the bed in which Melvin Bowie was resting.

He was seventy if he was a day. Thinning gray hair crowned his wrinkled face. But his eyes twinkled as he smiled the moment he saw Alec.

"This be Melvin," Kyth whispered to Leona. "He has no' been well fer some time."

"Good day to ye, Alec." The auld man sounded tired, his voice strained as if it took a good deal of effort to speak. Holding out his hand, he gave Alec's a squeeze. "And who be this lovely lass ye brought with ye?"

Alec smiled at Leona as he held out his hand and drew her to stand beside him. "This be me wife, yer new mistress, Leona."

"Och! The McLaren lass," Melvin replied with a smile. "They must truly believe ye want peace to give ye such a bonny bride."

"Down now, ye auld thief!" Alec said playfully. "Do no' get any ideas about stealin' away with her."

Melvin laughed, albeit weakly. "Ye ken I could, Alec. Were I thirty years younger." Facing Leona he said, "I was no' always auld nor weak. I had me fair share of lasses in me day."

Leona liked the man immediately. "I imagine ye neither jest nor lie," she told him. "Even now, ye be a handsome man."

He beamed with pride at her compliment. "I like her, Alec. Make sure ye treat the lass well."

Alec chose to ignore his remark. "How fare ye?" he asked, his tone turning serious.

"I have had better days, lad."

Having seen the dirty pots and dishes, Leona was concerned that he could not care for himself. "Have ye eaten this day?"

Waving away her concern with a gnarled hand, he replied, "Do no worry over me lass. I'll soon be joinin' me wife, me sweet Jannet."

Something told Leona he meant to join her in the afterlife, so she remained quiet. His tone, the way his eyes twinkled brightly at saying her name, told Leona he loved the woman, even if she were no longer here. She began to wonder what the woman had been like. Would Alec's eyes ever twinkle similarly at the mere mention of her own name?

"How long has she been gone?" Alec asked him.

"Four years now," Melvin replied. "Four years and three months come the new moon."

Awkward silence filled the tiny cottage. Leona was suddenly beset with an overwhelming need to be busy. Wanting very much not to shed any tears over the auld man's missing his wife, she began clearing the pots from the table. "Kyth, would ye fetch me some water? I should like to wash Melvin's dishes."

"Those be no' mine," Melvin said from his bed. "The women folk bring me a meal each day. They take turns, ye ken."

She stood at the table, a small pot in one hand and a bowl in another. "Ye eat only once a day?" she asked with one raised brow. No matter how auld or weak a body was, it still needed sustenance more than once a day.

"'Tis enough," Melvin replied. "They be busy with their own. 'Tis enough they think of me when they do."

Wrinkling her brow, she looked to Alec for some guidance. From his blank expression, he had none.

"Would it be all right if *I* too, brought ye a meal?" she asked Melvin.

His smile burned brighter. "Now, that would be an honor, mistress! An honor indeed."

Leona continued to tidy up while Alec and Melvin discussed the growing crop of barley.

"If all goes well," Alec told him, "we shall have a fine crop come October."

"And who do ye plan on sellin' it to?" Melvin asked.

"The McLarens and McLeods have agreed to purchase a goodly amount. In a few weeks, I plan on visiting neighboring clans in hopes of sparking deals with them."

Melvin thought it a good idea and told his laird so. "Ye can put those in the corner, lass," he told Leona, who was gathering tunics from the floor and chairs. "One of the women folk will wash them fer me."

Before Leona could volunteer to take care of the task, Alec brought the conversation back to barley. After tidying the cottage as best she could, she went to stand behind her husband.

For nearly an hour, the two men sat and discussed farming. Leona listened intently, but kept any opinions she might have on the matter to herself. It was quite apparent that Melvin had more than just rudimentary knowledge on the subject. Far more than she possessed. Alec was soaking up every bit of information he could from the auld man.

Melvin began to yawn, yet never once complained of being tired.

But Alec was not blind. Without commenting on the auld man's condition, he simply said, "I thank ye fer yer time, Melvin. As much as I would enjoy sittin' here all the day long to learn from ye, I fear we can no'. We've other people to visit this day."

"Ye ken I always have time to help ye, Alec," Melvin said with a tired smile. To Leona he said, "And ye, lassie, can visit me any time ye wish."

~

AFTER LEAVING MELVIN TO REST, THEY VISITED THE COTTAGE NEXT TO his. They were met with the same confusion and contempt as given to them earlier. So it repeated, one cottage after another, one upset woman after another. Why a simple loaf of bread was met with such repugnance, Leona could not begin to guess. Though he said not a word, she was quite certain Alec was thinking *I told ye so.*

The last cottage they visited was Dougall's. It sat at the far western edge of the glen, a good distance from the other cottages. A neat and tidy garden grew south of the home. Just beyond that a small barn, a chicken coop, and a good-sized pen that housed three cows with three calves.

Dougall was out of doors chopping wood. Two of his older boys were helping to stack the wood in a lean-to.

Seeing Alec and the others approaching, he leaned his axe against the large stump and wiped his sweaty brow onto the sleeve of his tunic. "Good day to ye!" he called out as they neared the cottage.

"Good day to ye, Dougall," Alec said.

Dougall smiled at Leona as he bowed at the waist. "Good to see ye, mistress."

"'Tis good to see ye, Dougall," she replied.

Dougall called for his sons. "This be me eldest boy, Wills, and me second born, James," he said proudly. "Lads, this be yer new mistress, yer laird's wife, Leona."

They each smiled at her, before giving a polite bow. "'Tis a pleasure to see ye again, mistress," Wills said.

"Aye," said James.

Dougall looked curiously at his sons.

"We met her earlier, Da," Wills explained.

"Aye," Alec said. "They helped escort us to a few of the other cottages."

Content with the explanation, Dougall rubbed a hand atop Wills' head. "Come inside," Dougall told Alec. To Leona, he said, "I shall introduce ye to me wife. She's been eager to meet ye."

Leona prayed 'twas with happy eagerness and not the same scorn as the rest of the women she had met today.

Dougall held the door open as the others followed inside. Almost immediately, Leona felt at home. This was the cottage of her daydreams. A large bed sat in one corner, with a pretty linen curtain one could draw for privacy. A few steps from that, a ladder led up to a loft. A low fire burned in the hearth, a pot of something delicious smelling cooking within.

Furs were pulled away from the windows, allowing in the fresh, crisp air. Under one window sat a loom with a newly begun project. Clean rushes lined the floor. A few tapestries hung on the wall.

Dougall's wife, heavy with child, was standing near her sink. "Och!" she declared. "I was no' expectin' company this day! Me house is a mess."

In Leona's mind, 'twas as immaculate a space as she'd seen in quite some time. "Nay, 'tis a beautiful home," she said.

"Och! I just swept and laid new rushes and ye beasties are all trackin' in!"

The men looked duly chastised.

"Ye must be the laird's wife," she said, approaching with outstretched arms. She took Leona's hands in her own. "Och! Ye be just as pretty as Dougall said ye were."

Leona felt her cheeks grow warm at the compliment. Relief washed over her. *Finally, someone who is kind!*

"Would ye like some cider?" she asked. Without waiting for a reply, she set about pouring two cups.

The men in the room chuckled. "Me wife has never kent a

stranger," Dougall said.

"Och, ye big lout!" his wife exclaimed. "Outside with all of ye. I should like to get to know me new mistress without all of ye hoverin' about."

"But I have no' introduced ye yet," Alec reminded her politely.

"I ken who she be, Alec. We can make our own introductions. Now, off with all of ye."

The men laughed again as they began filing out of the cottage. Leona liked this woman instantly. She was left to wonder how Alec would respond were she to take the same tone with him. Would he smile and laugh and do her bidding or would he bite her off her head?

"I be Effie Bowie. Dougall's wife. Mother to Wills, James, Aric, and Thomas," she said as she set the mugs of cider on the table. "And in here," she said as she patted her belly, "would be Craigh. Or Phillip, I have no' yet decided."

"Ye be certain 'tis a boy?" Leona dared ask as she took a sip of cider.

"What else *could* it be?" Effie jested. "I have birthed six boy bairns. But only four have lived beyond their third day." Gone was the playful tone. Now her voice was laced with sorrow.

Leona had no personal experience of that kind of loss, but she was a woman. She could well imagine the heartache Effie had suffered. "I be so sorry," she told her.

"'Tis the lot of all women, I suppose," Effie said as she absentmind-edly rubbed her large belly. "So to answer yer question, aye, I be certain it be another boy. He be just as ornery as his brothers, keepin' me awake all hours with his kickin'."

Slowly, her smile returned. "Would ye like somethin' to eat?" Effie asked.

"Nay, but I thank ye," she said.

'Twas then Effie noticed the basket on her table. "What be in there, mistress?"

Leona felt her face grow warm. Thus far Effie had seemed a kind and reasonable woman. The last thing she wanted to do was injure her feelings. "'Tis naught but bread. And please, call me Leona."

"Bread? What kind?" Effie asked with much curiosity. "Who be it fer? And please, sit."

She took the offered seat at Effie's table. Deciding there was no way to avoid the inevitable, Leona lifted the cloth and slid the basket toward her. "I was tryin' to do somethin' nice, by givin' a loaf of bread to those people I met today. But I fear I have insulted every woman in the clan by doin' so."

Effie looked at her as if she'd gone completely mad. "Insulted them?"

"Aye. They all said they could verra well make their own. Not one would take it. Alec had to give them to their husbands."

"Fools they be if ye ask me," Effie said as she looked inside the basket. "I say 'twas a kind gesture."

Relieved, Leona let loose a frustrated breath. "That was me intent. But I fear they took it as an insult."

"Can I have a loaf?" Effie asked with a hopeful expression. "I be no' due fer two more months, but I tell ye, it gets more difficult to move about each day. And bakin' bread? It tires me out, it does. I swear, I never got this tired so quickly with the others."

"I only have a few left, but aye, ye can have them all," Leona said with a warm and relieved smile.

With a grateful grin, Effie retrieved a loaf. "It smells heavenly," she said. Tearing off a hunk, she stuffed it into her mouth. "That be verra good!"

Leona was thankful for the compliment. Her spirits lifted rapidly. "Thank ye," she said.

They were silent for a while as Effie ate more of the bread. Leona sipped on the cider, uncertain what to say or do next, unaccustomed to just *sitting* and *talking* with someone other than Rose.

"So," Effie said, wiping the crumbs from her fingers. "Ye married Alec Bowie."

Leona smile and nodded.

"How be he treatin' ye?" Effie asked before bringing the cup of cider to her lips.

"Well," Leona replied before diverting her eyes from Effie's scrutinizing gaze.

"Well?" she asked. "Be that all?"

Leona giggled slightly. "We only married five days ago. But thus far, he has been quite kind."

Effie took in a deep breath. "I fear I do no' ken him well meself. He is a few years aulder than I. He spent many years away from here, either fosterin' or travelin' the world. He did not return until after Eduard died and Rutger took over as chief. But aye, he seems kind enough."

Leona had already learned as much. "What was Rutger like?" she dared ask, only because she wanted to learn more about her husband and his family. Mayhap gaining some insight into her husband.

Effie shrugged her shoulders with indifference. "Some liked him, some did no'. He was a difficult man to get to know."

It seemed to run in the family.

"And his parents? What were they like?"

Effie laughed aloud at that. "Och! Never in me life have I known two people who fought as much as they. Though they did love their sons, they apparently had a strong dislike for each other."

Leona quirked a brow. "But they were good to their children?"

"Aye, they were. Though Alec's father sent him away at a young age. I still think he did it to hurt Caitlin."

"That was his mother?" Leona asked. Thus far she hadn't heard any name but his brother's pass over Alec's lips.

"Aye. And what a beauty she was. She loved her sons, ye ken. Verra much. Doted on them, she did. But Roger — that be Alec's father — he hated his wife more than he loved his sons. He sent each of them away, ye ken. To foster, he said, but if ye ask Dougall, 'twas more to spite his wife than fer the lads' benefit."

Leona was suddenly beset with worry. What if she gave Alec a son? Would he send the boy away? She couldn't bear the thought of being separated from any future children they might have.

Seeing her distress, Effie smiled. "Do no' fash yerself over it. I do no' think Alec would be so cruel as his father was."

Leona could only pray Effie was right.

CHAPTER 10

They returned to the keep later in the afternoon. When they entered the courtyard, it was filled with at least one hundred men who were training. Swords clanging against swords, grunting, cursing, wrestling, throwing knives: the sounds of mock battle filled the air around them, bouncing off the walls and keep.

Taking Leona by the elbow, Alec led her to a safe place, where she would be safe and there would be no chance she could get hurt. "We work in the fields in the morn, then train in the afternoons," he explained quite proudly. "Ye will no' find a fiercer lot of men on God's earth."

Leona had to agree, but not with the same level of enthusiasm nor delight as her husband. She detested fighting. Oh, she knew 'twas a necessary evil, but that did not mean she had to take any enjoyment in watching.

When the McLaren and Mackintosh men trained, one could always find a group of women, either wives or women who wanted to be wives, watching with great interest. Often times they would take a picnic, making it a more festive affair. Leona never joined them. 'Twasn't as if any of them had extended an offer to begin with. But if they had, she would have politely declined.

"Och!" Alec exclaimed. "Did ye see how Andrew deflected Derrick's sword?"

No, no she hadn't. And she had no desire to. Unable to watch, she was staring at her boots.

Moments later, a man left the throngs and came to join them. "Good day to ye, Alec!" He greeted his laird with an extended hand.

Tearing her eyes away from her booted toes, she looked up. The man was massive. As tall as Alec, but he was built like a brick wall. Wide shoulders, broad chest, thick arms and legs. There was no mistaking he was a Bowie, what with his brown hair, dark eyes, and fierce countenance. 'Twas then she noticed a trail of blood running down the side of his face from a wound near his ear. "Good, lord!" she exclaimed. "Ye're injured!"

Momentarily forgetting who she was, she dropped the basket and grabbed the end of her apron. She was about to lift it up to wipe away the blood when Alec pulled her back.

"Lass, Derrick be fine," Alec told her.

The injured man, Derrick, was staring at her in wide-eyed confusion and shock.

"But he's bleeding," Leona argued.

"Aye," Alec said. "That often happens when we train."

Derrick laughed heartily. "'Tis naught but a scratch, mistress! But do no' fash yerself over it. I got Fergus back. Took him a while before he could breathe again, but I got him back."

It took every ounce of strength she had to bite her tongue, to keep from telling either her husband or Derrick, just what she thought of grown men fighting.

Smoothing down her apron, she stepped away, back to her husband's side.

"Lass, this be Derrick Bowie," Alec said, still smiling down at her. "Derrick, this be Leona, me wife."

Before she could offer a *pleased to meet ye,* Derrick turned away and shouted. "Down with yer weapons, ye pox-riddled whores and piss poor excuses of wasted flesh! Our laird be here with his wife!"

Leona jumped at the sound of his deep voice breaking out and over the crowd. A moment later, all weapons and fighting came to a halt.

"Thank ye, Derrick," Alec said.

"Ye're welcome."

Stunned, Leona was frozen in place when all attention was drawn her way. A few rapid heartbeats later, they were all walking toward her and their laird.

Grabbing her husband's arm, she held on to him for a sense of security. Just why she felt terrified, she could not begin to understand. But terrified she was.

"Leona," Alec whispered out of the corner of his mouth. "Do no' look so afraid. They'll think ye a weak woman."

Oh, but she was afraid. Afraid of the wall of men approaching, afraid of making a fool of herself, afraid she might say or do the wrong thing. Still, she willed her nerves to settle by taking a deep, fortifying breath. Lifting her chin ever so slightly, she stared straight ahead and waited.

"Lads!" Alec called out to them as the living wall approached. They stopped, ten deep, and just a few feet away. "This be me wife, yer new mistress."

None said a word. They offered what Leona could only hope were approving nods. 'Twas quite difficult to tell, for they all appeared so menacing.

"Now get back to work," Alec commanded.

That was it? Leona was dumbfounded. They all turned and went back to training.

Alec took her elbow in one hand and scooped up her empty basket with the other.

"That be it?" she stammered.

"What be it?" he asked as he guided her across the yard and toward the keep.

"The introduction to yer men," she replied as she stared up at him.

Glancing at her out of the corner of his eye, he said, "What more did ye want?"

She took in a deep breath and shook her head. "I—" she was

suddenly at a loss for words. At least not any that he wouldn't find offensive. "Ye did no' even tell them my name, where I come from. Ye did no' even ask them to declare their fealty toward me as your wife." She had seen it only once before, the public declaration made from the clan's warriors to the new laird's wife. She had also witnessed the laird giving a public speech on how proud he was in his choice of wife.

Alec drew to a halt and stared down at her in astonishment. "They already ken yer name, though they'll never use it. As fer where ye come from, they ken that as well. As fer their fealty, they already declared it to *me*. There be no reason to declare it to *ye*, fer ye are me wife. Ye already have it."

Oh, she knew she should have taken some measure of relief in what he was telling her. *They be Bowies,* she reminded herself. *'Tis too much to hope they would behave as others ye've known in yer life.*

Deciding it best to keep the rest of her opinions to herself, she offered Alec the warmest smile she could muster. "Thank ye fer settin' the matter straight in me head, Alec."

"Think nothin' of it, lass," he replied with a gentle pat on her hand.

OUT OF THE HUNDREDS OF PEOPLE LEONA MET, THERE WERE ONLY TWO — besides the children — who treated her with any amount of kindness; Auld Melvin and Effie. They were the only bright spots in an otherwise dark day.

She chose to focus on that; on the kindness she had received from Melvin and Effie. The day had not gone at all as she had hoped it would, but she would not lament it, nor would she feel sorry for herself. Although she was worn out and wanted nothing more than to take a nap, there was still much she needed to do.

As they walked into the gathering room, Alec asked how she enjoyed her day.

"Effie was verra nice," Leona said. She decided to focus on the pleasant woman who she was certain would be her friend and ally. "I think she and I will get along well."

"She be a good woman," he replied as he stopped near the large hearth. "I made arrangements with Charles to bring ye fresh milk in the morns. And Dewey, he will be makin' sure ye have plenty of firewood."

Taken aback, she stopped and turned to face him. "That was verra kind of ye." She was unable to read his expression and began to grow wary under his gaze. Had she done something wrong?

"And Phillip Bowie, he will be bringin' ye some venison on the morrow. He had a good hunt recently and I was able to purchase the meat from him."

Oh, she would very much like to serve her husband a fine meal of roast venison, with vegetables and fruits.

They stood staring at one another for a long while before Alec broke the uneasy silence. "I will be trainin' with the men the rest of the day. I should be back before nightfall."

"I shall have a nice rabbit stew ready when ye return," she said as she fidgeted with the empty basket in her hands. She could not help but feel there was something more he wanted to say.

"Verra well," he said with a slight inclination of his head.

And with that, he was gone, once again leaving without a proper kiss or goodbye.

AFTER ALEC LEFT, SHE WENT STRAIGHTAWAY TO THE KITCHENS. KYTH and Gylys were waiting for her when she arrived. "We fergot to give ye back yer baskets," Gylys said as he swung two empty baskets from each index finger.

"I had fergotten as well," Leona said as she entered the kitchen.

Setting her baskets on the table, she directed the men to do the same. Hanging her shawl on a hook by the door, she grabbed her apron. "I thank ye kindly fer yer help this day," she told them.

"Think nothin' of it, m'lady," Kyth said from a spot near the hearth. "It looked to be fine bread."

"I imagine 'twould be quite good with a bit of berry jam on it," Gylys offered.

"Aye, I agree," Kyth said.

It took very little time for her to realize what they were hinting at. "Sit," she told them with a nod toward the small table by the hearth. "I have some bread left, and jam."

Happy with her offer, they scurried to the table and sat.

Leona retrieved two loaves of bread, a jar of butter and some jam from the larder. "If ever ye be hungry, all ye need do is say so," she told them as she set the items on the table before them.

"Be careful what ye offer, m'lady," Gylys said with a devious grin. "Kyth will surely take advantage."

Kyth ignored the jest. Slathering his bread with butter and jam, he took a bite. "From heaven it be," he said as he closed his eyes. He bore the same expression Alec did after loving. 'Twas all she could do not to laugh at him.

"I swear I've never had better."

Having taken a bite, Gylys had to agree. "I bet the rest of yer cookin' be just as good."

Leona had to laugh at the two of them. "I fear I can only make a few things. Rabbit stew, venison stew, and the like. Just simple things, really. Nothin' fancy like stuffed peacock," she told them with a giggle.

"Och, 'twould be a good change from the bannocks and soup Derrick makes," Gylys said with a mouthful of bread.

"Be he a big man? Built like a stone wall?" she asked as she went into the larder to retrieve the vegetables she would need for the stew.

"Aye. He be the man who cooks fer us at the Armory. Verra good on the battlefield or as a smythie, but no' with cookin'," Kyth explained.

"But it beat starvin' since Alice left," Gylys added.

Kyth nodded in agreement. "Now there a woman who could cook."

"Who be Alice?" Leona asked as she grabbed an empty bucket.

"She was the cook here. But when Rutger died, she went to live with her daughter in Inverness. We have no' had a good meal since," Kyth said with a frown.

"Well, I be certain I am no' as good as Alice, but I shall endeavor to do me best," she said with a smile. As she opened the door and grabbed a second bucket, Kyth jumped to his feet.

"Allow me to do that, mistress," he said before popping another large piece of bread into his mouth.

"Aye, 'tis the least he could do fer eatin' all yer bread and jam," Gylys said with a grin.

She was growing fonder of these men the more she time she spent with them. Opening the door a bit farther so that Kyth could leave, she thanked him kindly. He was about to go when he stopped dead in his tracks.

He paled visibly, his eyes growing as wide as trenchers. "Do no' move," he whispered. "He be out again."

LEONA LEANED AROUND THE DOORJAMB IN ORDER TO GET A BETTER VIEW of what had Kyth frozen in place.

"Och!" she exclaimed happily. "'Tis just Alec's pup."

From behind her, she heard a chair scrape across the floor and the sound of Gylys withdrawing his sword from its scabbard. "Do no' move, mistress," he warned in a low hushed tone. "Shut the door slowly."

Leona rolled her eyes. She had made friends with Alec's hound two nights ago – a fact they'd both witnessed. Apparently, they still believed the bandogge was a danger. The dog caught sight of her and began to race toward her, with his tongue hanging out and his tale wagging.

Kyth began to slowly back up, visibly shaken by the sight of the bandogge coming toward him.

Confident she was in no danger, she stepped outside. "Good day, Patches," she cooed at the dog. She had already decided to rename the dog. He was not such an ugly beast to deserve the moniker Alec had given him. Nay, she thought him a sweet dog, and therefore deserving of a kinder name. She settled on Patches, because of the patch around his eye and his two white feet.

Kyth dropped his buckets and withdrew his sword. "M'lady!" he whispered harshly. "Come back in."

Ignoring him, she kneeled down and began to pet the dog. "That be a good boy, Patches. A right good dog."

The dog licked her face, whimpering happily as she patted his neck and head. "Why do these men fear ye so?" she asked. "Ye would no' hurt me, now would ye?"

The dog answered with a wag of his tail and another lick to her cheek.

"M'lady, ye do no' understand," Kyth whispered. "I've seen that dog chew a man's leg clean off!"

"Aye," Gylys said. "I have seen him tear a man's arm from his shoulder!"

Ignoring what she could only assume were gross exaggerations, Leona continued to pet the dog. "Be ye hungry, laddie?" she asked the dog.

Standing up, she patted the top of his head one more time. "Come inside then, I have a bit of ham ye can have."

Gylys and Kyth gave wide berth. So wide, in fact, they were at the back door, leaving Leona to wonder if they were not going to flee. "Lads," she said in a firm tone. "He will no' hurt ye."

"Ye can no' ken that, m'lady," Gylys said nervously.

"Och, if ye be worried, then leave," she told them.

"We can no' do that, m'lady!" Kyth replied. "If anythin' happened to ye, Alec would hang us both."

"Then sit down," she told them.

Patches was the only one to obey. The dog dutifully sat between the door and the table. The two grown men remained standing near the back door. "Lads, ye will be quite safe, I can assure ye. He will no' harm ye," she said as she went into the larder. She grabbed the ham and brought it back to the table. Using a large knife, she cut off a hunk and offered it to the dog.

"Patches, if ye promise no' to tear a leg or arm from Gylys or Kyth, I shall give ye a bit of ham."

The dog licked his chops, whimpered, but made no attempt to grab the ham from her hand. "That be a good dog," she said with a smile. Petting his head with one hand, she fed him the hunk of meat with the other. He ate it in two bites, swallowed it down, and sat patiently waiting for more.

"Nay, that be all ye get fer now," Leona told him.

"M'lady, please," Gylys pleaded with her.

Before she could offer him a sharp retort, she heard Seamus calling for *Satan.*

"Och! Why they have given such a sweet beast as ye such a name, I do no' ken."

Casting a glance at the two worried men at her back door, she was forced to surrender. With a heavy sigh, she spoke gently to the dog. "Come, Patches, we should return ye to Seamus."

The dog followed her out the door and across the yard.

"I fear our mistress be a bit tetched," Gylys said as he started to follow her out. "She does no' realize it be a bandogge and no' a kitten."

"I fear ye be right," Kyth agreed.

They remained close enough they could protect their mistress if necessary, but not so close as to anger the bandogge.

AFTER SEEING THE DOG SAFELY BACK INTO SEAMUS' CARE, LEONA returned to her kitchen. Gylys and Kyth were all too happy to get as many buckets of water as she wanted. But they left as soon as the chore was complete.

With the stew simmering nicely in the hearth, she set about making a few berry tarts for the evening meal. Gylys and Kyth had happily accepted her offer for them to sup with her and Alec later in the evening.

Once the tarts were baked, she set them to cool on the counter. Grabbing two buckets of warm water, she took them into the keep and above stairs to the bedchamber she shared with Alec.

He had left a pile of dirty clothes on the floor by the pitcher and basin. With a sigh, she set the buckets on the cold hearth before scooping the clothes up to put them in the hallway. After opening the furs to let fresh air in, she made the bed and lit a fire.

Her back and legs were beginning to ache. It had been a very long day. But no matter how tempted she was to take a wee nap, she refused. There was still too much to be done.

Leaving her chamber, she went in search of clean linens for the bed. Each of the chambers above stairs were empty and stark. Only two held any furnishings to denote their purpose.

Going below stairs, she continued her search. There had to be clean linens somewhere in the keep, but thus far, she was finding nothing.

When she left the eastern part of the keep and entered the gathering room, she came to an abrupt halt. Standing near the hearth was a woman she had not seen before.

To call the strange woman beautiful would have been an understatement. Her long, dark brown hair was drawn into a braid that cascaded over one shoulder. She wore an elegant burgundy dress, with long sleeves that tapered and fell past her wrists, almost to her ankles. The bodice was low-cut, giving just a hint of delicate breasts. Draped over the same shoulder as her braid was the Bowie plaid.

Leona felt inadequate at once. This stunning woman looked more the chatelaine and mistress of the keep than she. Prepared to turn and leave, she had almost gotten away when the woman spotted her.

"Good day, to ye," she said. "Be ye the new mistress?"

Even her voice seemed elegant.

Reminding herself that jealousy was a sin, Leona swallowed what little pride she had and stepped into the gathering room. "Aye, I am."

She was met with a warm smile and a graceful curtsey. "I did no' get to meet ye earlier. I was visiting me mum. She has a wee farm a long walk from here. I be Patrice, m'lady. 'Tis a pleasure to meet ye."

"'Tis a pleasure to meet ye, as well," Leona replied. The only thing she'd ever envied in her life were people's eyes. This new sensation was all together different; she was jealous of everything about this woman. *Why did Alec choose me when he could have had* her?

"If ever there be anything I can help ye with, all ye need do is ask. I have a wee cottage across the way. Just send word to me and I'll help wherever I can."

Her offer seemed genuine and from her heart. Leona knew she should feel grateful for it, for she had received so few kindnesses in her lifetime.

"I thank ye fer yer offer, Patrice."

"Are ye makin' yerself at home here?" Patrice asked. "Are ye findin' everythin' ye need?"

Wanting very much to rid herself of envy and jealousy, Leona sighed. *'Tis ridiculous to be jealous of this woman who is doin' nothin' but bein' kind.* "I can no' find clean bed clothes. I have searched every room below stairs, and they all be empty."

"They be above stairs," she explained. "We have a small room above stairs where we keep such things."

We? The question burned, the jealousy rising. Was this beautiful woman by chance Alec's mistress?

"Did ye work here before?" Leona asked.

Patrice's smile faded with Leona's question. "Nay, m'lady. I was betrothed to Rutger, Alec's brother." She looked almost pained to admit it.

Leona's eyes grew wide with surprise. The jealousy and burgeoning hatred she felt only a heartbeat earlier rapidly turned to guilt. How awful it must have been for her, this beautiful young woman, to have been betrothed to such an awful man as Rutger Bowie. At a loss for words, she stood silent for a long moment.

"I ken what Rutger did to ye, m'lady. There be no excuse fer it. But I can tell ye that he was no' always that way and he was never that way with me." Her voice turned forlorn and sad. "He was good to me. He was good to me family. I ken that be hard to believe, but it be true.

131

'Twas no' until that fool Donnel showed up, sportin' tales about massive treasures to be had, that Rutger changed."

Swiping away tears, Patrice finally looked into Leona's eyes. "He was no longer the same then. He was no longer kind and funny or generous. I can only blame greed fer changin' him."

Leona went to her at once. Taking her hands in her own, she said, "I be so terribly sorry." She could not fault Patrice for Rutger's sins.

"I could no' stop him. No one could, not even Alec."

"Wheest, now," Leona whispered, choking on her own tears. Her heart ached for this woman's loss. There was no denying Patrice had loved Rutger and felt guilty for not being able to stop him.

"I can only hope ye'll no' hold against me all the horrible things Rutger did to ye and yers," Patrice said as she swiped away more tears.

Leona knew it had taken a great deal of strength to walk into the keep and seek forgiveness. Forgiveness for crimes she had not been a party to nor committed.

Gone now were the ugly feelings of jealousy and envy. Instead, Leona felt pangs of guilt and sorrow for this woman. "There be nothin' to fergive ye fer, Patrice. Nothin' at all."

AFTER ALLOWING HER TO CRY IT OUT, LEONA HELPED DRY THE YOUNG woman's tears. Pulling her in for a warm embrace, Leona patted her back.

"I thank ye kindly, m'lady," Patrice said. "Ye're no' at all what I expected."

Setting her back, Leona smiled warmly, even though she was confused. "And what were ye expectin'."

Patrice gave a slight laugh. "I do no' rightly ken. Mayhap I thought ye'd be a hard woman and mayhap a bit tetched, fer ye *did* volunteer to marry a Bowie."

'Twas Leona's turn to laugh. "I suspect a sane person might no' have done the same," she admitted. "Mayhap I *am* a bit tetched." She would not admit to the true reasons for volunteering to marry Alec.

"Either way, I be glad to have ye here, mistress."

Leona gave a wave of her hand, dismissing the formality. "Please, if we're to be friends, call me Leona."

Patrice nodded, then dabbed at her eyes with a tiny bit of linen. "Ye would like to be me friend?"

"Aye, I would. I fear the other womenfolk, save fer one, did no' find me as kind as ye did."

Patrice tilted her head and drew her brow in. "What do ye mean?"

Leona did her best to make the cold greetings seem insignificant. "Alec took me to meet the clanspeople today. I took each family a small gift. A loaf of bread. Apparently, such things are no' done here."

Patrice remained confused. "I fear I do no' understand."

Rolling her eyes, Leona released a heavy sigh. "Where I come from, we like to give gifts to those we care about. Or as a means of welcome."

Patrice raised her hand to stop her. "Nay, I understand the reason for the gift."

"Ye do?" Leona was surprise to hear that finally, someone understood.

"Aye," Patrice replied with a nod. "Ye want them to like ye, ye want them to ken ye care. I would have done the same thing were I ye. What I do no' understand is why ye say the womenfolk did no' find ye kind?"

She had no good answer. "I do no' ken the why of it meself," she replied as she put her hands on her hips. "The men folk were confused, but each took me offerin' kindly. The women, however, they all acted as though I'd slapped them. As if I'd insulted them."

'Twas evident by Patrice's still knotted brow, that she did not quite understand. "That makes no sense. The women folk I ken would have accepted such an offer quite graciously."

Leona had to giggle. "Mayhap I did no' meet the same women ye ken?"

Either she did not understand Leona's jest, or she chose to ignore it. "Nay, I doubt that. I fear somethin' may be afoot here." Patrice had the look of a puzzled woman who was trying to figure out some great mystery.

"Ye say all but one treated ye poorly. Who was that 'one'?"

"Effie Bowie. Dougall's wife."

Leona saw something akin to fear flash in her new friend's eyes. But 'twas gone as quickly as it had appeared. "Effie be me sister," she declared.

Was that trepidation and fear Leona detected in her tone? Mayhap Leona was simply over-reacting. She was, after all, quite tired. "Och! She did no' mention a sister," Leona told her. "So kindness must run in yer family."

There was no doubt in Leona's mind that Patrice's smile was forced. "Aye, ye could say that."

A brief moment of silence passed before Patrice spoke again. "Would ye like me to fetch the bed clothes fer ye?" Apparently, the subject had been changed, but for what reason, Leona did not feel she should ask.

"Nay, but ye can show me where they be," Leona replied, happy for the offer and for the chance to make a new friend.

Patrice led the way out of the gathering room and above stairs, talking all the while. "'Twas nay always this stark and empty. I fear Alec wanted no memories of the past, so he removed everything. Most of it he put in the east tower. If ye do no' mind me sayin', m'lady, I think he went too far. Ye can no' even find a comfortable place to sit by the fire now."

"I have to agree with ye," Leona said. "Be he as stubborn as I think he be?"

Patrice laughed as she turned right at the top of the stairs. "Aye, he be just that stubborn."

Around another corner they stepped into a long, dark corridor. Leona stopped abruptly. The corridor was far too dark for her liking or comfort. She went back around the corner, grabbed a lighted torch, and soon returned. "'Tis too dark to see," she explained. Patrice smiled but said nothing.

At the very end of the hallway, Patrice took the torch, opened a door and stepped in. Leona followed behind her.

Once inside, Patrice found candles and began lighting them. As the room began to fill with light, Leona's spirits lifted.

The space was filled with all manner of furnishings, tapestries, and trunks. Along one wall was a bank of shelves that ran from the floor almost to the ceiling. "Here," Patrice said as she stepped toward it. "Enough sheets and bed clothes to see ye through ten winters!"

Leona was heady with glee. If it remained just she and Alec in this large keep, then, aye, Patrice was correct. 'Twould be a long time before she had to wash bedclothes.

"Thank God!" she exclaimed. "Och! Patrice, I thank ye kindly!"

Patrice beamed with pride. "Would ye like to take some of these things below stairs and start makin' this keep a home again?"

"I be sorely tempted," she said. "But I fear 'twould send Alec into an apoplexy."

Nay, if she were to do this, she'd do it one tiny step at a time. A tapestry here, a chair there, but slowly and gradually so as to keep peace between them.

CHAPTER 11

*P*atrice had offered to stay to help, but explained that her mother had not been well. Still, Leona thought it awfully kind of her to offer. She left with the promise of returning on the morrow. With Patrice gone, Leona returned to her bedchamber with an arm full of clean sheets and linens. She stored them in a trunk in the corner of their room.

After the room was as tidy as she could get it without scrubbing it from top to bottom, she returned to the kitchens. The stew was still simmering nicely, the tarts just where she had left them. 'Twould not be long before Alec would return and she wanted to make certain he had clean washing and drying cloths, as well as clothes to wear.

In her explorations of the keep and kitchens, she had discovered a tub in one of the empty rooms above stairs. What a luxury 'twould be to have a nice, hot bath instead of bathing in the loch.

So back above stairs she went, and back to the room Patrice had shown her. She had to remove a few chairs, one trunk, and a few small tables in order to make a path for retrieving the tub. That was much easier than actually moving the tub.

It did not budge. Not even after she put her hip into it. The base kept getting caught on the uneven floorboards. 'Twas more awkward and bulky than 'twas heavy. Not wanting to cause any further damage to the floors, she grabbed a soft sheet, unfurled it and spread it on the floor. Lifting each corner of the tub, then tugging the sheet under it, she soon had it where she wanted it.

"Bloody hell," she cursed under her breath as she tugged on the sheet with all her might.

'Twas a battle, but one she was fully prepared to win. Determined now, more than ever, to have a hot bath, she finally got the tub to move.

She had to stop twice to catch her breath, and it did take a good deal of effort and a fair amount of cursing, but she finally got the unyielding beast into their room. She was glad Alec was not inside for she didn't want him to know she knew those particular words. Giggling, she immediately thought of Rose. It had been she from whom she learned them.

With the tub positioned at an angle, but near the hearth, she sat down only long enough to catch her breath. "Well, I will need a bit more than two buckets of water," she told herself. "I truly wish someone would invent a way to get water into a tub without hauling buckets above stairs."

'Twould have been quite easy to fall asleep sitting up. If she didn't have a pot of stew cooking, she might very well have done just that.

With a tired sigh, she pushed herself to her feet and headed back to her kitchens to grab more water. Before Alec returned, she had hauled eight additional buckets of water above stairs to warm by the fire. Her hands and back ached and she was getting blisters on her fingers. But the thought of sitting in a nice hot bath until her skin turned wrinkly kept her moving.

"I do no' think I'll be doin' this every day. Mayhap Alec will help me with carryin' the water tomorrow."

She poured six buckets into the tub and set the other two to warm by the fire. Digging through her trunk she found a jar of clean smelling soap and set it on the chair by the tub. Excitement began to swell with the anticipation of climbing in.

Remembering she needed clean cloths, she returned to what she was now calling the linen room. She grabbed a few washing and drying cloths, blew out the candles, and left.

She all but skipped down the corridor to return to her awaiting bit of heaven on earth. Humming a happy tune, she entered her bedchamber. Much to her chagrin, Alec was there.

And he was stripping off his clothes.

When he saw her, his smile was enough to make her heart skip a beat. But what he said and did next was enough to make her want to scream and throw the chamber pot at him.

"Och! Lass!" he exclaimed happily as he climbed into the tub. No, not *the* tub, but *her* tub. Her hot water. Her bit of heaven on earth. "I can no' tell ye how glad I am fer a hot bath."

Oh, I can imagine, she mused angrily.

He sighed happily as he sat back and let the water surround him.

'Twas enough to make her want to cry.

"Every muscle in me body aches. I did no' think farmin' would be so difficult, but it is." He sat up and searched for the soap. Finding it on the chair, he looked up at her with a smile. "Do ye have a washin' cloth?" he asked with a nod toward the linens she was holding.

She counted to fifty before walking toward him for fear she'd be tempted to hold his head under the water. Without speaking, she handed him a cloth.

He took it, but did not immediately let go of her hand. "Leona, I be truly grateful fer ye thinkin' of me like this. 'Twas a nice surprise. I came in to get clean clothes before headin' to the loch and when I saw this, well..." he paused, as he smiled up at her with such warmth and gratitude it nearly made her heart burst with joy. "I be verra grateful to ye."

She could not remain angry with him. As far as she knew, a Bowie rarely, if ever, said *thank you.* To have Alec express his gratitude so sweetly meant the world to her.

It had been a very long day and he had worked all afternoon in the fields. His brow was covered in perspiration, his hands and arms filthy.

"I be glad ye are pleased," she told him, her anger gone.

He gave her hand a gentle squeeze before turning his attention back to bathing. "I came in through the kitchens looking fer ye. The stew and the tarts smell right good. Me stomach is growlin' somethin' fierce."

Hot, sweaty, and hungry. She reckoned it would be like this for some time to come and she should start getting used to it.

"Thank ye. I shall have it set out fer ye when ye come below stairs," she told him. And with that, she turned and left her husband to enjoy his bath.

THANKFULLY, KYTH AND GYLYS ARRIVED EARLY ENOUGH TO HELP HER set the table. They were all too happy to help, considering they were going to partake in a free meal, and one *not* cooked by Derrick.

She had washed up in the kitchens as best she could. *On the morrow,* she promised herself, *'twill be I who enjoys the hot bath.*

Leona was quite proud of the meal she had prepared for her husband. Rabbit stew, bread, berry tarts. 'Twas by no means a feast but she was hopeful that he would be happy with it just the same.

Alec came bounding down the stairs just as Leona set the heavy pot of stew in the center of the table. Curiously, he looked at Kyth and Gylys who were looking like young boys about to devour an endless supply of sweet cakes.

"Lads," he said as he approached the table slowly.

"Good eve, to ye, Alec," Kyth said.

"Yer bonny wife here invited us to sup with ye," Gylys explained as he eyed the pot of stew.

Alec was torn between wanting to have a quiet meal with his wife and *not* wanting to have a quiet meal with his wife. A good part of him wanted to eat quickly, then whisk her above stairs where he would make love to her for the next few hours. Another part of him worried that he was beginning to lose himself in her. And that would serve no good purpose.

The hot bath had done wonders to lift his spirits and reenergize him. Deciding he could have a pleasant evening with his men *and* take his wife above stairs, he smiled at them. "Then let us sup together, aye?" he said with a smile.

Looking forward to eating, he took his seat at the head of the table. "Pass me that stew, lads!"

LEONA WAS AT THE OTHER END OF THE TABLE, STANDING NEXT TO HER seat. Waiting. Waiting for her husband to pull out her chair. Waiting to hear a kind 'thank ye' for all her hard work.

And she waited.

While the men were happily ladling stew into their bowls.

She cleared her throat once. No one took notice. She cleared it again.

Alec looked up at her from his end of the table and smiled. "Sit, lass."

Och! The Bowie men have a lot to learn, they do! She thought as she pulled her own chair out and sat. *Ian always pulls Rose's chair out fer her. Men do that, ye mannerless louts! 'Tis just a sign of respect and kindness.*

What was she thinking? These were Bowie men. She seriously doubted they worried about manners.

"Would ye like some stew m'lady?" Kyth asked as he lifted a ladle out of the pot and plopped it into her bowl. The thick liquid splattered hither and yon. Only a small mess, but a mess she would have to clean.

Gylys tore off a chunk of bread and handed it to her.

Alec poured ale into his cup before handing it off to Kyth, who filled his cup and passed it to Leona.

Bread crumbs were falling here and there, ale sloshing and splashing over everything. Had these men never sat at a table before?

Even her own father, the cruel man that he was, possessed more manners than the men sitting at her table. Taking a deep breath, she decided to push it all aside and enjoy a fine meal.

Alec and Kyth had not waited until everyone had what they needed before digging in.

A moment later, with horrified expressions upon their faces, they were spitting the stew out.

"Gah!" Kyth declared.

"Good, God!" Alec exclaimed.

Gylys and Leona stared at the two men in wide-eyed confusion. Leona's heart began to sink. She'd made rabbit stew hundreds of times. No one had ever complained and certainly no one had ever spit it out!

"What be wrong?" she stammered. The men were too busy wiping their tongues and gulping down ale to answer. She dipped her finger into the stew for a taste.

'Twas as if someone had dumped a pound of salt into it. Wincing, she took a sip of ale to wash the taste out. *What in the world?* She stammered and fought for words. "I, I do no' ken what happened."

The men were staring at her, awash in uncertainty and pity. "I do no' ken what happened," she repeated. "I have made rabbit stew hundreds of times." It made no sense.

Quickly, she scooted away from the table, angry and humiliated. Without a word, she grabbed the pot and began to head toward the kitchen. "This makes no sense," she mumbled to herself.

Alec was behind her. "'Tis all right, lass. No one is a good cook on their first attempt."

"I told ye, I have made rabbit stew before," she shot at him over her shoulder. Stomping across the small yard, she flung open the door to the kitchen. Without a doubt she knew that her stew had been sabotaged. There was no way she would have added that much salt by accident.

Once inside, she slammed the pot down on the table nearest the door. Alec stepped in. "'Twas a simple accident," he said in a calm voice. "It could happen to anyone."

Spinning around angrily, she said, "Nay! 'Twas no' an accident. I did no' do this."

"We can have bread and cheese this night," he said, trying his best to comfort her.

She was about to give him a verbal assault when she caught sight of something over the hearth.

Her salt box.

'Twas laying on its side, as if it had been tipped over. "What on earth," she whispered as she crossed the small space.

"What is it?" Alec asked.

"The salt box," she said as she reached for it. "Someone has emptied nearly all of it, and they emptied it into me stew." Who could be so cruel? Who would be so wasteful?

"I'll send Gylys and Kyth to the village on the morrow to get ye more," Alec said as he took the empty box and inspected it.

"Who would do this?" she asked.

Alec scratched the back of his neck, confused and doubtful. "Could it have been an accident?"

"Nay!" she exclaimed. "I do no' keep me salt over the hearth. I keep it on the counter over there." She gave a nod toward the counter where the rest of her spices sat. Jars of varying sizes were lined neatly against the wall, out of sunlight and away from water. "I would no' be so careless."

Alec studied her closely for a long moment. "Are ye suggestin' someone did this on purpose?" he asked.

Finally, he understood.

"Aye, I be suggestin' just that."

ALEC WANTED VERY MUCH TO BELIEVE HER, BUT 'TWAS DIFFICULT. WHO amongst his people would do such a thing? Considering the less than warm greeting she was given by his people that morn, the list of suspects was quite long.

The cold manner in which his women folk had greeted his wife had not gone unnoticed. He had decided not to intervene nor mention it, believing it would be best to let things progress naturally. Was it not best to let his people come to know his wife, to see that she meant them no ill-will or harm?

"Mayhap 'twas meant as a jest," he said.

"A jest?" She looked utterly appalled by the idea. "To ruin food? To be so wasteful?" *To humiliate me?* "I be sorry if I do no' find the humor in it."

He let out a heavy breath as a thought occurred to him. "Mayhap 'twas no' meant as a jest, but as a way to test ye?"

She returned his question with a raised and dubious brow.

"The Bowie people are no' like the McLarens," he said.

She snorted in agreement. "They be like *no one else.*"

"In order fer them to accept ye, they will need to ken ye are no' some weak woman prone to tears. They want to ken ye be a good, strong woman."

"So they waste food and salt to see how I will respond?" She sounded very doubtful.

Alec smiled at her. "I ken it makes no sense, but the Bowie people are no' exactly known fer logic."

With that, she had to agree.

Kyth and Gylys appeared at the door just then. "Alec?" Gylys said in a low and soft tone. "We be goin' to the armory to sup."

Alec gave a nod of understanding.

"We be right sorry, mistress," Kyth said. Leaving no time for a response, the two men turned away and left.

"'Twas humiliatin'," Leona said on the verge of tears. "I wanted verra much to impress ye, and fer some reason, them."

Alec placed the nearly empty box on the table beside them. "Ye already have, lass."

Her brow furrowed, a blend of confusion and disbelief. He placed a kiss on the top of her head and hugged her. "Would ye feel better if I had locks installed on the doors?"

She nodded against his chest. "Aye, I would."

"Good. On the morrow, I shall have Seamus make new locks and keys that only ye shall have."

"Thank ye, Alec."

Rubbing a hand along her back, he said, "Now, what shall we eat this night?"

CHAPTER 12

I see the way he looks at her. He loves her. Already!

    And what is all this nonsense about peace? We be Bowies, fer the sake of Christ! We have no' ever kent peace. We be no' some band of holy men and women, who's only purpose in life is to serve God and mankind. Nay, we take what we want and when we want it. We be a ruthless, blood-thirsty lot of bloody sons of whores. Or at least we used to be.

    Somethin' in Alec has changed. He's gone soft. He wants us all to change, to become the same mealy mouthed, soft-hearted, ignorant fool he has turned out to be. And he wants to take the Bowies with him. And that idiot Dougall is standin' right beside him.

    To hell with Alec Bowie. To hell with Dougall and all the others who follow them.

    Alec will soon regret his feelings for her. I'll make sure of it. The bloody fool!

    I can no' allow it. I made a promise to Rutger, months ago when he lay dead on the floor of the stables. All mangled and bloody, with his eyes still open, even though he was dead. I made him a promise that day.

    I will do whatever I must to see his dream come to fruition. The Bowie clan will rise again. Stronger, more powerful, more ruthless than any clan ever to grace the lands of Scotia. I will kill Ian Mackintosh fer takin' his life.

But first, I must kill Alec's precious wife.
I have no other choice.

CHAPTER 13

The following morning dawned bleak and dreary. Rain fell in great waves, making Leona's morning ritual of going to the kitchens at the crack of dawn less than enjoyable. It did not help that she still ached from all her hard work the day before. It also did not help that she was still upset about the person who sabotaged her rabbit stew. The weather matched her mood.

Water seeped into her shoes as she quickly crossed the yard. 'Twas not a great distance, but in inclement weather such as this, it was far less enjoyable.

Once inside the cold and dark space, Leona hung her damp cloak on a hook, lit candles and torches before making a fire. Soon, the fire took away some of the chill, but not all. With her shoes and woolens quite damp, she shuddered. Quickly, she removed her shoes and set them on the hearth, then her woolens. The stone floor was cold enough to make her shriek. Quickly, she made for the table, sat, and pulled her knees up to her chest.

It would not take long for her things to dry. Digging into her pouch, she withdrew the handmade book she called her journal. 'Twas nothing more than scraps of parchment she had collected over time, bound together in auld, soft leather. 'Twas more precious than gold and held her innermost thoughts and secrets.

She read through past entries, the poems and sonnets she had written long ago. The parchment was precious, and while nothing more than scraps, 'twas still quite valuable. Someday, she hoped to be able to afford brand new pieces of parchment and not little pieces.

As predicted, her shoes and woolens were soon dry. It felt good to slip her cold feet into something warm.

Though Alec would likely not get much work done out of doors this morn, he would still need to eat. She also wanted to take a meal to Melvin. The poor man was all alone in this world.

Poking her head out of the back door, she was unable to gauge how long the rain would last. She'd need water, but all the buckets were empty. There was no way she was going to trod in the mud and rain to fill buckets. So she grabbed two and set them just outside the door to collect rain-water.

Thankfully, she had eggs left over from yesterday's collection. Not many, but enough to make Alec a nice morning meal.

Leona rather liked this quiet hour of the day. Alone with her thoughts yet busy enough to make her feel like her life had some purpose. Although she was still upset about the ruined stew from the night before. As she sat in the dimly lit space, sipping on warm cider, she wondered what she could do to prove herself to these people. Assuming, of course, that Alec was right.

She was not so naive as to believe one simple act would bring the clan around. Nay, the Bowies were used to hard living, to not trusting outsiders. For decades, they'd been a ruthless lot of thieves, raiders, and ne'er-do-wells. That would not change overnight, no matter how badly her husband wanted it, nor how hard he worked toward it.

They did not speak much of his plans for the future, other than in vague terms. Of course, they had been married less than a sennight. Hopefully, someday he would trust her enough to let her in. To allow her to help.

'Twas far too early yet to begin to demand such things.

Deciding she had sat long enough, she began to prepare Alec's morning meal. As she was slicing ham at the table, someone knocked at her back door. Setting the knife down, she wiped her hands on a cloth before pulling the door open. Standing in the rain was a young man she did not recognize. Tall and well built like Alec, and sporting the same dark hair and eyes, he stood in the rain.

"Good morn," Leona greeted him.

"Mistress," he said with a nod. "I be John Bowie. Charles asked me to let ye ken he can no' bring ye any milk this day."

She had forgotten all about the arrangement Alec had made with Charles.

"Charles is unable to bring ye milk. His roof be leakin' and he needs to repair it," he went on to explain. "He will do his best to send it tomorrow."

Leona didn't think she could fault a man with a leaky roof. "I thank ye for lettin' me know, John. Would ye like to come in out of the rain?"

"Nay, mistress, but thank ye. I have to return to the wall." And with that, he tipped his head and left.

He seemed an odd sort of young man, but then all the Bowies were odd sorts. Shaking her head, she went back to slicing bread.

As promised, Alec had ordered new locks to be installed in her kitchen. Seamus appeared late the following afternoon, apologizing for not being able to get to the task sooner.

"Do no' fash yourself over it, Seamus," she told him. "I be certain yer job is no' an easy one."

Pleased with her forgiveness, Seamus offered her an affectionate smile. "Thank ye, kindly fer bein' so understandin' about it all, mistress."

It had taken him a full hour to finish his task. Affixing the keys to a long, thin bit of leather, she draped it around her waist and felt instantly better. Determined not to risk another salt incident, she would be diligent in never leaving the kitchen without locking the door behind her.

L<small>OST IN HER OWN THOUGHTS, SHE WAS STARTLED WHEN</small> G<small>YLYS AND</small> Kyth entered the kitchen. Water dripped off their cloaks and boots, leaving puddles in their wake.

"Mistress, we be headin' into the village soon," Kyth explained.

Rather sheepishly, Gylys asked, "Will ye be needin' anythin' besides, well, salt?"

'Twas all she could do not to laugh at his discomfort. He was trying to be kind, something she felt wholly unusual for a Bowie. "Nay," she said, trying to maintain a straight face. "And I promise to use it sparingly in the future."

Then two men cast each other peculiar expressions. 'Twas Leona who laughed first. Moments later, they joined in.

"If ye be no' afraid to try again, lads, I invite ye to sup with us this night. If Phillip Bowie delivers the venison he promised to Alec, we shall dine on that. If no', I fear I will have to make another stew."

"Mayhap we should no' give ye the salt until *after* ye've prepared it?" Gylys offered with a laugh.

She liked these two men, she sincerely did. Like the brothers she never had. As they turned to leave, she was struck with the memory of her previous trip to the village.

"Wait!" she called out. "There *is* somethin' I would like ye to do."

Quickly, she reached into her pouch and pulled out her journal. At the very back of the book, she had drawn a likeness of the brooch she wanted to have made for Alec.

She gave a quick explanation of her idea for the brooch to Gylys and Kyth. "I would like to give it to him as a gift, ye see. I want it to be a surprise. Unfortunately, I did no' have the opportunity to ask the jeweler about the cost of makin' it fer me."

Another curious glance between the two men. "But why?" Gylys asked.

"Why what?"

He cleared his throat once before explaining his confusion. "Why do ye wish to give Alec a gift? And such a nice one as this?"

"He has a birthday in few months does he not?"

"Aye," Gylys said, still baffled.

"Well, I want to give our laird, me husband, a gift to commemorate it."

'Twas Kyth who said, "Ye be right fond of givin' gifts, aye?"

She felt her face grow warm with a blush. Clearly these people were unaccustomed to gift-giving. "Aye, I be quite fond of it. 'Tis me way of showin' him me gratitude."

"Gratitude fer what?" they both asked.

Her blush grew hotter. "Does it truly matter? I simply wish to give me husband a gift."

She was grateful when they gave up their questioning. "Ye want us to have him make it?" Kyth asked as he looked at her drawing.

"Nay, no' yet. I simply want to ken how much to make it and how long it will take him."

Although they did not quite understand the why of it, they agreed to do as she requested.

ALEC DID NOT LIKE WAKING UP TO AN EMPTY BED. 'TWAS AN ENTIRELY new sensation, this feeling of missing his wife, and he did not like it. Not one bit.

But he could not help but think of her as he lay on his back, looking up at the ceiling. She was a beautiful woman, his wife. He thought back to the disastrous supper the night before. If he were honest with himself, he would admit he was quite proud of how she handled the entire situation. She hadn't broken down into sobs, hadn't railed against the world, nor had she demanded he seek out the person guilty for ruining the stew. Nay, she'd taken it with graceful aplomb, even though he knew she was mad enough to bite steel.

And afterwards, when they ate their meal alone, here in their bedchamber, she had done her best to make him comfortable. He could not help but wonder, however, if her eagerness to please him was one more way to crack his otherwise stone-cold heart. One more way of getting him to appreciate her, to eventually fall in love with her.

Oh, he liked her well enough. Seriously, what was there not to like? Beautiful, kind, and oh so willing to please him in their marital bed. He found a little bit of heaven on earth when he was joining with her. The way she would call out his name, the way she would look at him with a smoldering heat, desire, and adoration.

'Twas enough to unsettle any man with a sound mind.

To his way of thinking, 'twas one more step toward the proverbial cliff, this sense of adoration for his wife.

'Twas not supposed to be like that. He was not supposed to have anything other than a warm regard for her. And he certainly was not supposed to follow her around like a hungry pup looking for its mother's teat.

Determined not to allow these dangerous feelings to guide his life, he left his warm bed, washed up in the basin and got dressed.

She be just yer wife, he told himself. *Nothin' more, nothin' less.*

Then why on earth was he possessed with the overwhelming need to see her?

LESS THAN AN HOUR LATER, ALEC CAME BELOW STAIRS JUST AS LEONA was setting the meal on the table. "Good morn, to ye," she said with a smile.

He stopped a few feet from the table and stared at her, for an uncomfortably long moment. "Be there somethin' the matter?" she asked as she nervously wiped her palms on her apron.

Aye, there was something the matter. *She* was the matter. Over her blue dress she wore that blasted apron. Why he hated the bloody thing, he doubted he'd ever fully know, but hate it he did. Perhaps because it hid so much of her fine figure. A figure he had enjoyed thoroughly the night before.

Her hair hung in a braid across her chest. Over it, she wore a kerchief, something else he was beginning to deplore, for it covered far too much of her gloriously soft hair.

Images of her naked, with her golden hair splayed out like the morning sunset popped into his mind. His arousal was instant.

Somehow he managed to reply, "Nay."

She studied him closely for a moment before turning back to the table. After fixing his trencher and setting it before him, she sat down next to him. "What be yer plans fer this day?" She asked as she spread butter onto a slice of bread.

"Prayin' the rain stops soon," he replied as he cut off a hunk of ham and popped it into his mouth. "And ye?"

"When the rain lets up, I plan on takin' Melvin a meal."

He gave an approving nod. "He will appreciate such a gesture."

And ye? Will ye appreciate it? She dared not ask the question.

"And as soon as I can, I plan on gatherin' rushes fer the floor. Get some of the chill out of this place," she told him, taking another delicate bite of her bread.

"It does get a bit cold, aye?" He remarked, again, with a mouth full of food.

Soon, he had consumed his meal. Wiping his face on the sleeve of his tunic, instead of the linen cloth she had placed next to his trencher, he pushed away from the table. "I will be in me study fer a time," he told her. "Then I have to see Dougall."

Before she could offer him a warm goodbye, he was strolling away from the table without a care in the world.

No sweet kiss goodbye. No kind word bidding her good day. He simply left.

She thought of Ian and Rose. Ian would not step a foot away from his wife without bidding her a pleasant farewell along with a kiss. Mayhap, had Alec spent more time with Ian, he would be able to see how a husband properly treats his wife.

But a visit to her former home was a long way off. 'Twould be too much to ask for one of the twice yearly visits he'd agreed to. Mayhap not until after the harvest would they be able to visit.

Should she wait until then to teach her husband the manners and things he would already know, had he not been raised by thieves and the like? Nay, that was too far off. She might grow too frustrated in the interim, and clout him over the head with a pot.

Nay, the best course of action would be to politely *teach* her husband the ways of the world.

The next time ye leave me, Alec Bowie, ye shall kiss me proper.

GOD DID NOT ANSWER ALEC'S PRAYERS REGARDING THE RAIN, THEREBY forcing him to stay indoors the entirety of the morning. He kept himself busy by going over the keep's ledgers and accounts.

Not much had changed since the first time he'd looked at them, not long after Rutger's death. His brother had a penchant for spending, and it hadn't been wise spending. Countless groats and sillars had been spent on frivolous things, such as silks, fancy clothing, jewels, gold necklaces, and the like.

Decades of thieving and marauding, of building up their coffers, had been wasted in a matter of less than a year. And for what? Silk tunics and baubles to adorn himself with? Alec wondered if Rutger would now agree 'twas all for naught. Unfortunately, he would never know the answer to that question.

He also wondered if, at the end of his life, in that brief moment right before the horse trampled him into the earth, if Rutger had a fleeting thought for anyone other than himself. Had he realized in that brief time that Alec had been right? Had he finally seen the error of his ways?

Again, 'twas doubtful.

Raking a hand through his dark locks, he let out a heavy sigh. Closing the book, he pushed it away and sat staring into the hearth. They had enough funds to see them through another year, *if* he were exceedingly frugal. If he'd been a praying man, he would be on his knees now, praying to the gods that their crops would be plentiful and that they might be able to sell enough to see them through another year.

Right after Rutger's death, Dougall, Kyth, Gylys and a handful of other clansmen had come to him and begged him to take over as chief. That had been the last thing he ever wanted. Nay, he would have been happy to stay in the shadows for the remainder of his days. He had not planned on staying here as long as he had. But when he saw how much his brother had changed and how he was leading the clan to utter ruin, he found he could not leave.

Months of pleading for change had fallen on deaf ears. Countless nights of trying to talk his brother into altering not only his ways, but the ways of the clan, had been for naught. His pleas, his arguments had been ignored.

And now, here he was with a handful of Bowie men who *had* been listening. They too, desired change. The kind of change Alec had been begging his brother for.

For reasons he still could not explain to himself, he had agreed to their request. He had become the chief of clan Bowie on one condition: they had to somehow manage to get the rest of the clan to agree to stop their thieving ways and work alongside them.

It hadn't been easy. But in the end, they agreed. But those skeptics who were not entirely loyal to him, had a condition of their own: they would put down their swords and pick up the plows for one year. If they did not turn a profit with their crops, then they would go back to the old ways.

The old ways that had left them with their current reputations as thieves, murderers, and criminals.

Thus far, the crops were doing quite well. Still, he worried. There could be too much rain or not enough. Too much sun or not enough. There was also the risk of blight or infestation.

In truth, he'd never farmed a day in his life. But he had read about it and had fostered with a family of warrior farmers. He referred to them as such for they were a fierce lot, the McGregors. But they were also farmers. They grew barley and wheat and raised cattle. Some of the best beef in all of Scotia.

That is where he wanted to lead his people: to a brighter future where coin was earned, as well as a reputation for being decent people. He wanted the Bowie clan to be the people one turned to in time of need and not the cause for the need.

Everything, his entire future, depended on the barley that was growing in the fields. He had yet to decide what he would do if the crops failed or if they did not turn a profit. Would he remain as chief of clan Bowie and sit idly by while his clan went back to their old ways?

The thought made his head pound.

He was about to pour himself a dram or two of whisky when a knock came at the door.

"Come!" he ground out in frustration.

The door opened and Leona stepped in. Gone were the kerchief and apron, for which he was grateful. Now, he could see just how beautiful she was. The blue dress clung nicely to every luscious curve of her magnificent body. Though her hair was still braided, he could see more of it now. The candlelight glinted across it most majestically.

Pushing away the lascivious thoughts that crashed into his mind, he asked, "What can I do fer ye?" Then downed the entire contents of his cup. The whisky would help steel his nerves against her.

She smiled then. That glorious smile that lit up the room. *Damnation,* he cursed inwardly as he tore his gaze away from her full lips and grabbed the ledger he'd just closed.

She laughed then, a sweet, melodious laugh. A laugh that unsettled him as much as her smile. "I came to see if I could do anything fer ye," she explained as she sidled up to the table. "Ye have been in here fer quite some time. Be there anythin' I can help ye with?"

Chancing a glance, he saw her hopeful expression. For the briefest moment, he considered showing her the books, sharing his worries and concerns with her. Then he thought better of it. The more time he spent with her, the more his heart betrayed him with skipping beats. "Nay, but I thank ye," he said, turning back to the ledger.

"I be verra good with cypherin'," she told him. "I kept me father's books fer him."

No. No. No. He looked up at her again. God's teeth, but she was a strikingly pretty woman. High cheekbones, full lips, breasts that he could all but feel under his hands. "Nay, I be done." He closed the book, pushed it away and stood.

"I have to go see Dougall," he said. 'Twas the only thing he could think to say, the only excuse he could come up with at the moment that would allow him to flee her presence with some of his dignity still in tact.

Her lips curved into that delightful 'o'. She did look rather disappointed.

"But it be pourin' rain," she said.

"Aye," he replied. Clearing the knot from his throat, he went on to say, "But 'tis important." He made a hasty move for the door.

"Will ye be back fer the noonin' meal?"

Her question brought him to a halt, with his hand on the door latch. "Nay," he said. Without looking, he *knew* her lips had formed into that 'o' again, that her eyes were filled with disappointment. "I'll be back fer the evenin' meal." And with that, he left her standing in the middle of his study with mouth agape.

THERE HAD BEEN NO OPPORTUNITY TO ASK FOR A KISS, FOR HE HAD retreated like a cat whose tail had just landed in hot coals. "What on earth is wrong with that man?" she wondered aloud.

Her idea to teach her husband the proper way to say goodbye was not going as planned. She would not allow his abrupt departure to spoil her mood. Eventually, she knew, he would have to stop running away from her.

There be time. Plenty of time.

JUST AFTER THE NOONING MEAL, JOHN BOWIE KNOCKED AT HER KITCHEN door again. She met him with a smile. "Good day to ye, again, John Bowie."

"Mistress," he said with a slight inclination of his head.

"Would ye like to come in fer some cider and sweet cakes?"

She thought her offer sincere and kind. He looked at her as if she had three heads.

"Nay, mistress," he replied. "I came to tell ye that Phillip Bowie sends his regrets. He does no' have any spare venison fer ye."

Spare venison? Hadn't Alec told her the night before he had purchased the venison? Confused, she asked, "Did he say when he *might* have more?"

The man swallowed hard, his adam's apple bobbing up and down. "Nay, mistress, he did no'."

First no milk, now no venison. She let out a frustrated breath. For a brief moment, she debated on whether or not she should let Alec know about the lack of milk and venison. *Nay,* she told herself. *He be a busy man and this be something ye should be able to take care of on yer own.*

"Thank ye, kindly, John Bowie. Please tell Phillip that if he cannot supply the venison, he can return the coin my husband gave him for it."

"Return the coin, mistress?" he asked, apparently confused.

"Aye, the coin Alec paid him fer the venison. If he can no' supply it, he may seek Alec out and return it." She hoped her consternation was apparent enough and that he would let Phillip know she was not pleased.

The man bobbed his head again and left without saying goodbye. Mayhap this leaving without a word was a Bowie trait passed on from one generation to the next? Either way, it irritated her no end.

The only way to change the Bowies would be to change her husband. Oh, she didn't want to change everything. Just the severe lack of manners.

Closing the door, she faced the empty kitchen. "Well, it will no' be roast venison this night," she said to no one. "I hope me husband likes mutton."

~

Thankfully, Alec had emptied the tub the night before. That was her only consolation considering the man had stolen her bath. Determined to hurry and bathe before he returned, she happily began hauling buckets of water above stairs.

If the bath had been food, her mouth would have watered at the sight of it. Warm, steaming, and luxurious. She had just emptied the last bucket and set it near the hearth when Alec walked in.

"Och, wife!" he declared with a smile. "Ye spoil me, ye do!"

She stood in stunned silence as he quickly stripped out of his muddy clothes, leaving the pile in the middle of the floor. Without a word, he stepped into the tub and sank back.

"'Tis heaven on earth, it is!" he declared happily. The steam rose upward, his face bearing the expression of a very happy man.

Her heart sunk. He was taking *her* bath again. The one she'd worked so hard to prepare. Did the man have some sort of mental ability that detected a hot bath? She had few choices. Scream that he was a bath thief, or smile and feign all was well.

"Leona, lass, I can no' thank ye enough fer thinkin' of me like this," he said as he reached for the empty pitcher. "Ye're a good woman, ye are." He dipped the pitcher into the steaming water and poured it over his head.

A good woman? 'Twas the closest thing to a compliment he had given her, at least outside their marital bed. *Aye, Alec. I be a good woman who has no' had a hot bath in far too many days to count!* She wanted to rail at him, scream, mayhap take the pitcher from his hands and bash it over his thick skull. Tears threatened behind her eyes.

But she couldn't scream or rail or injure him. He'd just told her she was a good woman. *A good woman.*

Deciding it best to leave now, before she said or did something foolish, she gave him the same kind of goodbye as he was so fond of giving her. Without a word, she rushed from the room and headed below stairs.

CHAPTER 14

*E*arly the next morn, she tried to slip out of bed without waking her husband. But the moment she lifted the furs, his hand slid her around her stomach as he pulled her into his chest.

"Why do ye flee our bed each morn?" he asked, his voice scratchy with sleep.

Leona giggled lightly. "I do no' flee, Alec. I leave early in order to prepare yer morning meal."

"What if it is ye I want to feast on?" he asked playfully as he nibbled at the tender spot of skin behind her ear.

"Although that sounds like a splendid idea, and one I could fully enjoy, I fear by the noonin' meal, ye'd be starvin'," she replied with a giggle.

He nuzzled his chin against her neck, his day old beard scratched, but in a thoroughly pleasant way. "'Twould be a most pleasant way in which to starve."

By the time she made her way below stairs and into her kitchens, the sun was already coming up. 'Twas a pleasant, bright morning, with only a hint of fog caressing the land.

Once inside, she lit candles first, then the fires, all the while humming a happy tune. While her husband had fallen asleep almost as soon as they were done loving one another, she had gained a good deal of energy. 'Twas a most delightful way to start the day.

With only a few eggs left in the larder, she grabbed her basket and stepped out into the early morn. She felt light today, with a sense of carefree abandon that she'd not felt since she was a very little girl.

God, I love the feel of yer hair, he had declared more than once. *'Tis softer than any silk. And yer skin? I love the way it feels against me own.*

With the warm memories of the night before, she gathered eggs with a smile. The chickens squawked and protested, but she was undeterred. With her eggs gathered, she thanked the chickens and returned to her kitchen.

SHE WAS SLICING HAM WHEN SHE HEARD A SCRATCH AT HER BACK DOOR. Wiping her hands on her apron, she opened the door to find Patches on the other side. A moment later, he was licking her hands, begging for her attention. She could not resist smiling at the beast. "Well, good morn to ye," she said as she scratched the top of his head.

Though he seemed content with her affections, he soon began to whimper and lick his chops. "Och!" she declared. "Do ye smell the ham?" He whimpered his answer.

"Stay," she ordered with a pointed finger. The obedient bandogge sat back, continued to drool and lick his chops but he waited patiently for her return.

Knowing Alec would disapprove, she gave the dog a few scraps of ham anyway. After he chomped them down, she gave him a few pats on his back, then ordered him to return to Seamus.

As she returned to her work, someone came knocking at the back door. He was a younger lad, maybe only five and ten years of age. A tall, skinny boy, with dark hair and eyes, and he looked rather nervous.

"Mistress, I be Caleb. Charles asked me to tell ye he can no' bring ye milk this day."

Leona sighed inwardly and prayed this would not be a daily occurrence.

"His cow was startled this morn and knocked over the bucket," he went on to explain.

Although she would have liked milk to help make a gravy, 'twas not the end of the world. "Thank ye, kindly, Caleb. Please tell Charles no' to worry over it. There is always the morrow."

He gave her a nod, bid her good day, and left.

"I hope Alec does no' tire of the same meal each morn," she murmured. "Ham and eggs, eggs and ham, it be the same no matter what ye call it."

Stepping into the larder, she looked around, ever hopeful that something would gain her attention, something delicious with which to break their fast. As she was perusing the contents, she was startled when she heard a familiar voice call out to her.

"Leona?" Came Effie's voice from the kitchen.

Stepping out of the larder, she smiled and greeted the woman. "Good morn, to ye."

"Och! There ye be!" Effie replied. "Ye look busy this morn."

"Just making Alec his mornin' meal. What brings ye here?" Leona asked.

Effie smiled. "I needed to stretch me legs. Dougall and the boys have gone fishin' and I thought 'twould be nice to visit with ye. To see how ye be gettin' along."

Leona thought it a most kind gesture. "Well I be glad ye thought of me," she said as she offered Effie a stool near the hearth. "Be ye hungry? Would ye like some cider?"

"I've already eaten, but a bit of cider would be nice."

Effie sat sipping cider while Leona returned to her work. "How are ye feelin'?" Leona asked, with a nod toward the woman's belly.

"It be gettin' more difficult to sleep at night," Effie replied with a slight giggle. "This one prefers the late night hours."

A twinge of envy struck Leona's heart before she pushed it away. Mayhap, just mayhap she was now carrying Alec's child. She smiled at the thought.

"What will ye be doin' later this day?" Effie asked before taking a sip of cider.

"Cleanin' this keep," Leona replied.

"I do no' envy ye in that task. Do ye have rushes?"

"Nay, I fear I do no'," Leona admitted.

"Well, after yer mornin' meal, come to me cottage. We can gather rushes together."

Leona was grateful for the offer. "I thank ye, kindly, Effie. I would like that verra much."

"Think nothin' of it. I be in need of fresh rushes meself," she replied.

A long moment of silence passed, with Leona busy at the table and Effie sitting quietly at the hearth. Something about Effie's countenance, the way she stared blankly into her cup, felt 'off'. "Be there somethin' the matter?" Leona asked.

"I hear ye met me sister, Patrice, yesterday," she said.

"Aye! I did. She was verra kind to me. I like her."

Effie glanced up from her cup. "Leona, I would like ye to be careful when it comes to Patrice."

Confused by the warning, Leona knotted her brow. "But why? She was verra kind to me."

Effie let loose with a heavy breath. "She has no' been the same since Rutger's death."

Of course not, Leona thought to herself. Who would be the same after such a thing?

"Patrice might seem kind to ye, but..." Effie's voice trailed off.

Leona could sense there was far more she wanted to say. "Effie, say what ye need to."

"I do no' like speakin' ill of me sister. 'Tis the truth I do no'. But, I ken her better than anyone. She will pretend to be nice to ye while she's with ye. But behind yer back?"

Leona gave this a good measure of thought. Effie seemed genuine in her concern. Mayhap Patrice *was* the kind of woman who could not be trusted. Usually, Leona was quite good at picking up on such things, for she had suffered at the hands of plenty of people like that in her lifetime. But not once had she detected even a hint of duplicity with Patrice.

Not wanting to argue it, and not wanting to find guilt in someone she truly did not know that well, she decided to wait and get to know Patrice for herself. But she would heed Effie's warning. "Thank ye, Effie, fer yer honesty. I shall be verra careful when it comes to Patrice."

Effie looked as relieved as she did embarrassed. "'Tis only yer best interests I have in mind, ye ken."

"Do no' fash yerself over it," Leona told her with a smile. "What time would ye like to gather rushes?"

~

WITH BREAKFAST SERVED, THE TABLES CLEARED, AND ALEX ON HIS WAY to work in the fields, Leona searched for something to tie bundles of rushes together. She was excited for the chance to be out of the keep as well as a chance to do something so mundane and ordinary as gathering rushes with a friend.

The only other time in her life she had experienced a true friendship was when she had lived with the Mackintoshes and McLarens. Leona could say, unequivocally, that Rose Mackintosh was her one and only friend.

But now she faced a new chapter in her life. A new way of living. Not only was she married — and if that didn't surprise anyone then nothing on earth ever would – she was married to a braw clan chief. The chatelaine of her own keep. Hundreds upon hundreds of people were now counting on her, even if they didn't know it.

She had learned from Alex that the last *married* Bowie chief had been more than twenty-five years and five chiefs ago. Mayhap, just mayhap, the cold reception she had received from the women, was due to that. Not only had their chief married, but he had married an outsider. Undoubtedly this was a change that would take some time getting used to.

She found the necessary twine in the storage room above stairs. Tucking the twine into her belt, she grabbed her cloak from her bedchamber and left the keep.

"Where be ye goin', mistress?" A voice called from the upper wall. Leona was standing at the drawbridge, waiting for it to be lowered.

"To Dougall's home," she called up to the man. "To see his wife, Effie." Though why he needed to know, she couldn't begin to guess, but kept the question to herself.

Without another word, the drawbridge was lowered. Taking that as permission to leave, she crossed over the thick timbers quickly and headed for the path that led to the cottages.

Having only been to Dougall's once before, it took more time than she had planned to find the place. Though many of the cottages were similar in size and appearance, there were enough differences to make it somewhat easier to discern one from the other.

Just as had happened the day before, she was at once surrounded by children. At least a dozen wee ones, ranging in age by her estimate from six to no more than two and ten. The girls outnumbered the boys.

"Good day, mistress!" one of the little girls said with a smile. Leona felt guilty for not remembering her name. Nor could she remember anyone else's.

"Good day to ye, lass," she replied with a warm smile. It did her heart a measure of good knowing that at least the children would treat her kindly.

"Where are ye goin'?" the cherubic little girl asked before slipping her hand into Leona's.

"To gather rushes with Effie, Dougall's wife."

"Can we go with ye?" she asked.

"Aye, we want to help!" another girl who couldn't have been more than ten summers said. Her smile was bright and so sweet. There was no way Leona could have denied their requests.

"Aye, I see no problem with ye helpin'," she told them.

The boys, wholly uninterested in gathering rushes, declined the offer to join the women folk. "We'd rather hunt with the men," one of the younger boys said. He looked so serious — a smaller version of her husband or Gylys or Kyth — Leona could have laughed aloud had she not worried she'd injure his young pride.

The girls kindly escorted Leona to Effie's cottage. As they walked along, they were filled with all manner of questions. "Do ye like bein' mistress?" "Do ye like bein' married to our chief?" "Is it true ye have to sleep on the floor because Alec took away all the furniture?"

'Twas difficult, but she managed to keep up with the questions. "Aye, I do like bein' mistress and I do like bein' married to Alec. And nay, 'tis no' true about the furniture. We sleep in a bed. He hasn't taken it all away."

One of the older girls chimed in. "Me mum said he took everythin' away because it be too painful a reminder of his brother."

Leona had surmised as much. "Well, he hasn't taken it *all* away. Just most of it."

"Because it reminded him of Rutger?" she asked.

"I am no' certain. Mayhap we should ask Alec," Leona said.

"Ask Alec what?" Leona nearly jumped out of her skin when she heard her husband's voice. She spun to find him standing but a few steps behind her, sporting a curious expression.

"What are ye doin' here?" she asked, completely perplexed at seeing him. He was supposed to have been working in the fields.

She had no doubt now, from his piercing gaze, that she had done something wrong. But what?

"Ye left without escort," he replied coolly.

Perplexity turned to confusion. "Escort?"

Standing with one hand on his hip, he crooked his index finger and bade her come forward. Uncertainty reigned supreme as she took a step toward him. He crooked his finger again and again until she was nearly stepping on his feet.

Leaning down, in a low, soft voice that did not match the glower he was giving her, he said, "Ye can no' leave the keep without escort. 'Tis too dangerous."

Not once in all her days had she ever required an escort and told him so.

"But ye were no' the chief's wife," he politely informed her. "Ye can no' leave the keep without an escort."

"But are we no' safe and sound on Bowie lands?" she asked, more than miffed with him, but for reasons she couldn't exactly explain at the moment.

"Aye, we are, lass. But I would feel better if ye did no' leave without an escort."

Was that tenderness she saw in his eyes? Her heart instantly warmed with a rapid beat. *He cares. He truly cares about me!*

"Ye do no' ken these lands well and are likely to get lost."

The warmth and fondness evaporated in the blink of an eye. "Lost? Ye can no' be serious. I was only goin' to Effie's and she was goin' to take me to gather rushes. And I do *no'* get lost!"

Before Alec married Leona, Ian Mackintosh had told him of the countless times Leona had wandered off, gone for days at a time. When Ian had asked her to explain those lost days, she had politely informed him that she wasn't *lost,* but merely taking time to herself, to write in her journals.

Alec was not about to risk her safety or welfare. For a whole multitude of reasons, the most important being one he did not want to admit. If anything were to happen to her, he didn't think he could bear it.

Instead of telling his beautiful wife — who was glaring at him angrily right now — the truth, he chose instead to say something else, something that ended up wounding her tender heart.

"Aye, I am quite serious. I'll no' have ye wanderin' off and gettin' yerself lost. I do no' have the time to form a search party. I have more important things to tend to."

He saw it immediately, the intensity of both her anger and her hurt. There was nothing to be done about it. He could not apologize in front of the dozens of little eyes staring at them. 'Twould be a sign of weakness, and one he'd not give in to. Pushing all his guilt aside, he stood taller, and glared back at her.

"WELL, LET ME TELL *YE* SOMETHIN', YE UNKIND, STUBBORN, LOUT! I WILL go where I damned well please and *when* I damned well please and I'll go without escort!" The words were out before she realized it. The only thing that would have stopped her tirade now, would have been an arrow to her heart.

A collective gasp filled the air behind them, the children more than a bit stunned to hear anyone talk to their laird and chief in such a disrespectful manner. Leona cared not what they might think.

"And another thing, if I ever do get lost, I would no' want ye to come find me! I'd rather be lost in the woods, starin' down a wounded bear and a pack of wolves than to have *ye* rescue me!"

Before she could utter another syllable, Alec grabbed her arms, pulled her in, and planted a firm, passionate kiss on her lips.

'Twas the only thing he could think to do. The only thing he *wanted* to do.

She struggled, albeit briefly, before melting into his arms. He took a good measure of pride in the fact that every time his lips touched hers, she melted and melded so sweetly into him, as if she had been made specifically by God for such a purpose.

'Twas the children's laughter and giggles that brought him out of his momentary lack of composure. Regaining that lost composure took a moment longer than he would have wished. "Are ye certain ye'd no' want me to rescue ye?" he asked playfully. Twining a lock of her hair around his finger, he waited for her answer.

~

Why on earth had he kissed her? Like *that*? With such abandon and passion? And in front of the children?

The answer was staring her right in the face, in the form of a very smug expression. She slapped his hand away from her hair and took a step back. "Aye, I be certain," she ground out. "Now, if ye'll excuse me, I have rushes to gather with Effie."

Though her legs had the strength of warm pudding, she managed to spin around and walk away from him. Haughtily, with her chin up, so he could not see just how his kiss had affected her. The children fell in around her, all a-twitter and giggle.

As she stomped toward Effie's cottage, she heard her husband's laughter. "Just follow the children. They ken how to get to Effie's!" he called out to her.

If his mission was to humiliate her, he had failed. However, if his intent was to anger her further, he could call it a rousing success. She stopped in her tracks and spun around.

There he still stood, just where she had left him. All smug and superior.

Two can play at this game, she thought to herself.

Masking her anger, she returned to him, grabbed his face with her palms and stood on her tip-toes. Without begging permission, she pulled his face to hers and kissed him just as soundly, just as passionately as he had her moments ago.

Pushing him away, she looked into his eyes, and spoke. "If ye were ever lost, *I* would no' take time out of my busy day to go lookin' fer ye. I'd let ye rot."

~

Pretending she was unaffected by the exchange of kisses with her husband, Leona set off for Effie's cottage. The children, bless them, were all too willing to take her there straight away. Thankfully, her husband did not follow after.

Biting her bottom lip was the only way to get rid of the still lingering tingle he'd left on them moments before. It also helped to remind her just how angry she was with him.

Standing in front of Effie's cottage, she decided to push away the anger and hurt. 'Twould do her no good to dwell on that which she could not change: her stubborn husband.

Before she could knock on the door, Effie opened it for her. Her bright smile faded when she caught sight of the children standing with Leona. There was a flash of disappointment behind Effie's eyes.

Instantly, Leona regretted her decision to allow the children to tag along. Mayhap Effie had been looking forward to time away from children, or time to have adult conversations without little ears listening.

"I seemed to have picked up a few new friends along the way," Leona told her. "I hope ye do no' mind if they join us."

Effie's frown was gone in the blink of an eye. "Nay, the more hands we have helpin', the quicker our task is done," she said before stepping away from the door. "Just let me get me basket."

Somehow, Leona didn't quite believe her attempt at sounding cheerful or agreeable. Then she remembered Rose, and how often her mood would change, especially the last two months before giving birth. Believing the sudden shift in moods was caused by Effie's being with child, she decided not to dwell on it any further.

Effie was still smiling when she left the cottage and closed the door behind her. "How be ye wee lassies this fine day?" she asked the horde of little girls. "How be yer families?"

Leona and Effie spent the next two hours gathering rushes and listening to the little girls giggle and laugh. The women did more gathering than the little girls, but Leona didn't mind. She thoroughly enjoyed watching them as they played together.

As she watched them picking flowers and chatting about all manner of things, she could not help but think about her own child-hood. How desolate and lonely it had been.

Never once had she had a friend. There had been no carefree days for her, where she giggled incessantly with even one other child, let alone a group of them. She had been an outcast in every sense of the word. Accepted by no one, not even her father.

Ingerame.

An overwhelming sense of heartache began to build. Not with missing him. Nay, on the contrary. She felt melancholy over the loss of the childhood she should have had instead of the one she'd been given.

Why? Why could he never accept her as she was? Why did he hate her so vehemently? Those were questions she'd been asking since she was a little girl. To date, she still had no answers.

'Twas then she made a silent oath. *My children will have* this *kind of life. Filled with carefree days, many friends, and they will always ken they are loved.*

EXPECTING HER HUSBAND TO GIVE HER ANOTHER LECTURE ON HOW TO behave when others were around, Leona was not eager to return to the keep. But knowing there was no way to avoid it, other than walking back to the Mackintosh keep, she decided 'twould be best to simply face the moment head on and get it over with.

But the lecture never came.

She and Alec ate their evening meal together with Kyth and Gylys, and not a word was said on what had transpired that afternoon. All in all, 'twas as pleasant an evening as any other.

Mayhap, just mayhap, he was coming to realize she was a strong, independent woman who was quite capable of taking care of herself. A woman who could be his ally and friend.

Or mayhap he was saving it for future use.

Either way, if he wasn't going to mention it, then neither would she.

CHAPTER 15

$\mathcal{W}$ ith her husband's habit of wiping his hands on his tunics, working in the fields each morn and training with his men in the afternoons, it didn't take long before he'd amassed a large pile of laundry. Married more than a week now, 'twas past time she washed his clothing.

'Twas the blood splattered on his clothes that upset her the most, even though 'twasn't his blood. Nay, 'twas from the men he trained with on a near daily basis.

The thought sickened her. Not that she couldn't stand the sight of blood. On the contrary, it wasn't the blood that made her feel ill at ease. It was what the blood represented: fighting.

She was doubtful she'd ever understand a man's need to fight, either with his bare hands or with weapons. Why were they so keen on destruction? The search for power? For wealth? And at any cost?

Mayhap, if she ever made it to heaven, she could ask God for the answers to those questions. Hopefully, He was not as stubborn as the men on earth, and would answer honestly. With words instead of the same annoying 'grunting' sound most of the men here were so fond of using.

With her arms filled with Alec's dirty clothes, she left the kitchen through the back door. It would have made sense that the laundry was near the well. Try as she might, she did not see anything that resembled what she was looking for. So she stood, staring at the buildings around her in hopes that something would stand out.

The armory was to her left, not far from the granary. To her right, and down a beaten down path stood the stables. In between were a few tiny, ramshackle buildings that she surmised were far too small to house a laundry. Behind her was the keep, her kitchen, and the chicken coop.

Worry began to settle in. What if, by chance, the lairds before Alec had never built a true laundry? What if they had to trek outside the keep and down to the loch to wash dirty clothes? Nay, that made no sense. Before Alec, the keep was filled almost to the rafters with men and guests and servants.

"Can I help ye, mistress?"

Startled from her reverie, she jumped at the sound of Patrice's voice. It had been several days since she had seen her. She looked just as regal and as beautiful as the last time they'd met.

"Och! Patrice! Ye nearly scared me out of me own skin!"

"I be terribly sorry! 'Twas no' me intent." Her smile was warm and infectious. "Ye looked lost. Be there somethin' I can help ye with?"

Leona let loose a breath as she struggled with the weight of the laundry in her arms. "Aye, ye can. Where be the laundry?"

"It be behind the granary," she told her. "I can take ye there if ye'd like."

"That would be wonderful," Leona said, relieved once again to have Patrice's assistance.

"Let me help ye with that," Patrice said as she took half the bundle of laundry into her own arms. "Though I do no' think the mistress of the keep should be doin' laundry."

Leona wanted desperately to agree out loud. "'Tis no trouble," she lied. In truth, this was the one area she was dreading the most. Spending an hour over a boiling pot of water was not her favorite way to spend a day.

"I do no' see why Alec will no' get ye some help with all the cleanin' and cookin'," she said as they made their way toward the granary. "'Tis no' like he'd be revertin' to the auld ways of the auld chiefs. 'Tis just a bit of help, after all."

Help would be nice, but she doubted Alec would be too keen on the idea. He had seemed adamantly opposed to it when she had asked him about it the first night she had arrived here.

Suddenly, it occurred to her that mayhap there simply wasn't enough coin for such a luxury? With what she knew about Rutger, he'd nearly bankrupted the clan with his penchant for extravagant clothing and lavish feasts. The thought saddened her. If that was the case, and she was completely certain it was, 'twas no wonder her husband was working as hard as he did. Not only was he trying to lead his clan toward a brighter and better future, he was also trying to restore the coffers.

"'Tis a bonny and bright day, is it no'?" Leona asked, changing the subject altogether.

Patrice looked up at the bright sky for a moment. "Aye, I suppose it is," she said as she led the way around the granary. A well-worn path had been beaten over the grassy space. "There be yer laundry," she said with a nod toward the structure. If one could call it such.

'Twas nothing more than three walls draped with dingy looking, auld panels of fabric. The roof was made out of the same ugly fabric. A large copper pot sat in the center of the space. It was suspended over a large, empty pit where a fire could be built. A long table sat against the back wall. Next to that was a narrow opening that lead to the yard behind.

Seeing Leona's disappointment, Patrice said, "Do no' fash yerself over it. At least ye no' be trying to do laundry for the entire clan. 'Tis just the two of ye after all."

Aye, 'twas just the two of them. But what if they had many children? And what about the winter months when the snow was deep or the wind bitter and cold? 'Twas a disagreeable thought.

"Aye," she said taking a deep breath. "At least I do no' have to find a stream and beat the clothes against the rocks." *Try to remain positive, Leona. Ye've suffered worse than this.*

"There be lines to dry the clothes behind it," Patrice explained. "If we're lucky, there might also be some wood left to build the fire. They used to store it back there." She set the pile of clothes in a large basket in the corner. "Now, ye'll be verra glad to ken there be a well back there as well, so 'tis only a few steps to fill the pot."

That information brightened Leona's spirits. *At least someone had given some thought to it all.*

Leona added her pile to Patrice's before following her around to the back of the structure. The stockpile of wood wouldn't last long, but at least the well was only a few steps away. 'Twould be enough to do at least this one load of laundry. Ten lines of thin rope on which to dry clothes had been hung from the structure, across the little yard, and attached to sturdy looking beams. All in all, 'twasn't nearly as bad as she had first surmised.

"I'll help ye get a fire started," Patrice said as she grabbed two nicely sized logs and headed back inside. Leona was right behind her with two logs of her own.

In short order, they had a decent fire built and had managed to fill the pot with several buckets of water. Grabbing two squat stools, they sat outside in the sunlight while they waited for the water to heat.

"How is yer mum doin'?" Leona asked as she stared at the back of the granary.

"Much better," Patrice replied. "She had fought the ague fer so long, I began to worry she would never get better."

"That is good to ken," Leona said as she enjoyed the sun beating down on her face. Off in the distance, she could hear the men training, the sounds of metal clanging against metal, the muffled sound of shouts and curses floating in on the air.

"What about your parents?" Patrice asked thoughtfully.

Leona didn't like talking about either of her parents. Whenever she thought of her mother, she often felt sad and quite lonely. Whenever she thought of her father, she felt angry and ashamed. "Me mum died when I was six," she said in a low, melancholy tone.

"Och!" Patrice turned to face her. "I did no' ken, Leona."

She gave an indifferent shrug, as if it didn't matter. But it did. "'Tis all right, do no' fash yerself over it."

"And yer da?"

Ingerame Graham was not a subject she wished to discuss. "He still lives."

Sensing her unease, Patrice decided it best not to press the matter. She fell silent for a long while. "Do ye have any other family? Sisters? Brothers?"

"Nay, I do no'," she replied before thinking on Rose. "I do have a cousin, though. Rose Mackintosh."

Patrice's cheeks flamed with shame.

Thinking of Rose led them both to think of Rutger and what he had done.

"I did no' ken Rose was yer cousin," Patrice said.

"I did no' ken it either until recently. Our mums, as it turns out, were cousins. I suppose 'tis why Rose and I look so much alike."

Patrice fell silent again, undoubtedly thinking about Rutger and how he had kidnapped Rose. Mayhap even the turmoil and strife he had brought to his clan.

"Patrice," Leona said, turning to face her. "I do no' want ye to dwell on what Rutger did. It all turned out well in the end. I do no' hold against ye anythin' he did to Rose."

Damp eyes filled with pain looked back at her. "What about what he did to ye?"

"Och! Nay!" Leona exclaimed as she took Patrice's hands in her own. "'Twas no' me first beatin', though I do pray it was me last," she said with a smile, hoping to add some levity to the moment.

"Had I been there that day, I would have stopped him," Patrice said, wiping tears away with the sleeve of her dress.

"I have no' doubt at all that ye would have."

"I did no' ken until it was too late, what he had done to ye."

Leona gave her a warm smile and patted the back of her hand. "Do no' fash yourself over it. I meant what I said. I will never hold what Rutger did against ye. Now, let us talk of somethin' far more pleasant."

Before a new topic of conversation could be decided, a man came walking toward them. He appeared to Leona to be in his early twenties. Every bit a Bowie with his long dark hair and piercing brown eyes. A handsome lad, tall and lean.

"Good day to ye, Allen," Patrice said as she wiped her face dry and pretended she hadn't been crying.

"Good day to ye, Patrice. Mistress," he gave a slight nod as he addressed each woman. No official introduction was evidently needed. Everyone would by now know the wee woman with the odd eyes and blonde hair was the laird's wife. "I saw the smoke and came to see if all was well."

Leona stood up and offered him a warm smile. "All be well. We are only doin' a bit of laundry."

He looked positively elated to hear it. "Thank, God! I hate doin' me own laundry."

Patrice giggled. "We're only usin' it fer the laird's and mistresses' laundry. We be no' openin' it to all."

Deflated, he kicked a pebble with his toe. "Well, damn," he muttered.

An idea popped into Leona's head, an idea that would hopefully allow her to help her husband rebuild the clan's coffer. She might even earn enough to purchase the plaid broach she wanted to give him. "Allen, is it?"

"Aye, mistress. Allen Bowie, son of Edgar and Kate."

Leona offered him her best curtsey. "'Tis a pleasure to meet ye, Allen."

"Likewise," he mumbled, apparently still distressed over the lack of laundry services.

"Allen, how much would ye be willin' to pay to have someone do yer laundry?"

He raised a brow, but didn't think long on the matter. "A siller, mistress."

Alec's gift was going to cost her far more than a siller, but it was a good start.

"'Tis a deal, then," she said as she extended her hand.

"What be a deal, mistress?" he asked, completely confused.

"I would be verra happy to do yer laundry fer a siller. A siller a load."

It took a moment before understanding set in and his eyes lit up. "Ye'd do that fer me, mistress?"

"Of course I would. Fer a siller a load, if ye're agreeable."

"I am, mistress, I am."

And with that, Leona MacDowall-Bowie's laundry service began.

Leona's first week at her new home proved to be as busy as it was challenging. Though the majority of the rooms were empty, it was a daunting task, but one she was fully determined to see to fruition.

Her relationship with Alec had improved after their argument in front of the children and anyone else who might have witnessed it. Something in Alec had seemed to change. He seemed happier, if such a thing were even possible. Though she dared not question it or ask him about it. She was doing her best to keep things on an even keel. Why bring up a thing if it might upset the ship, so to speak.

At night, in their chamber, he would make long, slow, and passionate love to her. So much so, that she was finding it more difficult to slip out of bed before dawn. Mayhap that was his intent, to wear her out in order to keep from waking alone. Another question she dared not put voice to.

Whenever they were alone, he was always charming and kind. But when they were near anyone within hearing distance or vision, he would become almost as cold as stone toward her. She could only assume he was putting on an air of indifference so as not to look weak in front of his people. 'Twas the only thing that made a bit of sense to her.

She was working hard to gain her husband's approval. Approval that she at times doubted would ever come.

She had taken two empty chambers down the opposite corridor from where she and Alec slept, and made them into nice, useable bedchambers. Should they ever have company — even though that was as likely as a pig flying — she would be prepared for such an event.

The days were long and laborious. What with all the cleaning, cooking, laundry, and everything else that went into running her household.

But no matter how busy her days were, she always took the time to take a meal to Melvin.

He was such a sweet, if not mischievous auld man. His greeting was always the same whenever she arrived. "Och! There be the prettiest lass in all these lands!"

She knew he was simply being kind, but still, his compliments always seemed to lift her spirits — even if they didn't need lifting.

Her blisters had formed blisters and were now turning into hard callouses, but Alec didn't seem to mind. The dark circles under her eyes did not keep him from loving her soundly each night.

Or soundly in the morn. For the past several days, she had awakened to find him watching her. He'd not say a word. Instead, he would simply give her that devious smile she was growing so fond of, then proceed to love her until she was breathless.

As much as she would enjoy falling asleep again after, she was unable to. Her mind simply would not shut off. It would inevitably remind her of all the tasks she needed to accomplish.

Besides, the early morning hours were the only time she had to bathe. While she was glad Alec appreciated the hot baths she prepared for him each evening, she was growing quite tired of hauling all those endless buckets of water above stairs.

She did it because she cared for him a great deal. She did it because she loved the smile that came to his face. She did it because she wanted him to care for her as much as she cared for him.

Aye, some might think her a fool for working so hard to gain the affections of a man who simply could not find the strength to give her more than a quick compliment on the meals she prepared. But what should she expect from a Bowie?

Practically asleep on her feet, with Patches right beside, her, she was kneading bread when a knock came at the door. She knew who 'twas, or at least what it was about, before she answered.

Wiping her hands on her apron, she told Patches to remain where he was. "Do no' be growlin' ye beasty," she told him sternly. "Whose turn do ye suppose it be to tell me there will be no milk this morn?" she asked the dog before opening the door.

'Twas a man she had only caught a glimpse of once or twice before when she'd been out of doors. He appeared to be around forty, with thinning, dirty hair, yellow eyes, and tattered clothes. He positively reeked of stale ale and sweat.

"Good morn, mistress," he said as he fidgeted with the dingy cap he held in his hands.

"Good morn," she replied. "Are ye here to tell me there will be no milk this day?" Accustomed now to the daily visits of one person or another who would inform her there would be no milk.

He swallowed hard before answering. "Aye, mistress," he said rather nervously.

"Ye can go back to Charles Bowie and tell them no' to bother anymore. I plan on buyin' me own cow." She was not necessarily angry with this poor soul, but with Charles Bowie and the fact he was not brave enough to face her in person. It should not be this difficult to get a bit of milk. Irritated with the situation as a whole, she was about the shut the door when he stopped her.

"Mistress?" he said, swallowing hard once again. "Would ye be havin' a chore I could do in exchange fer a bit o' bread?"

Whether 'twas his worn clothes, haggard appearance, or his countenance, she could not rightly say. But there was something about the man that indicated a tremendous amount of sadness. Feeling guilty for being so discourteous a moment ago, she said, "Of course!" as she pulled him into the kitchen.

Patches lifted his head and protested the intrusion with a low growl.

"Wheest!" Leona scolded him. Wagging her finger at the mutt, she said, "Ye do no' growl at our guests."

He whimpered once, then lay his head down to return to his nap.

To her guest she said, "Do no' worry over Patches. I'll make certain he leaves ye be."

Hunger apparently won over fear of the dog. Cautiously, he stepped inside and waited next to the door with his eyes glued to the big dog.

"What be yer name?" she asked politely.

"Willem Bowie, mistress," he answered.

"And what do ye do here, Willem?"

Behind his dull eyes, she caught a flutter of shame. "Odd jobs here and there," he replied.

Leona could not help but wonder if he worked only long enough to earn enough coin for drink, but kept her suspicions to herself. "I could use a few buckets of water," Leona told him. "And I will be givin' ye more than a bit of bread fer yer hard work."

"Thank ye, kindly, mistress," he said. Apprehensively, he donned his cap and took the buckets Leona offered him.

It did not take him long to return. "What else could I help ye with, mistress?" he asked from a spot near the door.

She studied him closely for a long moment, with her index finger tapping at her upper lip. Letting out a heavy sigh, she asked, "When was the last time ye had a good, hot meal? Or a bath?"

His face burned red with humiliation. "I get along well enough, mistress." He was clearly insulted by her questions.

"Oh, I am most certain that ye do, Willem. But ye see, I be in need of some help."

He eyed her suspiciously for a long moment. "What kind of help?"

"How are ye at choppin' wood?" she asked.

"I ken how to swing an axe, mistress," he said, once again insulted by the question.

Offering him her most sincere smile, she said, "Good, because I fear I used the last of me wood this morn. Now, I can no' pay ye in coin, but I can pay ye with hot meals and a hot bath, if ye'd be agreeable."

He thought on it for a brief moment before answering. "Aye. I reckon we could come to such an agreement."

"Good!" she exclaimed happily. "I would also like ye to see about gettin' me a cow."

Perplexed, he asked, "A cow, mistress? But I thought ye said ye were already gettin' a cow?

"The thought of getting me own cow just occurred to me when ye gave me Charles Bowie's message. So can ye help me?"

He rubbed a hand across his stubbled jaw and pondered the situation. "I could ask around. How much are ye willin' to pay fer one?"

She had no good idea what a milk cow might cost, but did not divulge that bit of information. "It depends on what the askin' price is," she replied with a wink.

Apparently amused with his mistress, Willem chuckled softly. "Well then, I shall see what I can learn fer ye."

With their agreement set, Leona went to the larder and pulled out the wood tub she'd been using for her own baths. "Fetch some more water, Willem," she told him as she stepped back into the larder.

"More water? Weren't the two I brought ye enough?" he asked curiously.

"No' for the bath ye're goin' to take."

It took some cajoling and a few threats to convince Willem Bowie that he did, in fact, need a bath. By threatening never to feed him again if he didn't agree, Leona got him out of the kitchen. He returned in a short while with clean clothes. He wasn't the first stubborn Highlander she'd ever dealt with. She learned much about Willem as he bathed behind the screen. For instance, he was a widower, his two children, both young men now, were married with children of their own. They lived in Kinbrea. He lived alone, in a tiny little cottage at the very edge of the glen, not far from Dougall's home.

After he had bathed, she fed him a fine meal of rabit stew, warm bread, and sweet cakes. Clean and with a full stomach, he was ready to do whatever she wished.

"I'll need ye to chop wood for me. I need wood for the kitchen, as well as inside the keep, and the laundry. I could use some fresh kindlin' as well."

When he wiped his face on his sleeve, Leona cringed inwardly. 'Twould take a good deal of scrubbing to get the stains out of his sleeves.

"As ye wish, m'lady," he said with a low, flourishing bow.

With Willem fed and on his way to chop wood, she decided 'twas a good time to take a meal to Melvin Bowie. She would take him the rest of the rabbit stew, some bread, butter and honey, as well as a few sweet cakes.

With her basket packed, she headed off to spend some time with the auld man.

THIS TIME, WHEN SHE LEFT THE KEEP AND CROSSED OVER THE drawbridge, Alec hadn't followed her. Apparently he had come to agree with her that she did not need an escort to visit the small village.

The day was quiet and still, with the sun bright and warm. Even the birds seemed to be at rest this day, for there was no continuous chattering or twittering coming from the trees. There were only a few children out and about. Mayhap this was the time of day they all rested.

Leona was quite surprised when she came upon Melvin at his cottage. For the first time since she met him, he wasn't abed asleep. Nay, he was sitting just outside, on a three-legged stool, soaking up the warm summer sun. He looked far better today than he had in her short time here. He actually had some color in his cheeks and his eyes sparkled.

"Melvin," she called out to him. "Ye look verra well this day!"

Using his walking stick, he tried to stand.

"Please, do no' get up on my account," she told him with a wave of her hand. "'Tis glad I am to see ye up and out of doors, and on such a fine day."

"It *is* a fine day. I do no' ken why, but I woke up this morn, full of

186

vigor and vim," he said with a warm smile. "And 'tis good to see ye, lass."

She set the basket on the ground at her feet before coming to stand beside him. He had a most excellent view. Just beyond the cottages to the north, were rolling, grass-covered hills. To the east, a vast woods that seemed to go on forever. She caught sight of something in the distance in those old woods. She could just barely make it out. The roof of a tower mayhap?

"Melvin, what be that?" she asked, pointing to the structure in question.

He turned slightly but could not see what she was pointing at.

"It looks like a tower made of stone."

"Och, that!" Melvin said. "It be the tower from the auld keep."

"The auld keep?" she asked, her curiosity growing.

"Aye. Bring that basket inside for me and I'll tell ye all about it."

Leona first helped Melvin inside before setting the food out for him. With cups of cider poured, she sat across from him and listened intently.

"Ye see, about a hundred years ago, our keep was nestled inside those woods ye saw. 'Twas a good keep, made mostly of wood, ye ken. Well, we were fuedin' with the Randalls back then. Who kens why or what started the feud, 'twas so long ago." He took a breath, then a few bites of the rabbit stew. "'Tis fine stew ye make lass, verra fine stew. Me Jannet, she was no' much of a cook, but she kept me from starvin' fer many a year."

Leona thanked him for his compliment. "Why do we no longer live in the auld keep?" she asked, helping him to return to the topic she was so curious about.

He swallowed a bite of bread and took a long drink of cider before continuing with his story. "Because they burnt us out."

"Who burnt us, I mean, the Bowies, out?"

"The bloody Randalls. The cowards waited until a time when our best warriors were out on a hunt. Then they attacked in the middle of the night, or so the story goes. 'Twas a blood bath, a dark, dark night fer the Bowies. The auld tower still stands, though God only kens why. I think because 'twas the newest structure built then, and built out of stone it was." His tone turned sad, the smile dwindled. "They burnt nearly everything to the earth. They killed many of our people, including women and children."

The Bowies had done the same thing to the McLarens not long ago, when they attacked in the dead of night to kidnap Rose. 'Twas difficult to feel any amount of sympathy, save for loss of innocent children. But she kept that opinion to herself.

"The chief at the time, his name was Alexander, he lost his wife and all but one of his children. Devastated he was at their loss. We rebuilt, where the keep now stands. 'Tis why we have a moat, and nearly everything built from stone. It took some ten years to build, or so the story goes."

She could not help but wonder if the Bowies were always so ruthless. Had they always been thieves and raiders? If so, she couldn't rightly blame them. Such a devastation would have a tremendous impact on a person. To lose everything, to have it all destroyed. "Melvin, is that when the clan turned to, well, to a life of, well, that is to say," she fought hard for the politest way to voice her question.

Melvin laughed then. A full, loud belly laugh. "Be that when the clan turned to reivin'?" He asked as he chuckled. "Nay lass, we've always been a ruthless lot of thieves and reivers and raiders!"

AFTER ENJOYING HER TIME WITH MELVIN, LEONA LEFT HIM SO HE could have a quiet afternoon nap. At the last minute, she decided she would first visit Effie before returning to the keep.

As she rounded the corner to Effie's, she spotted Dougall standing behind the cottage. He had one hand on the wall and he was doubled over. Leona ran down the little lane. "Dougall?" she said his name as she cautiously approached.

Hearing her, he looked up. He was as pale as a sheet. Sweat poured off his face, dripped off the tip of his nose. His green tunic was plastered to his body. "Good lord!" she exclaimed.

"Good day to ye, mistress," he said as he tried to stand to his full height. He winced as he rubbed his belly.

Leaving her basket on the ground, she went to him. The smell of vomit hit her nostrils as soon as she was next to him. Putting an arm around his waist, she said, "Let us get ye inside, Dougall. Ye look like death."

He chuckled slightly, but accepted her help without complaint. "I fear I must have eaten somethin' that did no' agree with me."

"From the looks of ye, I'd say it hated ye." When he put more of his weight against her, she let out a grunt.

When they made their way to his door, he leaned against the wall for support while she opened it. Effie, who had been sitting at the table peeling vegetables, jumped to her feet when she saw Leona struggling to get Dougall inside.

"What on earth?" Effie exclaimed as she came to her husband's side. "Dougall, what happened?"

With a groan, he fell onto their bed before Effie could pull back the furs. "I fear I do no' feel well," he said.

Leona gave a very un-ladylike grunt. "No' well?" She begged to differ. As Effie filled the basin with water, Leona explained what she'd seen. "When I came down the lane, he was doubled over. And he's been throwin' up."

Effie pulled a stool from near the hearth and sat down next to her husband. "Ye look like death," she told him.

"That seems to be the growin' opinion," Dougall said with a grimace. "But I assure ye, I be fine. I must have eaten somethin' that did no' agree with me."

Dipping a cloth into the basin, Effie said, "Is that a comment on me cookin'?"

Overcome by a stabbing pain in his belly, Dougall rolled over and hung his head over the edge of the bed. Effie grabbed the basin just in time for him to throw up.

"Shall I fetch the healer?" Leona asked, uncertain at the moment what she should do. Dougall looked awful and sounded even worse.

"Aye, please, see if ye can find her," Effie said as she handed the basin to her. "Would ye please dump this fer me?"

'Twas all she could do not to vomit herself. Holding her breath, she took the offensive basin out of doors, around the back of the cottage and tossed the contents out. When she returned to her friends, Effie was wiping Dougall's brow.

"Quit fussin' over me," he ground out. "I will be fine."

Effie was having none of it. "Ye'll be fine when the healer says ye'll be fine, ye big, stubborn lummox!"

LEONA ENLISTED THE HELP OF KYTH AND GYLYS IN FINDING THE healer. But within an hour of calling for her, Dougall appeared to be feeling much better. He had finally stopped vomiting and managed to keep down a bit of water.

All the while, Effie tended to him with great care, and the occasional threat of gutting him if he did not stay abed. Even when she was cursing him to the devil, he smiled at her with great affection and warmth in his eyes. Any fool could see they loved each other deeply.

The hour was growing late and Leona had yet to begin preparations for the evening meal. Seeing Dougall's improvement, she begged their leave.

"Thank ye fer yer help," Effie told Leona as she escorted her to the door. "These Bowie men we've married are a stubborn lot, are they no'?" She cast a worried look toward her husband as she spoke.

"Aye," Leona agreed.

Effie hugged her and thanked her again.

The evening air was cool and felt good against her skin. Retrieving her basket, she set off for her own home.

It had been a busy and full day, but one she had thoroughly enjoyed. As she walked along the path, she noticed some of the clanswomen standing in a small group. When she bid them a good eve, each woman gave her a spiteful look of reproach, as if she did not have the right to address any of them.

"It be a fine eve, aye?" she said as she walked past. She didn't think for a moment they would return her greeting or respond to her question. And she was right. They all turned away from her with indignant expressions. A turned back can be almost as painful as a slap to the face. She could *feel* their reproach

It hurt, it truly did.

What she could not figure out was *why*. Why did these women seem to despise her so intensely? They'd only just met her, did not know the first thing about her. With an inward sigh, she kept her head up and a smile on her face as she walked by and continued on down the lane.

Of course, 'twas nothing new, this harsh treatment.

But here? Not one person thus far had any comments on her eyes. Nay, on the contrary, no one said a word about them. The men all treated her kindly and with as much respect as a Bowie knew how to give.

But the women? Why did they seem to be so angry with her? Patrice and Effie were the only two women who had offered any kindness.

The only thing that made any sense at all was that *she* was not a Bowie. Mayhap they were upset Alec had married outside the clan. He could have married anyone here, she supposed, and they would have been happy for it.

It wasn't *Leona* per se that they hated. 'Twas the fact she was an outsider.

I must show them I do belong here, she thought.

With that tiny bit of hope, she felt better. On the morrow, she would begin to prove to these people that she did in fact belong here.

CHAPTER 16

I see the way they look at one another. Besotted fools that they are. They say no' a word when they be around others. But the eyes? The eyes say plenty.

And Leona's eyes? Who the bloody hell has eyes such as she? Only a witch would possess two entirely different colored eyes.

Can Alec no' see what is in front of him? Nay, he can no' because she has cast a spell upon him. A spell that means ruin for our clan. She's a witch I say. A witch!

She walks around all sweet and innocent. And no one seems to care she's cast a spell upon our laird. Oh, the women can see, fer I set that plan in motion before the witch set a toe on Bowie lands. But the men? I can see how they lust after the wench. The bloody fools. She's cast a spell on them as well. They will no' listen to good sense, so besotted they be with her.

I be plantin' the seeds of doubt. A word here, a word there, no' a shout or a battle cry. Nay, sometimes a whisper can do more to change a man's mind than screamin' or hollerin' ever could. So that what I be doin'. Plantin' seeds of doubt in all their minds.

Alec, however, he will be a much harder one to convince, so I shall no' even try.

I'm going to kill her.
Then he'll see.

CHAPTER 17

*L*eona was more tired than she could ever remember being.

Alec kept her awake for long hours at night, loving her until her body had the consistency of warm butter. She didn't mind the loving. In fact, she looked forward to it with great anticipation. 'Twas the one time of the day where she felt they understood one another. The one time of the day where he made her feel beautiful and important.

They might not have been able to talk to one another about feelings, ideas, or dreams of the future. But at least they could connect on a far deeper level when they were in each other's arms.

Mayhap her husband, being the leader of the ruthless Bowie clan, simply did not know *how* to express himself with words. Far too frequently, she would compare their relationship to the one between Ian and Rose. The differences were significant.

Where Ian and Rose's marriage had been a love match, hers and Alec's was not.

Where Ian was quite comfortable with telling Rose how much he loved her, no matter who was about, Alec did not have the same capability.

Oh, she was not so gullible as to believe Alec loved her. At least not in the same way Ian loved Rose. The only thing she could hope for was mutual admiration.

But deep down, she began to want something *more*. 'Twas futile and immature, she supposed, but she could not help herself.

'TWAS A BRIGHT AND SUNNY AFTERNOON, WITH THE BIRDS CHIRPING IN the trees, a light breeze, and nary a cloud in the sky. Leona had finished the laundry earlier in the morn and the clothes were now hanging on the line to dry.

She had obtained two more customers that morn. Men who would pay her the same amount of coin as Allen had agreed to. It did her heart good to know that soon she'd have enough coin to purchase her own milk cow. There would be no more dealing with Charles, or beggin' Effie for a mug of milk in order to prepare a meal. Aye, doing laundry for the unmarried menfolk added to her daily chores, but she didn't mind. She was earning much needed coin. Coin for a cow, and coin for Alec's gift.

With nothing to do while the clothes dried, she returned to the keep. She spread fresh rushes on the floor of the gathering room and looked about the large space. 'Twas a dull, depressing room. There was nothing to indicate people actually lived here. No tapestries, no flowers, no cushions on the chairs or benches.

'Twas all hard and cold and desolate. Her previous good mood was quickly dissipating the longer she stood in the center of the grand space. What on earth could she do to spruce it up, to make it more inviting? Lost in her own thoughts, she came close to jumping out of her skin when a voice startled her.

"Good day, to ye, Leona," Patrice greeted her warmly from the doorway. She'd apparently come in from the direction of the kitchens.

"Och, Patrice!" Leona declared, placing a palm to her startled heart. "Ye scared me."

Patrice came to her at once. "I be terribly sorry, Leona. I seem to do that to ye frequently. Please, forgive me."

Leona giggled at her own silliness. "Do no fash yourself over it," she told her friend.

"Ye looked to be thinkin' hard on somethin'," Patrice replied.

With a heavy sigh, Leona said, "Aye. I be tryin' to figure out how I can make this place a bit more homey."

Patrice placed her hands on her hips and looked about the room. "It be a bit cold, aye?"

Leona nodded her agreement. "I need to do things a little at a time, so Alec does no' notice it all at once."

"Ye could start with a tapestry," Patrice offered.

"I fear I do no' have any."

"Of course ye do," Patrice told her. "The room I showed ye when ye first arrived? It has a few tables, chairs and such. But that be only a *tiny* part of the treasures this keep holds."

She had no idea to what Patrice was referring. She had been in every room of the keep, and thus far, had not discovered anything that could be deemed *a treasure.*

Sensing her confusion and doubt, Patrice offered her a warm smile. "There be four floors in the north tower. Three of them be filled near to burstin' with all the things Alec had removed after Rutger died. Come, I shall show ye."

Taking Leona's hand in her own, she lead the woman out of the gathering room in search of supposed hidden treasures.

Patrice had not lied. 'Twas indeed a treasure trove of everything one could imagine. Candlesticks made of pewter, silver, even gold. Slavers and platters and goblets galore! Opulently upholstered chairs, some with matching hassocks. Chests, armoires, and items which she had no idea of their purpose. Shields, swords and weapons, as well as luxurious rugs, and yes, even tapestries.

'Twas all right there, in the north tower. Room after room of things she could use to turn this cold, dark place into a home.

"Lord, almighty!" Leona exclaimed with wide, astonished eyes.

Patrice smiled with a good measure of pride. "I told ye, did I no'?"

"Aye, ye did!"

Leona reckoned that if she added only one item a sennight to any of the rooms within the keep, 'twould take ten lifetimes before she had emptied the tower rooms. For the briefest of moments, she thought of hauling it all below stairs now, and surprising her husband. But only briefly. He'd have an apoplexy if she changed things too quickly.

"I do no' ken where to begin," she admitted out loud.

"If it were me, I would begin small. Put a tapestry up in the gatherin' room, and mayhap some of the simpler candlesticks in yer bedchamber."

'Twas as good a plan as any. "Verra well," she said, resting her hands on her hips. "A small tapestry today, mayhap a larger one in a few days?"

"I really do no' understand yer husband," Patrice said as she stepped over a hassock to get to a pile of tapestries draped across a long table.

"Ye be no' alone in that regard," Leona mumbled as she followed her friend. "I can no' understand his need to remove *everything* from all the rooms."

As they began to lift one tapestry up for inspection, Patrice said, "I have only come close to marryin' twice before. 'Tis times like these I feel I be the lucky one, escapin' the gallows, so-to-speak."

"Twice?" Leona asked absentmindedly as she lifted another tapestry.

Patrice fell silent for a moment, pretending she hadn't heard the question. "Do ye like this one?" she asked, changing the subject.

'Twas a beautiful tapestry, the needlework most excellent. But upon looking at it more closely, Leona decided against it. 'Twas an exceedingly graphic battle scene, complete with disemboweled men, dead horses, and much blood. "Nay," she said with a shake of her head. "I want somethin' a bit more *peaceful*." 'Twas bad enough she had to clean the blood from her husband's and her client's clothing. She did not want a constant reminder of what exactly they were doing or preparing for.

They continued to look through the heavy pile. All the tapestries seemed to be the same. One bloodbath after another.

"Is warrin' and fightin' the *only* thing this clan ever thought about?" she mumbled, growing more disheartened with each piece.

"Well, the men folk are quite fond of their *lovin',*" Patrice replied with a giggle.

Leona laughed in response. Alec was all the proof she needed in that regard. He was nearly insatiable most days. Like a man starvin', and she was the only bit of bread he'd seen in weeks.

Keeping her thoughts to herself, she continued to riffle through. Finally, nearly at the end of the pile, she found something that would suit. "This is quite nice!"

'Twas most intricately done, and quite elaborate. It depicted hills and heather, and a glorious sunset. It also showed several scenes of a man and woman, as well as them together with two little boys.

"It could no' have been a Bowie woman who created *that*," Patrice declared. "'Tis far too sweet!" She giggled once again at her own jest.

"I do no' care who created it," Leona said. "'Tis just the thing I want fer the gatherin' room. There be a peaceful feelin' to it. And it be no' too big."

With the decision made, they pulled and tugged until the tapestry was free. After rolling it up and setting it by the door, they went in search of smaller things they could add without issue.

"What about these candlesticks?" Patrice asked, holding up a pair of carved, silver candlesticks.

"Nay, I fear they be too grand. Somethin' more simple and less likely to have me husband accusin' me of turnin' his keep into a likeness of Stirlin' castle."

In the end, they settled on plain, wooden candlesticks and a hassock she could place in front of one of the chairs in their bedchamber.

"That should be enough fer now," Leona declared. "I be awfully grateful to ye fer showin' me these things, Patrice."

"Och, think nothin' of it. I am always glad to help."

ALEC DID NOT NOTICE THE WOODEN CANDLESTICKS PLACED IN THE center of the table when they sat down to sup. Neither did he seem to notice the tapestry she had hung. Of course, it was hanging in shadow, on the wall next to the fireplace on the far end of the room.

This night, they supped on roasted mutton with vegetables, a nice broth and dark bread. As a special treat, she made sweet cakes covered in raspberry jam. As had become the standard, Gylys and Kyth were dinning with them.

"Did Derrick tell ye he broke young Walden Bowie's arm durin' trainin' this day?" Kyth asked as he tore a hunk of dark bread from the loaf.

Leona came close to choking on that bit of news. "He what?" she cried out in a blend of shock and repulsion.

All three men stared at her as if she'd suddenly sprouted wings and taken flight.

"Derrick broke young Walden Bowie's arm durin' trainin' this day," Kyth repeated.

Exasperated, she said, "I *heard* ye the first time. But *why* on earth would he do such a thing?" As she often did when nervous, she began to ramble. "Surely it must be an accident. Yes, that is it, an accident. Pardon my surprise and outburst, Kyth. Would ye like more butter fer yer bread?"

He gave a slight shake of his head, as if he were trying to make some sense of her rambling. "But he did do it on purpose," he told her. "And aye, I would like more butter."

Leona's hand was suspended in midair, holding the small jar of butter. "Certainly, ye jest?" Looking to Alec for help, she said, "Tell Kyth no' to jest so, Alec. 'Tis no' polite."

"But he is no' jestin'," Alec replied. "And I would like more butter as well."

Stunned, she sat staring at these three men. The jar remained in her hand, hovering over the table. "Ye jest. Certainly, ye be all be jestin' with me." Shaking her head, she set the jar down on the table, next to her own trencher. "Ye men, ye certainly love to jest with me." She offered up a half-hearted laugh. "No man, no' even a Bowie, would break a young man's arm on purpose."

Kyth and Gylys looked to their laird for some guidance. All he offered them was a shrug of his shoulders.

"Lass, why does the fact that Derrick broke Walden's arm bother ye so? And may we please have the butter?"

"Stop jestin'," she told him, growing more certain that none of them were. Their own confused expressions said as much.

"I am no' jestin'. I want the butter," Alec said with a nod toward the jar.

Butter? Was the man insane? How could he even think of eating at a time such as this. "He truly broke the boy's arm?" she murmured.

Alec rolled his eyes, exasperated with his wife's line of questioning. And the fact she wasn't passing him the butter. "Aye," he said as he scooted his seat away from the table. "And Walden is no' a boy. He's ten and eight."

"Ten and eight?" she all but screeched as he made his way to her end of the table.

"At that age, he should ken better," Kyth offered up his own option.

"Know better than what?" Leona demanded to know.

Alec grabbed the jar of butter and returned to his seat.

Answering his wife's question, he said, "Walden should ken better than to try the patience of a man of Derrick's size — as well as his skill."

Good, lord! She was supping with savages! Stammering, she asked, "And if we have children, Alec, and they try yer patience, will ye break their arms?"

"Only if the situation calls fer it," he replied dryly.

"Ye can no' be serious?" she asked, totally dumbfounded. "Ye would truly break yer child's arm?"

In frustration, he handed Gylys the jar of butter. "If any of our children were *dumb* enough to come at me, as Walden did Derrick, supposedly unarmed, *and drunk* and proceed to call me every foul name under the sun, and declare they'd bloody well marry whoever the bloody well they pleased, then proceed to attack me by throwin' dirt in my face before he pulled a dirk out of his boot and slash me hand, then aye, I would break their damned arm! Ye can no' disrespect a man like Derrick, or me, in such a manner. The young man asked fer Derrick's daughter's hand. Derrick declined it, because he *kens* Walden. Walden is a hot-headed fool who thinks he can beat any man in any kind of challenge. Derrick kens Walden would treat his daughter poorly. And Lucinda does no' want Walden. So there ye have the entire story, lass. Are ye satisfied that the *poor boy* deserved what he got?"

Embarassed, she sat in silence for a long moment, only offering her husband a slight inclination of her head. A thought suddenly occurred to her then. "I did no' ken Derrick was married."

"Because he's no'," Alec said, glad the discussion of poor young men was over with.

"But he has a daughter?"

Pulling a bit of meat from his leg of mutton with his teeth, Alec nodded. "He has three," he said with a full mouth. "And four sons."

Unwilling to jump to any conclusions again, she asked, "He has seven children and is no' married? Has she passed?"

"Nay, they all be alive and well," Kyth said.

Turning to face him, Leona asked, "They?"

"Seven children betwixt three women," Gylys clarified. "And nay, he did no' marry any of them."

"Why no'?" Leona asked, her concern growing.

"Because they were already married."

Her head was beginning to throb. "Seven children with three *married* women?"

"Aye, Kyth said before stuffing his mouth with vegetables.

Not wanting to sound prudish, she let the matter go. 'Twas also the only way to keep her head from exploding. How could a man father children with three married women? It made no sense. But to try to make sense of it made her head throb.

Bowie men! Will I ever learn to understand them?

WHILE ALEC, KYTH AND GYLYS SAT NEXT TO THE FIRE, DISCUSSING THE future of their clan, Leona cleared away the table. With her tray filled with as much as she could carry, she left them alone whilst she went to the kitchens. Rain had begun to fall steadily while they supped, leaving the ground wet and muddy. Unprepared for the change in weather, she hadn't grabbed her cloak before leaving the keep. The wind picked up as she crossed the tiny yard, lifting the hem of her skirt, splattering rain against her ankles. The damp air, the wind and rain turned her skin to gooseflesh.

Once inside the warm kitchen, she set the tray on the counter next to the sink. Shivering, she rubbed her hands together to help ward off the cold. *Is there any place on God's earth where it be warm more often than no'?"* she mused.

Wanting to hurry back into the keep to grab the rest of the foods and dishes, she spun around to leave, and bumped right into a hard chest. In an instant, her heart was pounding against her chest. Fully prepared to let out a terrified scream, she took in a deep breath, but stopped when she realized 'twas her husband.

"Bloody hell, Alec!" she exclaimed as she fought to catch her breath and still her heart.

His reaction was not what she had anticipated. Instead of apologizing, he threw his head back and laughed.

"'Twas no' funny!" she scolded as she slapped his arm.

"Och, but 'twas!" he argued, still chuckling at her distress.

Beyond perturbed, she asked, "Would *ye* be laughin' were I to sneak up behind ye and scare ye half to death?"

Still smiling, he quirked one brow. "'Twould never happen, lass."

"What wouldn't happen?" she asked, her anger and fright slipping away, all because of that blasted smile of his. The one that warmed her to her toes.

"Ye could never sneak up on me. I am, after all, a trained warrior."

Be that a challenge in his tone? She wondered. "Ye're sayin' I could no' sneak up on ye?"

"Aye, I be sayin' just that. And if ye did manage to — though I still say it be impossible — ye'd no frighten me as I did ye. I do no' scare easily."

Tilting her head to one side, she smiled up at him. "Nay?"

"Nay, lass," he said with a slow shake of his head. "'Twould take far more than a wee lass such as yerself to scare me. I be a Bowie, ye see. And Bowies are never *scared.*"

She didn't believe it, not for a single moment. Ian Mackintosh had once told her that any man who says he is not ever afraid is either lying or insane. At the moment, she was quite certain her husband was both. "Remember yer words, Alec Bowie. They might just come back one day and bite ye in yer firm little arse."

Obviously, he did not take her threat as she had intended it: as a challenge. Nay, he began laughing at her all over again. She stood with arms folded across her chest, waiting patiently for him to regain control of what little good sense he possessed.

After a short while, he took her hands in his and kissed the tips of her fingers. "Ye're cold." 'Twas a statement of fact, not an inquiry.

"A wee bit, aye," she told him. "Now, be gone with ye. I have to clear the rest of the table." She made no move to leave, for she was enjoying his smile and the way his eyes were twinkling in the candlelight.

"I have already done that fer ye," he told her, kissing her fingers once again.

Surprised more than when she found him standing behind her like one of the king's spies, her eyes grew wide. "Ye what?"

Motioning to the table behind him with a nod, he said, "I brought the rest of the things fer ye. Ye work far too hard of late."

If he did not stop shocking her senses, she might have an apoplexy. 'Twas the first time since marrying him that he had taken notice of all her hard work. That made her heart soar as well as soften toward him even further. She stood in mute silence, staring up into those warm, brown eyes.

"I be no' a complete savage, ye ken." His tone was so warm, scattering her good senses hither and yon. 'Twas utterly disarming.

"I should like ye to stop," he said as he twined a lock of her hair around his finger. Why, oh why did that simple act have such an affect on her? His very touch, his low, soft voice, those brown eyes … they all made her feel as though she'd just drunk a dram of fine whisky; warm, content, and happy.

"Stop what?" she asked after she managed to find her voice.

"Workin' so hard," he said. "Now, leave these dishes for the morrow and let us go to bed."

Although she disliked leaving a task for later, her husband's invitation, with its hidden meaning and sensual undertones, was too much to pass up. Dirty dishes, be damned.

SLOWLY, BIT BY BIT LEONA BEGAN TO ADD LITTLE TOUCHES TO THE KEEP. One day, 'twas a beautiful green vase she had discovered in the tower. Filling it with flowers, she set it on the hearth, next to the wooden candlesticks. She had been forced to stand on a chair in order to reach it properly. Even then, she was barely able to set the candlesticks and vase upon it, for 'twas so tall.

When she wasn't cooking, or scrubbing something inside the keep, she was busy with her growing laundry services. Ostensibly, the single men absolutely loathed having to wash their own clothing. Which was good for Leona's purse, but not so good for her hands, for they were growing more chapped and calloused with each new day.

Before long, her list of clients had grown to nine. When she realized she could keep up with no more, she had to begin turning men away. *The first time in me life I ever had the attention of any man, let alone so many!* she had mused with a giggle.

There would be no laundry drying today, for the weather had turned. Pewter skies hung overhead with rain falling steadily. Today, she decided to tackle more of the empty rooms.

Thus far, she had counted a total of forty-one rooms. Only a few

— the bedchamber she shared with her husband, his study, and the two rooms she had previously made into guest chambers — possessed anything remotely homey. Everything else was cold, stark, and uninviting.

'Tis as sad a space as any there ever was, she mused gloomily. *I imagine the gallows at Stirling Castle possess more life and warmth.*

"There be no' a candle in either chandelier, no cushions upon the hard chairs, nothin' at all soft or invitin'," she muttered. Tapping a finger against her chin, she engaged in an inner debate betwixt heart and mind.

"Yer husband, he be a good man. Does he mourn the loss of his brother and that be why the keep is so cold and stark? Or be it somethin' more?" she wondered aloud.

A sudden breeze filtered in from some unseen place, bringing a chill to her skin. Was it the ghost of something or someone, that haunted her husband? Was that why he had everything removed?

"Certainly, I can find a way to get him to see that we can be comfortable here without being lavish or ostentatious."

But if ye do too much, he's liable to become verra angry with ye, her mind argued. *But he'll no' harm ye, no matter how angry he might be,* her heart reminded her. *After all, he did sign yer marriage contract. And he has said on more than one occasion he'd never raise a hand to ye, no matter yer transgressions.*

In the end, her heart won out. She was fully determined to rid this keep of Rutger Bowie's ghost.

With her mind made up and knowing she had several hours before Alec would return from the fields for his evening meal, Leona set off for the north tower and the treasures it held. She wouldn't bring everything out of storage in one day, but neither was she going to wait ten years to do it slowly.

Her mission this warm afternoon, was to bring down cushions for the benches and chairs for the gathering room table, as well as smaller tables upon which to place vases and candlesticks. But the largest item she needed, would require the help of a few men. 'Twas the long sideboard she had seen before on those treks where she pilfered and pillaged the tower rooms.

With a lighted torch in one hand, she made her way down the long corridor, across the short bridge that connected the main keep to the north tower. She had a skip in her step and her heart felt light, nearly giddy with anticipation.

The main door to the tower was a heavy, wooden beast. She had to rest her torch in the iron sconce next to it so she could use both hands to open it. It released far easier than the previous times she had entered.

Leaving it open enough so she could slip inside and then back out again, she grabbed her torch and stepped through into darkness. Certain the sideboard was on the second floor, she lifted her skirts and ascended the circular stone staircase. Though she and Patrice had cleared the cobwebs a fortnight ago on their first journey here, there was still something dark and forbidding about the place.

The wind whipped through the door she had left open. Though 'twas a warm, sunny day, the wind swirling around her felt cold. Like hands reaching out from the beyond to pull her down into blackness.

"Do no' let yer mind run away with ye, Leona," she warned her imagination. "There be no such thing as ghosts." Though she had spoken the words aloud, nothing heard her but the damp musty air.

As if the wind meant to argue , it seemed to grow stronger. It began to howl, wailing. It sounded plaintive, as if it were in some ungodly amount of pain and sorrow. Wanting to escape from the staircase, she hurried her pace, and all but ran to the second floor. She let out the breath she'd been holding the moment she reached the wide landing. Chastising herself for allowing her imagination to run wild, she said, "There be no such things as ghosts or goblins, ye eejit. 'Tis just the wind."

Still, she had the oddest sensation that something was watching her. Something unseen in the shadows, just waiting for a chance to … to do what? Scare her half to death?

Alec! She thought to herself. *He be right behind me, wantin' to terrify me out of me own skin. Bah!*

Cautiously, she stepped back toward the staircase, holding the torch out so she could get a better look.

Nothing.

No one was waiting in the shadows. Not Alec or anyone else.

Feeling very much like a bairn, she cursed her imagination once again. Turning away, she set the torch in the iron holder next to the barred door. Wiping her sweaty palms on her apron, she took a deep breath before lifting the heavy bar. It groaned an ever-so-slight protestation, but it gave way. Lifting it into the black wrought iron bar, she shoved it into the curved iron bracket intended to hold it open. She gave a good hard tug to make sure the bar wasn't going to fall back down.

On the morrow, I will have Gylys and Kyth remove these blasted bars! She promised herself. *Why on earth anyone would want to bar a door from the outside is beyond me.*

It suddenly dawned upon her, that perhaps this north tower was meant to house prisoners. *Good, lord, these Bowies! Did they truly house so many prisoners? Were the dungeons below no' enough?*

Pushing the thought aside, she pulled hard on the iron ring and drew the door open wide. It scraped against the stone floor, blending with the sound of the wind and her pounding heart.

"Good lord, Leona! 'Tis no' as if yer stealing into Stirling Castle to kill the king. Ye're here to find cushions!" With a shake of her head she expelled a short breath.

Just as she was about to grab the lighted torch, she felt a presence she could not identify. Before she could even react, two hands were shoving her into the dark room.

She stumbled forward and landed face first with a thud. Her breath was stolen away by fright more than the actual hard landing. The rough stone scraped against her cold skin. Quickly, she rolled over to scream at whomever had pushed her inside. The scream caught in her throat.

No one was there.

The door was closing before she could scramble to her feet. A moment later, it slammed shut and the bar fell into place.

She was bathed in darkness.

The wind continued to howl, but now, it sounded more macabre, even more unreal, as if it were laughing at her.

CHAPTER 18

The slamming of the door, the heavy thud of the wooden bar falling into place, echoed off the stone walls. Cloaked all at once in maddening blackness, her heart seized along with her lungs.

She was a little girl again. Terrified, alone, and in the horrifying darkness, locked in a trunk because she had angered her father. He knew how afraid of the dark she was and he had used it to frighten her. Upset over something she'd done, that she couldn't even remember now. Furious, he picked her up and forced her into the old trunk, kicking and screaming, crying out as she heard the click of the latch.

He left me there to die.

I was just a child but he did not care. He left me there to die.

She might not be in an old trunk now, but the fear was just as debilitating as it had been that day. Just as real, just as palpable, just as terrifying.

If Mrs. Macfaddon hadn't heard her distress and set her free, she could very well have died inside that musty old trunk. The image of her tiny corpse rotting at first, then turning to bones and eventually, dust, made her want to retch.

Breathe, she told herself over and over. *Breathe. Ye be no' a little girl.*

It took a long while before she could will away the tremble in her fingers, to still her rapidly beating heart.

Alec will come fer me, she told herself. *He will come fer me.*

IT HAD BEEN A GOOD DAY OF TRAINING. UNDER ALEC'S TUTELAGE, AS well as Derrick's and Dougall's, his men were improving. Albeit not as fast as Alec would have wanted.

They were used to taking a more defensive approach when it came to fighting — they were, after all, thieves. And as such, they were a stealthy, silent group of men. That skill might prove useful on the battlefield someday. But only if they were strong enough to actually *do* battle. Stealing into a place in the middle of the night was one thing. Defending your people against marauding hordes of other Highlanders or, God forbid, the English, was another.

For decades, the rest of the world had left them alone. To a certain extent, they'd all grown comfortable with knowing very few people were insane enough to attack them. However, there was always the small chance, that one in a thousand chance, that an attack from without might happen.

So after planting the fields of barley following Rutger's death, Alec had also immediately begun training his men. There were days when he questioned that decision. But today? Today, his men were finally *listening,* finally learning.

If he were able to cement *good* relationships with other clans, there might come a time his own clan would be called upon in time of war. He'd rather have his ballocks cut off with a rusty dirk than to have his men look foolish on the battlefield. Hence, his determination to make them as strong and as good as he possibly could.

He stood now with Derrick and Dougall, at the edge of the wide open yard, watching the men in mock battle.

"Keep yer shield, up, Connor Macpherson!" Dougall yelled out to the young man. "Else Andrew Bowie will separate yer head from yer shoulders!"

Connor listened without looking away from his opponent. As directed, he lifted his shield higher, just in time to fend off a mighty blow. However, he did not see Andrew strike out until it was too late. He'd brought his sword across Connor's shins. Thankfully, he hadn't used much force and only tore open the young man's trews.

"Well," Dougall said with a shake of his head, "do ye think this rag-tag bunch of thieves will ever be as good as we need them to be?"

Alec crossed his arms over his chest and watched. "God, I pray so."

Derrick, usually the most pessimistic of souls, added his own opinion to the conversation. "Ye have to admit, they be gettin' better."

Just then, Connor took great offense to something Andrew said. He threw down his shield and his sword and lunged after him. A moment later, they were rolling around in the grass and dirt. Connor was in a murderous rage.

"Ye take that back, ye son of a whore!" he screamed at Andrew as he pinned him to the ground.

"Go to hell, Macpherson!" Andrew yelled back.

Alec rolled his eyes in frustration.

"Shall we stop them?" Dougall asked.

"I have five groats that says Andrew wins," Derrick spoke out of the corner of his mouth.

Before any further wagers could be made, Alec thundered angrily towards the two young men. In one swift motion, he had pulled Connor off and thrown him several feet from Andrew. Andrew looked relieved and held out his hand to his laird. "Thank ye, Al-"

He hadn't any time to finish. Alec grabbed his hand, lifted him to his feet before shoving him hard with one hand. The surprised young man fell backward and landed soundly on his rear end.

"If this is how the two of ye will behave in the field of battle, ye both can stay at home and let yer mum's feed ye sweet cakes and warm milk!" Alec's voice boomed through the yard. All fighting came to an abrupt halt.

Connor struggled to his feet, murder still dancing in his eyes. "I was defendin' me sister's honor, Alec!"

Alec pinned him in place with an angry glare. "I do no' care *what* yer motive was."

Still angry, Connor stepped forward. "He said every man in the keep has lifted me sister's skirts, includin' *ye.*"

Alec turned to face Andrew, who was still sitting on the ground. "Did ye say such?"

Andrew gave a rapid nod of affirmation.

Turning his attention back to Connor, Alec said, "And ye believed him?"

Connor stammered, unable to answer immediately.

"Ye're a fool, Macpherson," Alec said as he took a step closer to Connor.

"Why are ye angry with *me?*" he asked, as he took a few steps back. "'Twas no' me that he insulted."

"He did no' insult *me,* Macpherson. When ye are in battle, yer opponent will say many things to ye, things ye *ken* will no' be true. They will say these things to set ye off, to get ye off balance. That is when they'll gut ye and leave yer carcass fer the scavengers!"

Duly chastised, the young man stared at his feet.

"And ye," Alec said as he turned back to face Andrew. "Do ye believe what ye said?"

Another rapid shake of his head. "'Twas Derrick who told me to say it."

Alec glanced at Derrick, who was smiling proudly.

"*Ye* told Andrew to spread rumors about Connor's sister?"

"I might have mentioned it, aye," Derrick said. "'Twas merely a suggestion. Connor has been beatin' Andrew soundly for weeks. He came to me and asked fer help in defeatin' him. I *suggested* he find out what Connor holds most dear, and insult it."

Clarity dawned. "In order to get Connor off balance," Alec said.

"Aye."

'Twas an age-old trick, used often. One Alec himself had deployed on numerous occasions.

"Pick up yer swords, Connor. Andrew," Alec told them.

Quickly, they did as they were told. Alec waited until they were standing before he withdrew his own sword. "I will train the two of ye myself," he said, slicing his sword through the air at nothing with the appearance of indifference. "And when I be done, ye will be able to hear a man say he tupped yer own grandminny and 'twill bother ye as much as a wee midge flyin' about yer heads."

TRUE TO HIS WORD, ALEC PUT THE TWO YOUNG MEN THROUGH HELL. Not only did he repeatedly insult their mothers, their mother's mothers, their sisters, he even went as far as to insult their fathers.

At first, the young men were furious with his copious insults. They would lunge at him, either one at a time or together in unison. And each time, Alec would fend them off with such ease, it was as if he were flicking a fly off a sweet cake.

The young men grew more irritated and furious with each insult and each deflection. More than once, he tossed them to the ground on their buttocks. Neither man was a match for his cool, steely-eyed determination, his strength, nor his experience.

Within an hour, the two men were soaked with sweat, out of breath, and in general, defeated. When he saw their shoulders sag, he smiled at them.

"Lads, have ye learned anythin' this day?"

They glanced at one another before looking dejectedly at him.

Alec nodded at them. "I see ye have no'. Pick up yer swords. We'll be here all bloody night long until ye can tell me what ye've learned."

He would be ruthless if he needed to be, if not for their sakes, then the sakes of those men who surrounded them now and were watching. Alec needed each of his men to understand three things: One) to always, under all circumstances, remain calm. Two) never surrender, no matter how tired you were. And three) never let your opponent see how tired, worried, or even scared, you really were. Thus far, these two students were failing on every level.

~

ALEC REFUSED TO LET THE TRAINING SESSION SOUR HIS MOOD OR HIS
hope for their futures. Most of the men had readily picked up on what
he had been trying to teach Connor and Andrew. He could only hope
that after a dip in the loch, a hot meal, and some time to think, they
too, would eventually see the soundness of what he was teaching.
Heaven help them both if they didn't.

Hot, sweaty, and covered in dirt and grime, he said good eve to his
men and headed toward the keep. A hefty breeze picked up, giving
him a better idea of just how bad he smelled. Though he knew there
would be a hot bath waiting for him, he decided that mayhap 'twould
be best to wash the top layer of filth off in the loch first, then proceed
to his bath.

The loch was not far from the main keep. Once there, he began to
strip out of his sweat-soaked clothes. After pulling his tunic over his
head, he noticed a tear in the sleeve, and a few droplets of blood. He
knew his wife hated the sight of blood, even if it wasn't his own.
Without thinking, he crouched at the bank of the loch and gave the
fabric a good scrubbing.

His thoughts immediately turned to Leona, who he knew was at
this very moment preparing him a fine meal. She was a fine cook, his
wee, beautiful wife. She worked hard to keep him fed, his clothes
mended, and in short, to be a good wife.

And she was. It had been a complete surprise at first, just how
good a woman he found her to be. He'd also been surprised when he
realized he *liked* the woman. More than he had anticipated when she
had agreed to marry him.

His plan had been simple: agree to marry her, get her with child,
then leave her the bloody hell alone.

Now, he knew that was going to be impossible. Hell, it already *was*
impossible to stay away from her, to not think about her nearly every
waking moment of every day. There was no reason to wonder what
his father might say about his current predicament.

"Ye're a bloody fool, Alec! I raised ye better than this. I warned ye, if ye

give yer heart to any woman, she'll crush it into dust. But no' before she beats ye dead with it."

As a small boy, he never truly understood what his father had meant. Now, much older and wiser, he understood all too well. Loving a woman, *any* woman, even one as sweet and beautiful as his wife, was dangerous. It would make him weak, and weakness, according to his father, was something a Bowie *never* was. Weaknesses made a man do foolish and stupid things.

But Leona was different. There wasn't a pinch of guile in her entire soul. She was genuine, honest, and kind. And, God, the way she loved him, without restraint, wholly and passionately each night? Loved him, at times, to the point where he could not walk after.

Thinking of his wife lying naked underneath his own nakedness, brought a smile to his face.

When he realized he was scrubbing his own clothing — and whistling a lively tune to boot — all in order to be kind to his wife, he nearly keeled over from the shock of it.

"What the bloody hell is happenin' to me?" he whispered incredulously.

Do no' fash yerself over it, his heart told him. *Ye're just bein' kind. Kindness does no' mean ye're weak or that ye have fallen in love with yer wife.*

When Alec stepped into the gathering room with Gylys and Kyth, he knew almost at once that something was wrong. The table was not set. No warm, delicious food waited for him. 'Twas completely empty and dark. Not a single candle was lit.

Not a day since they'd married, had he come in from the fields that a meal was not waiting for him. Not once.

Gylys and Kyth sensed it as well. They looked first at each other before looking to Alec.

"Do ye suppose she has taken ill?" Kyth asked.

Somehow, Alec doubted it. His wife was a determined, caring

woman. She'd have to be on her deathbed before she didn't make it to her kitchens.

Hopefully, Kyth's suspicions were correct. "Ye look in the kitchens. I'll look above stairs." Alec told them as he headed toward the staircase.

Not wishing to jump to any ugly conclusions just yet, he took the stairs two at a time. Mayhap his wife had listened to his suggestion that she had been working far too hard. Mayhap she had lay down to take a much needed rest and was now fast asleep in their bed.

Quietly, on the off chance he was correct, he slowly opened the door. The bed was empty. Sticking his head inside, his quick perusal told him she was not here.

Still unwilling to believe something had happened to her, he closed the door and headed back below stairs. Kyth was waiting for him at the bottom of the steps.

"She be no' in the kitchens," Kyth told him. "The hearth be cold."

"And neither is she above stairs," Alec said, his brow furrowed with concern. He was not worried. He refused to worry. Worry meant he cared for his wife far more than he was ready to admit.

Gylys came in from the rear entrance. "Did ye find her?" he asked with a hopeful tone.

"Nay," Alec replied.

"I checked behind the kitchens," Gylys told him. "She be no' with the chickens nor near the well."

"I be certain she is nearby," Alec said, though he was growing more concerned.

"Mayhap she is at Melvin's," Kyth offered. "She takes him a meal each day. Ye ken how the man can talk yer ear off."

"Aye," Gylys agreed. "Mayhap he is holdin' her prisoner with one of his stories of the auld days."

His jest made Alec chuckle, but only slightly. "Then let us go rescue me wife from him."

∼

ALEC STOPPED AT THE DRAWBRIDGE AND CALLED TO THE MEN ON WATCH above. "Did Leona leave the keep today?"

The man on duty shook his head. "Nay, m'laird, no' that I ken. But I've only just come on watch an hour ago. Do ye want me to wake up Kennith and ask him if she did? He was on watch earlier."

Believing there was no need to call for an alarm, Alec called back, "Nay, 'tis no' necessary."

With Gylys and Kyth beside him, he waited impatiently for the drawbridge to be lowered. *Where on earth could she be?* He wondered.

They stopped first at Melvin's cottage. The man was sleeping when they entered. "Nay, she did no' come to see me this day," Melvin answered sleepily to Alec's inquiry. "She comes to see me every day, usually after the noonin' meal."

Alec's heart began to race with worry.

"'Tis unlike the lass, no' to come here, or at least send word," Melvin added as he rubbed a hand across his belly.

"Word?" Alec asked with a raised brow.

"Aye, on those rare days she be too busy, she sends a meal with Willem or someone else. But she did no' do that."

Worry began to settle in around Alec's heart.

Sensing his worry, Gylys said, "Mayhap she be at Effie's. Mayhap Effie be havin' the babe and Leona is helpin'?"

Alec thought on it for only a brief moment. "Effie is no' due fer another month," he said. Although 'twas entirely possible her time had arrived earlier than expected. "Mayhap there be a complication and that be why Leona can no' be found." He wondered if Gylys was as unconvinced by his statement as he was.

They bid Melvin good day and headed toward Dougall and Effie's home. He refused to panic, to let worry or dread rule his actions. Leona, he believed, would be found. *Hell, she is probably back at the keep already and wonderin' where I am,* he mused.

Dougall opened the door, his expression turning from confused to worried as soon as he laid eyes on Alec. For reasons Alec could never figure, Dougall seemed to be able to read him better than anyone he'd ever known.

"What be the matter?" Dougall asked as he waved them into his home.

"We came to see if Effie has seen me wife," Alec said, as he looked hopefully to Effie, who was setting the table for their evening meal.

"I have no' seen her all day," Effie told him, with a raised brow. "Usually she stops by to check on me after she visits with Melvin."

"She did no' go see Melvin this day," Gylys told her.

"And she be nowhere in the keep?" Dougall asked?

"Nay," Alec replied. "But we have no' looked in every room. We thought mayhap she had been held up by Melvin, or stopped here to help Effie."

Dougall and Alec looked at one another for a brief moment. Dougall recognized at once that Alec was doing his best not to let anyone know he was concerned or worried.

"I shall come help ye look fer her," Dougall said before grabbing his sword and belt from the hook by the door. "I be certain she be fine," he added.

"Would ye like me to help?" Effie asked with a good deal of concern in her tone.

"Nay," Alec and Dougall replied in unison.

"'Tis best ye stay here," Dougall told her. "Ye were no' feelin' well this day."

For once, his wife decided against arguing with him, which only added to his concern for her well-being.

The men left the cottage, while Dougall closed the door behind them. "Did ye inquire with the watch if anyone saw her leave?"

Alec explained about the change in watch.

"I say we wake Kennith up then," Dougall said. "Just to be certain."

The hour was growing late, the sun painting the skies in deep crimson and amethyst. 'Twas the kind of sunset his wife would have oohed and ahed over. *Do no' begin thinkin' of her in the past tense, ye eejit,* he cursed his traitorous heart.

They hurried down the path, through the thicket, and to the draw-bridge. Someone had ordered it raised as soon as Alec and his men had popped through the thicket.

"Wake up Kennith Bowie!" Alec shouted to the men above.

~

HE'D LAST SEEN HIS WIFE AT THE NOONIN' MEAL. THAT WAS A GOOD eight hours ago. Not Kennith or anyone else who manned the wall that day had seen Leona leave the keep. Therefore, it stood to reason she was still inside the keep, or at the very least, its walls.

Men were called for to aid in the search. Alec assigned a group of men to each floor, where they would search from room to room.

When that first search yielded nothing, Alec was nearly overcome with dread. "Call for more men," he barked to Gylys. "I want every square inch of this keep searched. Even the dungeons."

Gylys, just as worried as anyone about his missing mistress, gave a curt nod. "Shall I send men to search the stables, granary and such?"

"Aye," Alec responded gruffly. "Every square inch, inside and out!"

~

HE WILL MOURN HER LOSS. MAYHAP NO' FOR LONG, BUT MOURN HER HE will. I tried to warn him she was a poor choice, but he would no' listen to reason. "If ye must marry, marry from within the clan," I told him. Stubborn fool.

'Tis a pity she has to die, for I was truly beginning to like her. 'Tis a small sacrifice if it means savin' our clan from ruin. I have made many sacrifices over the years for this clan. I will get my due, I will. I deserve it after all the hell I have gone through, after all I have done for these people. I'll no' stand idly by and watch Alec Bowie and his whore run us aground.

It was my good fortune seein' the witch headin' for the north tower. Och, but me heart pounded with the anticipation! Me fingers all but itched to be wrapped around that skinny neck of hers.

No one will think to look for her there. I did no' even have to remove me dirk. One small push, bar the door, and voila! Our problems are solved.

I imagine it will take a few days before she dies. She'll suffer, which *makes it all the sweeter in the end. Knowin' it took days fer her to die. And none shall suspect my role in it.*

I was no' there, but they say Eduard was dead before he hit the ground. His death near crippled me with grief, but I did no' show it. I could no' show it.

Rutger, they say, suffered for only a short time. 'Tis another death I could no' mourn as openly as I wanted. He was no' the man Eduard was, but at least he was no' tryin' to lead us down the path to 'peace'. Peace. Bah! The word makes me skin itch! This be no' what Eduard would have wanted. Nor Rutger. Nor any other of our chiefs before them.

I be tired of bein' ignored, of people lookin' at me as if I were less than nothin'.

They'll no' be ignorin' me much longer.

In the end, they will see the wisdom in my plan.

"I AM GOING TO DIE HERE," LEONA CRIED QUIETLY.

Just how long she had been locked away in the black-as-pitch room, she was uncertain. It seemed an eternity.

This room, she decided, would eventually become her tomb. No one knew where she was. The tower, though still connected to the main keep, sat too far away for anyone to hear her cry for help. That, along with the thick walls, the lack of windows, and the barred door, did not help matters.

Hours ago, she had given up screaming for help. It wouldn't do any good anyway. Besides, she had screamed so loudly and for such a length of time that she lost her voice. She had clawed and scratched at the door until her nails were broken and her fingers bled.

On her hands and knees, she had crawled around the floor of the room, looking for something, anything that might help effect an escape. Though she could see not a thing in all this blackness, nothing felt helpful. There was no axe, to fire stokers, not even a candlestick to beat against the door with. Nothing but big, heavy pieces of furniture, a few chairs and tables. Not even an old worn cushion on which to rest her head.

She had also given up trying to figure out *who* had shoved her in and barred the door. 'Twas no ghost, of that, she was certain. Nay, 'twas a flesh and blood person. And whomever he was, he most assuredly wanted her dead.

If his intent had been only to terrify her, he had succeeded. And would he not have returned at some point to let her out? If terror was his only thought, he'd have returned by now.

Nay, he wanted more. He wanted her to suffer and to see her die. If she hadn't known for a fact that her father was still on Mackintosh and McLaren lands, she would have thought him her captor and executioner.

She hadn't been here long enough to make an enemy as ruthless, as hateful as Ingerame. Or at least, she hadn't believed she had.

Who, who among these people despised her enough to want to see her dead? No matter which way her mind went, she came up with no good answer.

It mattered not, she supposed. For in the end, she would be dead before anyone discovered where she was. No one, not even her husband, would think to look for her here.

As she lay in the dark, with her head resting on her hands, she thought of Alec. Her silent tears fell down her cheeks and onto the cold stone floor. Fervently she believed he was at this very moment looking for her. But chances were, he was looking outside the keep and not within. His first thought would have been that she was lost, wondering about in the woods. Aye, he was probably angry for making her take time out of his busy day to go looking for her. But was he worried? Was he consumed with fear and dread?

A tiny part of her hoped that he would pine for her loss the same way Brogan Mackintosh still mourned over the loss of his wife. She no longer cared that it was selfish of her to want such a thing. She was going to die here, probably not for days, but die she would. And when she left God's earth, she wanted to believe someone would miss her. And she wanted that someone to be Alec.

⌒

ALEC HAD SPREAD HIS MEN FAR AND WIDE, BOTH WITHIN THE KEEP AND beyond it. As the sky grew inky black, so did his mood. Darker and more dangerous, the longer they searched for his wife.

Dougall and Kyth had stopped trying to offer any words of encouragement as they helped their chief search for Leona. 'Twould do no good. Dougall knew Alec would not rest until he found her. He could only pray they found her alive. For if someone had harmed her — as he was strongly beginning to suspect — there would be no end to the vengeance Alec would seek. Heaven help them then.

"We've searched every floor, the attics, and the dungeons," Dougall said as they were heading below stairs. He waited for a response, but none came. Alec was on a mission. Focused and intent on finding his wife.

Dougall could only imagine the distress and torment his friend and cousin was going through. If their roles were reversed and 'twas his Effie missing, he reckoned he'd tear this keep apart, brick by brick until he found her.

Entering the gathering room, they were met by Willem Bowie. He looked as though he had been drinking, which was not a surprise to anyone. His hair all a mess, his eyes bloodshot and ruddy, he stood next to the table.

"M'laird," Willem greeted Alec. "Be it true? Yer wife be missin'?"

Alec took note of the man's worried expression, the manner in which he twisted his cap in his hand. He also could not help but notice the odor of whisky upon his breath. "Aye, she be missin'," Alec answered dismissively as he walked past. Dougall and Kyth were following close behind.

"M'laird," Willem called out to Alec's back. Alec paused and turned to face him. But before he could utter a word, Patrice came rushing into the room.

She was as pale as a sheet, her eyes rimmed in red. "Alec!" she cried out breathlessly as she crossed the room quickly. "Be it true?" She placed her hands on his forearms and looked into his eyes.

There was no need for him to answer. His dark brown eyes all but stormed with a blend of rage and concern.

"Please, tell me, what can I do to help?" she asked.

Dougall stepped forward. "Mayhap ye could stay with Effie," he suggested. "She was no' feelin' well this day."

Incredulous he would even suggest it, Patrice said, "Ye ken Effie has no use fer me, Dougall."

"Ye're her sister," he politely reminded her. "She loves ye."

"Love? 'Tis no' the word I would use to describe how yer wife feels about me."

They argued back and forth for a long moment, before Alec could take no more. Irate, he said, "If the two of ye want to discuss yer family problems, please, take it to yer own home. I have more important things to do than to listen to ye squabble!"

Duly chastised, they began to apologize and beg his forgiveness.

"M'laird," Willem Bowie spoke up from behind Dougall and Patrice

"What is it?" Alec barked loudly.

Undeterred by his laird's booming voice, Willem stepped forward. "Did ye check the north tower yet?"

Alec eyed him suspiciously for a brief time. "The north tower?"

"Aye," Willem said with a nod of his head. "She has been goin' there off and on fer the past week or two. I helped her just the other day, to carry a table down."

Confused, Alec stepped forward and glared down at the man. "What on earth are ye goin' on about?"

Willem righted his shoulders and lifted his chin. "The mistress," he said. "She has been goin' to the north tower to bring things out of storage, tables and such. Mayhap she went there today?"

In truth, Alec hadn't given a thought to looking there, for he could see no purpose in his wife entering it. "And ye're just *now* comin' to me with this information?" Alec all but growled at Willem.

The man paled visibly. "I have only just returned from Kinbrea," he replied in shame. "I did no' ken she was missin'."

There was no time for Alec to apologize for all but biting the man's head off. Spinning on his feet, he headed toward the north tower. "Dougall! Kyth!" he called out over his shoulder. "With me!"

A DULL ACHE HAD BEGUN TO FORM AT THE BASE OF LEONA'S SKULL FROM lying on the cold floor. What she would not do for a cup of cider. Earlier, in her blind exploration of the room, she had found what she believed to be a crate filled with auld chamberpots, much to her bladder's relief and gratitude.

Now she lay on the floor, still and quiet, dozing in between bouts of quiet tears. God, how she hated being in the dark! Every creak, every noise was magnified in her imagination. At one point, she felt something scurry across her slipper, a mouse no doubt, which made her scream out in fright.

THERE HAD BEEN NO SIGN OF LEONA ON THE FIRST FLOOR OF THE tower. They'd looked in every nook and cranny and found nothing. Alec's heart pounded against his chest, filled with worry and anger. Anger that he could not find her, and anger that he allowed himself to fret so.

It was not supposed to be like this. *He* wasn't supposed to be like this. A worried simpleton, distressed because he could not find his wife. His gut, his heart, were knotted together in a confusing, nonsensical mess. Now was not the time to worry over his feelings for Leona. He had to find her. *Please, God, let her be alive!*

Taking the stairs two at a time, he all but ran to the second floor. "Leona!" he called out as the landing came into site. "Leona!"

He paused to listen, but heard no response. The light from his torch flickered, casting unearthly shadows across the walls.

The door was barred from the outside, just as it should be. His heart sank, hope dwindling. She couldn't be behind a barred door. He was about to turn away when his inner voice pleaded with him to take a closer look.

Crouching, he held his torch low so that he could look at the floor. There, he found what looked to be fresh scratch marks in a semi-circular pattern. No doubt they'd been made recently by the old wooden door having scraped against the stones.

Look inside, his inner voice niggled again. *Look inside.*

There was a cold torch in the sconce already. He lit it before setting his torch on the floor by his feet. Quickly, he lifted the bar and pulled the door open. It scraped against the hard surface, the sound bouncing off the walls. Blood rushed through his veins, pulsated in his ears as he grabbed the torch and stepped inside.

Time seemed to slow measurably as he held the torch high, then low, searching, hoping, begging God to let him find her.

At first, he didn't recognize the form lying on the floor. It took a moment for reality to set in.

"My God!" he cried out as he made his way around a pile of furniture. "Leona!"

She did not move. Not a twitch, not a sound. She lay there, all balled up, her head resting on her hands.

His heart seized, refused to beat. His lungs refused to take in a breath as he knelt beside her. Fear, sheer, unadulterated fear fell over him. Slowly, he reached out to touch her silky, golden hair. "Leona," he whispered her name once more.

CERTAIN 'TWAS ONLY A PLEASANT DREAM, LEONA IGNORED THE VOICE calling her name. She didn't want to wake up right now, because Alec was there, keeping her warm, scaring away the darkness.

"Leona, please wake up," Alec was whispering to her again. In her sleepy state, she thought he sounded worried or afraid. But that could not be, for Alec Bowie was never afraid.

It took Alec shaking her before she pulled out of her deep slumber.

When she opened her eyes, she was no longer in the darkness. There was light! And Alec!

"Ye came fer me?" she asked, relieved and confused all at once.

He expelled a relieved breath as he pulled her into his arms. "I thought ye dead," he admitted aloud.

She held on to him for dear life, refusing to let go. "Ye came fer me," she cried against his chest.

"Of course I came fer ye," he said. "Did ye think I would no'?" How on earth could she believe him so callous, so cold that he would not look for her.

"I knew ye would look fer me, but I believed ye'd no' think to look fer me here," she told him between sobs.

"Wheesht, now, lass," he whispered before pressing a kiss to the top of her head. "I will always come fer ye."

"I thought I would die here," she told him. "I hate being alone in the dark."

Alec did his best to soothe away her fears, to offer whatever comfort he could.

"Alec, please do no' be mad at me," she murmured into his chest, squeezing her arms around him more tightly.

"Mad at ye?" he asked incredulous she'd even suggest it at this moment. Aye, he'd been angry, but not with her.

"I was no' lost, ye ken."

He let out a breath and a chuckle. "Then why have I spent the last three hours tearin' this keep apart looking fer ye?"

She lifted her head away from his chest to look him in the eye. "I was no' lost. I was stuck. There be a difference," she told him. "Were ye really lookin' fer me fer three hours?"

"I've had the entire clan lookin' fer ye," he said.

"Ye were worried?" she asked, her voice filled with a blend of doubt and hope.

"Just a wee bit," he said.

Kyth called to them from the doorway. "Alec? Have ye found her?"

"Aye, I have!" he called over his shoulder.

He could hear a collective sigh of relief from his men who waited beyond. "Is she well?"

"I believe so," Alec called again. Turning his focus back to his wife, he yelled, "She be a bit cold, but she be fine."

"Thank, God!" Gylys exclaimed unashamedly.

"Let the others ken we have found her," Alec yelled to his men. He still hadn't taken his eyes off Leona.

Lowering his voice, he asked, "How did ye come to be locked in here?"

Something flickered in her eyes. Something that told him she was debating her reply. "Leona, I would have the truth, please."

"I am not certain," she told him as she turned away.

"Not certain?"

She took in a deep breath of air and let it out slowly. "Alec, someone pushed me. I did no' see who, but I *felt* their hands on me back. Before I could get back up, the door was closin'. Then I heard the bar bein' lowered."

Pushed? "Someone pushed ye, then locked ye in?" 'Twas difficult to wrap his mind around what she was telling him. *Who? Who would do such a thing?*

"Aye, they did." She sounded tired as well as wounded.

Fury swelled in his gut, making his hands shake, his voice tremble. "Who would do such a thing?"

"I fear I do no' ken," she said.

Swiftly, and with little effort, he scooped her up and stood to his full height. "Come, let us away this room and get ye to our bedchamber."

"Wait!" she cried out to him. "Please, set me down."

With a raised brow, he asked, "Why? Ye have been through quite a torment, lass."

"Alec, if the person who locked me in here is *out there,* watchin', I do no' want them to think I was so terrified that now I can no' walk."

Though he could see the wisdom in her line of thinking, he was not ready yet to let her go.

"I do no' want them to think they won, Alec. Please?"

Reluctantly, he set her on her feet. His pride in her increasing a hundred fold when she pulled her shoulders back and lifted her chin. She was going to leave this room on her own two feet, with her head held high. Leona was not about to let the bastard who had locked her in here win. Aye, she was a strong-willed lass.

And she was going to need to be if his instincts were correct.

Someone wanted to kill his wife.

CHAPTER 19

*A*lec was not about to let anything else happen to Leona. As soon as he saw her safely to their bedchamber, he stepped into the hallway to discuss the matter privately with Dougall.

"Are ye certain?" Dougall asked after Alec explained what he knew about Leona being locked in the tower.

"Aye, she seems to be. And I do no' doubt her recollection," Alec said. "The door is far too heavy for it to have been closed by the wind."

Dougall rubbed a hand across his stubbled jaw. "Aye. But Alec, who would do such a thing? The lass be far too decent and kind. She has no' been here long enough to make an enemy, even if she were able."

Alec had to agree with his assessment. "But I have."

Dougall studied his cousin for a moment. "Ye think 'twas meant to hurt ye?"

"Aye, I do." Though he despised having to admit to it, it would have been his undoing had anything happened to Leona. Thankfully, he did not have to say the words aloud in order for Dougall to understand.

"Any suspicions on who it might be?"

While he was nowhere near as ruthless as his predecessors, he was not so naive as to believe he had no enemies. "There are those among us who did not wish to take the path to peace," Alec reminded him.

"True," Dougall replied. "But I can think of no one angry enough or vengeful enough to bring harm to Leona or to ye."

"So ye've heard no rumblin's amongst the people?" Alec asked him.

"No more than usual."

Alec let out a frustrated breath. "Mayhap they are careful with what they say around ye? Ye are, after all, me cousin and friend."

"That is also true," Dougall replied. "So what are we to do?"

"I want Kyth and Gylys to watch over me wife at all times," he said.

"That should no' be a problem. They be quite fond of Leona. Especially her cookin'."

Alec chuckled. "They have yet to miss a meal she has prepared."

"I shall speak to them at once," Dougall said. "And after, I need to return to me own wife. She was no' well today."

Alec slapped a hand on the man's shoulder. "Go, be with yer wife. And tell Gylys and Kyth to remain sober, fer they shall start their watch first thing in the morn."

"Now *that* they will object to."

"I DO *NO'* NEED TO BE WATCHED OVER LIKE A BAIRN."

Alec was just as determined to see her watched over as she was to prohibit it. "As me wife, as chatelaine and mistress of the keep, ye are important to our clan."

'Twas late morning as she stood in her kitchen preparing the morning meal. She had slept in, exhausted from the ordeal from the day before, which had put her in a sour mood to begin with. Whenever she thought of her time in the locked room, her anger would bubble and rise.

But this? This was too much. "I can no' think with Kyth and Gylys standin' over me all the time," she groused. She tossed eggs into a pot of cold water and hung them over the fire to boil.

Alec stood with his feet apart, arms crossed over his chest. "Ye proved yer ability to take care of yerself yesterday."

Leona glowered at him. "'Twas no' me fault and ye ken that! But now, now that I know someone wishes to do me harm, I can take more precautions."

"As will I," he told her, his tone firm and unrelenting. "Ye *will* be watched over. When I can no' be with ye, Kyth and Gylys will be. I will no' argue the matter further."

She cursed under her breath as she yanked open the door to the larder. "What about when I need to bathe? Shall they watch over me then?" she called out over her shoulder as she stepped into the larder.

'Tis ridiculous, she thought to herself as she grabbed a loaf of bread and a length of sausage.

As she turned to leave the tiny room, she bumped into her husband. "Bloody hell, Alec!" she cursed at him. "Stop doin' that!"

He smiled down at her. "Stop doin' what?"

"Sneakin' up on me like ye do!" She tried to go around him, but he was blocking her path.

"If I can sneak up on ye when ye ken I already be in the same room, then *anyone* else could do the same."

She would hang before she admitted he was right. "Please move, else 'twill be the noonin' meal before we eat."

He didn't budge. Instead, he smiled down at her as he took a lock of hair and twined it around his finger. "As fer the bathin'," he drawled out his words seductively, "I shall be the only one to watch over ye then. I might even offer to help."

Blast this man! He knew just how to confuse her, to unsettle her nerves. "Stop that!" she said as she batted his hand away.

"Stop what?" he asked, his tone low and provocative.

"Stop tryin' to distract me. I ken what ye're doin', and 'twill no' work this day. Now move."

He laughed again before taking her into his arms. "Ye find me distractin'?" he asked playfully.

Of course she found him distracting. Almost to the point of madness. And 'twas especially so whenever he had *that* look in his eyes. She refused to give him the satisfaction of knowing it. "Nay," she lied. "Ye are nothin' more than a nuisance."

He smiled, smug with knowing she was lying through her pretty white teeth.

"Coward," he whispered playfully.

"Me? A coward?" she asked, exceedingly insulted.

"Ye can no' admit ye find me distractin'," he told her with a mischievous smile.

Offering him her most indignant expression as well as a roll of her eyes, Leona said, "Oh, I can admit to such, when 'tis the truth. And what of ye, Alec Bowie? Can ye ever admit to findin' me somethin' more than a nuisance?"

He had the audacity to throw his head back and laugh at her. "A nuisance? Mayhap at times," he said as he drew her into his chest and held her tightly. "But more often than not, I find ye a distraction. Such as now. All I truly wish to do," he kissed the top of her head before bending down to whisper in her ear, all manner of wickedly sinful and delightful things he wished to do with her and to her.

By the time he was done, she was holding her breath, her heart pounding ferociously against her breast, and her legs all a tremble.

Then he left her there, alone in the larder, with nothing to do but think about what he had said.

Willem came to see her just before noontime. Gylys opened the door and asked him what he needed.

"Do no' be ridiculous," Leona chastised him as she scooted him out of the way. "'Tis Willem. He is a friend."

He looked tired and a bit worn out, as well as confused by Gylys' brief interrogation. "Ignore Gylys," Leona said as she drew the man inside. "He's only doing his *duty*." A strong emphasis on the word 'duty'.

"Mistress, I only be doin' what Alec ordered me to do. 'Tis fer yer own safety."

"Willem, would ye like somethin' to eat?" she asked as she sat him down at her table. "I have some sausage and eggs left over from breakfast."

"Thank ye, m'lady. That would be verra kind of ye," he said, licking his lips. "But I did no' come here to eat."

"Bah!" Leona said with a wave of her hand. "Do no' fash yourself over it. I'll be verra happy to feed ye today." In truth, she was glad for the distraction. Gylys' presence was beginning to grate on her nerves. He stood as a constant reminder of what had happened yesterday. Oh, she knew he was only following Alec's orders. Still, it didn't mean she had to enjoy it.

"I would like some eggs and sausage, mistress," Gylys said with a hopeful smile.

With a roll of her eyes, she made a trencher for Gylys and handed it to him. Most eagerly, he took the trencher and sat down opposite Willem.

"So, Willem, what brings ye to see me this day?"

"I came to see how ye fared," he told her, using a bit of bread to sop up the grease from the still warm sausage.

"I fare verra well." She smiled warmly. "And I hear I have ye to thank."

"Me?" he asked with a raised brow.

"Aye," she patted his hand. "Alec told me ye were the one to suggest lookin' in the North Tower."

He swallowed down his bite of bread. "Well, they said they had looked everywhere," he told her. "But I figured if they had looked *everywhere*, they'd have found ye."

"Exactly!" she exclaimed. "Fer one can no' be nowhere, can they? Even if ye do no' ken where 'where' is, it be somewhere, aye?"

Gylys gave a great shake of his head as if it might bring some sense to what he'd just heard. Deciding it didn't truly matter, he returned his attention to his food.

"Well, I do thank ye, Willem. Were it no' fer ye, I'd still be in that tower, scared half out of me mind."

Willem's expression turned solemn. "We would have turned the world over lookin' fer ye, mistress," he told her. "Ye be one of the only truly kind people here. No one else would make me bathe or offer me a hot meal." He cast her a warm smile.

"Ye will always find a friend in me," she told him as she patted his hand.

"Did ye hear, mistress, that Effie be havin' her bairn?" Willem said as he took the last bite of his eggs.

"What?" she exclaimed. "Why did ye no' tell me that sooner?" She scooted her stool away from the table and headed for the door.

Gylys jumped to his feet as soon as she opened it. "Mistress, where be ye goin'?"

Rolling her eyes, she answered with a good deal of irritation. "To Effie's. She be a friend and she be havin' her babe. She be no' due fer another month."

When Gylys started to follow her, she said, "Stay, enjoy yer meal. Ye may find me at Effie's when ye're finished."

"Alec will kill me if I let ye go alone," he told her as he grabbed a length of sausage with one hand and a hunk of bread with the other. A moment later he was racing to catch up to Leona.

LEONA WAS OUT OF BREATH, FILLED WITH WORRY, BY THE TIME SHE reached Dougall and Effie's cottage. Gylys was fast on her trail, eating the bread and sausage as he kept up with her.

As far as she knew, Effie was not due for at least another month. In her experience — albeit limited — early babes rarely fared well.

Dougall and his four sons were standing out of doors, near the woodpile. One look at his face and Leona knew he was just as worried as she. The boys, however, were oblivious. They were on the ground in a tight circle, playing some game with round stones.

"Dougall!" Leona called to him as she raced down the path. He met her halfway.

"Mistress," he greeted her. "I fear Effie can no' have cider with ye this day," he began.

"I ken that, Dougall," she told him. "I have just learned her time has come. How does she fare?"

He ran a worried hand through his hair. "I do no' ken. The midwife be with her now, as well as Margaret and Leesa."

Leona was glad to know the midwife was already in attendance. "If I ken Effie at all, she will be fine. She be a stubborn, strong woman."

Gylys offered his own opinion then. "That be right true, mistress. Effie be too stubborn to allow anything to happen to the babe or herself."

Dougall chuckled and gave a nod of agreement. "Aye, that she is."

"I shall go and see how she fares and let ye know, aye?" she asked, placing one palm on his arm.

"Thank ye, mistress. I would like that. I am certain Effie would as well." Dougall offered her a weak smile as he looked back to his sons.

She turned then, to look at her guard. "Gylys, ye are no', under any circumstances, to follow me into Effie's cottage."

His eyes grew wide with horror. "Of course no'! I would no' think, that is to say, I mean ..." he was at a loss for words.

If her assessment of him was correct, he'd rather be gutted with a splintery board than to step one foot into a cottage where a woman was giving birth.

"Ye can watch over Dougall," she told him with a grin. "I shall no' be long."

With that, she left the two men to do whatever it is men do whilst a woman is birthing.

Reaching the door, she smoothed down her skirts, then swept away an errant strand of hair before gently rapping at the door. A moment later, the door opened.

Leona recognized the woman at once from the group who had ignored her days ago. "Good day," Leona greeted her with as warm a smile as she could manage. She tried to step into the cottage, but the woman stepped in front of her.

"What do ye want?" she asked, her tone haughty and cold.

"I wish to see my friend," Leona told her, confused by the woman's menacing stance.

"She be busy. She has no time fer ye this day."

Her rudeness and supreme, indignant tone, was the last straw. Leona drew back her shoulders, lifted her chin and looked directly into the woman's eyes. "Might I remind ye that I *am* the mistress of this keep and ye shall address me as such. Now step aside and let me pass." She kept her tone even and smooth, belying the fact her insides were raging with anger.

The woman looked as though she could not believe Leona had the audacity to order her to move aside.

Ignoring her, Leona pushed past her and into the cottage. Effie was standing near the table, bent over, with one hand on her back. She was covered with sweat, holding her breath and gritting her teeth.

"Effie?" Leona whispered as she stepped toward her.

The strangest expression came to Effie's face when she lifted her head. Leona could not have described it if someone had a dirk to her throat. The other two women were looking at Leona as if she were an apparition. The tension and unease was palpable. It filled the room as heavy as smoke from an open fire.

At once, she knew her presence was neither needed nor wanted. Effie, she could forgive, for she was in a good deal of pain. Nothing a woman said or did during this time could ever be held against her. She had learned that only recently, when she had helped Rose Mack-intosh birth her son.

"Dougall is quite worried," she told Effie. "I promised him I would see how ye fared."

The pain passed, as did the odd expression. Effie let out a deep breath as she gave a quick nod. "Thank ye, Leona," she said. "I fear 'twill be some time before this babe arrives." She took another deep breath and tried to right herself, but was unable. "Could ye please take them away from here? Mayhap to the keep? Watch over them until the babe arrives?"

Relief washed over her. She might not be needed *here*, during the birthing, but she *was* needed. "Of course," she said happily. "'Twill be an honor to do so."

Thus far, the other women in the room had remained rooted and mute. Leona gave each one a curt nod before quitting the cottage.

Out of doors, she let out the breath she'd been holding. Forcing another smile to her face, she sought out Dougall and his sons.

It took a good deal of cajoling on her part before Leona could convince Dugall that Effie was doing well and wanted him to take their children and go with Leona to the keep. Finally, he relented, but only after she and Gylys promised to send messengers back and forth with hourly updates.

The boys were all too happy to leave. "We have no' been to the keep in forever," the youngest lad, Thomas, exclaimed as they raced down the path.

"'T'as only been a few months," James, only a year older, corrected. "Ye eejit."

Dougall rolled his eyes and called out to his sons, "Lads, ye shall be on yer best behavior when we get to the keep. And James, do no' call yer brother an eejit. Thomas! Get out of the mud! Yer mum will skin us both alive!"

Amused, Leona could not help but smile. *This could be Alec and yer sons some day,* she thought. The vision of Alec walking along with a passel of their children made her heart all but sing with joy. *Alec will be a good da.* Of this she had no doubt at all.

She watched as Dougall scooped up James, lifted him high and then settled him on his shoulders. The little boy, no more than five summers, squealed with delight.

Thomas looked wounded. "I want a turn!"

"I just got my turn," James told him right before sticking his tongue out at his older brother.

"That's not fair," Thomas groused as he kicked at a pebble with his toe. His two older brothers, older and wiser of course, shook their heads in dismay.

Without warning, Gylys scooped the lad up and set him on his shoulders. Thomas beamed with delight, looked at his younger brother and stuck his tongue out at him.

"Lads, I do believe I have a few sweet cakes at the keep," Leona told them.

All at once, they were discussing how much they loved sweet cakes, then began to argue over who could eat the most without throwing up.

THE HOURS PASSED BY AT AN AGONIZINGLY SLOW PACE. LEONA DID HER best to keep the boys entertained, though in truth, they did not require much supervision., Leona took great delight in watching the energetic little boys race through the keep, pretending to be warriors protecting their lands.

With Dougall there to watch over her, Gylys left them alone to tend to what he called *matters of a personal nature.* At which the boys giggled and rolled around on the floor in a heap of laughter.

For a late afternoon respite, she fed them bread with butter and honey, apples, cheese, and dried meats. They wolfed down their food and guzzled their cider like true Highland warriors. Instead of calming them down, as had been her intent, it only seemed to rejuvenate them.

While the boys laughed and played, Dougall paced and fidgeted. Occasionally, he would absentmindedly reprimand them for screaming too loudly or running too fast. 'Twas Leona who politely told them her table was not *the wall* and they shouldn't traipse upon it.

When it came time to prepare the evening meal, she corralled the boys and told them to follow her. "Where are we goin'?" James asked as he skipped beside her. "Are ye goin' to show us the tower room ye were locked in?"

"I heard 'twas a brownie that locked her in," Wills told his brothers.

Leona came to an abrupt stop and turned to listen.

"'Twere no brownie," he told him. "'Twas the ghost."

"What ghost?" James and Thomas asked, all wide-eyed.

Leona watched as Wills and Aric exchanged a knowing glance. She knew they were up to no good, but decided to see where they went with this story.

"Ye do no' ken about the ghost of the keep?" Aric asked with a quirked brow.

Both boys shook their heads and begged to be told.

"Ye think they be old enough, Wills?"

Wills studied them closely, with an index finger to his cheek. After a long moment, he nodded. "Aye, I think so."

"Well then," Aric said, "ye should tell them about the ghosts who inhabit this keep."

"All of them?" Wills asked with a quirked brow and feigned expression of astonishment. "I do no' think they be old enough to hear about the gray lady."

"What gray lady?" James asked, his eyes nearly as wide as trenchers now.

"Och! The gray lady who haunts this keep. They say she was killed here, by her husband's own hands. They say he killed her near *samhain* time, more than a hundred years ago, ye ken? He found she was bein' unfaithful to him."

"What does that mean?" James asked. "Unfaithful?"

Wills and Aric exchanged a knowing glance before Wills answered. "It means she had made a babe with a man who was no' her husband."

James and Thomas did not quite understand what their older brother meant. They looked at one another, shrugged their shoulders, and begged him to go on.

"Well, the laird, her husband, when he found out about her betrayal, they say he went mad with jealousy and hanged her. Right here in this verra room. Right next to her lover. On the eve of *samhain.* They also say, she haunts the keep to this verra day. They both do, the gray lady and her lover. They wander the keep at all hours of the day and night, tryin' to find one another. But the laird, he had a curse put on their souls right before he hanged them. Now, they can no' find one another."

"That be right," Aric agreed with a nod of his head.

What the two young men did not know, for they were too engrossed in their own story to notice, was that Kyth and Gylys had come to stand behind them. Leona remained quiet, wondering where on earth Wills and Aric would take their story.

"The gray lady," Aric began. "She be all covered in blood. It drips from her eyeless sockets, from her fingertips—"

Before he could terrify his younger brothers any further, Gylys and Kyth reached out and grabbed Wills and Aric without warning.

The two young men nearly leapt out of their own skins. Each lad gave a mighty scream, with eyes wide and arms all akimbo.

'Twas all Leona could do not to fall to the floor in a fit of laughter.

James and Tomas looked mighty confused, for they'd apparently never witnessed their brothers so terrified before.

"*That*, lads, is what ye get when ye try to terrify yer younger brothers," Gylys chastised the pair, as he tried not to laugh.

"Aye, they be far too young for such a story!" Kyth added as he set Aric down on his shaking legs.

"That was no' fair!" the older boys argued.

"No' fair?" Gylys asked. "Aye, I do believe it was. And I believe yer da will agree. Shall we ask him?"

The boys looked more terrified of their father finding out than they had moments ago when Gylys and Kyth had grabbed them. "Nay!" they protested.

Suppressing a smile, Kyth looked to Leona. "How do ye think we should punish these heathens?"

Punish? Leona cried inwardly. Her first thought was of belts, floggers, and dark places. 'Twas only when she saw the mischievous grin on Kyth and Gylys' faces that she realized they were not speaking of beatings. "I say they should wash the dishes after dinner this night," she offered. "And give their younger brothers the sweet cakes I had set aside for *them*."

The boys began to protest until Kyth pointed out they could take the matter to their father to settle.

Once it was settled that as long as they apologized to their brothers — and accepted Leona's proffered 'punishment' — then no one would bring up the matter with either their father *or,* worse still, their mother.

~

LEONA HAD AS MUCH EXPERIENCE WITH CHILDREN AS SHE DID WITH newly born bairns. That is to say, none at all.

So when it came time for the evening meal, she was astonished at the amount of food four little boys could eat. The older two ate almost as much as the men, and just as vigorously.

They had received word not long before they sat to sup, that nothing much had changed from the last update. Effie was still in labor, but no one should worry. These things took time.

Dougall barely ate at all, for he was far too worried over his wife. Alec and the other men did their best to keep his spirits high. "Effie will be well," Gylys told him as he poured Dougall another cup of ale. "She be a strong, fine woman."

Dougall offered his friend a wan smile. Of course, none of the men at the table could understand the worry and torment one felt when his wife was trying to birth his child. He imagined Alec would learn what this torment felt like at some point within the next year, if not sooner.

'Twas difficult to take advice from men who had not walked in his boots.

When he could take no more of the waiting, he scooted away from table and shot to his feet. "I am going to go see for myself how she fares," he declared solemnly.

"Are ye sure that is wise?" Alec asked as he cut off a bite of baked fish.

Dougall pinned him in place with a glare reserved only for murderers. "Aye. I am sure 'tis wise." He looked then to Leona. "Mistress, would ye mind keepin' an eye on me boys?"

Leona gave a nod of her head. She thought it awfully sweet that he was so worried about Effie. *I wonder, if I do get with child, if Alec will worry over me like Dougall worries over Effie.* "Of course," she told him. "Go now, be with yer wife."

The rest of the men shrugged their shoulders with disinterest. The boys all began to clamor around their father. "Can we come with ye?"

'Twas Gylys who shot down the idea. "Do ye no' remember? Ye promised to help Leona," he reminded them.

Dougall looked relieved. "Then they should keep their promise. I shall return soon." And with that, he quit the gathering room without a glance backward.

~

BECAUSE WILLS AND ARIC HAD NOT COMPLAINED ABOUT THEIR punishment, and because Leona had a soft spot in her heart the size of Edinburgh, she gave each of them a sweet cake after their work was complete.

They licked their lips as they looked at the cakes. "Thank ye, kindly mistress. We shall go give these to James and Tomas," Wills said, a bit dejectedly.

"Nay," Leona stopped him. "Those are for the two of ye. James and Tomas have had theirs."

Confused, they looked to her for clarification. "But ye said," Aric began.

Leona gave them each a warm smile, then tousled the locks on Aric's head. "Aye, I ken what I said. Think of this as yer reward fer no' complainin' or grousin' about washin' the dishes. And fer doin' such a fine job of it!"

The lads smiled and thanked her. They had the sweet cakes half eaten before they were out of the kitchen.

Leona swept up the last of the dust from the kitchen floor, smiling all the while. Oh, how she hoped she would have sons as sweet and as energetic as the boys who just left her kitchen.

After making certain everything was in its place, she blew out all but one of the candles and locked up for the night. As she headed toward the keep, she thought she heard a great commotion coming from within.

Worried that the boys might be getting into more mischief, she hurried inside.

~

LEONA'S JAW ALL BUT HIT THE FLOOR. THERE, IN THE MIDDLE OF HER gathering room, was her husband, along with Gylys, Kyth and Aric. They were standing on top of her table, with swords drawn.

Surrounding them, with little wooden swords, were James and Tomas. "Down with ye, ye bloody bastards!" James yelled as he jabbed at the men.

"Never!" Kyth yelled, the tip of his sword meeting the end of James'.

It took a long moment and several rapid heartbeats before she realized they were simply playing.

"I'll hang ye from yer bullocks!" wee Tomas yelled up at the men. "Give us yer coin purses!"

"Ye'll have to pry it from me cold, dead hands, ye mangy, filthy, son of a whore!" It had been her own husband who yelled that last bit.

Oh, no, no, no! She exclaimed inwardly. A vision of her husband and his men teaching *her* children how to fight, curse, and - oh lord! Aric just spit on her clean floor! She would have none of it.

"What in the name of God are ye all doin'?" She hadn't realized she was shouting until all the men and boys turned to face her.

"I will *no'* have ye teachin' these innocent boys how to curse!" She called out to the men on the table. "And Aric, I swear if ye spit on me clean floor one more time, I shall skelp the hide right off ye!"

She thundered toward the lot of them. "I will no' have this kind of rough-housin' in me home!" Her voice was firm, unyielding. "And to teach these little boys how to curse? 'Tis, 'tis downright disgustin'."

Wee James smiled up at her. "They did no' teach us how to curse, mistress. Our da' did!"

Her head began to throb. Taking a deep, cleansing breath, she said,

"I do no' care *who* taught ye. Ye will no' use that kind of language in *my* home, do you understand? And there will be no spittin' either. And if ye want to behave like a bunch of savages and ruffians, you can take it *out of doors!*"

She did not give one wit if her husband was upset. Not one wit! And if he even as much as thought of yelling at her for the way she spoke to him in front of his men, why, she'd clobber him over the head with his own sword!

Each and every one of them simply shrugged their shoulders. Alec and his men jumped down from the table. Kyth and Gylys began to usher the boys outside. Once they were gone, Alec turned to face his wife.

She hadn't expected him to be smiling at her. But he was. Uncertain if that should terrify her more than outrage or fury, she took a tentative step away.

Alec grabbed her about the waist and kissed her. Deeply, passionately. Once he was done, he set her back, still bearing the same devious smile. "I believe ye will one day make a fine mum," he told her.

Stunned, nay, completely astonished, she could only stand there as he turned around and left.

Her heart soared, for Alec was never one to give out compliments at the drop of a feather.

He believes I will make a fine mum!

Did that also mean he thought her a fine wife?

CHAPTER 20

'Twas long after the midnight hour before they received word on Effie. Alec and Dougall had been sitting near the fire in the gathering room, sipping on fine whisky as they talked of old times as well as the future of their clan.

Leona had settled the four lads into a room across the hall from hers. After numerous stories — far less terrifying than the ghost story of earlier that day — the boys finally succumbed to exhaustion and fell asleep. Afterward, she went to her own room and collapsed into her own bed.

After the long day she had had, with chasing after four rambunctious young boys, she had made up her mind to have only daughters.

Alec woke her with a tender kiss on the forehead. "We have a babe," he said as he caressed her cheek with the backs of his fingers. "A fine, healthy, and verra big boy."

Relieved to hear the babe was well, she sat up and rubbed the sleep from her eyes. "I should go to Effie," she said, her voice husky from sleep.

"Nay," Alec said as he began stripping out of his clothes. "Effie is doing well. Dougall has gone to be with her now. I told him we would keep the boys and bring them back in the morn."

That was good news, she supposed as she fell back into the bed and drew the covers up to her ears. In the morn, she would take the boys back to their mother and father, where they would be introduced to their new brother and future partner in crime.

EFFIE INSISTED ON NAMING THE BOY ARCHIBALD. DOUGALL DID NOT like it. He wasn't adamantly opposed to it, he simply did not like the name.

And Alec sure as hell did not like it. 'Twas his father's name.

He stood with Dougall in the late night hour, near the hearth in Dougall's cottage. Effie was in bed, the curtains drawn around her. Alec stood quietly as Dougall held his seventh son.

When word had come 'twas a big lad Effie had birthed, they had not been exaggerating. Alec wondered silently, how on earth something *that* large could come out of a woman as small as Effie. He left it up to the miracle of birth and all that.

Wrapped in a cocoon of linen, the boy slept contentedly in his father's arms. Thick dark hair encircled his head and covered his wee ears. A round little nose and rosebud mouth, he did look rather cherubic. But that name!

"Did ye say why she chose the name?" Alec asked as he peeked at the handsome boy child.

"Nay, she did no'," Dougall whispered.

"And she is set on it?"

Dougall nodded his head. "Aye, she is. And after all she's been through, and seein' the size of this boy, I will no' go against it."

The babe yawned and sighed sweetly. "He is a fine lookin' boy, aye?"

That, Alec could not argue.

"He be the biggest one yet, ye ken. All our others were wee in comparison," Dougall said as he rocked back and forth on his feet. "I do no' think is too soon to say he will be a fine warrior someday, aye? Look at the size of the boy's hands!"

Alec bit back a laugh. "Aye, I agree. When would ye like to start his trainin'? Is next week too soon?"

Dougall smiled down at his son. "I think he could handle it."

A tickling sensation began to form deep in Alec's stomach. He wondered if Leona would be able to give him a son? Mayhap more than one. It could be him standing here months from now, holding his firstborn for the first time.

I wonder if me da was proud on the day I was born? Where that thought came from, he was uncertain. He tried to think back to his youth, to his younger years. For the life of him, he could not recollect ever seeing his father smile. At least not at him or Rutger.

"I fear me wife will object if we start too soon," Dougall told Alec. "Mayhap we will no' tell her just yet."

Alec chuckled softly and gave his friend a pat on the back. "Well done, Dougall, well done."

Dougall finally tore his gaze away from his son long enough to look at Alec. He bore the most peculiar expression. "'Twas me wife who did all the hard work. 'Tis she who deserves the praise."

Since he'd never witnessed a birth before, he could not argue that point. "Aye, and praise her I will, in a few days. After she has rested."

Dougall turned his attention back to the babe sleeping in his arms. Alec bid them both good night, eager to return to his own wife.

A son, he mused as he walked along the moonlit path. *I should verra much like to have many sons.*

As soon as she had served Alec his morning meal, Leona set off to visit Effie and the new babe. She had the four boys in tow, along with a basket of food to help get the family through the next day.

The boys chatted excitedly and skipped along as they headed out of the keep, across the drawbridge, and down the path. They were quite eager to meet their new brother.

As they approached Dougall and Effie's cottage, Leona felt compelled to stop and speak to the boys first. "I ken ye be verra excited to see yer new brother. But please, remember, yer mum is goin' to be quite tired for the next sennight or so. Ye must be quiet, so ye do no' wake the babe or upset yer mum."

Each boy nodded his head earnestly, as if they understood and would obey. Oh, they might for the first hour or so. But after that? She really didn't know how Effie was going to survive this lot of heathens she had borne.

Wills was the first to arrive at the door. Slowly, he opened it and stepped inside. He paused briefly to look at his brothers and reminded them to be quiet. More nods of agreement before they all filed in.

Effie was sitting up in the bed, holding her babe in her arms. He was swaddled in a soft yellow blanket. Dougall was sitting on the bed beside her, with his back to the door. Effie looked up when she heard her sons enter. She smiled warmly at them. Dougall turned to see what had drawn her attention.

"Me heathen sons have returned," Effie said playfully.

The boys swarmed their parents. The younger two climbed on the bed in order to get a better look. Wills and Aric stood next to their father, as they all looked in awe and wonder at the new arrival.

"Och! He is huge!" James declared, to which his brother Tomas agreed.

Leona's heart swelled with happiness for the family. She stayed near the door, so as not to disturb the reunion. Dougall smiled as he approached her. "Thank ye fer takin' care of me sons, mistress."

"'Twas no' problem, Dougall," she replied. They hadn't necessarily been a problem. More like an unexpected invasion.

Effie was busy introducing Archibald to his brothers. Leona's arms ached with longing. She wished for all the world it was she who was abed, introducing her own babe to his father.

"I should leave ye be," Leona said. "Please, let me ken if there is anything I can do." She handed Dougall the basket and began to leave.

"Mistress," Dougall said as he placed a hand on her arm. "'Tis glad I am that ye are here. Ye've been a good friend to Effie, as well as me and me boys. Bowies are no' known fer showin' gratitude. But I just wanted ye to ken."

Her eyes grew damp as her heart swelled with gratitude and appreciation. "Thank ye, Dougall. Thanks to ye, and to Effie fer being so kind to me. Now, go and be with yer family."

LEONA HELD HER CRAMPING, ACHING STOMACH. HER MENSES HAD arrived in the middle of the night, deflating her hopes that she was with child.

"These things can take time," Alec told her as he held her close. "Do no' worry it."

She knew she should appreciate his kindness. At the moment, it was not making her feel any better. *One would think with all the lovin' we've been doin' I would be with child by now!*

Alec kissed the back of her head. "We've only been married a few weeks, Leona. Please, do no' worry. It will happen."

"But when?" she whispered.

He hugged her tight. "Wheest now, and sleep."

Although she was tired, 'twas impossible to sleep. *What if I never get with child? Will Alec set me aside?* That was a real, deep concern. She was growing quite fond of this man. The last thing she wanted was to disappoint him. She was not comfortable with asking all the burning questions, for she was uncertain she wanted to hear the answers. *Will ye keep me? Even if I never give ye a child?*

THREE WEEKS HAD PASSED SINCE EFFIE HAD GIVEN BIRTH. LEONA WOULD stop by every day, after visiting with Melvin, to check on her friend. Rain or shine, Leona was there to offer whatever assistance she could. Some days, she could only stay for a moment, others, if her chores were complete, she would stay longer and visit.

There were a few times when Effie would ask her to hold Archibald whilst she took a bath, or tended to her other sons. 'Twas those quiet moments of holding the rather large babe, that she looked forward to most. Sometimes, she would pretend it was her own babe she held in her arms.

August turned into September, the days growing shorter, the rains heavier. Alec worried over their crops like a mother over her first born babe. Soon, far sooner than she wanted, he would be leaving for a week or so, to visit neighboring clans. His hope was to forge business relationships that he prayed would turn to mutual alliances.

He shared little else with her. His worries, his concerns, he kept to himself. Leona did not want to push the matter, for she didn't want to appear to be a nagging, interfering wife. Instead, she let him know in quiet ways, that she was there should he ever need to unburden himself.

She and Alec had fallen into a comfortable routine. Her days were spent within the keep, trying to turn it into a comfortable home. His days were spent in the fields or in training.

'Twas at night, when they would retire to their bedchamber, that she felt closest to him. When they were *here*, alone and away from the distractions of the outside world, Alec was different. Attentive, kind, and oh, so very sweet! Not a night or a morning would pass that he did not make love to her.

Leona was growing more comfortable, and more brazen, and there were times she would instigate their lovemaking. Alec allowed her to be herself, to be free to do or say whatever she wished.

Afterward, they would fall asleep in each other's arms. She felt content, safe, and cared for there, in those late night hours. Wrapped in his arms, listening to his soft steady breaths, feeling his warmth radiating against her skin. 'Twas the most wonderful of times, the most wonderful of places.

She could only pray that it would last a very long time.

CHAPTER 21

*W*here the bloody hell were Alec's men? They seemed to be disappearing one by one.

They had been working in a field east of the keep since early morning, to prepare it for planting the following spring. They'd been having a rather difficult day, fighting a battle with a very stubborn auld tree trunk. The tree itself had been easy to cut down. But the roots were deep, wide spread, and entrenched. No matter how far down they dug, no matter how hard they pulled, it refused to budge.

Alec had sent Gylys to the keep first, for a team of horses and a message for his wife, asking her to bring his lunch to the fields. When Gylys hadn't returned in what Alec deemed a reasonable amount of time, he sent Kyth after him. A half an hour later, he sent Willis after the both of them, with the threat of disembowelment if they didn't hurry the bloody hell along.

Thus far, none of the men had returned. His patience was growing as thin and fine as a rabbit's hair. He, Derrick and Dougall were left to battle the deeply rooted tree alone.

"Would ye like me to go fetch the lot of them?" Derrick asked as he wiped the sweat from his brow.

"Nay!" Alec ground out as he stabbed his shovel into the earth. "I shall do it meself."

"Would ye like me to have a platform erected? So ye can hang the lazy lot of them?" Dougall asked.

He knew the man's offer was not in jest and he was half-tempted to give the order. "Go with me and gather the bloody horses I asked for. I shall find out what the hell the men are up to that keeps them from their work."

As they headed back to the keep, Derrick grunted his agreement. "Knowin' Gylys and Kyth as I do, the two of them are most likely sittin' at yer wife's table, gobblin' down that stew she makes. 'Tis all they talk about, yer wife's cookin'."

He looked positively perturbed, if not wholly wounded. "I make a good stew as well. But did ye ever once hear them say as such? Ye'd think she be the only woman on the planet ever to cook anythin'. Well they can bloody well rot as far as I be concerned."

Amused by Derrick's tirade, Dougall patted him on the back. "Do no' worry it over much, Derrick. Ye will find ye a lass someday. One who will appreciate yer cookin'."

ALEC, DOUGALL, AND DERRICK SPLIT WAYS AFTER PASSING THROUGH THE second gate. Derrick went off to do what Gylys, Kyth, and Willis were to supposed to have done more than an hour ago. Alec went in search of the defectors. Somehow, he couldn't help but believe Derrick was correct and his wife was to blame. The men were likely all sitting down at Alec's table, eating *his* food, and enjoying the company of *his* wife. The ungrateful curs.

Mad as hell, he stomped up the steps, flung open the heavy doors and went inside. "They'll be cleanin' chamber pots for the next six months," he mumbled under his breath.

The sound of voices, men's voices, filtered from the gathering room into the foyer. *I knew it!* He screamed silently. *The lazy bastards are enjoyin' a fine lunch while the rest of us are workin'...*

His angry musings were brought to an abrupt halt when he stepped from the shadows and into the room.

There, on the far side of the gathering room, was Gylys. On a ladder, with a wet rag in one hand, a drying cloth hanging from his sword belt. Chatting happily away as he cleaned the mantle. "I used to help me mum clean when I was a lad," he said. "But if ye e'er repeat that, I'll deny it while I gut the lot of ye. Save fer ye, mistress."

In the center of the room, were Kyth and Willis, next to a chandelier that had been brought to the floor. They seemed to be as happy as Gylys as they cleaned the iron with rags. "Do no' fash yerself over it, mistress. We be glad to help ye."

Two other men were sweeping the floor. Another was hanging a tapestry on the wall.

To his right, was his wee wife. Sitting on a chair, directing the men. Nay, not *the* men. *His* men.

"The candles be in a crate in the hallway. If ye could put those in before ye raise the chandelier, I would be verra grateful."

"Aye, mistress," Kyth answered with a bright smile.

Alec could not have been more stunned. Or more angry.

He thundered into the room and stood before his wife. "Me men are warriors. Me men are farmers. They are no' bloody maids!"

His booming voice all but shook the rafters. Everyone in the room halted what they were doing. Hands were suspended in midair, eyes were wide with fear and shock.

Leona sat frozen, staring up at her husband, her eyes as wide as trenchers, and her mouth had fallen open.

"What in the bloody hell is goin' on?" he demanded through gritted teeth as he towered over her. 'Twas then he noticed a trickle of blood on her forehead. "And why the bloody hell are ye bleedin'?"

Gylys gave her no time to answer. "Now Alec, as God is me witness, I tried to keep her from harm, I swear it. I caught her, but no' before she hit her head on the table goin' down."

Alec spun to face his wife's champion. "Goin' down?"

Gylys climbed down from the ladder, wiped his hands on the dry rag in his belt before tossing the wet into a bucket on the table. "I swear to ye, I'd rather be gutted than any harm come to yer wife. I do no' think I was ever more terrified in me life. And I never moved so fast in all me life. But I was no' fast enough."

Alec let out a breath of frustration. The man was blathering on, and it didn't make a damned bit of sense. "Just tell me what happened."

Gylys glanced at Leona before turning his attention back to his laird and chief. "Well, I was just comin' into the keep, to give her the message, like ye asked. She was up on the ladder, cleanin' the mantle." He gave a quick nod toward the other hearth. "Well, she leaned over a bit too far, ye ken. When I saw she was goin' to fall, I all but flew across the room to catch her. I did, I did catch her, but she still hit her head on the table as we were fallin' to the floor."

Alec paled. *She could have been killed.*

Turning back to his wife, he said, "Why in God's name were ye on a ladder?"

She swallowed twice before she could answer. With a bloody rag pressed against her scalp, she answered. "The mantle needed cleanin'."

Tamping down the anger, pushing aside the thought of what he would do if he lost her, he crouched low to look at her injury. Gently, he pushed her hand aside for closer inspection. 'Twas an awful gash that would no doubt require stitches.

Speaking over his shoulder to Gylys, he asked, "How soon before the healer arrives?"

Gylys' silence and the fearful expression on his wife's face said plenty.

He knew the answer before asking the question. "Ye did no' call fer the healer, did ye?"

Leona gave a slow shake of her head. "I will be fine, truly I will."

Before he could give her his own assessment of the situation, a young lad appeared beside him. "Here be the salve ye asked for, mistress. And the bandages."

Alec could only stare in confusion at the salve and bandages in the extended hand beside him.

"Thank ye, kindly, Albert," Leona said as she carefully took the items and placed them in her lap.

"Ye can no' fix yer head with salve and bandages." Was his wife insane? Had she gone mad?

"Those be no' fer her head, m'laird. Those be fer her hands," the young man explained.

Alec stared at his wife for a long moment, waiting for an explanation. With a roll of his eyes, he handed the items back to the boy and took her hands in his. She winced slightly when he turned her palms upward.

In addition to the blisters and callouses on her fingers — things he had not noticed until this very moment — there were long, red abrasions running across her palms. Several blisters had been torn open, oozing and red. "What happened?" he demanded to know.

Again, she remained silent as he waited yet again for an explanation. When none was forthcoming, he stood to his full height. "Will someone explain to me what the bloody hell happened to me wife's hands?"

The men had gathered around him. None was quick to offer an explanation. Were they protecting his wife?

"Gylys?" Alec said as he crossed his arms over his chest.

"Well, Alec, now, do no' be mad at yer wife. 'Twas nay her fault the pulley broke."

"Whether or no' I be mad at me wife is none of yer concern, Gylys. What should concern ye is how I might kill ye if ye do no' start givin' me straight answers."

There was just enough anger in his tone to let all those standing about know he was going to have them all drawn and quartered.

"Well, ye see, after I volunteered to clean the mantles for her, she decided to clean the chandeliers. She was bringin' the first one down when the pulley broke," Gylys explained.

"Aye," Kyth interjected. "And I was standin' under it, fer I had just come in to see what was keepin' Gylys."

"Aye, 'tis the truth, Alec," Gylys agreed with a nod.

"And then what happened?" Alec asked as he began rubbing his forehead. A dull throb was beginning to form behind his eyes.

"Well, she saw what was about to happen, that Kyth was about to get killed by the fallin' chandelier, so she grabbed the rope and let out a scream. She did her best, she did, to keep it from crashin' down on him." Pride filled eyes and another warm smile directed at Leona.

"And that is how she got the burns on her hands," Alec surmised.

"Aye. But ye'll be glad to ken I *did* catch her that time," Gylys added.

Alec looked up at him, wholly confused.

Gylys swallowed hard. "Ye see, the chandelier weighs a hell of a lot more than yer wee wife. The weight of it was pullin' her into the air. I reckon 'twas terrifyin', bein' lifted so high into the air so quickly. So she let go without givin' it much thought."

Leona spoke up then. "I did apologize to ye, Gylys. Several times."

Gylys gave her a warm smile. "Aye, ye did, lass."

"Apologized fer what?" Alec asked.

Another glance exchanged betwixt the two of them. "Fer scarin' him half to death. And more than once in the same day." Leona replied softly.

At then end of his own rope, Alec gave his head a shake. "And that be when ye caught her?" *Please, God let this be the end of the story for I fear I can no' take much more.*

"Aye, I did." Gylys beamed proudly.

Alec took a step back as well as a deep breath. When he saw the fear in his wife's eyes, 'twas all he could do to keep from screaming, from demanding she never look at him that way again.

She could no longer hold back the tears. They streamed down her cheeks and dripped off her chin. "I be terribly sorry, Alec. I try, I truly do. But I can no' do it all, all the time. Sometimes, I need a little help."

His chest tightened, his gut twisted with guilt. He scooped her up into his arms and headed toward the stairs. "Call the bloody healer now, you eejits! Or I'll have ye all hung by nightfall!"

"I can walk, Alec, truly I can," Leona told him as he thundered up the stairs.

"With the day ye're havin', ye'll break yer neck fallin' down the stairs," he ground out.

She winced when she wrapped her arms around his neck. Her hands stung, her muscles ached, but fear kept her from complaining. *Lord, what is he goin' to do?*

He said not a word as he stomped down the hallway. Muttered not a sound when he kicked open the door to their bedchamber. Didn't so much as bat an eye as he gently laid her on their bed.

Good lord, he has lost his mind! He's goin' to kill me.

He studied her closely for a brief moment. Lifting the hair away from her forehead so he could look once again at her wound. A large knot had formed, the skin just beginning to turn purple. 'Twas not bleeding as much now, but it would still require stitches. But what bothered him most were the dark circles under her eyes. He'd noticed them before and had told her days ago he thought she was working too hard. Now he knew, they weren't brought on by lack of sleep. She was utterly exhausted.

"Gylys!" he shouted over his shoulder.

He hadn't needed to, for Gylys and Kyth were standing right behind him. "Aye, Alec?" Gylys replied, startling Alec.

"Bring me hot water and cloths. And find out what is taking the healer so long!"

"Ye've only just sent for her, Alec," Leona politely reminded him as soon as the two men left the room.

He responded with a furious glower.

A long moment passed before he finally spoke. "I told ye days ago ye were workin' too hard. I told ye to stop."

Stop? He *was* mad. Completely insane. "And just which of me chores would ye like me to stop doin'?" Her head throbbed, and not just from the knot gained from hitting the table. "The cookin'? The cleanin'? Or the laundry or gatherin' eggs, or haulin' the ten buckets of water up here each night just so ye can have a hot bath? Or should I give up the mendin' and sewin' or gatherin' rushes?" She was growing angrier by the moment.

His brow furrowed in confusion and she had only given him a small list of the things she did each day.

"Ye bring up the water for me bath?" he asked, completely stunned and perplexed.

Leona rolled her eyes, wishing she was brave enough to clout him on his dense noggin' with a chamber pot. "Who did ye *think* was bringin' it? Faeries?"

He opened his mouth, but the words wouldn't come. "But …"

Letting loose an exceedingly frustrated breath, she closed her eyes and counted to ten before going on. "Ye will no' allow anyone to work inside the keep. Ye told me the day we arrived that none work here, do ye no' remember?"

In truth, he didn't remember the conversation in its entirety. Oh, he remembered being overcome with lust and desire, as was typical whenever she was near. Or whenever he thought of her. But their conversation? Nay, he could not say he remembered it.

"Why did ye no' ask me fer help?" he murmured.

She swiped away an errant tear. *Would ye have given it to me?*

"And why do ye do it? The bath I mean."

Silence filled the space between them. Hanging as dense and heavy as morning fog. Another tear trailed down her cheek. She wiped it away with her fingertips.

"Leona?" His voice was scratchy with a blend of guilt and curiosity. For the first time since marrying her, he had a need that went beyond the physical. "Please, tell me why ye do that for me."

Wiping her cheeks again, she gave a slight shrug. "The first time, the bath was no' for you, but for me. But ye stole it."

More guilt washed over him. *I am a fool and an eejit.*

"But it made ye so happy that I could no' tell ye the truth of it. And the next day, when ye did it again, well…"

Aggravated by his own ignorance, he ran a hand through his hair. "So ye only did it because ye were afraid to tell me the truth?"

She gave a shake of her head. "Nay," she answered. "I just want ye to be glad ye married me." *I want ye to be proud of me. I want ye to like me.*

Sensing there was more she wasn't saying, he asked, "Ye wanted me to be glad?"

Nodding her head rapidly, she said, "Aye. I want ye to be proud of me. I never want ye to regret marryin' me. Ye could have had any woman ye wanted, but ye agreed to *me*."

Any woman I wanted? No, that was far from the truth. He was a Bowie for the sake of Christ. Women had never exactly fallen over themselves to warm his bed or become his wife. In fact, the only woman to ever voluntarily share his bed — without need of monetary compensation — was Leona.

"I am glad I married ye," he whispered.

His words were meant to give her some relief from her worries. He had hoped they would put an end to her misery. Instead, they seemed only to add to them, for she broke down completely then. A heaping mess of sobs. Sobs and tears that tore through his heart.

He took her into his arms, uncertain what he should do or say.

"Do ye speak the truth?" she asked, sobbing against his chest. "Ye are truly glad? Ye do no' regret marryin' me?"

For a brief moment, he felt like crying himself. Taking in a slow, deep breath to help quash the feelings of guilt, uncertainty, and aye, even adoration toward his wife, he said, "Nay, lass. I have no regrets."

WERE ANYONE TO ASK HER WHY 'TWAS SO IMPORTANT TO HAVE ALEC'S approval, she could not have given them a reasonable explanation. Most of the time, it made little sense to her own mind the *why* of it. That intense need for his approval, for his happiness.

Leona would never ask him for his heart. That would be far too much to ask of any man, let alone Alec Bowie. Nay, she was not the kind of woman a man could or would happily give his heart to.

Far from graceful, elegant, witty or beautiful, with very little to offer other than her cooking and cleaning skills. Nay, she knew all these things to be true. As common as a blade of grass, she was.

Still, there was a little part of her that *needed* someone on this earth to think her more than simply 'common'. Something a notch above would be nice.

Yet when she heard him say he had no regrets, that he was glad he married her, she came undone. Knowing there was a strong possibility he had said the words only as a means of comforting her, didn't truly matter. He had said them.

Nay, they weren't the kinds of words a poet might come up with. Not the kind of words a man deeply and passionately in love with his wife might say, but at the moment, she didn't care.

"Thank ye, Alec," she cried softly against his chest. Melting against him, she felt safe and cared for in his arms. 'Twas not a deeply profound romantic love they felt for one another. 'Twas far from that. But feeling safe and cared for by another person was something she had always wished for. Nay, had *prayed* for on a daily basis for as long as she could remember.

"Wheest, lass, do no' cry," he murmured softly.

'Twas impossible at the moment to keep the tears from falling. Mayhap the tears were due to exhaustion, or the bump on her head, or the burns on her hands. Who knew?

Before he could say anything else that would bring forth more tears, Gylys came into the room. "I have the hot water, Alec. And fresh bandages."

A part of him was relieved his friend was there. Another, larger and far more dangerous part of him wanted to drown him in the bucket he carried. Instead, he simply thanked him, and set about pouring the hot water into a basin.

"Mistress, Allen Bowie is below stairs. He wonders if his laundry be done. I told him ye were indisposed, but that I would at least ask."

Alec was almost too afraid to ask what Gylys was talking about.

"Aye," Leona said. "It be in the laundry, in his basket. Ye can accept his payment on my behalf."

Alec stood in stunned disbelief. "Why in the bloody hell is my wife doin' Allen Bowie's laundry? And what *payment?*"

He took note, once again, of the exchanged glances between his wife and Gylys.

"I needed the coin, Alec, to buy a milk cow," Leona told him as she rubbed her forehead with her fingers.

As if that explained the situation or brought any clarity to the matter.

Seeing his confusion, Leona tried to explain the matter better. "I need a milk cow, but I did no' have the coin. One day, when I was in the laundry, Allen saw me and we got to talkin'. Well, before I knew it, I was agreein' to doin' his laundry fer a set price. Word spread. Now with all the coins earned from the laundry, I can buy a milk cow."

"And do no' ferget the other thing, mistress," Gylys added with a smile.

Leona's face burned crimson. "Almost, Gylys. Mayhap in a few weeks time."

"*What* other thing?" Alec asked her. Forgetting the task at hand, he had filled the basin to overflowing. "Bloody hell," he cursed under his breath as water splashed onto his boots.

"I will no' tell ye about the other thing," Leona answered in a firm tone.

"Why the hell not?" he asked, growing more irritated with what he was learning. He dropped a cloth on the floor and using his booted foot, tried to wipe up the spilled water.

"Because it be a surprise," Gylys explained happily. "And I've been sworn to secrecy, so do no' even think to try to get me to tell ye. I'd rather be drawn and quartered."

Leona giggled at Gylys' reply to his laird and chief.

The more he learned this day, the more he realized he didn't know a damned thing about his wife or the goings on in his own keep. Gylys knew more about her than he did. Infuriated and filled with self-reproach, he had no response. His mind went blank for a long moment.

"Well ye can tell the men they can do their own laundry from now on. Me wife is the *mistress* of this keep, not a bloody laundress!" His heavy boots thudded against the wood floor as he went to tend to his wife's injuries.

Angrily, he set the basin on the table beside the bed and sat beside her.

"But Alec, I need the coin," she argued, visibly horrified that he'd even suggest she give up her laundry services.

"I will give ye whatever ye need." He dipped a cloth into the basin and wrung it out.

"But I must do this one thing on me own."

"Why?" he asked as he began to gently wash away the blood from her forehead.

"Ye would no' understand," she told him.

He sighed inwardly. Aye, there were many things that he did not understand, especially when it came to his wife. "Ye think me so dumb? Too dumb to understand a thing?"

"Nay," she said, wincing when he touched the cut. "I think ye're too easy to anger."

The cut began to bleed again. Cursing again under his breath, he shouted at Gylys. "Where the bloody hell is the healer?"

Startled, Gylys gave a curt nod to each before quitting the room in a hurry.

"Please do no' yell, Alec. It hurts me head."

"I am no' yellin'!"

A quirked brow told him she begged to differ.

"'Tis impossible no' to yell this day," he began in a harsh tone. "Me wife is nearly killed no' once, but twice. Then I learn she's been carryin' countless buckets of water above stairs each day fer me bath. I also learn she has been hired by me men as a laundress. What will ye tell me next, lass? Have ye been choppin' wood as well?"

"No' any more," she replied. "Willem Bowie does that fer me in exchange fer a hot meal or two. He also gets water from the well for me, that is when he remembers and is sober enough."

Chopping wood. Hauling water. Laundry. Cooking, cleaning, and God only knew what else his wife had been doing these past weeks. 'Twas enough to make a grown man lose his mind.

None of it made a damned bit of sense. "I had agreements with men to take care of those things fer ye. The milk, the wood, the water, venison, all those things were to have been given to ye or done fer ye."

Embarrassed, her cheeks flamed red. "I ken that. But, well …"

"Well, what?"

"Charles had one problem after another with bringin' me the milk. First, his child was sick, then the cow kicked over the bucket and he had none to spare. Another day 'twas too rainy. And another day, he was ill. I finally sent word that he need no' bother, I'd buy me own cow."

"And the wood? The water?" He wasn't so sure he wanted to know the answers.

Ashamed, with eyes downcast, she answered, "Much the same."

His anger flared again. But this time, for far different reasons. He crossed the floor in a few short strides and flung open the door. "Gylys! Kyth!" His deep, booming voice rattling Leona's nerves.

"I asked ye no' to yell," she whispered. Apparently, he hadn't heard her plea for quiet.

"Gylys! Kyth!" he yelled again.

"Ye're goin' to run them ragged with all the runnin' up and down the stairs," she told him.

A moment later, the two men appeared, out of breath.

"Bring Amartha and Felicia Bowie to me, along with their oldest sons."

"Before or after we find out where the healer be?" Kyth asked.

The intense throbbing in his head intensified. Oh, he tried gallantly not to yell, he truly did. "I think betwixt the lot of ye," he began in a low voice. But his anger continued to swell. "Ye might be able to do both. Before I hang ye! Fer the sake of Christ, ask someone to help ye if ye must!"

Alec slammed the door shut on the two men before spinning around to face his wife.

Reposed in the bed, with the bloody rag once again pressed against her injury, she looked utterly and wholly exhausted. Worry settled in around his heart. From experience, he knew a head injury, even a seemingly insignificant one, could kill a man. Or, at the very least, leave him addlepated and unable to function normally. For the first time in as long as he could remember, he began to pray. Pray silently that God would watch over his wife and not take her from him. *Please,* he said silently. *Please do no' take her from me.*

WITH THE MEN OFF TO FIND THE HEALER AS WELL AS THE OTHER PEOPLE he'd asked to see, he was left alone with his wife. She leaned back against the headboard with her eyes closed, and the rag still pressed against her forehead.

"Leona." He had to clear the knot from his throat before he could continue. "I…" The words were there, in his heart, but he'd grown cowardly. No matter how much he wanted to speak them, he couldn't.

Finally, he went to sit on the bed beside her. Gently, he took her free hand in his own. "Leona," he began, in a low, hushed tone. "I will no' have ye workin' so hard again. I swear it."

She said not a word. A long moment passed by before he realized she had fallen asleep. "Leona," he called to her again, more loudly this time.

Her eyes flew open at the sound of her name. "What?"

"I need ye to stay awake, lass. At least until the healer gives ye permission to sleep."

"I was no' sleepin'," she groused. "I was merely closing me eyes." *And doin' me best no' to clout ye over the head with a candlestick.*

"Ye can no' sleep until the healer sees ye," he told her, ignoring her previous declaration that she was doing no such thing.

"Why no'?" she asked, irritated with him as much as she was with her self.

He gave her an incredulous look. "Because ye have had a serious wound to yer head."

"We have already established that. Now, tell me, why I can no' just close me eyes fer a wee moment."

"Because ye might no' wake again."

Skeptically, she rolled her eyes. "Ye're daft."

"Am I?" he asked. "I've seen it happen. In battle."

Before he could explain what he'd seen in battle, Gylys reappeared at their door. He had Derrick with him.

Leona watched as the men huddled together. She couldn't hear what they were discussing at first. Occasionally, they would look her way. They were behaving like conspiratorial spies, speaking in hushed tones that were at times, harsh, and others, nearly sorrowful. Instinctively, she knew that whatever they were discussing, it was not going to bode well for her.

"The healer is over at Tom Bowie's," Gylys told him, in a low voice, as soon as Alec opened the door. "His wife is birthin' their first bairn and is havin' problems. They say she might no' make it through."

As much as Alec cared for his own wife, there was no way he would drag the healer away from her current situation. "Damn," Alec whispered his reply.

"I've sewn up plenty of wounds," Derrick told him. "But I'll no' lay a hand to yer wife."

"Why the hell no'?" Alec demand to know.

"Because she be *yer* wife. And ye're fond of her. And I fear if I cause her the slightest discomfort, ye'll gut me like a trout."

Alec let out a long breath as he raked a hand through his hair. "I would do no such thing," Alec told him. Without saying a word, Derrick's expression said he knew Alec was lying through his teeth.

Derrick spoke nothing but the truth.

When next he looked to Gylys for help, the man shook his head. "Nay, do no' ask me to do it."

There would be not a Bowie man around who would volunteer to sew up his wife's head. Not because they did not care, but because they were not brave enough to anger their chief and laird.

"Verra well," he ground out. "I shall do it meself."

They all turned to look at Leona then. Her brow furrowed with a good deal of suspicion.

"I shall get the mendin' kit," Derrick offered hastily.

"I shall help him," Gylys said with a curt bow as they both left the room in a good deal of haste.

"Really, Alec, I do no' think stitches be necessary," Leona told him as she tried scooting away from her husband.

He was sitting on the edge of the bed, with Derrick, Gylys, Dougall, and Kyth flanking them on all sides.

"Leona," Alec said as he scooted her back to the edge of the bed. "This *needs* to be done. The gash continues to bleed."

She stared into her husband's eyes, her own filled with a good deal of trepidation. "It will eventually stop," she argued.

"Aye," Alec said. "When ye've lost every drop of blood in yer wee body."

Certainly he must be exaggerating. She looked to the men surrounding them. Nay, she'd find no help there. Each man looked quite serious, and kept nodding their heads in agreement with her husband.

"Mayhap, we should wait for the healer?" she all but begged for a delay.

Alec was doing his best to maintain his composure. "It could be hours before she is able to help. By then, it could be too late."

Too late?

Convinced her husband was simply over-reacting, she ignored the threat in his comment. She also realized there was no other way around it. If he had to drug her and have his men hold her down, he was going to stitch up her head. No matter her own opinion on the matter.

With a roll of her eyes, she sat up in the bed and straightened her skirts. "Verra well," she began. "But do no' tarry. I have much work to do."

Her statement elicited expressions from each man of astonishment that questioned her soundness of mind.

"Would ye like me to knock her out, Alec?" Derrick asked thoughtfully. "So she will no' feel anythin'?"

"Ye'll do no such thing!" Alec and Leona replied in unison.

Derrick replied with a shrug of his shoulders and nothing else.

"What about a tonic?" Gylys asked. "I could make one up that will put her to sleep."

"That might no' be a bad idea," Alec replied.

Leona held up her hand. "I would appreciate it if you would all quit behaving as though I'm no' even here. I will *no'* be knocked out. No' by Derrick or by a tonic."

"Stitches can be a might painful," Dougall offered up.

"Aye," Kyth replied. "Ye're such a wee thing, mistress. 'Twill hurt like the devil."

Just what her size had to do with the matter, she could not begin to guess.

"If I were a *Bowie* woman, would ye still wish to knock me out?" she asked them.

"Ye *are* a Bowie woman," Alec replied, his tone firm and resolute.

Her heart swelled with pride then, and the tears began to fall.

The men shared puzzled expressions. "What be the matter, mistress?" Kyth asked.

"Be ye in pain?" Derrick asked with a hopeful expression. As if he could not wait to *knock her out.*

"Nay," Gylys answered for her. "I fear she does no' want to be a Bowie." He was unmistakably sorrowful with that thought.

Alec let out a long, heavy breath as his men discussed why his wife was crying. "Lads," he called out to them. When he'd gained their attention, he said, "Shut up. Me wife is neither sad, nor in pain, nor does she not wish to be a Bowie."

"Then why be she cryin'?" Gylys asked.

Leona sniffed, swiped away a few tears, and smiled up at him. "Because I be so happy!"

〜

It took every ounce of strength Alec had to keep his hands from shaking. With nerves of steel, he stitched together her skin, wishing for all the world the needle was in the hands of the healer and not his own.

He had to give credit to his wife, though, for she barely flinched as he poked the bone needle through her skin. She didn't utter a word of protest, neither did she complain it hurt. Nay, she lay as still as death, with her eyes closed, as she held onto Dougall's hand. The rest of the men watched with keen interest, occasionally offering words of encouragement.

"Thank ye, Alec," Leona said when he announced he had completed the task. She wasn't certain, but she thought she heard a tremor in his voice.

When all was said and done, it took seven stitches to mend the gash. Gylys smiled proudly, as he stood at the foot of the bed and held out his hand, palm up. One by one the other men placed a coin into his palm. Apparently a wager had been set betwixt them.

Staring at the sight, she asked, "What on earth?"

The men smiled at her. Alec busied himself with the basin filled with bloody water and pretended not to know what was happening. He didn't care. All he wanted was to sit in a quiet corner and knock back a few drams of whisky.

It wasn't as if that was the first time he'd ever stitched someone back together. But they'd all been men. Not his wee, sweet wife. 'Twas an altogether unsettling ordeal and one he wished never to repeat.

"Will someone tell me why ye're givin' Gylys coins?" Leona asked, perplexed.

"'Twas just a friendly wager, mistress," Gylys told her.

Appalled, she gave a slight shake of her head. "Did ye wager whether or no' I'd cry or complain? Or that I'd pass out from fright?"

The men were doing their best not to smile or laugh. Dougall's shoulders were shaking as he turned his back and stepped away. With one hand on the doorjamb, the other on his waist, he continued to shake, holding onto the laughter he wished he could let go of.

"Well?" she asked, growing more frustrated with their silence.

Gylys cleared his throat, came around the bed and bent down to whisper in her ear. "The wager was no' about ye cryin' or passin' out, mistress. We all wagered on whether or not Alec would."

~

LEONA WOULD RATHER DIE THAN ADMIT TO HOW BADLY IT HURT. THE entire ordeal left her feeling exhausted. But she'd not let anyone know that, least of all her husband. She'd do nothing to diminish herself in front of him or his men.

After the men left, Alec returned to sit beside her. "Would ye like to cry now?" There was a playfulness to his tone. One she didn't appreciate.

"Ye act like I cry at the drop of a feather," she groused. "Now, if ye will stop hoverin' over me, I need to begin preparin' the evenin' meal."

Alec reached out and held her hand down on the bed. "Ye'll be doin' no such thing," he told her. "Ye are goin' to rest."

"But I thought ye said I could no' sleep until the healer saw me?" she asked sarcastically.

He pinned her in place with a hard stare.

"If ye do no' want me fallin' asleep, then I must remain busy. Now, quit bein' silly and let me leave. I have much work to do."

"Ye're no' leavin' this bed until the healer sees ye and until *I* say ye can."

"Really, Alec, do you no' think ye're overreactin' just a might?"

He gave a slow shake of his head. "Nay, I do no'. Ye have worked yerself to the point of exhaustion as it is. Ye have blisters and callouses on yer hands. Ye nearly killed yerself twice today," he ticked off his reasons one by one. "And I'll be damned if ye're goin' to be cookin' or cleanin' or anything else this night. Or any other day."

He left her alone on the bed while he went to her trunk. Searching around, he finally found what he was looking for. "Put this on," he said as he handed her the garment. 'Twas one of her auld, heavy sleeping gowns. Since she'd married him, there had been no need for such things.

"Ye can no' be serious."

"Aye, I am," he told her. As he was about to tell her she was not to leave this bed for the foreseeable future, someone knocked on their door. He hoped it was the healer and that she would be able to talk some sense into his stubborn wife.

'Twas only Kyth.

"Alec," he whispered in a hushed tone. "Amartha and Felicia Bowie are below stairs."

Alec had almost forgotten he had sent for them. He turned to speak to his wife. "Ye are to remain in that bed until I return," he ordered. "And to ensure ye do that, Kyth here will be keepin' ye company."

Leona rolled her eyes for what seemed the hundredth time in the past hour. "Ye be a cruel man, Alec Bowie. A stubborn, cruel man!"

He smiled warmly at her. "Thank ye, kindly, wife. I am glad ye think so."

To Kyth he said, "If she makes any attempt to leave this room, ye have me permission to tie her to a chair if ye must. And do no' allow her to sleep until the healer sees her."

"I'll no' let her leave, nor allow her to sleep," Kyth said.

Alec studied him closely for a moment. With a heavy sigh, he quit the room. *Knowin' me wife, she'll be orderin' the poor man around left and right.*

AMARTHA AND FELICIA BOWIE STOOD PERPLEXED BEFORE THEIR LAIRD, looking at him as if he'd just sprouted two tails. Where Amartha was squat and round, Felicia was tall and slender. Where Felicia's face was clear from any blemish, Amartha's sported a most distracting mole on her lower jaw. A prickly hair had sprouted from its center. Alec was doing his best not to stare too long at it.

Felicia was younger by a good ten years. Both were widows with children of varying ages.

"What be the matter?" he asked, confused by their response to his offer.

The two women cast a glance at each other before turning back to him. 'Twas Amartha who spoke up first. "M'laird, I have three children to tend to. I can no' possibly come to work fer ye."

He knew for a fact that her children were nearly grown. Hell, her oldest was nearing six and ten and already training with his warriors.

"As do I, m'laird," Felicia Bowie added.

While her sons were not as old as Amartha's, they were still old enough to help in the keep. Why were they so reluctant?

"Amartha, yer children are old enough to tend to themselves. As fer ye, Felicia, I thought yer lads old enough to work in the keep. They could fetch water and kindlin' and the like."

Another furtive glance between the two women. Aye, there was something definitely amiss.

"I fear I can no' help ye, m'laird," Amartha reiterated.

Felicia nodded her head rapidly in agreement.

Alec crossed his arms over his chest and studied each of them closely. Instinct was telling him there was much more to their unwillingness to assist his wife.

"Could ye no' use the extra coin?" he asked. "I am willin' to pay ye quite handsomely."

Their furtive glances back and forth were beginning to annoy him. Letting out an exasperated sigh, he gave a slow shake of his head. "Why do ye both just tell me the real reasons why ye are refusin' to work in the keep."

Felicia swallowed hard and stepped noticeably closer to her cohort. Amartha, mayhap because she was older, was far less afraid of her laird. "I will tell ye the why of it m'laird," she said as she pulled her shoulders back and lifted her chin. "There be no' a woman in this clan who will come to work fer yer wife. No' a one."

Her explanation did nothing but raise his ire. "What do ye mean?" he asked, as he placed his hands on his hips and leaned over to look her in the eye.

She barely flinched. Felicia, however, let go her grip on her friend's arm and took a few steps back.

"I mean exactly what I said, m'laird," she said with an affirming nod. "There be none here who will work in this keep, at least no' fer *her*."

Her. The word dripped venomously from her tongue.

"Why?" he asked, through gritted teeth.

"Because she be no' a Bowie," Amarath replied haughtily.

It made absolutely no sense to him. For clarification, he asked, "Do you mean to tell me, that no one will come to work in the keep because me wife is no' a Bowie?"

"Aye, I mean just that, m'laird. No one wants her here. Ye should ne'er have married the likes of *her*. Ye should have married within the clan."

With that, he reached the end of his patience.

Spinning on his heel, he began shouting for his men as he made his way toward the foyer. "Gylys! Kyth!" he bellowed as he stomped across the room. Before leaving, he turned to face the two women. "Neither of ye are to leave that spot until me order! Do ye understand?"

There was no mistaking his fury. The women remained silent, answering with fast nodding heads.

Gylys came from one side of the gathering room, while Kyth entered through the foyer. "M'laird, what be the matter?" Kyth asked.

"I want every woman within five miles of this keep assembled at once. In the courtyard in the next quarter hour. *Every one of them*," he ground out through gritted teeth. "If they refuse, they can bloody well consider it an act of treason and will be thrown as far away from this clan as possible!"

Neither man had the courage to ask why he was making such an order. Bounding up the stairs two at a time, Alec went to his wife. He would need more information about who had refused his orders before he set his clan on its side.

~

WITHIN HALF AN HOUR, THE WOMENFOLK AND THEIR HUSBANDS, WERE assembled in the yard where the men trained. Alec chose that spot for two reasons. One, 'twas the only place large enough to hold all of them, and two, 'twas far enough away from their bedchamber that Leona would not be able to hear what was about to take place.

Stepping onto the small stage they sometimes used to watch the men during training, he made no attempt to hide his anger. Gylys, Kyth, and Dougall stood directly in front of the stage, with arms crossed over their chests and feet planted apart.

Looking out at the crowd, Alec shook his head with disgust. His people were as quiet as they were perplexed by the sudden demand for their presence. As per his order, Amartha and Felicia stood front and center, just steps away from the stage.

"It has just now been brought to my attention," he began as he glared at Amartha and Felicia, "that me clan has decided they do no' like me wife. They have decided amongst themselves to treat her poorly and with disrespect. Nay because she be a mean, vile woman. Nay, ye do this because ye're angry with *me* for marryin' outside the clan. Ye're angry with *my* choice of a bride."

As he spoke, he could see some women shrinking away, whilst others donned proud, haughty expressions. The men, however, were looking at him as if he'd lost his mind. 'Twas just as he thought; 'twas the womenfolk and their jealousy at play here.

"Because ye be angry with *me,* ye've taken it upon yerselves to make me wife suffer. Instead of comin' to me with yer concerns or worries." He gave a slow, appalled shake of his head. "Never in all me days have I been more ashamed of a group of people!" He drew out his words slowly.

Next, he spoke directly to Charles Bowie. "Charles, ye and I had an agreement, did we no', fer ye to bring me wife a bit of milk each day?"

Charles blinked in confusion. "Aye, we did. And I have sent milk to her nearly every morn, Alec, just as ye asked."

"No' according to me wife," Alec replied angrily as he looked directly at Charles's wife.

"But, Alec! I swear we have sent it!" 'Twas then he noticed Alec staring directly at his wife. Turning his attention to her, Charles asked, "Myra?"

She refused to look at him. Instead, she stared at the ground at her feet. Her cheeks burned brightly with either shame or embarrassment. "Myra?" he asked again, this time, taking her shoulders in his hands and forcing her to look at him. "Ye said ye were takin' her the milk. Why did ye lie?"

In a low, harsh whisper, she said, "I will no' discuss it with ye here, Charles."

While Charles chastised his wife, Alec turned to his next target. "Philip!" he shouted, drawing the man's attention. "Ye sold me venison, did ye no'?"

"Aye, I did, and fer a good price," the man replied with a raised brow.

"Then I would like me money back, fer 'twas never brought to us."

Astonished, Philip first turned to his son, a lad of mayhap three and ten. "Did ye no' take the venison to our mistress as I asked?"

His son was just as surprised as his father. "Mum said no' to!" he exclaimed as they both stared at May Bowie.

"Dewey Bowie!" Alec called out at the crowd as he searched for the man and his wife.

The man stepped forward with a look of shame. "Let me guess, no wood was brought to ye."

Alec nodded and looked out at his people. His thoughts turned to the day his wife had been locked in the tiny room. He wondered if the person responsible was out there, amongst his people. Had their anger over his decision to marry Leona reduced someone to the point of attempting to murder his wife? Had that been their intent all along? Were they so incensed, so angry over it they would stop at nothing to undo his decision? It was entirely possible they hadn't meant just to scare her.

His people.

There stood someone among them who had tried to kill his wife.

The thought sickened him.

As the crowd murmured and men argued with their wives, he

closed his eyes and counted to ten before speaking again. "I married Leona MacDowall to bring peace to our clan. She be a fine young woman who has done no' a thing to deserve yer mistreatment." He paused long enough to draw a breath. "It ends here. It ends now."

He gave one last lingering glance at his people before stepping down from the stage and returning to his wife. Alec could only pray that the person responsible for locking his wife away understood, unequivocally, the underlying message of his words.

OH, POOR, POOR LEONA! BAH! 'TIS NOTHIN' MORE THAN A BUMP ON HER *head. No more than wee scratches on her hands and they all look after her as though she'd just been wounded in battle. Just wait until I get my hands on her. She'll know true sufferin' then.*

But I must be careful. I can no' move too quickly. I need to wait until Alec realizes just how much he really loves her. Then, and only then, can I make my move.

I lay in bed at night just thinkin' of all the ways I can kill her. So far, I be favorin' the knife. Oh, to slice that pretty face! To carve out those wicked, witch eyes of hers. To make her scream and suffer and pray fer mercy. But I shan't show her any, for she deserves none.

CHAPTER 22

The healer had finally arrived, long after the midnight hour. In the interim, Alec had done his best to keep his wife awake, though 'twasn't easy. The poor lass was exhausted, and he knew 'twas all his own fault. He had treated her with little care or respect these past weeks. Paying no attention to her unless she was in his bed.

I am such a fool. No better than a cur.

Though he didn't have the courage to apologize outright, he had decided he would do his very best to make it up to her. Just *how* he would manage to do that remained a mystery, but he was going to try.

He let Mairi into the bedchamber, glad and relieved to see her. He hoped he hadn't muddled the stitches or made his wife's condition worse.

Leona remembered her, albeit vaguely, from her very first visit to the Bowie keep. Mairi had been the one to tend to the injuries she had received at Rutger's hands. Mayhap in her mid-thirties, she was a beautiful woman, with bright, light brown eyes and light brown hair, twisted into a long braid.

Alec greeted her at the door, looking much relieved to see her.

"I got here as soon as I could," she explained as she stepped into the bedchamber.

"How be Tomas's wife?" Leona asked as she sat upright in bed.

"She had a beautiful girl. A *big* beautiful girl. Deanna will be well in a few days," she explained as she sat on the bed next to Leona.

"That is good to hear," Leona replied with a tired smile.

"Ye look exhausted," Mairi remarked.

"She is," Alec interjected as he stood beside her.

"I am fine, truly," Leona argued gruffly, giving her husband an frustrated look of reproach.

"Ye can leave us now, Alec," Mairi told him.

"I will stay." His voice was firm, determined.

"Nay, ye will no'," Mairi told him. "Ye're goin' to leave and ye're goin' to leave now. Elst I'll no' tend to yer wife."

"Might I remind ye that I am yer chief and laird?" he asked, in perturbation.

"Ye can remind me of it all ye want *after* I look to yer wife. Now, be gone with ye."

Leona had to bite her lip to keep from laughing. Oh, how she wished she was a bit more like Mairi and able to speak to her husband in the same firm, no-nonsense tone.

For a long moment, Alec debated on whether or not he'd listen. "Verra well, but I shall be right outside the door should ye need me."

"Nay, ye will no'," Mairi said. "I need ye to go to the kitchen and heat water fer me."

"I'll have Gylys do it," Alec told her.

"Nay, Alec, I need ye to do it," she said. She still hadn't looked at him. She was riffling through her satchel. "Please, Alec, do no' argue it."

Realizing he wasn't going to win, he gave up and quit the room.

"Thank ye!" Leona exclaimed in a hushed tone.

"Ye be verra welcome, lass."

"He has been hoverin' over me all the day long."

Mairi fished out clean bandages and several pouches. "Tell me what happened," she said.

Leona explained the events of the day as best she could. "And he has had me in this bed ever since. He will no' even allow me to use the chamber pot without his help. 'Tis maddening."

Mairi smiled and gave a shake of her head. "'Tis because he cares, lass."

After the way Alec had behaved this afternoon, she no longer doubted he cared about her. Aye, it did make her feel happy and content to come to that realization.

"Ye should take advantage of this time, lass," Mairi told her as she began to examine the stitches.

"Take advantage?" Leona asked.

"Would it no' be nice to rest fer a day or so? From what I am told, ye've been working quite hard these past weeks."

That much was true. "But I *like* takin' care of Alec and our home. It makes me feel as if I have a purpose."

Mairi frowned. "Yer purpose is to be his wife, the future mother of his children, and his strongest ally. No' his personal slave."

Leona laughed. "Alec did no' make me his slave, Mairi. I am merely trying to ..." She paused, trying to find the right words to explain everything without sounding like a simpleton.

Mairi quirked a brow. "Ye were tryin' to impress him, aye?"

Leona gave a quiet nod. If she were to admit it, she was trying to get him to *see* her. To see her as more than just the woman who warmed his bed at night. She wanted, nay needed, more than that.

"I saw the way he looked at ye, lass. Ye needn't worry."

"Worry?" Leona asked with a furrowed brow.

Mairi smiled warmly. "Ye've impressed him."

Much to Leona's delight, Mairi had given her permission to sleep. Alec was not as certain as his healer that sleeping just yet was a good idea. "Verra well," Mairi said as she packed up her satchel. "I now declare ye, Alec Bowie, the healer of our clan. Make sure ye check on Maude, down by the creek, on the morrow. She be due to give birth next month. And do no' forget to check on Seamus. He has a boil that needs lancin'."

Alec rolled his eyes, understanding full well what his healer was trying to do. "Fergive me, Mairi," he said. "I shall no' question ye again."

Standing at the door, she smiled up at him. "Ye be forgiven. Most men do worry after their wives, especially those who are as fond of theirs as ye are of yers. Ye be no different than all the rest, Alec Bowie."

Whether it was her knowing smile or the inflection in her tone, the way she said it set his teeth on edge. *I am no like other men,* he told himself. *I am no' some simple-minded weak fool.*

He stood near the open door for a long while after Mairi left, staring at the dark, empty corridor. *I am different,* he mused. Aye, he cared for his wife, but that meant nothing. Any good man would.

Quietly, he closed the door, wondering just how his healer had come to the conclusion that he was fond of his wife and no different than all the rest. Never did he behave as Dougall did, kissing his wife in the presence of others. Nor would he ever give Leona a playful pat on her rump, at least not publicly. And he certainly would never declare his feelings for her with the same brazen passion as Dougall often did for Effie.

Nay, he was not like Dougall, or any other love-struck fool. *Bah!* He declared silently. *Mairi is a foolish woman.*

Leaving the matter to rest, he turned to look at the object of his consternation. She was asleep, on her side, with her hands resting on a pillow. Her lovely, honey colored hair splayed seductively across her pillow and onto his.

Desire rose spontaneously and instantly. Cursing it, he went to the basin and splashed cold water on his face. *Me desire has nothing to do with me feelin's,* he whispered in his mind. *What man wouldn't want such a beautiful and desirable woman?*

Quietly, he removed his clothes and tossed them to the floor by the door. 'Twould be the first night since marrying her that he would not join with her. Nay, tonight she needed her rest, she needed to sleep.

Mayhap in a few days, after her injuries had healed. Then, and only then, would he allow his ardor and lust for his wife to take a strong foothold.

~

HIS INNER PROMISE TO LEAVE HIS WIFE ALONE WAS LONG FORGOTTEN BY morning time. He awoke to the warmth of her round bottom resting against his groin. The scent of her soap, feminine and floral, hung in the cool morning air. Her soft, steady breaths seemed to echo in the silent morning.

Alec made slow, passionate love to her, careful to avoid her injured head and hands. Leona did not seem to mind his early morning loving. In fact, she rather enjoyed it.

Once they both found their pleasure in one another, Leona fell fast asleep. 'Twas wholly unlike her to do so. Typically, she would wait until *he* fell asleep before she would slip out of their bed to go below stairs and begin her day.

But not this day. Nay, their roles would be reversed for the time being. Without giving much thought to it, Alec pressed a tender kiss to her forehead, slipped from the bed and dressed. As he entered the gathering room, he came upon Gylys, who had apparently slept in the chair beside the hearth.

"Gylys," Alec called out. The man jumped to his feet and reached for his sword.

"Bloody hell, Alec!" Gylys ground out before letting lose the breath he'd been holding. "Ye scared the hell out of me!"

Alec laughed at his friend's distress. "Me apologies, Gylys," he said with a bow.

Confused by his laird's unnaturally good mood, Gylys stared at him. "Ye seem to be in fine spirits this morn," Gylys remarked.

Aye, he was. At any other time, he would have forced his smile away and glared angrily at anyone who might comment upon it. But not this morn. "I suppose I am," he said with a shrug. "Leona is asleep. I have something I need to do. Keep a close watch on her, aye?"

Still confused, Gylys offered a simple nod as he watched his laird quit the room.

Alec soon found himself locked out of his wife's kitchen. He made another trip above stairs to retrieve her keys, paying no attention to Gylys who sat in the chair by the hearth. Moments later, he was unlocking the door and stepping inside.

Everything was so neat, tidy, and orderly. And he hadn't a clue as to what most of the implements were for.

"I am the chief of a mighty clan. Certainly, I can scrounge up a bit of eggs and ham fer me wife," he said to the empty room. Bolstering his spirits, he set about to prepare a lovely breakfast for Leona.

By the time he finished wreaking havoc on his wife's most prized possession — her kitchen — he had managed to burn a half dozen eggs as well as three thick slices of ham. And he took three skillets to manage it all.

Letting loose a heavy breath, he decided to make the best of it. Choosing the least burnt of the ham, and the least undercooked eggs, he set them on a trencher. It took a long while to find a tray, for she stored them in the most unusual place — on the shelf under the massive center table. He managed not to cut his fingers as he sliced off a few pieces of brown bread. The honey was not in the larder, as he would have assumed, but out on the long counter next to her spices.

By the time he finished finding what he needed and setting it all on a tray, the ham was cold and the eggs were beginning to congeal. "I never said I was a cook," he said aloud. "And I have certainly eaten far worse than this."

Deciding 'twas the thought that counted more with his wife than the actual outcome, he hurried to take the meal to her.

As he crossed through the gathering room, Gylys and now Kyth, were standing next to the hearth, speaking in hushed tones. Alec said not a word as he walked by, his focus on the tray in his hands.

Alec barely managed to keep from spilling its contents as he struggled with the door to his bedchamber. 'Twas the bundle of dirty clothes he had left by the door that nearly sent him tumbling to the floor.

Righting himself, he crept to his wife's bedside and set the trencher on the floor. "Leona, sweeting," he whispered warmly.

She rolled away, grumbling something incoherent. Something along the lines of how rude it was to wake a person up before the sun.

Chuckling, he took a lock of her hair and tickled the end of her nose. "Leona, I have a surprise for ye."

She snuggled further into the bed. "Thank ye," she whispered, but made no attempt to open her eyes. "But I fear I am too tired fer lovin' just yet. Can we wait until the sun is up?"

He chuckled again and gave her shoulder a gentle pat. "'Tis no' *that* kind of a surprise."

Curiosity won over sleep. Leona rolled over and peeked at him from under the covers. "What kind of surprise is it?" she asked sleepily.

He lifted the tray up and held it before her. "I made ye something to break yer fast."

Stunned, she sat upright and stared at the tray. "Ye cooked for me?" she asked.

He offered her a proud smile. "Aye, I did."

Once she was settled in, Alec set the tray on her lap. "I fear it be no' as good as what ye accomplish."

To Leona's way of thinking, he could have been offering her soup made from grass and it wouldn't have mattered. 'Twas the sentiment, the sincere gesture on his part, that brought tears to her eyes. "Och! Alec!" she exclaimed.

"'Tis no' *that* bad," he said as he poked a knife at the ham. "Just a wee bit burnt around the edges."

"I do no' mean that," she said. "This is one of the nicest things anyone has ever done fer me!"

He quirked a brow. "'Tis just a meal, Leona, no' a ruby encrusted crown."

Of course he couldn't' possibly understand what she meant.

Wholly unused to acts of generosity such as this, she could not help but cry over it. Taking in a deep breath or two, she willed her tears away. "Thank ye, Alec. Thank ye verra much."

∾

AFTER LEONA HAD FINISHED EATING AS MUCH AS SHE WAS ABLE —EITHER from lack of appetite or the unappealing meal — Alec took the tray back to the kitchen, but not before ordering her to stay abed and rest. She made no attempt to argue. Instead, she snuggled back into the covers and closed her eyes. He was quite certain she was asleep before he closed the door.

Once again, he ignored his men, who had now been joined by Derrick. The three men stared with furrowed brows as Alec crossed through the gathering room. Mayhap 'twas the skip in his step, or the smile on his face, or the fact that he was whistling a lively little tune, that stunned them. In truth, 'twas all those things.

They'd never seen their laird quite so happy before.

Alec had made quite a mess preparing the meal for his wife. As he stood amongst the dirty pots and pans, he wondered how his wife was able to keep the space as immaculate as she did. Letting loose with a sigh of resignation, he grabbed two buckets and fetched water from the well.

With the water heating by the fire, he realized he had no idea what to do with the scraps of food. *Mayhap she saves them for the pigs.*

Grabbing an empty bucket from by the door, he scraped the left over bits into it and returned it. Once that task was complete, he tested the water with his fingertips. Still cold. 'Twould do no good, he supposed, to use frigid water to clean.

Once again, he stood looking around. He wondered what his wife would do while she waited for water to warm. *She probably would have done that* before *she started cooking.*

His appreciation for all his wife did increased by leaps and bounds.

"I shall go check the fields first," he declared aloud. "The water should be warm upon my return."

~

DECIDING HE WOULD CHECK ON HIS WIFE BEFORE HEADING TO THE fields, Alec left the kitchen. The sun was shining brightly in the robin's egg blue sky. 'Twould be a good day to be in the fields.

Upon entering the gathering room, he found a small crowd had formed. Derrick and Gylys were still near the hearth, with Kyth standing guard at the bottom of the stairs. In addition to his men, two clanswomen — Hexie and Matildis Bowie, in their early forties — were huddled near the table. The two women could have passed for sisters. Each possessed the same dark brown hair and brown eyes as most of the Bowies. Roundish and buxom, they were each far too old to be wearing such tight and revealing gowns as they wore today. If Matildis were to sneeze, he reckoned the ties on her bodice would break and the goods she had proudly on display would spill out. Probably with much relief.

He could tell by the hushed and harsh tones in which they spoke that there was a problem. A problem he would undoubtedly be expected to solve.

A third person, a bonnie lass whose name he could not recollect, stood apart from them, in the corner by the entrance. Although she was staring at her shoes, Alec took note of the frequent glances she was giving the two other women.

When he had first agreed to become laird, he had decided early on to hold court once a month. There, he would listen to the concerns of his clanspeople, help solve any disputes, and otherwise act as a true laird and chief. But *only* once a month. The rest of the time, his people knew where to find him. As far as he was concerned, he had far more important things to tend to, such as getting his clan out of the financial hole his brother had dug for them.

His last court had been held the day before he left to marry Leona. That was more than a month ago.

"Good day to ye," he said to the women as he stopped a few feet from the table. Inwardly, he hoped this would not take long.

Hexie and Matildis quit whispering to turn their attention to Alec. They each returned his greeting and offered up little curtsies.

Choosing his next words carefully, for he did not want to be all day with trying to fix whatever problem these women had, he said, "I am on my way to the fields."

The two women cast quick glances over their shoulders at the young girl. In a low voice, Hexie said, "We need to speak to ye about the girl, m'laird."

Alec gave a cursory look toward the young girl in question.

"Ye see, m'laird, there be five of us livin' together," Hexie said.

"Aye, 'tis awfully crowded, m'laird," Matildis added, nodding her head at her friend.

"Do ye no' have the biggest cottage?" Alec asked, knowing full well they did.

"Och!" Matildis said with a smile. "'Tis a verra nice cottage, m'laird. The biggest one and we be quite grateful fer it."

While Matildis might have forgotten why they were there, Hexie hadn't. She nudged Matildis with a hard elbow to her ribs. "It might be the biggest, but it still be crowded. We be steppin' on one another left and right, ye ken."

Alec began to wonder if Matildis had a mind of her own, for she was once again nodding her head in agreement with Hexie.

"And the girl, m'laird," Hexie said with another glance her way. Lowering her voice, she said, "Somethin' be no' right about her."

A dull ache began to form betwixt his eyes. "I fear I do no' remember her name nor why she be livin' with ye," he said, ignoring the 'no' right comment altogether.

Matildis quit smiling. "The poor thing," she whispered. "Her parents and brother died last year. The ague. She be all alone, so we took her in."

"*Ye* took her in," Hexie corrected with a frown.

"Where else was she to go?" Matildis asked.

Whilst the women argued, Alec rubbed his eyes with his index finger and thumb. "What is it ye would like me to do?" he asked, breaking through their argument.

"Well, now, m'laird," Hexie began. "We ken ye was lookin' fer someone to work in the keep, to help yer wife."

They wanted him and his wife to take in the orphan? He looked across the room at her again. She could not be more than three and ten, he reckoned. Wee, as wee as his own wife. The girl did not possess the same dark brown hair as most of the other Bowies. Nay, hers was a few shades lighter.

He turned "Why?" Certainly there was more to it than a lack of space in their cottage.

The two women exchanged a knowing glance before Hexie answered. "As I said, there be somethin' wrong with that one."

He waited patiently, and with a stern expression, for her to continue.

Clearing her throat, Hexie said, "She be quiet, m'laird. *Verra* quiet. Always starin' at us as if *we* were the daft ones."

Alec had to wonder if she had ever been given a chance to speak her mind, especially if Hexie or Matildis were near.

"Ye see, m'laird, we likes to entertain on occasion. And we find it a wee bit difficult to do with *that* one around. Always lookin' so smug, so high and mighty. She does no' like to entertain the way the older women do, ye ken?"

Aye, he was beginning to understand with a clarity he wouldn't wish on his worst enemy.

"And her temper? Och! 'Twould put to shame any other Bowie, that I can tell ye without exaggeration. Why, just last eve, she slapped poor Marvis Bowie, the one who lives down by the creek, so hard, he almost lost an eye!"

The ache in his head was increasing with each word that spilled out of Hexie's mouth. "Why would she do such a thing?" He wished immediately that he hadn't asked the question.

"Because she does no' like to entertain like the rest of us."

He was appalled. "Do ye no' think she be a bit young to be *enter-tainin'* like the rest of ye?"

She gave him an exaggerated blink before responding. "She be five and ten, m'laird. Nearly six and ten! Why, by all rights, she should be married by now. But she does no' like anyone we have suggested to her. A haughty thing she be."

Alec was reaching the limits of his patience. "'Tis nay up to *ye* to be arrangin' anyone's marriage." He politely reminded them. Instantly, he felt sorry for the young girl. And unfortunately, he could well imagine the kind of men Hexie and Matildis would offer up for the poor girl.

"I shall bring the matter to me wife," he said, hoping to bring it to a close. "In the meantime, please be kind to the girl. She has, after all, lost her entire family."

From their stunned expressions, one would have thought he'd just asked them to join St. Agnes's convent.

"We have been nothin' but kind, m'laird. 'Tis she that—"

He cut her off with a raised hand. "I said, I would bring the matter to me wife. The girl shall stay under yer protection until further notice." He began to step away but paused. "And by kind, I mean do no' force the girl to *entertain* anyone. And it would serve ye well to let those ye entertain to ken that should anything happen to the lass, ye all will be answerin' to *me*."

By the time he finished inspecting the crops and training, Alec had completely forgotten about his visit from Hexie and Matildis.

A bit tired and worn from his afternoon, he headed to the keep, eagerly anticipating the hot bath that would be waiting for him. Then he remembered it had been his wife seeing to that luxury. With her on much needed bed rest for the next few days, there would be no soothing bath to go home to.

Begrudgingly, he turned around and headed for the loch. The water was a tad warmer than ice, but it served its purpose. He was soon clean of mud and muck and felt a bit invigorated.

The gathering room was empty and dark when he entered the keep. At once, he realized he did not enjoy coming home to such a dark and empty place. He could hear muffled voices floating down from above stairs. Undoubtedly 'twas his wife and men.

Taking the stairs two at a time, he was soon standing just outside the doorway to his room. There, in front of the hearth, was the tub, filled with steaming water. His anger flared, until he heard Gylys.

"Will ye be wantin' anythin' else, Mistress?" Gylys asked.

"Nay," he heard her reply. "And again, I thank ye both fer doin' this fer me. Alec has been workin' verra hard. And he does enjoy his hot baths."

Relief settled in when he realized it had been his men who saw to the bath, and not his wife. Guilt, however, was in hot pursuit.

Stepping into his bedchamber, he searched for Leona. She was still abed, just as he had ordered. Gylys and Kyth were gathering up buckets.

"Alec!" Leona exclaimed happily. "Yer bath be ready."

She couldn't see to his bath herself, but she still made certain he had one by enlisting the help of his men.

He said not a word as the men quit the room. Quietly, he closed the door behind them before going to his wife's side.

"Ye've already bathed?" she asked with a confused tilt of her head.

"In the loch," he replied.

Her lips formed into that seductive 'o' shape as she stared longingly at the tub.

Gently, he helped her to sit upright. "I say it be time *ye* enjoyed the fruits of yer labor," he said as he helped her to her feet.

THE FOLLOWING MORN DAWNED GRAY, THE CLOUDS PREGNANT WITH rain, not a beam of sunlight to be bought or found.

Inside their bedchamber, Alec woke to Leona snuggled against him for warmth. One would think that after the two hour 'bath' he had shared with her the night before, his ardor would have been sated for the next fortnight. But such was not the case this morn. Nay, he woke with the same fervent desires and need as last night. And only his wife would be able to quench it.

As he twined a lock of hair around his finger, the skies opened up.

The rain came down in great sheets and waves. God be with any man or beast caught unawares outdoors, for 'twas likely the rain could tear clean through a man's skin.

Leona snuggled in more closely, dangerously wiggling her bottom against his groin. Wrapping an arm around her tiny waist, he held her close. Inhaling deeply, he drew in her scent and held on to it, as if burning it into his memory.

How did it happen? He asked himself. *How have I become so attached to ye? How can I be filled with so much desire and need for one woman?* 'Twas dangerous, he knew it, to feel so strongly toward a woman. But Leona was not just *any* woman.

Nay, she was remarkable. Strong, determined, and sweet. Oh, so very sweet. He wondered what his father and his father before him might think of him. Undoubtedly, they'd condemn him for caring so deeply for a woman. But this morning, he didn't rightly care about the opinions of men long dead.

All he cared about was his wife.

He was not ready to concede to anything just yet. And he was nowhere near ready to admit he had more than a strong liking for Leona. Nay, he was not ready to give her the words.

Deciding for once, to let his wife sleep without intrusion or interruption, he slipped quietly from the bed. *Hell, half the reason she is so exhausted is due to yer selfish need to bed her five times a day, ye big, foolish lout!*

LATE THAT AFTERNOON, ALEC MADE HIS WAY BACK TO THEIR bedchamber to see how his wife fared. 'Twas a good thing he arrived when he did or she would have made her escape.

She was just stepping into her brown dress when he opened the door. She paused midway, her eyes wide with surprise. "Alec!" she said. "I thought I would no' see you until this eve."

Of course ye thought that, ye little minx. "I came to see how ye fare."

Knowing she'd been caught attempting to leave, she pretended nothing was wrong. "I am doing much better," she said. "I thought I would go below stairs and begin the evenin' meal."

He gave a slow shake of his head as he crossed his arms over his chest. "I will prepare the evenin' meal."

"You?" she all but squawked in horror.

"Aye," he replied. "Me."

He knew what she was thinking. The meals he had prepared for her thus far had been nothing short of dismal.

"Mayhap I could go with ye?" she began. "Only to *instruct*," she quickly added. "I would no' lift a finger. Just encourage ye a bit."

'Twas nearly impossible not to laugh at her horrified expression. "Ye are no' going to instruct or encourage. Ye're goin' to stay here. In bed. As I ordered."

She dropped her dress, her brow furrowed in anger. "Now listen here, Alec Bowie. I be yer wife, no' one of yer men. Ye do no' order me to do anythin'. If I want to go below stairs to cook, then I shall."

He let out a short breath. In two long strides he was in front of her, lifting her into his arms. "Then do no' consider it an order. Consider it a request."

Alec would be damned before he allowed her to work herself to the bone again. He kissed her forehead before depositing her onto the bed.

Sullenly, she folded her arms across her bosom. "I really do feel better Alec," she told him.

"I can see that you do," he said. "But ye're to remain abed."

"I am no' a child," she mumbled under her breath.

Alec leaned in and kissed her, sweetly at first. But it soon turned wild and passionate. He knew that if he did not stop now, he'd soon have her naked and writhing in passion underneath him.

"I ken verra well ye be no' a child," he told her after breaking the kiss.

Her lips were swollen, her eyes sparkling in the candlelight as she tried to steady her breathing. Playfully, he added, "Now do as ye're told."

Contentment turned to fury in the blink of an eye. Swinging her legs over the bed, she tried to escape. He caught her around the waist. "If ye do no' wish to be treated like a child, then stop actin' like one," he chuckled against her ear. "Else ye will force me to take away yer clothes and leave ye naked."

"Ye would no' dare!" she exclaimed as she fought to free herself from his tight grip.

Once again, he put her in the bed. "Gylys! Kyth!" he called out.

With wide, uncertain eyes, she asked, "What are ye goin' to do?"

"Tie ye to the bed if I must. The choice be yers."

CHAPTER 23

*T*wo days had passed since Leona's battle with table and rope. Two full days where Alec would not let her out of their bedchamber. He'd caught her once, the day before, trying to slip out of their room. Being the stubborn lout he was, he did the only thing he could think to do. He removed her trunk, her cloak, her boots, and left her with nothing but her nightdress. He even had the audacity to take her robe! He knew full well she'd rather die than have anyone, least of all his men, see her in such a state.

I told ye that ye were no' leavin' this room again until I gave ye permission. Ye are to rest.

Oh, she understood, she truly did, the reasons behind his actions. In truth, it *did* make her feel cared for. However, a body could only take so much *looking after* before she lost her mind.

To add insult to injury, she was hungry. Bloody hungry! Oh, she appreciated her husband's efforts to cook for her. But he failed at every attempt. The food was either burnt or horribly undercooked. She had taken to having Kyth and Gylys smuggle her apples, cheese and bread after each of Alec's meals.

What she would not give to have a bowl of stew. Or a hunk of venison. Anything but burnt ham or apples and cheese.

She sat now, alone in her chamber, trying to remain hopeful that on the morrow, he would ease up on her restrictions and allow her to do that which made her happiest: take care of him and the keep.

~

ALEC WAS DOING HIS BEST TO PROVIDE A GOOD MEAL FOR HIS WIFE. HE decided that instead of cooking as *she* would for him, he would cook the only way he knew how: on an open fire and out of doors. 'Twas not exactly like he would were he on a hunting trip or travelling across the country, but 'twould do for now.

Thankfully, the rains had let up that morn, leaving behind a muddy yard, but an otherwise fine, bright day. The chickens squawked each time he walked by. In the distance, he could hear the occasional snicker from the horses in the stables. Birds flew silently overhead: little black dots against the pale blue sky and wispy white clouds. In a small pen, in the farthest corner of the yard, a sow and her babes slept contentedly in the mud.

Earlier, he had sent a handful of men to fish and he was grateful that they'd been quite successful. They'd just returned with baskets filled with fine, good-sized trout they'd caught from the wide, meandering stream that ran through the northern part of their lands. It lay not far from the old keep, crooked and twisted. Deep in many parts, it could almost always be counted upon to provide a good bounty.

Alec took what fish he wanted — three goodly sized trout — and left the rest to his men. Before they left, he asked for their assistance in pulling one of Leona's tables out of doors, to use as a workspace to clean the fish and prepare the meal.

Once the table was placed where he wanted it, he fetched two buckets of fresh, cold water. One, he set on the hearth to warm, the other, he kept on the table. Before long, he not only had the perfect fire built, he also had the fish wrapped in clay and baking in the fire.

Knowing his wife as he did, she would appreciate a wee bit more than fish. Loping along to her garden he picked carrots, leeks, onions, and various other vegetables. He'd roast those in the fire along with the fish.

For once, he did not leave the mess to wait for another day. Tossing the scraps and scales into a bucket, he took them to the pig pen and tossed them in. The pigs squealed their appreciation, and fought over the bits and pieces.

Grabbing cloths from his wife's kitchen — which he had yet to clean — he wiped down the table as well as his knife. 'Twould take a while for the fish and vegetables to bake in the open fire. With time on his hands, he decided it might be best to tackle the messes he'd been leaving in Leona's kitchen.

Once he stepped back into the building however, the task seemed daunting. *Ye've certainly mucked it up,* he thought with a heavy sigh. *'Twill take hours to clean it all. Mayhap ye should just wait and start in the morn.*

Although he knew his wife would have a fit if she saw the destruction he'd wrought in her favorite place on earth, he convinced himself he would get to things on the morrow, when he had more time to devote to it. For now, he had to tend to the foods cooking in the open fire.

Setting the stool against the outside wall, he sat down. With his long legs stretched out, he rested his head and shoulders against the wall and closed his eyes. Immediately, his thoughts turned to his wife, who was above stairs at that very moment. *Why do I think of her so often?* He wondered silently. *Has she put some sort of spell on me, to make me forget all that my father taught me?* 'Twas doubtful. Nay, there was not an evil bone in Leona's body. She was no more a witch than he was the King of Scotia.

He could not remember falling asleep and was startled awake by the sound of someone speaking softly to him as they nudged his shoulder. He flew to his feet, his hand immediately reaching for the sword at his side.

It took only a moment for his eyes to focus, another moment to realize he was in no danger.

"Yer food was burnin', m'laird." 'Twas the wee lass from the day before. The one Hexie and Matildis were so eager to be done with.

Instantly, he went to retrieve the foods, but they were no longer in the fire.

"I took it out," the young girl said. "It all be on the table."

Glancing at the table, he could see the smoke rising from the clay.

"I think it be no' too far done," the girl offered.

Alec looked back to her. "Thank ye," he said, unable to recall her name.

A long moment passed as they looked at one another. 'Twas the girl who finally broke the silence. "I be Adhaira," she told him. "We met yester afternoon."

"I remember," Alec told her. 'Twas only a partial untruth. He recognized her face, but his mind had failed to produce a name to go with it. "What brings ye here this day?"

She neither hemmed nor hawed, choosing instead to get right to the point. "Hexie and the others have asked me to leave."

"Bloody hell," he cursed under his breath. Frustration rose. Had he not specifically told the women that he expected them to keep the lass under their protection? At least until he had discussed the matter with his wife? He was fully prepared to have them brought to the keep immediately so that he could mete out an appropriate punishment.

"They have been askin' me to leave fer some time now," Adhaira added. "I ken ye said I was to stay with them until ye talked to yer wife. But m'laird, I simply can no' do it any longer."

Confused, he asked, "Do they ken ye be here?"

She gave a quick shake of her head. "Nay, m'laird. They be too busy *entertainin'.*"

He was in no mood at the moment to deal with the insignificant arguments of a group of women. "Unfortunately, I have yet to discuss the matter with me wife."

Disappointment flashed in her light brown eyes. "I understand, m'laird," she said with a curtsy. "Ye might want to tend to yer meal before it grows cold." Without saying another word, she picked up a satchel from beside the fire and left him.

He grabbed a tray and set the still smoking foods on it. *On the morrow,* he told himself. *I shall clean the kitchen and discuss the matter of Adhaira Bowie with me wife.*

＊

LEONA WAS ASTONISHED AT THE MEAL ALEC HAD PLACED BEFORE HER. A trencher of fine baked fish and roasted vegetables, fresh fruits, bread, and he'd even remembered the butter and jam. "Who prepared this meal?" she asked.

"I did," he replied with a proud smile. "The fish was caught just this afternoon. I built a wee fire out of doors and cooked it like I would have were I on a huntin' trip."

She pulled off a bite of the steaming fish with her fingers, inspected it as she blew it to cool it off. It smelled heavenly and tasted even better. She closed her eyes, as if in the throws of ecstasy. It all but melted in her mouth. "'Tis divine," she said with a happy moan. "I did no' ken ye could cook so well!"

Just why he felt so proud at the moment, he couldn't rightly say. Neither could he explain why it made him so bloody happy to see her so happy, so content.

While his wife dived into the meal with the same fervor as a religious zealot, Alec watched, barely eating, for he was too enraptured with Leona.

"I swear," she said with a mouth full of vegetables, "that I shall never complain about being ordered to bed. Especially if ye'll be cookin' like this."

He could only chuckle at her declaration, for he knew that, come the morrow, she'd be back to complaining and insisting she was well enough to get back to being the chatelaine of the keep.

They ate the rest of their meal in companionable silence. Leona finished before he did. "If I dare say it, Alec Bowie, ye have surprised me this night! I thank ye fer such a fine meal." She smiled as she tried to suppress a yawn, but failed miserably in the attempt. Snuggling back into the bed, 'twas her turn to watch as he ate.

"Ye be a confusin' man at times," she said as she folded her arms behind her head.

"Me?" he asked with quirked brow. "I be as easy to understand as any man."

Leona laughed. "Which be no' at all," she told him. "Most men are as confusin' as the day is long."

Setting his trencher on the floor by his feet, he leaned over the bed to look her directly in the eye. "Now, what be so confusin'?" he asked playfully.

"Sometimes, I think there be two Alec Bowies," she told him. "And at times, I do no' ken which one I will be speakin' to."

He had no earthly idea what she meant, and told her so.

"When we be alone, ye be the kindest man. Verra carin', and aye, even sweet."

He raised an insulted brow. "I am *never* 'sweet'," he told her.

"Think ye no'?" she asked. To her way of thinking, the way he'd been caring for her was beyond kind. Sweet was the only word she could think to describe it. "Would ye feel better if I called ye a bloody bastard?"

"I would!" he declared with a devilishly handsome smile.

"As I was sayin'," she said with a roll of her eyes. "There be two of ye. The one ye are when people be about and the one ye are when we be alone."

"I am the same at all times, lass," he argued.

Leona gave a slow shake of her head. "Ye never kiss me when others are around. And ye never tell me ye think me beautiful, like ye do when we be alone."

"Of course I do no' do or say those things when others are about." He looked appalled at the notion of such public displays.

"That be what confuses me," she told him.

Alec was dismayed. "What happens when we are alone, is betwixt ye and I. 'Tis private, lass." What he did not say was that he found it special, something he wanted only unto himself. The rest of the world could find their own special moments, their own little bit of paradise.

Believing she had upset him, Leona apologized. "I be sorry, Alec. I only meant to say it be confusin'."

He realized that Leona was always herself, no matter who was about. She did not know how to put on a false front, to present herself differently in public. It struck him then that never had he met a more honest person, nor a more giving or caring one.

Would it be so wrong, on occasion, to show the rest of the world what he thought of his wife? That he appreciated her goodness, her generosity? Uncertainty fell over him. This, this he would have to give much thought to.

ALEC WOKE, THE SUNLIGHT STREAMING IN THROUGH A TINY CRACK betwixt the furs covering their window. As was beginning to become ritual, Leona's round bottom was pressed against his groin, his arm around her waist. He had to admit 'twas an awfully nice way to wake each morn.

In all his adult life, he'd never actually *slept* with a woman. He thought back to the days before he was married, before he was chief. Back to those days of drinking and visiting the whorehouses in Edinburgh.

Not once, in all his days, had a woman voluntarily shared his bed. And those that he purchased, he'd never bothered to stay with for more than a few moments after the deed was done.

My, how his life had changed in just a few short weeks. Was it simply his life that had changed, or had he become someone different as well? Circumstance alone, or something more? Something deeper and far more profound?

Leona stirred next to him, drawing his arm more tightly around her waist. Experience and time told him she was still asleep. His heart began to pound ferociously against his chest. *In her sleep, she seeks me out. Draws me nearer and holds on to me. Even after my mistreatment of her.*

Was it truly mistreatment or ignorance? Definitely 'twas ignorance. He had never intentionally mistreated her. 'Twas his own lack of experience, he supposed, with the opposite sex, that made him ignore the signs that most men probably would have seen.

Mayhap, just mayhap, his wee wife saw something in him that he could not see himself.

Or mayhap, they were simply two tetched and daft people who fate had brought together.

$\sim$

THERE WAS LITTLE DOUBT IN ALEC'S MIND THAT HE'D BE UNABLE TO keep his wife abed for much longer. He simply needed one more day in which to get her kitchen back in order. If she were ever to see the hopeless, chaotic state in which he'd left it, she'd most likely kill him with her bare hands.

Quietly, he dressed in the near dark room and slipped out without waking Leona. Though he dreaded the task that lay looming before him like a scourge, he knew he must face it head-on.

Bracing himself for the chore ahead, he swung open the door to the kitchen and stepped inside. Shock turned to abject confusion when he saw the condition of the kitchen. 'Twas as clean and organized as if Leona herself had cleaned it. Nary a dirty pot or spoon was anywhere to be found. The flour he'd spilled on the floor had been swept away, the tables and counters cleaned of the debris and messes he'd created over the past few days. A fire blazed in the hearth, the candles were lit and all aglow.

Had his wife somehow managed to slip away from bed during the night, seen what he had done, and set it to rights before he'd even known she was gone?

'Twas then that someone stepped out of the larder.

Adhaira?

"Good morn, m'laird!" she beamed happily. "I ken ye said to return to Hexie and the others. But when I came back last night and saw the state of this kitchen, well, I could no' just leave it. And rumor has it, ye have been burnin' one meal after another, tryin' to take care of yer wife."

For a long moment, he could not find his own voice.

"I kent ye would no' mind a *little* bit of help," she said as she began to unload the items from her arms. "Gylys was tellin' me last eve, that were yer wife to see what ye had done to her kitchen, she would be sorely upset. So the two of us set it all back to rights. Up quite late we were."

"How?" he stammered. "How did ye get in here?" His memory of the night before answered his own question.

"Through the door, of course," she answered. "How else would I get in?"

He had not returned after supping with his wife, had not come back to lock the doors. "We usually keep the kitchen locked," he mumbled.

"Well, it were no' locked last eve," she said as she placed one hand on her hip. "M'laird, be ye angry?"

Alec shook his head. "Nay, lass. I be quite grateful to ye." Although it might have been considered a sweeping intrusion, he was so ecstatic with how clean everything was, he did not care. Were he not a married man, he would have swept the young woman up and kissed her, so great was his relief and gratitude. He'd also have to thank Gylys for his help.

"I can leave if ye wish," she told him, eying him closely.

"Nay!" he all but shouted. "Nay," he tried once again. "I am certain me wife will be grateful to have ye here." *I ken that I be!*

"Good!" she replied with a relieved smile. "I was about to make ye a bit of somethin' to break yer fast. Unless ye'd like that chore to yerself?"

"Good, God, no!" he exclaimed. "I mean, I would thank ye kindly if ye'd see to it."

Her expression said she thought him awfully odd. He couldn't rightly blame her.

"Would ye like me to take a tray to yer wife?" she asked.

"Nay," he said. "I shall see to that meself." Remembering how his wife had rewarded him for the fine meal he had prepared the night before, he could only imagine more gratitude once he fed her yet another decent meal.

~

ALEC HAD LEFT ADHAIRA ALONE WHILST HE WENT TO CHOP WOOD. Once he had a good amount for the kitchen, he kept going so that he would have enough for the gathering room and their bedchamber.

When he was finished, he was soaked with sweat and covered with bits of splintered wood. Drawing water up from the well, he washed as best he could with the frigid water.

Plunging his face into the bucket, he swiped his hands across his face. Shaking out his wet hair, tiny droplets flew hither and yon. As his hands dried, he looked out at the empty yard. 'Twas then he saw Patrice stepping through the second gate. She looked worried as she rushed toward him.

"I came as soon as I could!" she exclaimed breathlessly. "How be Leona?"

He chuckled slightly as he shook water from his hands once again. "She be fine," he told her. "Although I dare say she is no' likin' bein' cooped up in our room all the day long."

Patrice let out an anxious breath. "I only learned just this morn," she told him. "I have been at me mum's for a few days. Tell me, is the scar as horrific as rumors have it?"

Rumors flew as fast as eagles in these parts. "Nay, 'tis no' at all bad. Just a few stitches along the top of her forehead."

"Och!" Patrice exclaimed as she placed a hand on her heart. "I hear it took five men to hold her down whilst ye mended her."

"She did no' even flinch. No one was forced to hold her down."

"I knew it!" she cried. "I swear ye can no' trust people to tell ye the truth these days."

Alec had to agree.

"May I see her?" she asked hopefully.

"Aye, ye can. I am certain she would like the company."

⌒

WHILE PATRICE HURRIED INSIDE, ALEC RETURNED TO HIS PILE OF WOOD. He scooped up an armful and headed into the kitchens.

Adhaira was just finishing spooning porridge into a bowl when he stepped inside. The room was warm, the scent of rising bread and freshly prepared food filled the air. His stomach began to grumble as he stacked the wood next to the hearth.

"There ye be, m'laird," Adhaira said as she placed the bowl on the tray. "I assume ye will be wantin' to eat with yer wife, so there be plenty for the both of ye."

Alec thanked her, grabbed the tray and left to take it to his wife.

When he neared his bedchamber, he could hear his wife and Patrice giggling about whatever it was that made women giggle. Using the toe of his booted foot, he carefully nudged open the door.

Leona was sitting up and Patrice was on the edge of the mattress. "Speak of the devil," Leona giggled when she saw Alec enter the room.

For some unknown reason, Patrice found the comment quite funny. Hilarious, in fact, for she nearly tumbled from the bed with laughter.

"Although I be quite curious as to why Patrice is in such a state, I am no foolish enough to ask for an explanation."

Leona continued to smile up at him. "'Tis probably best," she said. "I fear the answer would confound ye."

Alec rolled his eyes and set the tray on the opposite side of the bed. Patrice finally regained some control of her senses. "I be disturbin' yer meal," she said.

"Nay," Alec argued politely. "I have work to tend to." 'Twas true that he had work he needed to do. But he did not want Patrice to feel uncomfortable. And he knew his wife would probably prefer her company to his.

"Enjoy the meal and the morn," he said with an inclination of his head. "I shall see you later this day," he told Leona.

Before he was even out of the door, they were once again giggling like lasses who'd just seen their first naked arse.

～

"THOSE WOMEN SOUND HORRIBLE!" LEONA TOLD HER HUSBAND. 'TWAS just past the noonin' hour and Alec had just finished telling her about Adhaira.

"Horrible might be a bit strong," he told her. "Remember, they be Bowie women."

Leona shook her head in disagreement. "Believe me Alec, fer I've been witness to such things more times than ye can count. People can be cruel, no matter their bloodline."

On that, they could both agree.

"She be a bit shy at first," Alec explained.

If anyone understood *shy* 'twas Leona. People had often mistaken her for shy, when she was anything but. "Do no' worry over it, Alec. She and I may have more in common that either of us ken."

He was glad that his wife did not argue over his decision to have Adhaira stay and work in the keep. Leona was not too proud to admit she needed help.

He left her long enough to go below stairs and fetch their new charge. They returned a short time later. Leona was standing now, beside the hearth with a fur draped around her shoulders. She had run a brush through her hair and braided it. Alec supposed she did not want to appear weak when meeting the girl for the first time.

"Adhaira, this be yer mistress," Alec said by way of an introduction. "Leona, this be our new charge and scullery maid, Adhaira Bowie."

Adhaira dipped a short curtsey as she eyed Leona suspiciously for a long moment.

"'Tis a pleasure to meet ye, Adhaira."

"Thank ye, m'lady," she whispered softly.

They stood eyeing one another for a long moment. "Alec, would ye please return me robe to me?" Leona asked. "I should like to sit a while with Adhaira and talk with her."

Mayhap it was time to return her clothes to her, he supposed. "Verra well," he said before quitting the room.

"Please," Leona said with a nod toward the chairs. "Sit with me a while."

Reluctantly, Adhaira took the chair opposite Leona.

"Do ye truly wish to be here?" Leona asked. "And, please, tell me true."

The girl looked at her feet. Leona knew she was uncomfortable and tried to put her at ease. "Adhaira, I ken what people say about me behind me back. I ken the womenfolk here do no' much care for me — though I do no' rightly understand why, for they've made no attempt to get to know me."

Adhaira remained silent as she fidgeted with her fingers.

"I be no' a witch," Leona told her. "Though many believe so because of me eyes."

That statement drew her attention away from her fingers and feet. Adhaira looked up, took one look into Leona's eyes before abruptly turning her gaze away.

Leona laughed. "Ye can look at them, lass. Ye'll no' burst into flames."

"I be sorry, mistress," she said in a soft voice.

"Do no' be sorry, Adhaira. Ye can ask me anything ye wish about me eyes, or me."

"Were ye born that way?" she asked.

"Aye, I was," Leona answered. "Me da took one look at me and tried to convince me mum to put me in a fairie tree, or even drown me."

Aghast, Adhaira looked up. "Nay!"

"Aye," Leona said with a nod and a smile. "Thankfully, me mum refused."

"Did yer da grow used to them? Yer eyes I mean? Was he glad he did no' leave ye to die?"

It hurt, it truly did, to answer the girl's questions. "Nay, lass, he never grew used to them. Even on the day I married Alec, he told me he wished me mum had listened to him, had let him drown me."

'Twasn't pity she saw reflected in Adhaira's eyes, but a blend of confusion and sorrow.

"Now, I ask ye again, child. Do ye wish to be here? If no', I will no' be insulted, fer I *have* grown used to me eyes and the unsettlin' they give people. Though, I will tell ye, I would verra much like to have ye here."

"'Tis no' that, m'lady. I mean, no' yer eyes. People are eejits at times. Hexie and Matildis oft made fun of me."

"Of ye?" Leona asked with a raised brow. "Why?"

"Because I would no' lift me skirts for the men who like to visit our cottage. Because I do no' like to sit around drinkin' wine or ale all the day long. I did no' fit in with their way of livin'."

"I see," Leona said.

Hesitantly, Adhaira got to the real reasons why she did not want to live in the keep. "They told me that I *had* to come live here. I was no' given a choice. They also told me that I would no' be able to say nay to the laird or his men when they came knockin' on me door."

Leona knew at once the meaning of what she left unsaid. Anger bubbled in the pit of her stomach. No matter how old she grew, she would never understand how some people could be so cruel. "Adhaira, ye have my solemn word that neither my husband or any of his men will come knockin' on yer door. And if any of them ever do, ye have my permission to knock them senseless with the nearest object. Be it a chamberpot or fryin' pan. Then, ye are to find me at once, so that *I* can beat them senseless."

Adhaira's shoulders sagged with relief. "Ye mean, I am no' here to entertain them?"

"Entertain them?" Leona stammered. "Nay! Ye are here to help me in the kitchen and the keep. Cookin' and cleanin'. Nothin' more than that."

Adhaira leapt from her chair and knelt before Leona. "Och! Thank ye, m'lady! Thank ye!"

Leona gave her a warm smile and a pat on her hands. "Now, tell me, can ye cook?"

ALEC HAD TO ADMIT 'TWAS NICE HAVING SOMEONE ELSE DO THE cooking. Having help now, he was able to stay abed with his Leona, and enjoy loving her before he started his day.

This morn, he loved her languidly, taking his sweet time to love every bit of her. Soft yet deep kisses that matched the pace of their joining. Joining with her was unlike anything he'd ever experienced. No matter how many times, nor how many different ways in which he loved her, each time felt more magnificent than the last.

When they finished, they lay side by side, out of breath, staring up at the ceiling. Leona's cheeks were flushed, her eyes sparkling in the late morning light. A light sheen of perspiration covered her forehead as she smiled contentedly.

"'Twill it always be like this?" she murmured softly.

Although he was certain he knew to what she was referring, he asked, "Will 'what' always be like this?"

She grew quiet for a time. "Be ye hungry?" she asked, intentionally changing the subject.

"I could eat a bit," he replied, wondering silently what it was she was not saying.

She made an attempt to slip from the bed.

"Nay, lass. Ye have one last day of rest before I allow ye out of this room."

Leona let out a heavy, dejected sigh. "Alec, truly, I am well. There be no reason to keep me locked away."

He chuckled and smiled broadly. "And if I like havin' ye all to meself?" he teased as he pulled her against his chest.

He caught a glimpse of something behind her bright eyes and half-smile. Something he couldn't recognize. "Are ye well lass?" he asked as he stroked her back with his palms.

"Aye, I am well. I fear I simply be tired of being cooped up all the day long."

Uncertain if she was telling the truth or not, he kissed the tip of her nose. "Later this day, after I am done in the fields, would ye like to take a wee walk with me?"

"A walk?" she asked as she tilted her head to the side.

"Aye, a walk. Ye do ken what that is, aye?"

She rolled her eyes at his silliness. "Ye're daft, Alec Bowie. Daft."

He'd no argue it, for lately, he did feel quite daft. Especially when he was with her.

"Verra well, then," he said as he patted her rump. "Ye shall rest for the remainder of the morn. And after the noonin' meal, ye and I shall take a wee walk together."

"Then ye shall be givin' me back me clothes?" she asked hopefully.

"Of course I will. I can no' have ye walkin' about half naked. 'Twould drive the men mad with lust."

Another roll of her eyes before she slid away. "Ye be as daft as the day is long, Alec Bowie."

Again, he did not argue with her, for he knew she spoke the truth.

ALEC HAD RETURNED FROM THE FIELDS NOT LONG AFTER NOONTIME, just as he had promised. As a courtesy to his wife, he bathed in the loch before heading back to the keep.

Wanting to eat before they left, he went to the kitchen in search of sustenance. The door was standing wide open. Adhaira was there, bent over a bubbling pot of something that smelled savory and delicious.

At hearing him enter, she stood upright to look at him. "M'laird," she said with a nod. "Can I help ye?"

"What smells so good?" he asked, as he noticed the back door was also standing wide open.

Adhaira glanced at the pot behind her. "Venison stew. It be fer the evenin' meal. There be dried meats, fruits, and bread there on the counter fer yer noonin' meal."

Disappointed, but still thankful, Alec went to the counter and took a few pieces of meat. "Be there a reason ye have the doors open?" he asked.

"Fresh air be good for the body and the soul," she replied.

Whatever made the lass happy was fine with him. "Have we any cheese?" he asked.

With a nod, she laid the spoon on a damp cloth on the table before stepping into the larder. Alec was stuffing his face with a hunk of bread when he caught movement out of the corner of his eye.

"Satan?" he said the dog's name, confused by his presence. "How did ye get out?"

The dog sauntered to his master and summarily began to lick Alec's fingers. Before Alec could grab the dog's collar, Satan was walking away.

"Satan!" he called out to the dog.

His bandogge did not heed his command, which in and of itself was highly unusual. What confused Alec was the fact the dog had left through the opposite door and toward the keep.

"Satan!" he called out once again. The dog continued to ignore him. He went to the rear door of the keep and barked at the door, as if he were begging entry. Alec, wholly confused by his dog's actions, could only run after him.

Just as he grabbed the dog's wide, black collar, Gylys opened the door to step outside. But upon seeing the bandogge, his eyes grew wide and he stepped back and away.

The dog lunged forward, as if he were in fast pursuit of a rabbit, jerking himself free from Alec's grasp. He raced inside the keep at a full run, with Alec fast on his heels.

He didn't bother to call after the animal because 'twas apparent it wasn't going to listen. Entering the gathering room, he caught only a brief glimpse of the dog's rear end as it bounded up the last few stairs and rounded the corner.

Leona! Alec was suddenly beset with dread. He raced through the gathering room and up the stairs. As soon as he made it to the doorway to his bedchamber, he heard his wife speaking sweetly to the dog. He paused to listen.

"Ye wee beastie!" she exclaimed happily. "How did ye get in here? Och! If Alec catches ye 'twill mean both our necks."

Alec took a tentative step forward so that he could see better with his own eyes what exactly was taking place. His wife sat in a chair by the fire, with her back to the door. She was kissing and petting the bandogge as if it were a house cat!

Before he could utter a word of reproach, she spoke again.

"'Tis glad I am to see ye, Patches."

Patches? No wonder the bloody thing had not listened to him. His wife had re-named him!

"It has been a verra long while since ye and I have talked, aye?"

Alec could see the dog resting his paws on his wife's lap as she continued to show it much affection. "Ye be such a fine dog," she told it.

Silence filled the room as Leona petted the back of the dog, not looking at it anymore. "I have a wee problem, Patches," she whispered into the air. "Nay, it be a verra big problem, and I fear I do no' ken what to do about it."

'Twas as if the dog understood her discomfort. He rested his head in her lap. Gently and slowly, Leona stroked its massive head as she continued to look at something only she could see. Alec's curiosity was piqued, so he remained quiet, waiting and hoping she would disclose to the dog that which she could not share with him. More likely than not, she was going to complain about being 'cooped' up all the day long.

The room became silent for such a long while that Alec began to believe she wasn't going to tell the dog anything. 'Twas a silent, inner battle his wife was fighting. For reasons he couldn't quite understand, he wanted to go to her then, take her in his arms and whisper against her cheek that whatever was distressing her, she could share with him.

"Patches, if I tell ye a secret, do ye promise no' to tell?" she asked the dog as she lifted his head and looked into his eyes. The dog whimpered and licked her hand as if to agree to her request.

"Ye see, I fear I have fallen in love with me husband. I did no' mean fer it to happen, but it did."

Alec's eyes grew as wide and as round as wagon wheels. That was the last thing he was expecting to hear from his wife's lips.

She looked away from the dog, once again focusing on something far away. "I ken he and I agreed this would never be a love match. Therein lies me problem. I feel as though I have broken the promise I made to him, that day back at Mackintosh lands when I agreed to marry him."

Aye, they had agreed 'twas not and never could be a love match.

Terror seized his heart.

"I can no' say how it happened. Mayhap, 'twas how kind he has been these past few days. Och, he's been kind, in his own way, since the first time we met. But somethin' has changed betwixt us. Or mayhap in him? I do no' ken, Patches, what I am to do. I can no' tell him, for I fear he could no' ever love me back."

He could take no more. Silently, stealthily, he turned around and walked away.

CHAPTER 24

My wife loves me.

He ran the words over and over in his mind. His father's voice, which he believed he had finally locked away, came roaring back to life.

If ye give yer heart to a woman, she will wield it like a weapon. She will use it against ye and beat ye to death with it ... do no' e'er trust a woman, Alec. They all lie and cheat to get what they want. And what do they want? Yer bloody ballocks in a sack they can wear around their waists. They all be the same. Ye can no' trust a one of them.

'Twas a staggering piece of news.

In a daze, he walked around the gathering room for a time, his mind battling with his heart on what he should or should not do, or say, or feel. Confounded — and perturbed for reasons he could not grasp — he found himself in his study, pacing back and forth.

Just because she loves ye, does no' mean ye have to give her yer *heart,* he told himself.

His father's voice kept ringing in his mind, like the clanging of a church bell. *Fool. Fool. Fool.*

The walls seemed to close in around him. Suddenly, he felt

confined, restricted. If he stayed much longer, he thought he might suffocate.

He all but ran out of the keep. While the cool afternoon breeze felt good against his skin, he still felt much confined.

I need to ride, to be away from these walls. I need space to think.

A heartbeat later, he was heading around the keep and storming toward the stables. "Seamus!" he called out for his stable master. "Seamus!"

The man came rushing out of the stables with a look of concern etched across his brow. "M'laird?" he asked, wiping his hands on an oily cloth.

Alec thundered past him. "I need to ride." Alec ground out as he headed toward his horse's stable. Ares nickered and snorted, undoubtedly sensing his master's mood.

As Alec brought the horse out into the shed-way, Seamus was bringing his saddle. "What be the matter, m'laird?" Seamus asked with much concern.

Alec ignored him as he hooked Ares to the cross-ties. With his anger quite apparent, Seamus decided it might be best to give his chief and laird a wide berth. He tossed the saddle onto Ares's back and stepped away.

Alec's shouting had apparently drawn the attention of Derrick, for he soon appeared in the stables, with three other men.

"Alec?" Derrick called out as he entered. He glanced at Seamus, who offered him nothing more than a shrug and confounded expression. "Alec, what be the matter?" Derrick asked as he approached with a good deal of caution.

"There be nothin' the matter!" Alec bit out. "I simply want to ride."

Derrick had known Alec all of his life. He knew him well enough to deduce two things: one) his laird was upset about something. And two) inquiring as to what that something was would undoubtedly leave him with a black eye or a broken neck.

Whispering to his men, Derrick said, "James, ye and Robert go back and let Gylys and Kyth ken that the laird and I be goin' fer a wee ride. Fergus, ye come with me."

~

ALEC MADE NO ATTEMPT TO ARGUE THAT DERRICK'S PRESENCE WAS NOT needed this day. He was too consumed with raw emotions, emotions he couldn't quite understand, to care if his men followed or not.

As soon as the gates were opened at his command, he thundered over the drawbridge and down the lane. Veering to the west, he kicked his steed into a full run as soon as he was past the cottages.

The cool air whipped and stung against his sweat covered skin. With his heart pounding mercilessly against his chest, he rode hard and fast, trying to outrun his father's voice. *Fool. Fool. Fool.*

Through glens, across the wide stream, over hills, he rode as fast and as hard as Ares could go. His men kept up the grueling pace, but kept a fair distance.

Does it truly matter that she loves ye? What does that knowledge change? What does it matter? Leona loving ye, does no' make ye weak.

There was nothing to be done about his wife's feelings, no matter how misguided they might be. As he did his best to persuade his heart that it meant nothing, his heart begged to differ.

Ye ignored her. Ye ignored all the signs that she was workin' too hard. Ye refused to give her help when she needed it, until it was almost too late. She could have been killed when she fell from the ladder that day. She could have died when she was locked away in the north tower.

And still, she loves ye.

'Twas then that a voice, a long dead voice, tickled at the back of his mind. 'Twas his mother's voice.

He slowed his horse to a trot, doubt and uncertainty crashing into his mind. *Alec, I have loved yer da for a long while,* he could hear his mother speaking just as clearly as if she rode with him now. *'Tis truly painful to love a man who can no' or will no' love ye back. He has made me life a livin' hell on earth. And all because I loved him.*

He was transported back in time, to his youth, to when he was a little boy of six, standing as witness to one of the many horrible arguments betwixt his parents.

"All I ever wanted was to give ye a happy home!" his mother would cry.

"And ye have failed at every turn! 'Tis hell on earth to be married to such a demandin', cold woman!" his father would reply.

"Why do ye hate me so?" she wept.

"Yer tears be no' real, ye she-devil!"

That was not the life he wanted. *Hell on earth.*

Not for himself or any children he and Leona might be blessed with. Never would he wish that life upon a child. To be confused and afraid, wondering who he should listen to.

Wondering which of his parents he should love more.

An hour into his journey across his lands, they came upon a deep, dense forest. The line of trees acted as a border betwixt his lands and the MacLeods. 'Twas considered a bit of neutral territory as both clans would often hunt there with never an issue.

He veered west, walking slowly betwixt the glen and tree line. The sun was making its afternoon descent, the air crisp and cool. His heartbeat slowed to a more tolerable pace.

If I give Leona me heart, it will weaken me. Will I become the same as me father? Will our children suffer for it? Did my parents ever truly *love one another?*

Back and forth, a battle betwixt heart and mind. More than an hour had passed since they'd left the keep and he was no closer to enlightenment than when he'd left.

He realized then, he would find no answers in his past. Mayhap instead of looking to his parents, he should start looking elsewhere.

Never a praying man, he suddenly felt the urge to turn to God for advice. No one, least of all his father, would ever know he had turned to a force, a power, far stronger than himself.

Alec pulled his horse to a stop and craned his head to look skyward. "Lord," he whispered. "Please, tell me what I should do."

He heard nothing but the Highland wind, birds twittering in the trees, and the sound of his own heartbeat.

Undeterred, he asked. "Could ye no even see to it to give me a wee bit of a sign?"

'Twas then that something seemed to have spooked the birds, for they left the trees and took to the sky in great haste. Ares was similarly startled as he nickered twice, then stomped his foot.

Chuckling at his own folly, he looked to the heavens one more time. "'Tis no' much of a sign—"

Before he could finish speaking, he heard Derrick calling out to him.

"Alec! Look out!"

HAD DERRICK NOT CALLED OUT WHEN HE HAD, ALEC WOULD NOT HAVE turned at the right time, and the arrow would have pierced his heart.

Taken by surprise, he was frozen in place, but only for the briefest of moments. More arrows began flying through the air, coming from the treeline.

Quickly, Alec unsheathed his sword and returned his men's war cries with one of his own. Ares whinnied and reared, the highly trained animal eager and ready to help his master battle whatever enemy lay hidden amongst the trees.

Instead of turning and running away, Alec kicked his horse and tore across the glen to his men.

"Did ye see anyone?" Alec yelled as the arrows continued to fly.

With the horses screaming, pounding at the earth, the men had their swords drawn as they tried to determine what the bloody hell was going on. "Nay!" Derrick ground out.

"Do we take to the forest?," Fergus asked.

"Nay!" Alec and Derrick shouted in unison.

"Retreat!" Alec called out as he kicked his horse to a full run.

Derrick and Fergus pulled their horses beside his own, heading back the way they'd come.

"Be it the MacLeods?" Fergus asked nervously.

Before anyone could answer, an assault from ahead ensued. Arrows ripped through the air. One made its way into Derrick's left shoulder. "Bloody hell. The bastards shot me!"

There was no time to stop to tend to his wound. They were forced to head west, away from their attackers, and away from the keep.

They pounded across the glen, kicking up dirt, tearing through the tall late summer grass. In the open, they were at a distinct disadvantage. Alec surmised there had to be at least ten of them, because of the number of arrows.

Moments later, they could hear the sound of thunder coming from behind. Alec dared take a quick glance over his shoulder. He was off in his estimation by five. There were at least fifteen masked men chasing after them.

Out-numbered and out-weaponed, he could only pray they weren't outwitted. They did the only thing they could do: veer west and north, toward Kinbrea. But even at their current breakneck speed, 'twould be hours before they could reach the village. If they survived.

LEONA WAS NEVER ONE TO WORRY, AT LEAST NOT WITHOUT GOOD reason. The noonin' hour had come and gone without a word from her husband. Thus far, her only visitor had been Patches, whom she'd sent back to Seamus more than an hour before.

Wrapping a fur around her shoulders — because Alec still had not returned her clothes — she opened the door in hopes of asking Gylys or Kyth about her husband.

The landing was empty. Oh, she truly did not wish to go wandering about the keep in nothing but her nightdress, but she was growing hungry. And a little concerned.

Tiptoeing to the edge of the landing, she peered down and was relieved to find Kyth sitting at the table, partaking of fresh bread, dried beef, and an apple. "Kyth!" she called out to him. "Have ye seen Alec?"

He looked up and smiled at her. "No' fer some time, mistress."

Well that was no help and it made no sense. "We were to have lunch together," she informed him.

Kyth stood up and leaned back to look at her. "He might have been distracted. I shall ask Adhaira to bring ye a tray."

"Thank ye. And if it would not be too much trouble, could ye at least bring me my robe? I ken verra well ye ken where Alec put my things. I be cold today. Ye would no' want me to catch my death, would ye?"

He smiled up at her, apparently unbothered by her complaint of cold. "I shall see ye are fed, mistress."

Bah! "And would ye please find me husband? I need to speak with him."

Kyth inclined his head. "I can no' do that until Gylys returns," he said. He raised a hand to stop her protest. "But I promise, we will find Alec fer ye. Do no' fash yourself over it."

Who is fashin' themselves over anythin'? She thought bitterly. With a snort of derision, she turned on her heals and went back to her room.

HAD SHE NOT BEEN CONFINED TO HER ROOM, SHE WOULD BE BELOW stairs right now, heading to her kitchen in order to begin preparing the evening meal. But much to her vexation, she *was* confined. And growing more confused as the afternoon wore on. Where on earth was Alec?

Her frustration grew with each moment that passed. She had not seen him since morning. There was nothing unusual about that. What *was* unusual was that he had specifically told her he would return at noon time, and he would take her for a walk out of doors. Noontime was five hours ago, and thus far, no one would tell her where he was. Her stomach warned that something was wrong. Alec was a man of his word. If something had happened whereby he could not keep his promise, he would have sent word.

Having had enough of pacing around her room, she stormed out, and went to the banister that overlooked the gathering room. She didn't bother with grabbing a fur to cover herself.

"Gylys! Kyth!" she called down, angrily.

Both men were standing in the middle of the gathering room, talking to a young man Leona did not know. All three turned in surprise to look up at her.

"Have you received word of me husband yet?"

She caught the conspiratorial glances they shared betwixt one another before Gylys answered. "Nay, mistress, we have not. But we are certain all is well. Ye should return to yer room."

They failed miserably in their attempts to placate her. Instinctively she knew there was something they were not telling her. But what?

'Twas doubtful any of them would tell her the truth. 'Twas also likely none of them would bring her clothes to her. Frustrated, and with her worry building, she called down to them. "Send Adhaira to me at once. And see if ye can no' find Patrice as well."

Quickly, she returned to her room and her pacing.

Where is Alec?

THE PLAN HAD BEEN FOR ALEC AND HIS MEN TO SPREAD OUT IN THE attempt to outrun their faceless attackers. Alec continued west, while Derrick and Fergus were to split off and try to get back to their keep for reinforcements.

In a perfect world, it would have worked.

But they were outnumbered.

Alec could only watch in stunned horror as an arrow found its way through Fergus' neck. The man fell forward, slumped over the neck of his mount. An arrow hit the flank of the horse, which caused him to rear and toss Fergus to the ground.

Alec cursed under his breath, his heart pounding with dread and fear. "Bloody hell!" he shouted.

Were they to have fought one on one, instead of acting like cowards and ambushing them, Alec had no doubt he and his men could have defended themselves.

They were on their own land, for the sake of Christ! Should not a man be able to ride through his own lands without worry of attack?

Attacking unawares was something *his* people would have done in the not so distant past. Now that he had a taste of what it felt like to be on the receiving end of such treachery, he didn't like it. Bile rose in his throat as he continued pounding across the wide open glen.

A hill came into view. Derrick was still riding right beside him. "Go back!" Alec called out. "Go back and get help!"

Derrick spat at the ground. "The bloody hell I will!" he said. "And leave ye to these sons of whores?"

Mayhap if he had listened to his chief, the arrow would not have torn through his back, nor pierced his heart. But he hadn't listened and now, an arrow was thoroughly lodged inside his chest.

Blood began to ooze from betwixt his lips. His skin turned a deathly pale. Alec wanted to cry out, to curse and then kill the bastard who had just felled one of his oldest friends. With the impact of the arrow, Derrick let loose the reins and the horse began to slow.

Alec could not look back. There was nothing to be done for either Derrick or Fergus. And if he wasn't careful, there would be nothing to be done for him.

ARES WAS BEGINNING TO TIRE. HE'D ALREADY BEEN RIDDEN HARD before the attack had occurred. Who knew how well rested his pursuers horses were.

The ground was turning from wide open glens to a much hillier landscape. With each upward ascent, the horse grew more and more tired. Lord, Alec hated having to push the animal, but push he must if he were to have any hope of escape.

Alec had no idea how long they'd been riding; he could only estimate it had been at least an hour, with the way the sun was hanging low in the western sky. He prayed the attackers would soon give up their pursuit.

Over another hill the landscape turned hopeful. Ahead lay a forest in which he hoped he could hide.

"Come on Ares!" he all but begged his horse. The animal was

covered in froth and foam, his breathing labored. Although he struggled, he still pushed forward at Alec's command.

A wide meandering stream ran through the middle of the forest. Ares pushed up and down the embankment. The icy cold water was deeper than Alec had anticipated. But Ares did not let him down. They made their way through the stream, splashing water all around them. Alec's trews were soaked to his knees by the time they made their way across.

Ares struggled to climb up the next embankment. For a moment, Alec thought his trusty steed was going to fall down and die.

Once they were up the other side, Alec took to the dense trees. Quickly, he scanned the area for a place he could hide. Ahead, the forest thickened across uneven, jagged spaces. Felled trees, wet grass, black earth, gnarled and uneven and broken land.

He could push Ares no farther, not across this terrain. Quickly, he slid from his back, grabbed his reins and led him down a narrow crevice. Kneeling down, he waited, straining his ears to listen for any signs of his attackers. 'Twas difficult to hear anything over his own jagged breaths and the blood rushing in his ears.

Time passed by, agonizingly slowly. Overhead, what he could make out in the little breaks in the green canopy, the skies darkened, signaling that rain was on its way. He might be able to use the weather to his advantage.

As he waited and listened, his mind raced for an explanation. *Who were these men? What the bloody hell did they want? Why had they attacked?* He could only hope he lived long enough to find the answers.

His breathing finally slowed, his heart not beating quite as profoundly as before. The sounds of the forest were all around him. Birds chirping, cawing, squirrels squeaking as they raced through the trees. Still, he heard nothing that said his attackers were near.

Alec knew 'twas too soon to leave his hiding place. The aggressors had already proven they were determined. Doggedly pursuing him across countless miles. But for what purpose?

Ares's own breathing had begun to slow along with Alec's. The well-trained steed did not so much as snicker or paw at the earth. He remained as still and as quiet as a churchmouse.

Derrick and Fergus. He could not help but think of the loyal men who had risked their own lives to save his. There was no time to mourn the loss of the two brave men, men he had known for most of his life.

Hopefully, there would be time for mourning later. And revenge.

Alec's thoughts turned to Leona. What would happen to her should he die this day? Would she stay on or go back to Ian Mackintosh? The thought of her all alone in the world sickened him. And what if she were already with child? 'Twas quite possible she was, though 'twas too soon to tell just yet.

The thought of Leona alone in this world, carrying his child, strengthened his resolve. *I will get back to ye, Leona, come hell or high water.*

～

It had taken very little effort on Leona's part, to convince Adhaira to either find the clothes Alec had hidden, or find something else she could wear. The girl was gone so long, Leona was rummaging through Alec's clothes to find something suitable.

Thankfully, Adhaira did return, and with Patrice. Proudly, Adhaira told her, "I promised Gylys I'd make him sweet cakes for the next fortnight if he would tell me where yer trunk was."

Leona didn't care if she had promised to marry him, as long as she could get dressed. "Thank ye, Adhaira!" she exclaimed as she took the dresses and chemises out of her arms.

"What be goin' on?" Patrice asked. "Why did Alec take yer clothes?"

Leona quickly explained the why of it as she slipped out of her nightdress and into her chemise.

"Daft men," Patrice murmured. "I would be fit to be tied were I married and my husband had done that to me!"

"Speaking of my daft husband," Leona said as she stepped into her blue gown. "Has anyone seen him?"

"I have not seen him since around noon time, when that bandogge of his came into the kitchen," Adhaira told her.

"And I have not seen him since last I was here," Patrice added.

'Twas mightily peculiar. Leona knew something was afoot. But what?

"And ye have no heard anyone whisperin' of his disappearance?" Leona asked as she tied the laces on her dress.

Patrice and Adhaira looked to each other with confusion. "Nay, no' a word," Adhaira said. "But I keep to the kitchens."

"And I have only just arrived," Patrice pointed out. "Do ye think something be wrong?"

"Aye, I do," Leona replied. She grabbed woolens from her bed. "Did ye find me boots?" she asked Adhaira.

"Ye asked fer dresses, no' boots," she told her. "But I'll get them." She hurried from the room in a rush.

"What on earth is going on?" Patrice asked. "Yer husband takes yer clothes then disappears?"

Leona tied the laces of her woolens. "He took those the other day. I do no' think that has anything to do with him disappearing."

"Ye truly think something be wrong?"

"Aye, I do!" she exclaimed. She explained how Alec was supposed to have had lunch with her then take her for a walk afterward. "That was hours ago. And I can tell ye that Gylys and Kyth have been huddled together for the past hour or two, whisperin' over somethin'. Aye, somethin' be wrong. I can feel it in me bones."

THE ARROW CAME FROM BEHIND.

There had been no time to move. The arrow pierced Alec's right arm, his sword arm.

Who the bloody hell is trying to kill me? He screamed silently.

Too stunned to think of anything but fleeing to safety, Alec jumped from his hiding spot and onto Ares's back. In a flash he was off and running again, in a hail of arrows.

'Twas difficult to navigate over the uneven terrain. He kept his head down, low over Ares's back, and he weaved through the thick trees and brush. With his heart pounding and blood rushing in his ears, he tried to think of his next plan of action. If he had only brought his own arrows and bow!

Ducking under low lying branches, tearing through brambles and bushes, he tried to find his way out of the forest. Though 'twas not a forest he was used to visiting, he was certain he was still on his own lands.

Where were his warriors who patrolled this part of his lands?

Finally, the landscape leveled off again. Still hilly, 'twas not nearly as treacherous as he had left behind. Kicking Ares into a full run, he continued west, hoping to veer south at some point so that he might come across one of his border patrol warriors. Or, God willing, back to his keep.

"Mistress!" Gylys called out to Leona as she bounded down the stairs. Patrice and Adhaira were right behind her. "Ye're no' supposed to be out of yer room."

As if she didn't know that. "Thank ye for stating the obvious, Gylys," she said as she headed toward the foyer. Patrice and Adhaira were acting as supporters, and if necessary, they'd provide interference should anyone try to stop her.

Gylys was right behind them. "Mistress!" he called out. "Ye're no' supposed to leave the keep!"

"Again, Gylys, your talent fer statin' the obvious is profound."

Out the door and down the stairs Leona went. It would be another hour or two before nightfall. Hopefully she would find her husband before then.

"Mistress!" Gylys called out.

Leona noted the tone of uncertainty in the man's voice. She stopped and turned to face him. "If ye even think to stop me, Gylys, I shall tell me husband ye were starin' at me earlier, when I wore nothin' but me nightdress."

He stopped his forward progression and stared at her with wide eyes. "But I did no' such thing!"

'Twas a threat she'd not keep, but he did not need to know that. Leona looked around the courtyard. 'Twas was busy, far busier than was ordinary. "Where be my husband?" she asked him. Her words were clipped, her tone firm.

"Yer husband be fine, mistress. Now please, go back to yer room. I am certain he will be home soon."

Before she could offer a terse reply, she saw Kyth racing across the yard. He was coming from the stables. "Mistress?" he asked. "Ye're supposed to be abed."

These men were driving her mad. Doing her best to keep her temper in check — lest she do something she might later regret — Leona took in a deep, cleansing breath. "Kyth, do ye ken where my husband be?"

There it was. That same knowing, conspiratorial glance the two men had shared earlier when she asked the same question.

"I be certain Alec is fine. Ye need no' worry," Kyth told her.

And there was the same answer, if one could even call it that.

"'Tis a wife's duty to worry over her husband," Patrice told him. She looked just as angry as Leona. "Now, if the two of ye do no' explain to yer mistress what the bloody hell is goin' on, I shan't hold her back when she starts beatin' ye senseless."

Leona had already possessed a fondness for Patrice. Considered her a dear friend. But now? Now she absolutely adored the woman.

Adhaira stepped forward, nodding her head. "And I shall give her the heaviest pot in the kitchens to beat ye with!"

Finally! For the first time in a very long while she did not feel quite so alone.

"Lads, I be no' as naive or dimwitted as ye might think," Leona told them. "I have noticed the absence of me husband. I have also noticed that there be men comin' inside the walls. And I can also see the men comin' out of the armory, wearin' their chainmail and battle vestments. Pray, tell me if the two are no' connected?"

Kyth let out a heavy sigh. Gylys ran a hand across his stubbled jaw.

"Alec went fer a ride, around noonin' time. Derrick and Fergus followed," Kyth explained. "Now, I be no' sayin' anythin' be wrong, but we did expect them back by now."

Her heart plunged to her feet and bounced up again. "I have only been married to Alec a little over a month now. Still, I can no' help but think this is no' his usual behavior."

Gylys shook his head. "Nay, mistress, it be no'."

"But Alec is quite capable of takin' care of himself," Kyth added. "As are Derrick and Fergus."

"Aye," Gylys agreed. "Now, if ye ladies would no' mind just goin' back into the keep?"

"Are ye headin' up a search party?" Patrice asked, ignoring the request to return to the keep.

Kyth nodded his head. "Aye. We are goin' to give them another hour before we head out."

"Because I be certain they are all fine," Gylys added forcefully.

Before Leona could reply, shouts came from the upper wall. Everyone turned and headed toward the main wall to see what was the matter.

They stepped out of the secondary gate and into the larger courtyard. The gates had been opened, the drawbridge lowered.

Leona's mouth turned painfully dry as she watched a lone horse come racing across the drawbridge.

Kyth ran forward to catch the reigns. Leona was frozen in place. A group of men surrounded the anxious, nervous animal. Even from where she stood, she could see blood on the saddle and trails of it down the horse's side.

"This be the horse Fergus rode," Kyth declared.

Leona felt lightheaded, almost faint. Patrice and Adhaira stood beside her for support.

Gylys turned away from the horse to look at Leona.

"Can I start worryin' *now?*" she asked sarcastically.

No one answered.

CHAPTER 25

'*T*was a befitting sunset: A blood-red sky, with traces of mulberry and plum, and only a hint of gold. Dark, forbidding, it seemed to Alec it might just be an omen.

His arm pained him, the arrow still firmly lodged betwixt flesh, muscle and bone. There was nothing he could do to stop the flow of blood, for he was far too busy trying to outrun his pursuers. But if he didn't do something soon, he knew he was going to bleed to death.

With Ares at a full run, he crashed through a thick and tall bramble bush. Immediately, he knew he was in trouble. Just a few feet ahead, the land gave way. Before he realized what was happening, Ares was in a panic. A heartbeat later, time slowed down as he was tossed from Ares's back, and flying through the air. Unable to hold on with his injured arm, the reins slipped from his grasp.

Over the cliff he fell into darkness.

It would have taken God himself coming down from the heavens to hold Leona back. Never had Kyth nor Gylys met a woman as determined and stubborn as their laird's wife.

There was no time for arguing with her, Kyth and Gylys knew it. Somehow, she would find a way to follow after them. So they decided 'twas best to give in to her demands that she join the search party. Aye, they knew Alec would be fit-to-be-tied when he found out they'd set her atop a horse and agreed to her going with them. That was *if* he was still alive.

'Twas Leona's idea to use Patches to help find their laird. As far as the men were concerned, 'twas probably the best course of action and best idea anyone could have had.

Leona had sent Adhaira above stairs for her cloak, as well as one of Alec's tunics. None of Alec's men were brave enough to get near the bandogge, save for Seamus. And he'd only gone so far as to release the animal, who immediately went to Leona.

"Patches," she rubbed the top of the dog's head. "We need to find yer master." She didn't know what commands Alec might have used in order to get the dog to go after a scent. Holding the tunic under the animal's snout, she whispered, "Please, patches, find him."

The dog took several sniffs, even going so far as to lick the tunic. He whimpered once, then again, before he grew eager and excited. Leona held on to his collar, afraid to let go until she knew someone would be fast on his heels. Kyth, who was mounted and standing nearby, gave a nod of his head.

Leona released the dog, who took off like the devil was chasing him. Gylys immediately helped Leona to her mount before he took his own. Soon, more than one hundred Bowies on horseback were filing out of the courtyard and chasing after the bandogge.

Over hill, through glen and dale, they rode fast, keeping up with the bandogge. Occasionally, the dog would pause to sniff the ground for a few moments before he picked up the scent again.

All the while, Leona prayed. She prayed her husband was safe, that they'd find him and his men soon.

The sun was just beginning to set when they came upon Fergus. "Mistress, look away," Kyth told her. But it was too late. She'd already seen the poor man's lifeless body lying on the ground.

His corpse lay crumpled and bloody, his arms askew, one leg

broken. The arrow was still lodged in his throat. His cold, dead eyes staring up at nothing.

Bile rose in her throat, her stomach roiled with despair, sorrow, and disgust. She thought of Maisie, Fergus' wife, and their children.

They stopped for a moment while Kyth and a few men dismounted, looking for any evidence of what might have occurred. The other half of their team pressed forward, following Patches.

"It looks like an ambush," Kyth said. He was crouched low, looking at the ground filled with arrows. "Many men on horseback from the looks of it."

"An ambush?" she murmured.

"Aye," Kyth said as he tossed an arrow aside and stood up. "Were it a fair fight, Alec would be back at the keep right now, telling us the tale over a few drams of whisky."

Leona was glad Kyth held such a high regard toward her husband. She had never been witness to his fighting skills and would have to put her faith in Kyth's words. Which led to her hope that Alec was still alive.

"Who would do such a thing?" she asked, in a low, reverent tone.

'Twas apparent no one had the answer to that question.

SHE REFUSED TO BELIEVE ALEC WAS DEAD. THERE WAS A GOOD CHANCE he and Derrick were still alive. He *had* to be alive! Without him… nay, she could not allow her mind nor her heart to go there. 'Twas too painful, too gut wrenchingly painful.

They pressed on, leaving a handful of men behind to take Fergus' back to his unsuspecting family. Leona clung to hope like a drowning man clings to driftwood. 'Twas all she had.

Her hope was tested a mile or two later, when they came upon Derrick's body. He lay on his side, blood pooling all around him. The arrow that took his life protruded from his chest.

There was no way for her to hold back her tears. She wept quietly.

Made no attempt to wipe the tears away. She cried for Fergus, for Derrick, and for her husband.

Kyth pulled their group to a halt and began to give orders. "Phillip, I want ye and twenty men to spread out. Whoever attacked our laird and friends could still be about. Find the bloody bastards. Ye may kill as many as ye wish, but find out the reason behind the attack first."

Phillip gave a curt nod, before pulling back and choosing the men who would follow him.

"Do no' give up, Mistress," Kyth told her. "Alec be a smart man. Do no' give up hope."

As much as she wanted to believe him, 'twas nearly impossible. Tears slowly fell down her cheeks as they continued riding.

Please, God! Do no' let me come upon him, as we did Fergus and Derrick! I fear I would want to lay down next to him and die.

"Mistress," Kyth's voice broke through her quiet reverie. "Ye must keep hopeful. Alec be alive, and when he sees ye next, he will ken ye thought him dead. 'Twill be his end if he thinks ye did no' have enough faith in him."

She blinked away her tears, uncertain if he was simply trying to make her feel better or if he truly believed what he said. She studied him closely for a long moment, as they rode west and north. His jaw was set as he looked deep into her eyes. Aye, he believed what he said.

"Verra well, then, Kyth," she said as she dried her eyes and cheeks with the sleeve of her dress. "Let us go find me husband and take him home."

Night had fallen, a sliver of moon hidden behind heavy, dark clouds. Rain fell, lending to the depressing night.

Someone had possessed the wherewithal to bring torches. Even with the lit torches, 'twas a painfully slow pace they kept. Soon, they came upon the rest of their search party. Patches was walking around in circles sniffing the ground, apparently trying to pick up the scent again.

Leona shivered as the rain splattered across her face. Drawing her cloak more tightly around her, she donned her cowl. 'Twas late, cold, and rainy, but they would not give up their search for Alec. Even if it took all night, or even days.

Mayhap the men who had attacked them had not killed Alec. Leona wondered if mayhap he hadn't been kidnapped. Kidnapped was far better than being dead.

Patches picked up the scent again. With his nose close to the ground, his pace was much slower than before.

"Mistress," Kyth called out as he trotted back toward her. "The hour grows late. Mayhap ye should go back. I can spare enough men to guard ye."

Leona shook her head. "Nay, Kyth. I will be fine."

"We have no' heard from the scouts and the attackers could still be about," he argued.

"At this hour?" she asked. "If ye were worried over me safety, ye should have sent me back the moment we found poor Fergus."

Kyth rolled his eyes and let loose a frustrated breath. Seeing her determination to stay, he said, "Verra well. Please, stay next to me and Gylys. If anythin' were to happen to ye, Alec would have our heads on pikes."

Oddly enough, his words lifted her spirits. Knowing Alec would be upset should anything happen to her made her smile. Even though she believed the real reason he wanted her to return to the keep was his fear of what they might come across.

IT BECAME TOO DANGEROUS TO RIDE, SO THEY HAD TO DISMOUNT AND walk their horses. Kyth cut through bracken and bramble bushes, making a path for Leona. They were almost to the edge when they heard Patches howl and bark.

Kyth furiously worked to get them through the mess of twisted limbs and branches. Soon, they spilled out into a clearing.

Leona nearly fell to her knees when she saw Alec's mount,

pounding the earth, ready to trample Patches. "Patches!" she called out to him. "Here! Now!"

The dog left the horse and immediately came to stand beside her. He whimpered and fussed while Kyth went to settle Ares.

Gylys came to help, holding a torch out against the blackness. Leona heard something familiar then. The sound of crashing waves.

"Gylys!" she called out to him. "Take care!"

If her instincts were correct, the ocean lay not far from where they stood.

Cautiously, Gylys raised his torch and took tentative steps forward. His heart seized when he realized he was precariously close to the edge of a sheer cliff! "Stay back!" he called over his shoulder.

He lay on his stomach and held the torch out. Just as he had suspected. Alec lay on a very narrow ledge some ten feet below him. "Alec!" he called out. "Alec!"

FOR CERTAIN, HE THOUGHT HE WAS GOING TO DIE.

He had scrambled and clawed for something to hang on to during his fall. With his left hand, he'd managed to grab onto a thick vine, but he'd only been able to hold on for a little while. Finally, he dropped another five or six feet where he landed safely on an exceedingly narrow ledge. A bit of the earth had given away when he landed, threatening to send him tumbling another hundred feet or so to his doom.

Once he caught his breath and stilled his fearfully beating heart, he scooted backward and rested against the face of the cliff. He'd been close to dying far too many times to count this day.

Once his hands no longer shook or trembled, he examined his wound. There was a good deal of blood seeping around both the entry and exit. The arrow had pierced the tender flesh of his underarm. The tip was covered with blood and flesh, protruding out a good six inches. Experience told him the arrow was acting to help stop the complete and total blood letting.

Tearing the sleeve of his tunic off, he bunched it together and set it next to him. 'Twas painful, but he managed to get out of his plaid and the remainder of his tunic. Wincing with pain, he pulled the dirk from his boot and stuck it betwixt his teeth. Next, he removed his sword belt and placed it next to the bits of cloth.

He needed to get the arrow out.

"What I would no' do for a flagon of whisky!" he cursed as he began to carefully cut the tip of the arrow off. 'Twould be impossible for him to reach the fletching because of the angle of the arrow. He could not cut it, but hopefully, he could manage to pull it back out the way it went in.

Using his thumb to help keep the shaft of the arrow in place, he carefully carved at the wood until it was cut clean through. "Bloody hell, that hurts!" he groused, taking in deep cleansing breaths.

Making sure the tip was free of debris or splinters, he raised his arm up and over his head so he could both see and grab the fletching.

With his tunic torn into makeshift bandages, he took in more deep breaths. As with any unpleasant task, 'twas best to make quick work of it. In one swift motion, he gave out a loud yell as he pulled the arrow out of his tender, pained flesh.

Quickly, he wrapped the strips of tunic around the arm before wrapping his belt around it. Using his teeth, he pulled the belt taught. 'Twas only then he let loose the breath he'd been holding.

"Bloody hell," he cursed. The world around him began to sway and spin until he thought he might throw up. Instead, he passed out against the face of the cliff.

When Alec woke next, he was soaked with rain, the sky an inky black. At first, he thought he'd been dreaming, hearing discombobulated voices swirling in his mind. A few blinks of his eyes, a great shake of his head, and he began to regain his faculties.

"Alec! Speak to me!"

Was that truly his wife's voice calling to him?

"Alec, please!"

He took in a deep breath and dared turn his head to look up. He could just make out her face, lit by the torch she was holding out over the edge. "Leona?" he called back to her, disbelievingly.

"Och! Thank, God!" she cried out to him.

His mind raced, with worry and fury. Either she had escaped the keep and had found him on her own, or — and it was highly probably — that she had brow beaten the two men until they capitulated and brought her with them.

"Where are Gylys and Kyth?" he yelled up to her.

"Tryin' to figure out how best to get ye off that ledge!" she called down to him. The relief in her voice was undeniable.

"Then what in the name of God are ye doin' here, woman!"

"I swear, Alec Bowie, if ye tell me I am supposed to be abed, I will strangle ye with me bare hands!"

He could not resist the urge to laugh. Whether 'twas from his injury, the events of the day, or sheer insanity, his laughter came in great waves. It occurred to him that his wife was just as insane as he.

"Alec!" 'Twas Gylys calling down to him. "Are ye hurt?"

Now, if he were to answer that question honestly, his wife might be reduced to histrionics. Without a doubt, he knew she had been worried, probably frightfully so, when he hadn't come for her at noontime. Knowing her as he did, she'd probably been reduced to tears more than once this day.

"Other than me pride?" he called back. "Nothin' a few drams of whisky will no' fix."

"Och! Thank God!" He heard Leona cry out.

Someone scurried above, sending bits of earth and rock tumbling down.

"We are goin' to throw down a rope to ye," Gylys called to him. "We will pull ye up when ye give the word."

A few heartbeats later, the rope fell and landed on his head. Gritting his teeth against the pain in his arm, he pulled the looped end over his head and cinched it tight. "I be ready!" he called up.

Oh, he knew it was going to hurt, being yanked and pulled. He grunted, but managed to keep from yelling out.

It seemed to take a year before he was pulled over the ledge and back on to solid ground. He lay on his back, out of breath, and forever grateful to be off the bloody narrow ledge.

"Alec!" Leona flew to his side and sank to her knees. She began kissing his face, his cheeks, his eyes. "Where are ye injured? Did ye break anythin'? How long have ye been down there? Who did this to ye?"

Relieved, glad to be alive, he took a good deal of pleasure in her kisses and attentions. But he also knew he needed to be seen by the healer.

"Lass?" he said as he smiled up at her.

"Yes?" she asked anxiously. "What is it ye need? What can I do?

"Ye found me," he told her as he placed a palm on her cheek.

Bewildered, she scrunched her brows together. "Of course I found ye! I was worried sick over ye!"

He offered her his most sincere, if not devious smile. "But I do remember, not long ago, that ye told me were ever I lost, ye'd let me rot."

Her mouth fell open. She punched his arm. "Och! Alec Bowie ye are the most stubborn, pig-headed, ridiculous man I have ever met in me life! I should have let ye rot, to punish ye for makin' me worry all day and into the night!"

He laughed at her distress, which infuriated her.

"But ye did come fer me," he said. "And I be truly grateful."

She stopped her tirade, but continued to glare at him.

"Leona, I am goin' to tell ye somethin', but I need ye to swear to me, ye'll no' cry or make a fuss."

"Me? Cry or fuss?" she asked. "I never cry or fuss, Alec." What on earth was he thinking? Why, she was the most level-headed, stalwart person she knew.

"But I need ye to swear it lass. Please."

For the life of her, she could not begin to guess what was so important that he would need her sworn oath not to make a commotion. "Verra well, Alec, ye have me word."

With her help, he sat up. "Ye swear it?"

"I do!" she said, exasperated with him.

He turned so the she could see his injured arm. "I was shot with an arrow, lass. I pulled it out, but 'twill need stitches."

Leona kept her word. She did not cry, or scream, or otherwise make any sort of commotion or fuss. She took one look at his wounded arm, the bloodied bandages, and fainted.

TRUE TO HER WORD, LEONA DID NOT CRY OR OTHERWISE MAKE A spectacle of herself. Oh, she was not unaccustomed to the sight of blood. Raised around carpenters and laborers, bloody wounds, cuts, even the occasional missing finger, were as common as sheep. And she had certainly washed enough blood out of her husband's clothes of late.

Mayhap 'twas all the worry of the day. Mayhap 'twas her lack of sleep. Or, mayhap, 'twas the garish glow the torches cast against his arm, the way the light flickered over the blood that made her feel light-headed.

Whatever the reason, the moment she saw the blood seeping through the fabric, everything went black.

Gylys and Kyth were at her side at once, patting her hands, speaking to her, their worry quite evident.

"What happened?" Gylys asked, confused and worried all at once.

"That would be me wife tryin' not to cry or make a fuss over me injury," Alec explained.

Leona's eyes fluttered open. "Why am I lying down?" she murmured. It felt as though she were on a boat in rough seas.

No one answered.

She looked up at her husband. He bore a warm smile. Then she remembered.

"Ye need the healer," she said as she struggled to sit up.

"Mayhap ye do as well," Alec said. There was not the faintest hint of sarcasm in his tone.

"Nay," she argued. The last time she'd seen Mairi, she'd been ordered to stay abed for three days. "I am well." With fierce determination, she willed her stomach to settle. *The last thing Alec needs is fer me to act or look a fool.* Pulling on every ounce of willpower and energy, she began to take control of the situation.

"Come, let us get ye back to the keep," she said as she sat up. "Gylys, could ye please send men ahead to get Mairi? And tell Adhaira to heat plenty of water."

Kneeling next to Alec, she asked Kyth to hold the torch down low so the she might assess his injury. She knew better than to remove the belt. With no supplies, no bandages, no bone needle or thread, 'twas best to wait until they returned to the keep before she did anything else. The only thing she could do was try to determine the amount of blood loss thus far.

The tunic he'd used for bandages was soaked through. But it did not appear to be bleeding now, or at least not so much that she needed to worry significantly. She grunted, as she'd often heard men do. "'Tis naught but a scratch," she told him, looking him directly in the eye. Fervently, she hoped he could not see or detect the worry eating away at her heart.

"Aye, lass," Alec murmured. "'Tis naught but a scratch."

CHAPTER 26

*A*lec refused to ride Ares, for the animal had been put through too much already. Instead, he rode back to the keep on Leona's mount, with her nestled in front of him. One of his men took charge of Ares's reins, the steed following behind.

Someone had given them a fresh plaid, which Alec draped first around his shoulders before pulling his wife in close and wrapping her in it. It felt good to have his arms around her again. As much as he wanted to deny it, he needed her.

'Twas that time of night, between midnight and dawn, when even the night creatures were asleep. The sky could not make up its mind on whether or not it wanted to rain. Heavy, gray clouds moved in and out, the wind chilling them all.

They said not a word during the three-hour journey back to the keep. Alec was too tired, his mind too busy with trying to figure out who and why they had been attacked.

Leona, putting on a brave face, had concerns of her own. If they did not get her husband help, and soon, his wound could fester. If that happened, the best he could hope for was to lose an arm. The other alternative was death.

With dignity and grace, she kept her worries to herself. She would have been no use to anyone, least of all Alec, if she burst into tears at every turn.

Mairi had been found and was waiting at the keep when they arrived. With Leona's help, they tended to Alec's wounds as best they could.

He had bled ferociously when they removed the belt. The only thing they could do was pack the wounds tightly, with thick, heavy gauze. "I fear I can no' stitch him," Mairi explained. "He be bleedin' too much. We will have to wait."

'Twas the waiting that nearly did her in. Waiting to see if the bleeding would start up again. Waiting to see if a fever would set in. Waiting to see if he'd still be alive from one hour to the next. After Mairi and the men left, Leona helped Alec out of his boots and trews and bathed him as best as she could.

"Leona," Alec asked as she was washing his arms with a soapy cloth. "How did ye convince Gylys and Kyth to allow ye to ride with them, to search for me?"

She refused to look him in the eye and chose to focus on bathing him.

"Leona?"

"I told them I would tell *ye* they were oglin' me inappropriately whilst ye were away. I had only me nightdress, if ye remember. I forgot to wrap myself in a fur when I stepped out of the room."

He laughed, low and deep. "And they believed ye?"

Raising a brow, she finally looked him in the eye. "Would *ye* have believed me had I told ye such?"

His smile disappeared in an instant. Jealousy rose rapidly. "Do ye mean to tell me they were lookin' at ye like ye were a common bar wench?" his voice was rising in pitch. He shoved her hand away and tried to leave the bed. "I will kill them. I will kill them both!"

Leona laughed and shook her head. "Lie down, ye foolish man!"

He paused and cocked his head to one side.

"I told them I would tell ye they were ogling me inappropriately. 'Twould have been a lie."

He shook his head, hoping it would bring him some clarity. "So they were no' oglin' ye?"

Smiling, she gave a slow shake of her head. "When I came out of me room without the fur? Their eyes were glued to their feet. Nay, Alec. Ye can trust Gylys and Kyth."

A chuckle escaped as he lay back in the bed. "Ye're becomin' more and more a Bowie each day, lass."

"How so?"

"Well, he said as he patted her hand and closed his eyes. "Ye've learned how to blackmail a man."

She didn't know if she should feel proud or appalled at the notion.

Leona never left his side.

Not even when he ordered her to leave when his men returned late the following afternoon with news of the attackers.

"Nay," she told him firmly. "Yer men can speak just as freely as if I were no' here."

Either he was too weak to argue or he had come to realize she was stronger than he gave her credit for. It mattered not to her. She would stay and listen to everything. No matter how violent or lurid things might turn.

She sat in a chair next to the bed, and held his hand. More for her own benefit than Alec's.

Gylys and Kyth stood at the foot of the bed. Both men were road weary, with dark circles under their eyes, stubbled jaws, and damp, mud-covered clothing.

"Tell me what ye have learned," Alec said. Leona helped him to sit, propping pillows up behind him.

"We came upon the attackers before dawn," Kyth explained. "They were camped out at the forest we share with the McLeods."

"That was where the attack began," Alec told them. "They were McLeods, then?" Alec asked, a look of concern etched on his pale face.

"Only two were, but they were cast-outs. The rest were simply thieves."

That made very little sense to Leona. "Why would thieves kill them? Why would they hunt them down like animals?"

"'Twas revenge they sought. No' purses," Kyth replied. His jaw was clenched, working back and forth. His anger was unmistakable.

Revenge? Leona dare not imagine the reasons why they sought revenge with such blood-thirsty determination.

"Be they all dead?" Alec asked.

"Aye," Kyth replied. "Every last one."

Leona shook her head in dismay. There had to be more to it than that. "Ye killed them fer seekin' revenge? Revenge fer what? And do ye no' fear retaliation? Does yer killin' them make up fer what they did? Will it bring back Derrick or Fergus?"

There were too many unanswered questions for her liking. Anger rose from the pit of her stomach.

"Mistress, they sought revenge fer somethin' Alec had no part in. And nay, their deaths do no' make up fer anythin'," Kyth told her. He sounded tired and angry and sorrowful. "And it sure as hell will no' bring me friends back."

"Then why kill them? Why no' think of another form of punishment?" She hated fighting and death and all this talk of revenge.

He glanced at Alec before answering. "Mistress, they attacked because they thought they could get away with it."

"What do ye mean?" she asked, wholly confused.

"We've laid down our weapons. We've picked up plows. The world now believes we are lead by a weak-minded fool. That we will no' do anythin' to defend ourselves."

Leona looked to her husband, her stomach a jumbled mess of knots. "They attacked because ye wanted peace?"

A tic had formed in Alec's jaw. He knew, he understood all too well the implications of what Kyth had just told him. Unfortunately, the same could not be said for his wife. "Those men were foolish to believe such a thing. They misunderstood our desire for peace for weakness. We can have peace. We *will* have peace, and remain a strong people. Killing them shows anyone else who might believe as they did, that while we might be plantin' crops and raisin' cattle, we will defend what is ours."

It took a long while for his meaning to sink in. While they were no longer thieves themselves, nor marauders or murderers, they'd no' lie down or turn and run like cowards.

The Bowies were far from cowards.

Unfortunately, it took the deaths of two good men and more than a dozen thieves to get that message across.

And it sickened her to know she understood it.

THE FUNERAL FOR FERGUS AND DERRICK WAS HELD TWO DAYS AFTER THE attack. Leona had been so busy tending to Alec that she had not had time to visit Fergus's widow, Maisie, or their children.

Alec, though still quite weak from his injury, insisted on attending. 'Twas important he show his people that he was well and would continue to get well. Derrick had been a good friend to him over the years. And Fergus had been one of his earliest supporters for peace.

They woke to heavy rain that morn, so 'twas decided the funeral be held in the gathering room of the keep. The bodies, draped in linen, as was their custom, lay side by side on tables brought in specifically for that purpose.

With Leona at his side and Kyth and Gylys behind them, they left the bedchamber and went below stairs. The gathering room was unable to hold all those people who had come to pay their last respects. The foyer and hallways were packed as well, and more people spilled out the doors, rain-be-damned.

Maisie sat on a chair next to her husband's body, as she held their youngest babe in her arms. Their other two children, just weans really, clung to her legs. A few of the womenfolk stood next to her, one with a hand on her shoulder, offering their support. In that small group stood Effie, holding Archibald. Next to her was Dougall and their sons. Leona thought Dougall looked pale, a bit gaunt. Perhaps he was simply tired from the events of the past few days.

The Bowies, for the most part, were God-fearing folk. However, there was not a priest in all of Scotia brave enough to tend to this flock. Neither did they posses a kirk or chapel in which to pray. When it came to weddings or funerals, 'twas left to the chief of the clan to act as officiant.

A small dais had been brought in for Alec to stand on to address the people. With his shoulders back, his head high, he took to it. Never once did he wince or otherwise show how much pain he was in, either physically or emotionally. Leona, Kyth and Gylys stood next to the dais as their own display of support for their chief.

The crowd hushed as Alec began to speak.

"As many of ye ken, Derrick, Fergus, and I were attacked recently, by a band of thievin' whore-sons. Without warnin', they ambushed us on our own lands."

Angry murmurs spread throughout the crowd. Leona was surprised to hear her husband speak in such a manner at such a solemn occasion.

"The bastards who attacked us are also dead, our men saw to it."

A cheer erupted from the crowd. The people waved their fists in the air, nodded and cheered their approval, glad that revenge had been sought on behalf of these two fine men.

Alec raised his hand to call for quiet. Slowly, the cheers faded and people stood in wrapt attention, eagerly waiting to hear what else their laird might have to say.

"This be no' the first time such a thing has happened to us. And 'twill probably no' be the last. But we are Bowies. We will defend our lands, our people, to the verra end if we must."

Another cheer broke out over the room. To Leona's way of thinking, this was less a funeral and more a call to war. Still, she remained silent, watching and listening.

"We come here today, to say goodbye to two of the finest men I have ever kent in me life," Alec spoke out over the din of the crowd. They fell silent once again.

"The rest of the world thinks we be nothin' more than a bunch of thieves and murderers." He paused briefly as he looked out at his people. "At one time, that was true."

The crowd laughed and looked proud.

"I imagine this room be filled with more thieves and reivers than all the gaols in Scotia!"

More laughter, more proud looks from the throngs of people.

"But the outside world does no' ken the *true* Bowies. Aye, we might be a lot filled with questionable characters, but we are a proud and decent people," Alec said, his face filled with pride.

"To the outside world, Fergus Bowie was a cow reiver. 'Tis true, he was. One of the best. But what they do no' ken, was that he was also a fine musician, a man who was good with animals, and a man who loved his wife, Maisie, and their children with all that he was. He was a good man. A man you could count on in time of need. He'd no' turn his back on ye. Unless, of course, ye were a sassenach."

Chuckles and laughter filtered through the crowd.

"And Derrick Bowie, now there was a man's man. If ever ye were in battle, ye wanted a man like Derrick at yer side. Mostly, because he was so bloody big, ye could use him as a shield!"

Raucous laughter spread throughout the room. Alec smiled warmly at his people. "Now, the outside world, they thought he was nothin' more than a brawler, a man who would break yer neck for lookin' at him the wrong way," he smiled and leaned over the podium as if he were sharing a secret. "That only happened twice and both times, 'twas a sassenach who had insulted him."

He waited a long moment for the laughter to subside. "To the outside world, Derrick was a defiler of women; he stole countless women from their husbands and fathered countless children with them. That is *almost* true."

Heads nodded all around them, for they knew the truth of the matter.

"What they do no' ken is the entire truth of it. 'Twas three women, and they be here today," Alec looked at the three women who sat near Derrick's body. They were surrounded with numerous children of varying ages. From babes to boys old enough to shave, and girls old enough to marry.

"What they do no' ken is that Derrick saved each of those women from husbands who were crueler, more vile, and meaner than the whole of us combined."

Leona watched the women closely. One of them bore a jagged scar across her face. It started at her forehead, down the side of her cheek, back up, across her nose to the opposite side of her face. Tears of grief streamed down her cheeks and off her chin. Her sorrow was as real as the sun coming up each morn.

"What some call stealin', we call rescuin'. Derrick saved each of them and their children from beatin's. From rape. From bein' sold from one man to the next. From hell on earth. *That* was the kind of man Derrick was. He could no' allow them to suffer, so he brought them here. To live amongst us, to protect them."

Leona looked out at the crowd. There was not a dry eye to be found. She felt it then, the pride, the love this clan had for one another. 'Twas not something they took lightly or for granted. Each of them understood what their reputation was. They took pride in it for they knew the *truth*. And Leona was seeing and hearing that truth for the first time. She didn't even try to hold back her tears.

"These men," Alec choked back a few tears of his own. "These good, decent men were loved by all. Their absence will be felt for a verra, verra long while." He took a deep breath before going on. "I will miss them. They were me friends."

He gave a final nod to his people before stepping down from the dais. For the first time since they had married, Alec came to her and wrapped his arms around her. 'Twas the first time he ever displayed his affection for her publicly.

WITHIN THE HOUR, THE CLAN BOWIE WAS FILING OUT OF THE gathering room and heading toward the cemetery. Alec had taken

Leona's hand in his as they led their people out of the dark room and into the dull, dreary afternoon.

Big, strong men carried the bodies of Derrick and Fergus Bowie with a blend of pride and grief. They're families followed behind, clinging to one another as they walked across the drawbridge and headed south. The rain had let up only slightly. Gray skies and dark clouds overhead matched the somberness of the moment. Someone played a melancholy tune on a lute as the procession walked along the path.

The cemetery sat not far from the original Bowie keep, in a serene and well kept little glen. Graves of varying ages were marked with wooden crosses, all in neat rows. Leona wondered which of these people were in charge of keeping the cemetery. Whomever it was, 'twas quite evident they took their duty seriously. 'Twas free from weeds and bramble bushes or other unwanted plants. Neat, tidy, and well kept.

They went to the far side of the cemetery where holes had been dug. The bodies were lowered into the darkness. Raindrops fell like tears from heaven, splattering against the linen covered bodies as well as the living.

Gylys appeared at Alec's side. He handed him Fergus's sword. Alec kissed the hilt before kneeling down. Closing his eyes, he whispered something Leona could not understand, before laying the sword across Fergus's body. A long moment passed before he stood and resumed his position next to Leona.

Next, a lad Leona thought to be about six and ten, stepped forward. She recognized him as one of those children standing with the women Derrick had rescued. Soon, a dozen children lined up beside him. The youngest, a boy who could not have been more than four years of age, was holding Derrick's sword reverently with both hands. He had to lay it sideways in order to kiss the hilt. His little eyes were filled with tears as he passed it on to the next child.

Down the line Derrick Bowie's sword went, from one child to the next. Each of them whispering something unintelligible before kissing the hilt. The oldest of the children finally received that heavy, oft used sword. It tore at Leona to see this lad who was trying so hard to be brave, break down. His shoulders shook as tears fell from his eyes. Gylys went to stand next to the young man to offer his support. The young man had to take several deep breaths before he could proceed with the ritual.

When he finished, he handed the sword to Alec, who repeated the phrase and gesture. Once again, he knelt and placed the sword atop Derrick's body, just as he had done with Fergus's.

Once the ritual was finished, Alec took Leona's hand once more and began the slow trek back to the keep. After leaving the cemetery, Leona dared ask the burning question.

In a low, reverent tone, she whispered, "Alec, what was the phrase ye all said when kissin' the hilt of their swords?"

He gave her hand a gentle squeeze before answering. "Fare thee well, my friend. Ye were loved."

THE FOLLOWING FEW DAYS SEEMED TO FLY BY. THANKFULLY, ALEC WAS healing nicely and no fever set in. But much to Leona's vexation, he refused to rest for more than two days. "I have important duties," he told her. "I can rest when I am dead."

"And ye will *be* dead sooner than ye think if ye are no' careful!" she argued.

They reached a compromise of sorts.

He could work as long as it wasn't physical and Leona promised not to nag him over it. She also promised not to beat him senseless should he injure his arm again.

On the fourth day of his recovery, Leona finally left his side. At her request, Adhaira had been taking meals to auld Melvin, faithfully each day. Leona wanted to thank her for her kindness as well as plan out meals for the next few days.

Leona was in the kitchen with Adhaira when Patches came scratching at the back door.

"Och! That beast has been here every day!" Adhaira cried, refusing to open the door to him.

Leona rolled her eyes heavenward. "That *beast* saved yer laird's life," she told her as she opened the door and let Patches inside. Leona crouched low and loved on the dog. "Is that no' right, Patches? Ye are no' the ferocious beast every one says ye be."

When Leona looked up, Adhaira was standing behind the larder door, peering around it with one eery looking eye.

"Och! Do no' be so silly!" Leona told her. "If ye toss him a bit of ham, he will forever be yer friend."

"I'll decline yer offer, mistress," Adhaira whispered.

Leona stood up with her hands on her hips, and said, "Have we any ham? Or mutton?"

"Aye," she whispered. As if she were afraid the dog would hear her and come charging.

"Then please bring it to me. I promise, I shall protect ye."

The eye disappeared, replaced moments later by an outstretched hand holding a leg of mutton. Realizing Adhaira was not going to get anywhere near the dog, Leona retrieved the proffered food. "Patches, lie down."

The dog licked his chops before dutifully taking his spot by the hearth. "Good boy," Leona praised him. Patting him on the head, she then gave him the leg of mutton.

"Now," she said as she wiped her hands on a drying cloth. "Lets ye and I discuss upcoming meals. Do ye ken, be there anythin' we're runnin' low on?" she asked as she retrieved a bit of parchment and the ink and quill she kept stored in a box on a shelf under the counter.

Refusing to leave the safety of the larder, Adhaira's voice, though muffled, came filtering through. "Aye, there be a few things we could use."

While Adhaira rattled off the items they were low on, Leona wrote everything down, adding a few necessary things of her own. On the morrow, she would send Gylys and Kyth to Kinbrea to procure those things on her list.

"There ye are!" 'Twas Alec's voice speaking to her from the door.

Leona stood abruptly, surprised to find him out of bed. "What are ye doin'?" she asked, rushing to his side.

"I woke up and ye were gone," he smiled at her. "Besides, I've laid abed long enough."

"Ye will have laid abed long enough when *I* say ye have," she told him as she wrapped an arm around his torso.

"I thought ye promised no' to nag?" he said playfully.

"Ye be confusin' me concern fer ye with naggin'. Now, back to bed with ye."

He refused to budge. "Will ye be joinin' me?" he asked, his tone low and warm and oh, so very inviting.

"Nay," she told him, though she was truly tempted. "I have work to do."

Before she had time to think, Alec had her in his arms and was kissing her. Deep, passionate, knee-knocking kisses. "Then I shall take my pleasure with ye *here,*" he said as he walked her backwards, kissing her all the while.

'Twas then he heard someone clearing their throat. A muffled sound, coming from the larder.

He pulled away from Leona's lips. "We be no' alone?"

Leona giggled sweetly and shook her head. "I fear no', husband."

For the first time since she had met him, Alec looked utterly embarrassed. A deep red blush crept up from his neck before spreading across his face. Even his ears turned red! Leona pulled her lips in to keep from laughing at his distress.

"Good day to ye, m'laird," came Adhaira's voice from behind the larder door.

He cringed, his skin turning even darker. He buried his face against Leona's neck. "Why, pray tell is she in the larder?"

"She be hiding from Patches." She nodded toward the hearth where his dog was happily devouring the remnants of the bone.

Patches! He had forgotten about his bandogge and that his wife had changed his name. He spun around in the direction she indicated.

"Satan!" he called out. The dog looked up once before turning his attention back to the bone.

Now, he had a choice to make. He could rail against his wife and chastise her for breaking his bandogge. Or he could simply let it go.

Before he could make his decision, Willem opened the back door and stepped inside. Patches was on his feet in an instant, standing next to Leona, growling low and gutturally, giving fair warning that he was the protector of his mistress.

"Patches!" Leona called out, resting a hand on top of the dog's head. "Be nice!"

Alec gave a slow shake of his head, wholly confounded. *Satan* sat dutifully at his wife's feet, never once taking his eyes off the invader. Mayhap the dog wasn't broken after all.

With Alec summarily embarrassed, Leona sent him back to his room and Patches back to his keeper. After finishing the list, she decided 'twould be a good time to begin a few batches of bread. It did not take long before she and Adhaira had a dozen loaves rising.

Leona was about to take her leave to go see to her husband, when Patrice came to see her. The poor woman's eyes were red from crying.

"Patrice, what be the matter?" Leona asked as she ushered the woman to a chair at the table.

While Patrice fought back her tears, Adhaira poured a mug of cider and offered it to her. "I have just come from Dougall and Effie's," she began as she dabbed her eyes with a bit of linen.

Leona's heart seized with dread. Her first thought was of the babe. "Is it Archibald?" she asked.

Patrice shook her head and swallowed hard. "Nay, 'tis Dougall. He became ill again. The healer thinks he has the wastin' disease."

Leona sank into a chair opposite her friend. "Nay," she murmured, her heart stinging with disbelief. Adhaira made the sign of the cross before pouring Leona her own mug of ale. Leona ignored it.

"Aye, 'tis true. Effie just told me and I came here straight away."

They sat in stunned silence for a long while. Leona's heart broke for the poor family. Alec would take care of them, making sure they did not starve, as he was doing for Fergus's and Derrick's families. He would ensure they always had a home and would want for very little. Save to have their fathers back.

With Alec recuperating from his wounds, she felt 'twas up to her to visit with the families. "Adhaira," she said, her mind still reeling from the awful news. "I need ye to prepare baskets of food. I want to take them to Maisie and the other women. While I am out, I will stop to see Effie and Dougall."

"Would ye like me to help deliver them?" Patrice asked.

"Aye, but only if ye're up to it. I fear we have had far too much dyin' and mournin' of late."

"I will help ye too, mistress, if that be all right with ye?" Adhaira offered.

"I can use all the help I can get this day."

EACH OF THE WOMEN CARRIED TWO BASKETS OF FOOD WITH THEM AS they left the keep. Leona had decided to see for herself how Dougall was faring before she shared anything with her husband.

They stopped at Maisie's home first. Patrice knocked softly at the door. Moments later, Maisie opened it. Her eyes were red with tears and she was taken aback by the presence of the three women.

"Maisie," Patrice said in a warm voice. "We have brought ye a basket of food."

Maisie took it without uttering a word. From inside the cottage, they could hear a babe crying. Leona stepped forward to speak to her. "Maisie, I want ye to ken that should ye need anythin', we are all here fer ye. All ye need do is ask."

"I want nothin' from *ye*," she spat out.

Leona was surprised at her harsh tone and words. Before she could offer a reply, Maisie went on. "'Tis *yer* fault me Fergus is dead!"

"Maisie, that be no' true," Patrice exclaimed.

"It is! Had Alec no' married her, we would no' be layin' down our weapons! 'Tis all her fault. She turned his head, she did! Look what peace has gotten us!"

Leona's stomach churned. Though she knew in her heart she was no more responsible for the deaths of Fergus and Derrick than Maisie was, it still stung to think anyone could blame her.

"Maisie, ye *ken* that be no' true," Patrice told her in a soothing voice. She draped an arm around her shoulder. "Alec has long wanted peace fer our clan. Yer Fergus wanted it too. Long before any of us even knew of Leona."

Maisie wiped her tears on the shoulder of her dress. "I shall never ken peace. No' now. No' without me Fergus. Peace!" she all but spat the word out. "Peace was no' worth me husband's life."

She turned away from the women and went back into her cottage, shutting the door softly behind her.

Oh, how Leona wanted to weep! To cry and beg for the woman's forgiveness, even though she knew she was not at fault.

"She be hurtin'," Patrice said as she pulled Leona away from the door. "She needs someone to blame."

"Then she should be blamin' the men who killed Fergus, and no' our mistress," Adhaira said as they returned to the narrow path.

"Will they ever accept me?" Leona asked to no one in particular.

"Aye, they will. Eventually," Patrice said.

"I have accepted ye, mistress," Adhaira said. "So has Melvin. Och! He adores ye! As do all the men folk."

But I can no' sit with the men folk and talk of womanly things, she mused.

"And I have accepted ye as well," Patrice offered with a warm smile. "The rest will come a long, with time. Ye'll see."

Leona was not nearly as hopeful or as confident as her friends.

By the time they reached Dougall's cottage, Leona felt light-headed, her stomach still churning. Patrice took note of her pale face and the sheen of perspiration that had broken out across her brow.

"Leona, why do ye no' let Adhaira and I take these baskets to Derrick's women? Ye look like ye're about to faint."

She wondered briefly if either of her friends would think her a coward if she agreed. "In truth, I am no' feelin' well."

"Ye rest here a bit, with Effie and Dougall. We shall return fer ye in a little while," Patrice said as she gave her a gentle hug. "In truth, I fear I can no' look at him just yet. Knowin' what I ken."

If Patrice could openly admit to being somewhat of a coward then Leona saw no harm in doing the same. "Verra well," she said. "Please, tell Derrick's family how sorry I am for their loss."

Patrice agreed to extend her condolences. They left Leona on Dougall and Effie's doorstep as they set off to visit with Derrick's family.

Leona rapped at the door and waited. No sounds came from within so she knocked again, a little louder. She heard a muffled voice coming from within. Worried Effie might be needing help, she opened the door and stepped inside.

The furs had been drawn away from the windows, letting in a cool breeze. No candles were lit, so it took a moment for her eyes to adjust to the semi-dark space.

"Leona?" came Dougall's voice from the bed.

Leona stepped forward so she might see him better. He looked as weak as he sounded. Dark circles had formed under his eyes. His lips looked painfully dry. He lay against a few pillows, covered with only a light sheet. "Dougall," she said as she drew nearer. "Where is Effie?" She pulled up a stool and sat beside him.

He coughed slightly, holding his stomach. "It feels like me guts are afire!" he groused, wincing with pain.

"I be so sorry, Dougall," she told him as she felt his forehead with the back of her hand. No fever, which was probably a good sign. She spotted a basin with wet clothes on the small stand by the bed. She dipped a cloth in, wrung it out and placed it on his forehead. "I would ask how ye fare, but I think 'twould be a most ridiculous question."

He gave a slight chuckle and nodded his head. "I feel as though I have been trampled by a team of horses. Carryin' a wagon filled with lead."

By the looks of him, she did not doubt his description. "Dougall, where is Effie?"

He closed his eyes and drew his arm over them. "I sent her away for a bit."

"Away?" Leona asked incredulously.

"Aye."

Certainly he did not mean on a permanent basis. "Why?" She ran the cloth across his neck. It pained her to see him in so much pain.

"Because I do no' want her or me sons to sit around and watch as I die!" he ground out.

Sadness enveloped her. Were it Alec abed dying such a horrible and painful death, she would not leave his side, no matter what he might want. 'Twas her right to be there until the very end. "So, 'tis true then?" she asked, already knowing the answer.

"Aye, 'tis true."

Leona thought back to how poorly he looked at the funeral. "How long have ye been ill?"

He shrugged a shoulder. "Off and on fer a month or so. After the funerals, it got worse. I have been throwin' up and shitin' somethin' fierce fer a few days."

'Twas no' fair. Dougall was one of the first Bowie men she had met. She had always thought him a good and decent man. Knowing how he felt about compliments, she resisted the urge to speak from her heart. "I have no' yet told Alec, for I have only just learned ye were ill an hour ago. I came here first, to see for myself."

She knew Alec adored his cousin. Dougall was more than just a cousin, however. He was Alec's closest friend, his staunchest supporter. Lord, how she dreaded having to tell him that Dougall was dying.

He lowered his arm. "Do no' tell him."

"What?" she asked, surprised he would make such a request.

"I do no' want Alec to come here and look at me with pity in his

359

eyes. I want no one here. 'Tis why I sent Effie and the children away. Just let me die in peace."

She grew instantly perturbed with him. "I kent ye were a mean, despicable son of a whore, Dougall Bowie. I did no' ken ye were also selfish."

His brow furrowed. "What are ye goin' on about? I may be a mean, despicable son of a whore, but I am no' selfish!"

"Think ye no'?" she challenged. "Yer wife, yer children, they love ye. They adore ye. As do Alec and I, and as far as I ken, everyone who kens ye. Ye want to die all alone? 'Tis selfish. Yer wife, yer children, they want to offer ye whatever comfort they can at this time. They want to be there to tell ye good bye."

"Bah! That is a pile of horse shite!"

"Really?" she countered. "Think to Fergus and Derrick's deaths. They died all alone. Think of *their* families. Nary a one of them had a chance to say goodbye, to tell them how much they were loved. How much they would be missed. Think ye no' that those men would have loved to have had one final moment to look at each of them and tell them *I loved ye best?*"

His frown disappeared and she could see that he was giving some weight to her words. For the sake of his family, and for Alec, she prayed he would heed her good advice.

LEONA MADE SURE DOUGALL WAS AS COMFORTABLE AS SHE COULD MAKE him before leaving to return to the keep. She didn't bother to wait for Patrice and Adhaira. After sitting with Dougall, all she wanted was to get back to her own husband.

She loved Alec, there was no denying it. Soft, lonely tears fell from her cheeks as she walked back to the keep. There was next to nothing she wouldn't give to be brave enough to give him the words of her heart.

Coward that she was, she simply couldn't. Her worry, her true fear, was that the words would upset him so much that the comfortable, safe existence they currently shared, would be no more. She worried he would pull away, would not want her anymore. Oh, she knew 'twas probably a ridiculous thing to worry over.

But Alec, Alec was cut from a different cloth. Unlike anyone she'd ever known. Aye, she had no doubt at all that he cared for her. But love? Nay, he did not love her, at least not like in the fables and tales of auld. He did not love her deeply, nor passionately, nor with all that he was, as he had spoken of Fergus' love for his wife and family.

THE CONVERSATION WITH ALEC went about as horribly as she had expected. "Nay," he said, shaking his head as he paced around the gathering room. "There must be some mistake."

"I wish I could have that hope for ye, husband. But I saw him with me own eyes no' more than a half an hour ago. I wish it were no' so, but it is." Her heart ached for her husband, for the sorrow and shock he was feeling at learning his closest friend, his last living direct relative, was dying.

He raked a hand through his hair before taking a seat. "The healer confirms it?"

Leona nodded. "Though I have not spoken to her directly, Patrice tells me Mairi was there just this morn. She believes he has the wastin' disease. Mayhap only a few weeks left."

"I must go to him at once," Alec said as he stood back up.

"Would ye like me to go with ye?"

He let out a short breath. "Aye, that would be awfully kind of ye."

Selfishly, she liked knowing he wanted her there, beside him, during this most difficult time.

Leona grabbed her shawl and together she and her husband left the keep to begin saying goodbye to his dearest friend.

DOUGALL TRIED PUTTING ON A BRAVE FACE FOR ALEC, AND ALEC DID the same. He did not want Dougall's last days on earth to be so solemn. "So when do ye plan on given' up this charade and gettin' back to yer fields?" Alec asked.

Dougall laughed. "Aye, 'tis true I be enjoyin' the attention. Why just this afternoon *yer* wife bathed me. 'Twas a most delightful moment in my otherwise bleak life."

Alec looked over his shoulder at Leona. She stood just a few steps away, her eyes wide with horror. "'Twas no' like that, Alec, I swear it! He was so ill, and covered in sweat—"

Alec stopped her explanation with a wink and a smile.

"Och! Can ye no' leave a dyin' man to his fantasies?" Dougall asked, tongue in cheek.

Leona burned crimson.

"I would thank ye kindly, ye bloody bastard, if ye would keep me wife out of yer fantasies," Alec responded with a wry smile. "Else, I will have to kill ye."

Dougall turned serious then. "I swear, I would much rather die at yer sword than the way I am."

Leona wanted to weep, silently praying her husband would not grant the man his wish. One never knew with these Bowies, just when to take them seriously.

"And take that pleasure from yer wife?" Alec asked. "Nay, I like Effie too much to do that."

"Bah!" Dougall said. "Effie would no' kill me. She loves me too much."

Alec chuckled softly. "She would if she heard ye talkin' about ye fantasizin' about *my* wife."

Dougall turned pale. "Ye will no' tell her, will ye?"

Alec patted his arm. "Nay, my friend, we will take it to our own graves."

By the time they left, more than an hour later, Dougall had agreed to allow Effie and the children to come back home.

CHAPTER 27

*A*lec was healing nicely. While Leona was convinced 'twas due to her prayers and Mairi's powers at healing, Alec was convinced 'twas his strong Bowie blood. 'Twas only because she had nearly lost him that she did not argue.

The man was impossible to keep in bed. Unless, of course, she was with him. His injury certainly had not affected his desire for joining with her.

Thankfully, he had agreed to leave any farming and training to his men, at least for a short while. He refused, however, to give up or set aside all of his chiefly duties.

He spent a good part of his day in the gathering room, either visiting with those who had come to see how he was, or solving disputes that sometimes arose. When he had had his fill of those pursuits, he would retire to his study, where he would pour over the books and think of ways he and his clan could earn an honest living.

Leona, Patrice, and Adhaira soon had the entire keep in order. Patrice had been spending more and more time there, now that her mother's health had improved. She and Leona became closer and Leona was beginning to think of her as her dearest friend.

Willem was a tremendous help to their pursuit at making the keep more inviting — at least when he wasn't drinking. But with his help, the gathering room felt homier. 'Twas he who would go to the north tower to retrieve pillows, tapestries, and anything else he could carry by himself.

Alec's contentment with resting and staying indoors lasted a full seven days. By the eighth, he was antsy and ready to get back to work. Leona, however, was not convinced 'twas such a good idea.

On a particularly chilly evening, she and Patrice were in the gathering room, mending one of the few dresses Leona owned. They were at one of the tables, with Leona's brown dress spread out on it.

"Ye have no other fabric?" Patrice asked as she studied the dress closely.

"Be it that bad?" Leona asked as she chewed on the nail of her thumb. The dress was several years old. She had worn holes in the middle, just below the knees. Because she had none of that old fabric left, she had tried to patch it using some heavy linen she had found in the storage room above stairs. The linen was several shades lighter than the rest of the dress.

Patrice puffed her cheeks and let the air out slowly. "Mayhap we could dye the patch?"

As if she hadn't thought of that. "I *did* dye it."

"Oh," Patrice whispered.

Leona sighed. "'Tis as bad as I thought, then."

Patrice placed a comforting hand on her shoulder. "On the morrow, I will bring ye one of me old dresses. We should be able to adjust it to suit ye."

While Leona appreciated the offer, she refused. "Och! 'Tis no' necessary. I shall keep this one back and only wear it when I be cleanin'."

"Really, Leona, it be no problem at all," Patrice argued. "Rutger gave me many a fine dress. I do no' wear most of them."

Leona did not think her husband would like that very much; her wearing dresses his brother had purchased for Patrice. And she could not have been more right.

~

ALEC HAD ENTERED THE GATHERING ROOM LONG MOMENTS BEFORE. THE women, so lost in their own thoughts, had neither heard nor noticed his presence. He stood quietly, eavesdropping on their conversation.

Guilt filled his gut, for he realized there were still many things about his wife that he did not notice. Such as her lack of suitable or even usable dresses. Aye, he had made a promise to himself not long ago, to pay far closer attention. He made certain she was no longer working in the laundry for coin. Had blessedly been able to find someone to help her with the daily workings of the keep.

But dresses? Nay, he had not put a thought to such things.

Anger filled his gut when he heard Patrice's offer to give his wife her old dresses, which Rutger had given her before his death.

There was no way on God's earth he was going to allow that to happen.

Leona deserved far better.

"Leona," he called out as he stepped forward. Startled, both women jumped and spun to face him.

"Alec!" Leona exclaimed as she held a hand to her breast. "Ye scared the wits out of me!"

He smiled warmly as he bowed slightly at the waist. "My apologies."

She quirked a brow and cocked her head to one side. "What is wrong?"

"Wrong?" he asked.

"Ye just apologized. Ye do no' do that unless something be horribly wrong."

He could not help but laugh. "Nothin' be wrong, lass. How are ye this cold night, Patrice?"

They exchanged curious glances before Patrice answered. "I be fine. And ye?"

"I be quite well, thank ye fer askin'."

Leona rested a hand on one hip. "An apology *and* a thank ye, all in the same day? Have ye hit yer head?"

Alec crossed his arms over his chest and sighed heavily. "Leona, did ye no' say ye wished I used all those fancy manners ye speak so highly of?"

"That was months ago," she politely reminded him.

He no longer wished to discuss the matter, especially not in front of Patrice. "Leona, I need to go to Kinbrea on the morrow and I would like ye to go with me."

His wife was quiet for a long while, as she studied him with a suspicious eye. Confused by her demeanor, he said, "Well? Would ye like to go with me or no'?" He had assumed she would jump at the chance.

"Aye," she finally answered. "I should like to go."

"Good," he said as he clapped his hands together. The action sent a shock of pain radiating up and down his injured arm, but he ignored it. "I shall leave ye to it then." He gave a slight bow and returned to his study.

THE TWO WOMEN WATCHED AS ALEC LEFT THE ROOM. PATRICE SHOOK her head in confusion. She left her equally confused friend standing next to the table while she went to the window and pulled open the fur.

"What are ye lookin' at?" Leona asked.

"I be lookin' to see if there be any pigs flyin' about."

Leona's brow knitted. "What are ye goin' on about?"

Patrice laughed. "With Alec bein' so polite and mannerly, I thought mayhap the day had come where pigs fly."

"Bah!" Leona exclaimed with a giggle. "Ye be daft!"

Patrice turned and gave Leona a cheeky smile. "Nay, I think it be yer husband who be daft. I believe he has fallen in love with ye."

Leona rolled her eyes. "Now I *ken* ye be daft."

"Am I?" she asked. "I think no', Leona. Why else would he be so polite?"

Leona gave a dismissive shrug. "Can a man no' change?"

"Of course he can," Patrice said. "But usually he only changes when there be a woman worth changin' fer."

Leona turned back to the dress. *He does no' love me,* she reminded herself. *He only cares.*

"Come help me figure out what to do with this dress," she said, speaking over her shoulder.

"I recommend the rag bin," Patrice said jokingly.

Leona found no humor in it. "I be sorry if *my* husband has no coin," she ground out. "Mayhap he would have had yer Rutger no' run this clan to ruin."

Immediately, she regretted uttering those words. Tears filled her eyes when she looked up at Patrice, who's own eyes had filled.

"Och! Patrice! Please fergive me!"

"Ye speak only the truth," Patrice said. Her voice was filled with sorrow. "'Tis I who am sorry. I should no' have made fun of yer dress."

"Nay, 'tis I who am sorry," Leona argued as she wiped away an errant tear. "I ken 'twas no' yer fault what Rutger did."

"Do no' be so certain," Patrice said.

"What do ye mean?" Leona asked, mystified.

Patrice shook her head and pulled a bit of linen from the sleeve of her dress. "Please, I wish no' to speak of Rutger any more this night."

Deciding it was best to let the matter drop, at least for now, Leona nodded in agreement.

"Now, let us see what we can do to fix this dress," Patrice said as she sniffed and picked up the gown.

"Have ye gone mad?" Leona asked her husband incredulously.

"Why do ye assume so?" he asked.

They were standing at the wool merchant's stall in Kinbrea. They'd arrived not long ago. Leona had assumed they'd be purchasing supplies for the keep. But she had been wrong. However, he was fast proving her earlier assessment that he'd lost his mind.

She leaned in so that she could speak without the wool merchant hearing. "We do no' have coin for such luxuries."

Alec leaned in and whispered in her ear "I can no' buy ye yards and yards of silks, but I *can* get ye a few lengths of nice wool." He stood back and smiled. Turning to the wool merchant, he picked up a bit of wool and said, "She would like enough of this to make a dress."

Leona put a hand on his. "What are ye doin'?"

"If ye will no pick out the fabric, I will."

She heard Kyth and Gylys chuckling from behind them. Whether their laughter was born of Leona's distress or their laird's delight, she couldn't say. Either way, she found it annoying.

There wasn't a doubt in her mind he meant what he said. Letting out a breath, she said, "Nay, no' that one." 'Twas mayhap the most hideous yellow she'd ever laid eyes on.

"But I like ye in yellow," Alec argued.

"No' *this* yellow," she said. She lifted the corner of a bundle of soft, yet bright yellow fabric. Just a few shades brighter than the dress Rose had made her for her wedding day. "And I'd like a bit of the dark blue there."

The wool merchant gave a polite nod before removing the bundles.

"Are ye satisfied?" she asked her husband.

"Nay," he answered with a shake of his head. "We'd also like a bit of the burgundy."

As much as she would have liked to argue, the burgundy was too beautiful to decline. The wooler smiled at Alec. "She'll be quite bonny in that burgundy."

Gylys and Kyth apparently agreed. "Aye, but our mistress be bonny no matter the color of dress she wears," Kyth said proudly.

Alec simply nodded.

Leona's cheeks flushed.

"I can see," the wooler smiled. "Yer mistress would be bonny wearin' nothin' but flowers in her hair," he jested.

All three Bowie men immediately unsheathed their swords and

held them to the wooler's neck. Appalled, they were, that the man would say such a thing.

"Ye keep yer filthy thoughts to yerself, ye bloody cur!" Kyth ground out.

"'Tis me wife ye're speakin' of," Alec seethed.

"Would ye like to keep that filthy tongue of yers?" Gylys asked as he moved the tip of his sword to the man's mouth.

Leona, completely stunned by their actions, raised a hand. "Alec! I am certain he meant nothin' untoward or unseemly!"

The wooler, whose eyes were as wide as wagon wheels, swallowed hard several times. "Aye, m'laird, I meant nothin' unseemly! Please, fergive me!"

"What, pray tell, *did* ye mean, old man?" Alec asked. The malice in his tone was undeniable.

"I only meant that yer wife be so bonny, so beautiful, nothin' she wore could match or enhance the splendor of her face, m'laird!"

The poor man was visibly shaken by the turn of events.

Alec smiled at him. "I think I would be more inclined to accept yer apology if ye were to throw in a bit of that purple silk," he said, inclining his head toward the piles of silk on the table behind the wooler.

The wooler nodded his head so rapidly that the thinning gray hair on his head shook along with it. "Aye, m'laird, 'twould be me great privilege to do so!"

"Ye will do no such thing!" Leona said defiantly. With her index finger, she lifted her husband's sword out of the way and stepped between the two men.

"Leona, move away," Alec ordered. "The wooler and I are negotiatin'."

"'Tis no' a negotiation," Leona pointed out. "'Tis extortion!"

"But he insulted ye, mistress," Kyth pointed out.

"Nay, he most certainly did no'. He was merely offerin' me a compliment, to which the three of ye took offense."

"Be that no' the same thing?" Gylys asked with a confused brow.

Leona rolled her eyes. "Nay, 'tis no' the same thing." She took a deep breath. "Alec, if ye force this kind man into givin' ye the silk fer free, 'tis the same as stealing. And I will make a dress fer me milk cow out of it, before I make one for meself! I will no' wear stolen goods."

"M'laird," the old man said, his voice shaking with fear. "Mayhap I could offer it to you at a discount?"

Alec quirked a brow, looked at his wife before turning his attention back to the old man. "A huge discount."

Leona supposed it was the best she could hope for. She apologized to the wooler repeatedly. The poor man's hands shook as he cut an extra long length of the purple silk.

～

ONCE THEY'D COMPLETED THEIR TRANSACTION, ALEC TOOK THE FABRIC and placed it under his arm and led her away. Kyth and Gylys, of course, were right behind them.

Since the attack, Alec had doubled the patrols at their borders. He'd also increased the number of men who traveled with them. Some thirty Bowie men were spread out amongst the crowd of villagers and merchants, each keeping a close and watchful eye on their laird and mistress.

"If I offer to buy ye a meat pie, do ye promise no' to give it away?" He was, of course, referring to their first visit to Kinbrea when Leona had given their meal to a poor woman and her babes.

"Nay, I will make no such promise," she told him.

He had to appreciate her honesty.

The fabric was the kindest gesture anyone had ever bestowed upon her. Though the entire ordeal had left her reeling and light-headed. 'Twas rather difficult not to cry tears of happiness or distress. Would her husband and his clan ever change?

Mayhap they had. Leona had to believe that if such an occurrence happened six months ago, the Bowie men would have gutted the poor merchant.

Shivering slightly in the cool morning breeze, she pulled her cloak a bit tighter.

"Ye're chilled," Alec said as they walked along.

"Aye, it is a bit chilly this day."

"Mayhap we should leave," he suggested.

Leona was not ready to leave just yet. "Nay, I would like to eat a bit of somethin' first." Lately, ever since the attack on her husband, food had not been settling well in her stomach. She supposed 'twas nothing more than worry and the distress of that awful day and the night-mares that had been disturbing her sleep ever since.

Alec conceded to her wishes. With a hand resting on the small of her back, he guided her through the throngs of people in search of meat pies. This time, he would purchase an extra, in the event his wife felt compelled to feed more of the downtrodden.

THE MEAT PIE DID NOT TASTE HALF AS GOOD AS THOSE THEY HAD EATEN the first time Alec brought her here. She managed only a few small bites before handing it off to her husband.

"I thought ye were hungry?" he asked as he took the offered pie.

"I was. But it be no' verra good. It tastes off."

Alec disagreed but said nothing. At least she hadn't given it to a complete stranger.

As they walked past the jeweler's stall, Leona looked over her shoulder and gave a nod to Gylys and Kyth. This morn, before they'd left the keep, she had given Kyth the coin necessary to finish paying for the plaid brooch she had ordered as a gift for Alec. 'Twas to commemorate the day of his birth, which was in October. Kyth smiled and gave her a wink as he fell away from their small group. A different warrior stepped in to take his place.

Ahead, the street split off in two directions. Alec took the one that led to the sea. The scent of ocean spray tickled at Leona's nose. The air grew considerably cooler along the path. The wind whipped at her skirts, chilling her further. But she cared not, for she was going to see the ocean once again.

The winding, rocky path spilled onto the beach. Waves crashed against the sand and rocks, spraying salty seawater all about.

"'Tis the most spectacular thing I have ever seen," Leona remarked. "I swear, I should never tire of seein' it."

Alec smiled as he handed the fabric off to Gylys. "Where be Kyth?" he asked, finally noticing his absence.

"He had to piss," Gylys replied.

Leona had grown accustomed to men cursing around her. It still irked her when they were so crass, but she kept her thoughts and opinions on the matter to herself. Alec took her hand in his. "Stay here," he told his men as they walked away.

Leona caught the movement of something out of the corner of her eye. A small figure, standing on the beach. 'Twas a little boy, tiny and fragile, and he appeared to be fishing. Quickly, she scanned the area for an adult, but found no one.

"Alec?" she whispered as she let go of his hand. Instinct warned the boy was too small to fight agains the waves that crashed against the rocky beach. He was far too close and in great danger of being sucked into the frigid water.

Alec looked to see what had pulled his wife away. When he saw the little boy and the danger he was in, he acted immediately. As he rushed forward, a large wave came in, crashing over the child. He went under, flipped to his stomach and tried to crawl away.

Alec was lifting the child out of the frigid water and pulling him to safety before Leona got there. The boy coughed and sputtered, his little hands still holding onto the fishing line. "Lemme go!" he cried weakly.

"What in the name of God were ye doin'?" Alec ground out as he laid the boy down on the sandy beach.

"I have to catch a fish," the child answered between coughs. Gylys and Traigh, upon seeing the commotion, came racing down to help.

Leona knelt beside him, looking him over for any sign of injuries. She recognized him immediately. He was the same boy she had given her meat pie to weeks ago.

"Och! Ye could have drowned," she told him, her tone filled with concern.

"I have to catch a fish," he cried out as he struggled to sit.

Leona glanced at her husband. Both were as concerned as they were confused. "Why?" Leona asked.

Tears streamed down his gaunt little cheeks. He began to shiver violently. Alec removed his plaid and wrapped the boy in it. "Me mum is sick. I have to catch a fish. If I can feed her, she might get better."

Gylys removed his own plaid and gave it to Alec. "Here." He said nothing else, but Leona could see he was quite disturbed.

"Where be yer mum?" Alec asked as he wrapped the second plaid around the boy.

"In the village," he replied, fatigued and distressed all at once. "I *have* to catch a fish."

Alec let loose a frustrated breath before lifting the child into his arms. Standing to his full height, he said, "We shall feed yer mum, lad. Just show us where she be."

WITH THE BOY'S DIRECTIONS, THEY WERE SOON MAKING THEIR WAY down a dark and dank alleyway. 'Twas filled with garbage, days old slop, and debris from unrecognizable objects. It smelled of urine, feces, and sickness.

Leona's stomach roiled at the odors that assaulted her senses. Only a few feet inside and she felt lightheaded. A few more steps in and she was ready to vomit.

Alec came to an abrupt halt, sensing danger or death ahead. "Traigh, take me wife from here," he said. "Gylys, come with me."

Leona could make no false pretense to argue against waiting. She was grateful to be out of the dark, depressing gloom as Traigh led her back out and several steps away.

"Are ye ill, mistress?" the tall, slender man asked.

She took in deep, slow breaths in hopes of steadying her stomach, her head, as well as her nerves. "I will be fine," she replied.

As they waited, Leona wondered what her husband was doing. Was the child's mum dying? And what of his sibling, the sickly bairn they had met all those weeks ago? Her chest ached with worry over the little family. In her heart of hearts, she wanted to take that little boy home, along with his family. Desperately, she wanted to feed them, clothe them, and give them a life away from this horrid place. But would Alec agree? Or would he do nothing more than give them a few coins and leave them to their fates?

'Twas a good long while before she saw her husband step out of the darkness. He was still holding the little boy. Leona's heart seized momentarily with an intense dread. Mayhap they were too late!

But a few moments later, Gylys appeared. In his arms was the boy's mum. Gaunt, pale. Nothing more than skin and bones.

"Come, Leona," Alec said with a nod of his head. "We be leaving."

THERE HAD BEEN NO NEED FOR HER TO CHAMPION THE FAMILY. PRIDE swelled, her love for her husband growing by leaps and bounds, all in a few rapid heartbeats. She could only nod her head in agreement.

Rushing ahead to walk beside her husband, she whispered, "But what of the bairn?"

When she saw the expression of sadness on Alec's face, she knew the answer.

"The bairn passed a few weeks ago," he replied.

They said nothing else as they made their way through the back streets, to avoid the crowds along the wharf. The only sounds were of a shivering little boy still convinced he needed to catch a fish in order to save his mother's life.

THEY HAD RIDDEN HARD AND FAST BACK TO THE KEEP. ALEC HAD handed the boy off to Traigh, for there simply wasn't any room left on Ares. He and Leona had ridden to Kinbrea together that morn. They had learned along the way the names of the two people they had rescued. The lad was named Fionn, his mother, Slaien. Though they could assume by their names they were Irish, neither of them were in any condition to verify or deny it. Gylys kept Slaien wrapped in his arms and the plaids offered up by the other men in their party, for the entirety of their ride back.

Alec had sent a few men ahead of them to have Adhaira heat as much water as she could, and to prepare a room for their guests. He had also called for the healer and Patrice. Both women were waiting on the steps of the keep when they rode through the gates.

Before nightfall, Fionn and Slaien had been bathed, dressed in warm clothing, and put together into a warm, comfortable bed across the hall from Alec and Leona's bedchamber. When they had removed all of Slaien's tattered clothing, they were struck by the horror of her illness. Leona had never before seen anyone as thin as this poor woman. Literally, she was nothing more than skin and bones. And when they had removed the dirty kirch covering her head, Leona gasped, astonished at what she saw.

"Good lord," Mairi said through clenched teeth.

Slaien's hair, what little of it remained, was matted against her scalp.

"She sold her hair," Patrice whispered, stupified.

"Sold her hair?" Leona asked rhetorically. She had heard of women cutting their hair to sell it to wigmakers. But she had never actually witnessed such a thing before.

Mairi tended to each of her new patients for a good long while. Below stairs, next to a fire roaring in the hearth, she gave Alec and Leona her prognosis.

"The woman, Slaien, has yet to wake. Her fever be quite high, her lungs filled with fluid. If she makes it through this night, 'twill be a miracle."

Leona could not help but weep for the poor woman and her son. Soft tears fell from her lashes as she held onto Alec's hand. "And the boy?" she asked.

Mairi released a heavy breath. "He too, is fevered, but his lungs do no' sound as bad as his mum's. I have more hope for him than I do her."

"I thank ye kindly, Mairi, for helping them," Alec said.

"If they had been brought to me days ago, I might have been able to do more. I have applied plasters to their chests and given them a licorice root tisane. All we can do now is pray."

Leona wiped her cheek with her fingertips. *If only they had been brought her days ago... nay,* weeks *ago. The bairn would have lived. A woman would no' have lost her babe.*

"Patrice has offered to help me with them through the night," Mairi said. "I must return to them now. If anythin' changes, we will send word."

Leona thanked her once again as she watched her ascend the stairs. *What will happen to Fionn if his mother dies?*

She and her husband sat in silence for a long while, each lost in their own thoughts. 'Twas Alec who broke the silence. "Leona," he said, his voice soft and low, "should anything happen to the boy's mum, I should like to give him a home here. Would ye object?"

Object? Relief flooded her senses. She leapt from her chair and wrapped her arms around her husband's neck. Alec drew her in until she was sitting on his lap. "Nay, Alec! I would never object!" Never did she think it possible to love someone so deeply, so profoundly, as she loved Alec. Pride, relief, happiness, danced around inside her stomach.

Alec chuckled softly as he twined a loch of her hair around his index finger. "I thought as such," he admitted. "Still, I felt compelled to ask."

She rested her head against his chest, glad for the warmth his body and arms gave her. "What if they both survive?" she asked.

"Then we should give them a home here," he replied. "If that be what she wants."

Leona hugged him tighter. "'Tis times like these that I wish we had a kirk, or even a small chapel."

Alec grunted, but whether 'twas in agreement or disgust, she could not tell. "Ye do no' need a kirk or chapel to pray, lass."

"I suppose no'," she agreed. "Still, there is somethin' to be said for havin' a quiet, peaceful place to go at times like these."

He shrugged once, but otherwise had no response.

~

HOW DARE HE BRING THOSE LICE INFESTED CREATURES INTO THE KEEP? *Rutger would never have allowed such a thing. He would have let them starve, as Alec should have done. Now they be stinkin' up the place. But everyone is acting as though Alec and Leona saved the life of the king! Bah! A good deed? I think no'.*

Dougall will be dead soon enough. Then I can put into play the rest of me plan. I can no' act too quickly, it might bring about suspicions. I can no' afford that.

Derrick and Fergus dyin', that was a blessin'. I've already begun to put the seeds of doubt into the minds of their women. Blamed Leona, I did. Soon, I will start speakin' of witchcraft and blamin' her for all who are dyin'. "Dougall was as healthy as an ox before she arrived. And now look at him." Aye, seeds of doubt that will grow and grow until all the clan will be believin' she is naught but a witch. A witch who is here to destroy us. A witch who turned Alec's head.

But 'tis difficult to wait. My fingers itch to be around Leona MacDowall's throat, to squeeze hard as I watch her eyes bulge out of their sockets, to watch as she takes her last breath. Och! What a happy day that 'twill be!

Once she be dead, Alec will go back to actin' like the Bowie he was meant to be. He will no longer care about peace, or farmin'. I will make certain of it.

CHAPTER 28

*L*eona did not consider her concern for his wellbeing 'nagging'. Neither did Alec, but he refused to admit it. His wife was motivated by a kind heart, and he could not hold that against her. Besides, he did rather enjoy all the attention she had been bestowing on him.

Her kind heart extended to perfect strangers as well. When she wasn't fussing over Alec, she was fussing over Fionn and Slaien. Fionn had improved, but was far from being out of the woods just yet. Poor Slaien, however, was not doing as well as Leona would have wished. The fevers still ravaged her frail body. Occasionally, she would drift in and out of consciousness, but as far as any of them could tell, she had no idea where she was or what was happening to her.

Just two short days after bringing Slaien and Fionn to the keep, and a little more than a sennight after the attack, Alec informed Leona he was leaving. She very nearly became unhinged. "Are ye daft?" she asked him.

They were in their bedchamber, preparing for bed. She was slipping out of her dress as she stood beside the bed.

Frustrated, Alec shook his head. "I told ye weeks ago about this trip." 'Twas vitally important to the future of their clan that he begin forging bonds with their neighboring clans.

"That was *before* ye were nearly killed!"

"But I was no' killed, was I?" he ground out.

"There still be time to be killed, Alec," she told him.

Apparently, he was unbothered by her veiled threat to finish what the attackers had started. "Do no' worry over it!" he exclaimed as he removed his sword belt and hung it on a peg next to the bed. "I be taking Kyth with me, and fifty of my best men. I will back before ye've even realized I am gone. I shan't be away for more than a sennight."

She grunted derisively. "If yer wound opens again, and ye bleed to death, ye will have no one to blame but yerself. Do no' expect me to feel sorry for you either!"

He laughed at her distress as he climbed naked into the bed. "I believe what ye are tryin' to tell me is that ye will miss me."

She glowered at him. "Miss ye? I think no'!"

He offered her a seductive smile. "I will miss *ye*."

Caught by surprise, she stood half undressed beside the bed. "What?" she asked, uncertain she had heard him correctly.

"I said that I would miss ye," he said as he smiled warmly.

Blast it if she didn't begin to cry! "Ye will?"

He scooted across the bed and helped her undress the rest of the way. "Aye, I will. Be ye tired lass?"

She shook her head. "Nay, why do ye ask?" She swiped at her cheeks with the backs of her hands.

"I remember ye tellin' me once, that ye sometimes weep when ye be tired. Lately, ye have been weepin' quite a bit."

"I have not!" she argued, her mood shifting so suddenly it surprised even herself.

Alec chuckled softly as he pulled her into the bed. "Nay, ye have no'."

"Make up yer mind, Alec," she told him as she snuggled against his chest. "Have I truly been weepy?"

"Aye," he nodded as he kissed the top of her head. "Ye have."

Unable to deny the truth any longer, she said, "There has been much sadness of late. First Derrick and Fergus, and now Dougall."

"I ken I do no' have to ask, but will ye promise me ye will check in on Dougall and Effie whilst I am away?"

She hugged him tight and made the promise.

THE SOUND OF THE HORSES CLIP-CLOPPING OVER THE HEAVY WOODEN bridge echoed ominously in the early morn. Alec and his men left at dawn on a dreary late September day. Leona and Adhaira followed as far as the drawbridge, waving goodbye and wishing them good luck and safe travels.

Leona refused to cry in front of Alec or any of his men. She would save her tears for later, after he was gone and she could return to the privacy of her bedchamber. Though 'twas no easy feat to hold back the tears of longing, of wishing he didn't have to leave.

She stood at the entrance of the keep and watched in quiet turmoil until the last horse had crossed. Closing her eyes, she prayed silently. *Please, God, keep them safe. Bring my husband back to me.*

The sound of hooves on the bridge broke through her prayers. Leona opened her eyes only to see her husband trotting back over the bridge.

Alec pulled his horse to a stop halfway over. Ares snorted and shook his big head. Alec crooked his finger at her, bidding her come forward.

A delightful tingling sensation burst from her stomach to her fingertips as she hurried to her husband. "What are ye doin'?" she asked as she stood next to his mount.

Alec smiled that devilishly handsome smile she so adored. She took his outstretched hand in hers, uncertain what he was doing. He surprised her by hauling her into his lap. "Remember," he whispered against her ear. "I shall miss ye."

Then in front of God and everyone, he kissed her. The kiss, wild and wholly inappropriate, considering the number of people who were witnessing it, left her breathless and stunned.

A few wild heartbeats later, he was setting her back on her feet.

Leona stayed on the drawbridge until the band of Bowies were nothing more than tiny dots on the horizon

LEONA KEPT HERSELF BUSY AS SHE COUNTED DOWN THE DAYS HER husband would return. Keeping her loneliness to herself as she presented a happy front to anyone she encountered.

Before Alec left, he increased the number of men who would watch over her in his absence. At Alec's insistence, Kyth and six other men had been moved into the keep. They made temporary barracks, three to one of the empty rooms above stairs and three to one below.

'Twas not easy for Leona to be surrounded by so many men — only one of which she knew well at all. Patrice had also moved into the keep, though 'twas only temporary. She had come to help with Fionn and Slaien days ago and hadn't left. Leona was exceedingly grateful for her help and her company.

Fionn had improved remarkably. With Leona and Adhaira's good cooking, and Patrice and Mairi's healing skills, the boy no longer looked like the same gaunt, vacant-eyed living skeleton as when he had arrived. Leona wished she could say the same for his mother.

The little boy refused to leave his mother's side. Gylys kept the lad company for most of the day. With so many guards inside the keep, it mattered not to Leona. She was glad he had taken an interest in the boy.

"He guards ye like ye're the queen of Scotia," Patrice whispered as they sat next to the hearth in the warm, cozy kitchen.

There was a man posted at each door. "While I can appreciate my husband's concern, I must admit it is a bit—" she paused, searching for the right word, "uncomfortable."

Patrice giggled. "At least ye have Adhaira here with ye, to keep ye company."

"I fear she does no' like all the attention the men bestow upon her," Leona said as she sipped on warm cider.

"Where is she?" Patrice asked.

"Doin' laundry. But if ye ask me, she escaped."

They giggled quietly. "Och!" Patrice said, a thought suddenly occurring to her. "Have ye even begun to make new dresses with all the fabric Alec purchased for ye?"

Leona slapped a hand against her forehead. "Bah! I had completely forgotten." She'd been so busy tending to her sick guests, making sure auld Melvin was fed, as well as all the guards within the keep, she hadn't given any thought to dresses.

"Well, let us take advantage of this quiet time and start," Patrice suggested.

Leona welcomed the idea.

Soon, the two women were in Leona's bedchamber and Patrice was taking her measurements. "I can no' remember the last time I had a new dress made just for me," Leona admitted happily.

"Then where did yer current dresses come from?" Patrice asked.

"Hand-me-downs mostly. Though Rose did make me a fine yellow gown for my weddin' day!"

Patrice paused briefly. "Rose Mackintosh?" she asked.

"Aye," Leona said, momentarily forgetting about Rutger kidnapping Rose. The event had led to his death.

"Ye, Patrice, be the second woman I could ever call me friend," Leona told her warmly. "And I be truly grateful for it."

Patrice offered her a shrug of indifference as if she were embarrassed by Leona's kind words. Leona reckoned 'twas the Bowie way and left it at that.

"How be Effie?" Leona asked. "I fear I have no' had time to see her of late."

"Effie is Effie," Patrice said as she removed the pretty burgundy fabric from the bed. She said nothing else as she carefully unfolded the fabric and shook it out. "This be a fine burgundy wool," she said in an attempt to change the subject.

Leona could not understand the relationship betwixt Patrice and

Effie. Certain she was that had she ever been blessed with a sister, they would have been close. In her mind, nothing could or would ever have come between them.

"Why do ye and Effie no' get along?" Leona asked.

"Do ye want tight fittin' sleeves, or loose?" Patrice asked, ignoring the question. Carefully, she folded the fabric in half and laid it on the floor.

Undeterred and more than just a bit curious, Leona said, "Loose. And why will ye no' answer me?"

"Because I do no' want to discuss me sister," Patrice replied in a firm tone.

Leona stood, perplexed. "I never had a sister," she said. "I fear I do no' understand why ye do no' get along."

Patrice finally looked at her with hands on her hips. "Do ye want me help or no'?"

'Twas apparent she was not going to get the answers she sought. "I do," she replied softly.

"Then let us get on with it, shall we?"

Leona could only nod in agreement as she hoped she hadn't hurt their friendship.

THOUGH LEONA WOULD HAVE BEEN MORE THAN HAPPY WITH A SIMPLE, serviceable gown, Patrice would have none of it. She insisted on adding some elegant stitches to the bodice and sleeves. She had run back to her own little cottage and returned a short time later with all manner of pretty silk thread.

"I think the dark green would be nice against the burgundy," Patrice said. Leona agreed. They sat together by the hearth, each working on a sleeve.

One of the guards came to Leona's room to let her know the evening meal was ready. Leona was glad for the break, for her eyes were beginning to feel strained.

"Thank ye," she told the young man. "We shall be down straight away."

Carefully, she laid the lovely dress out on the bed and went below stairs. Leona felt tired and famished. She had not been eating as well as she should have these past few days. Too much had happened that kept her mind and hands busy, and she did not take the time to eat well.

As they descended the stairs, a smell coming from the gathering room assailed her senses. "Good, God!" she exclaimed. "What is that awful smell?"

Patrice was behind her on the stairs. "'Tis just fish," she said, confused.

The smell was simply too much. Leona's stomach roiled and churned in protest as she began to grow quite dizzy. Then her world turned black.

~

THANKFULLY, PATRICE CAUGHT HER BEFORE SHE COULD DO ANY REAL injury to herself. "Leona!" Patrice exclaimed as all manner of people rushed to the stairs.

Oh, she wanted to vomit. If she could throw up, it would alleviate the roiling in her stomach. "I be sorry," Leona whispered as she fought to still her spinning head.

"Help me get her back to her room," Patrice said.

One of the guards lifted her into his arms while she complained. "Och! I will be fine," she said. "Please, I can walk."

He ignored her request, as well as her demand. Moments later, he was laying her on her bed while Patrice and Adhaira hovered over her. Adhaira was fanning her with the end of her apron. Patrice was checking for signs of fever.

Someone had called for Mairi, who came rushing into the room. "What happened?" she asked as she gently pushed Patrice aside to see for herself.

"I do no' ken," Patrice said. "We were headin' to sup. She complained of somethin' smellin' horrible, then she collapsed."

"I did no' *collapse*," Leona argued. "I simply felt light-headed for a moment. Truly, I be fine."

"Ye most certainly are no' *fine*," Patrice argued.

"Och!" Leona said as she threw a hand over her achy eyes. "'Twas just that God-awful smell! What *was* that?"

"I smelled nothin' but the fine fish Adhaira had prepared. And mayhap leeks."

The mention of fish and leeks did not settle well; the faint odor still lingered in her nostrils. A wave of nausea, overwhelming and intense, washed over her. Quickly, she rolled onto her side, reaching for the chamberpot. Mairi grabbed it and held it whilst Leona threw up.

Adhaira stood with tears in her eyes. "I did no' think the fish smelled bad," she murmured.

"It did no' smell bad," Patrice told her as she wrapped an arm around her shoulder. "'Tis just that Leona is no' feelin' well. I am certain it be a fine fish."

"Adhaira, go below stairs and heat some water," Mairi directed. "And Patrice, fetch me bag from Slaien's room."

Once the women were gone, Mairi set the chamber pot aside and looked at Leona. "So how far along do ye think ye be?"

LESS THAN A QUARTER OF AN HOUR LATER, LEONA WAS SHEDDING TEARS. Tears of joy she could not suppress if someone had a dirk to her throat.

"Ye be certain?" she asked for the tenth time.

Mairi shushed her sweetly. "Aye, lass, I be certain. I'd say ye'll be a mum come spring. Mid to late April if I ken anything about babes."

The joy was overwhelming. "I am goin' to be a mum," Leona repeated breathlessly, still unable to believe the good news. "I am goin' to be a mum."

"Aye, ye will be a mum," Mairi said as she wiped her brow with a damp cloth. "Mayhap ye should send word to Alec?"

Alec. Suddenly she felt miserable that he was not here to share in the good news. Now she was crying for altogether different reasons.

"Wheest, lass," Mairi said with a smile. "It does ye no good to cry."

"I can no' help it!"

Mairi hugged her for a long while, patting her back and telling her all would be well.

Finally, her tears began to wane. "Please, tell no one yet," Leona said. "I want to tell Alec myself. I do no' want him to hear it from anyone but me."

Mairi agreed, suggesting they tell anyone who asked that she simply ate something that did not agree with her.

Leona could barely contain her happiness. Finally, she would have someone who would love her without question or condition.

CHAPTER 29

*A*lec had planned on being gone for only a sennight. 'Twas a fortnight later before he and his men trod over the drawbridge.

Road weary, covered in grime, drenched to the bone, he was tired. More tired than he could ever remember being. And he was furious. Furious, deflated, and feeling hopeless.

Of the eight clans they had visited, only three had even allowed them entry. Of those that did, only the McLeod's and the Mackintoshes agreed to purchase their grain.

Acres and acres of fine grain, better grain than even he had anticipated when he'd planted it last spring. And very little of it could he sell. He did not possess enough granaries to store it all.

In a foul mood, he handed his horse off to a stable boy and thundered into the keep. He wanted a bath, a hot meal, and nothing else. Feeling worthless, he wasn't even sure he wanted to see his wife.

He had let his clan down. Had convinced them that farming was their only path to a brighter future. He could not have been more wrong.

And Leona. Knowing her as he did, she would put on a happy face and try to make him feel better about it. She would convince him that there was hope, no matter how bleak the present situation might be.

Angry with himself, angry with those arrogant clan chiefs who had refused to see him, and angry at the world, he thundered into the keep.

Leona was waiting for him in the foyer. She looked radiant. Resplendent. Beautiful. But not quite radiant or sweet enough to calm his tortured soul.

"Alec!" she exclaimed as she raced to greet him with open arms.

How on earth was he going to tell her the truth? He'd led his clan down a path of ruin. No better than his brother, or those chief's before him.

"Leona," he said coldly. "I be tired and weary." Half-heartedly, he returned her warm embrace. He felt completely unworthy of her love or devotion.

She stepped back, her brow twisted into a line of confusion. Aye, he caught the glimmer of hurt flash behind her odd eyes. 'Twould be nothing compared to how hurt she was going to be when she learned of his utter and total defeat.

"A bath awaits ye in our bedchamber," she said, as she painted a happy expression on her face.

He offered her a curt nod before hurrying above stairs.

Do no' take it to heart, Leona tried convincing herself. *He is tired and weary from his travels, nothing more.*

Holding her tears at bay, she decided it might be best to leave him alone for at least a little while. She would give him time to bathe and rest, without her hovering over him like flies over honey. Besides, she had a feast to help prepare.

She had been planning tonight's meal for days. As soon as she had received word that Alec was returning, she set her plans in motion. Many people had been invited to attend the feast, as a surprise for her husband. Then afterwards, when they were alone, she would share her good news with him.

Though his response to her embrace and joy stung like a slap in the face, she knew that once she told him about their babe, his attitude would improve by leaps and bounds. Or at least that was her fervent prayer as she left the foyer and went to the kitchens.

'TWAS UNDENIABLE: HE DID NOT DESERVE TO HAVE A WIFE SUCH AS Leona. Why could he have not told her that he had missed her desperately? Why couldn't he compliment her on her new dress, or how pretty her hair looked all loose and flowing down her back?

Alec stood alone in their bedchamber, staring at the hot water rising from the tub. Clean clothes were laid out neatly for him on the bed. Clean boots sat on the floor next to those. She'd even thought to have a fresh plaid waiting.

A tray of dried meats, cheeses, breads and fruit sat on the table by the fire. Along with it, a flagon of fine whisky. He poured a large dram into the mug and tossed it back as easily as if it were water. It didn't burn, for he'd been drinking for the last few days.

She had done all of this for him. Undeserving, foolish lout that he was.

As much as he wanted to go below stairs and apologize as well as thank her for her thoughtfulness, he couldn't. Coward. She deserved more, she deserved better.

He stripped out of his muck-covered clothes and slid into the hot bath. The warm water was soothing, helping to ease his tense muscles. But it did little to clear his mind.

After scrubbing from head to toe, he stepped out of the bath, wrapped a cloth around his waist before pouring himself another dram of whisky. This one he drank slowly as he sat by the warm hearth and stared into the flickering flames.

'Twas probably not wise to drink alone, especially when one's personal opinion of oneself was at an all time low. But Alec cared not for anything wise. He was awash in self-loathing.

In the hour that passed by, he had finished the whisky. Every last drop of it, all the while his self-appreciation dwindling until he felt as worthy as a slug. Lowlier than a worm.

How much more time passed before a knock came at his door, he couldn't say. He was too far into his cups. He growled at whomever it was to enter.

'Twas Traigh, one of the men he'd left behind to guard his wife.

"What?" Alec ground out harshly.

Traigh blinked once before answering. "Yer wife would like ye to ken that she waits below stairs. 'Tis time fer the evenin' meal."

Alec grunted as he stared blurry-eyed at the young man. "Tell her I shall be along shortly."

Traigh gave a curt nod before quitting the room.

ALEC DRESSED, PULLED ON HIS BOOTS AND SWORD BELT WITH AS MUCH enthusiasm as a man going to the gallows. *God, I do no' want to face her. No' yet.*

Much to his surprise, he found his gathering room filled with guests. An additional table had been brought in to seat everyone. His men took up two full tables. At the main table sat Patrice, Willem, Gylys, auld Melvin, Mairi, and Adhaira.

"What are ye all doin' here?" he asked as he took his seat at the head of the table.

Patrice was the first to notice his odd mood and did her best to explain. "Leona wanted to give ye a fine welcome home, m'laird."

He grunted before reaching for his mug. 'Twas empty.

"Would ye like some ale?" Patrice asked. Without waiting for a response she stood, picked up the pitcher, and came to stand beside him. She had to hold his hand steady while she poured the ale.

"Thank ye kindly, fair maiden!" he said as he knocked back the ale. "Pour me more!"

All eyes in the room were on Alec. Aye, they'd seen him drunk before, but never to this extent.

"Mayhap a bit of cider would be best," Patrice suggested. "Leona has put a good deal of thought into this meal."

Alec laughed heartily. "Patrice, ye'll make some man a fine wife someday! Now, pour me more ale."

Not wanting to cause a disturbance, Patrice debated on what she should do. Leona had returned to the kitchen to grab a pot of Alec's favorite jam. She leaned in closely to whisper into his ear. "Alec, please. Leona will return soon. Mayhap ye should have some cider."

Apparently, he found her pleas for decency humorous. Throwing his head back, he laughed heartily again. "Och! Patrice! Have ye learned yer naggin skills from me wife?"

He gave her no time to answer before he pulled her into his lap. She was still holding the pitcher of ale, and the sudden action caused it to spill and splatter all over her skirts.

"What else has me wife been teachin' ye in me absence?" Alec's words were slurred, his eyes bloodshot from far too much drink.

Patrice giggled nervously. "Alec, I think ye should let me go."

"Bah!" he said before laughing again.

The next voice he heard was that of his very angry wife.

LEONA HAD NOT SEEN EVERYTHING THAT TRANSPIRED BEFORE SHE entered the room. But she had seen enough.

Anger and hurt filled her already weak stomach. She marched across the floor and stood but a few steps from Alec and Patrice.

"Kindly remove yer person from me husband's lap," she seethed, glaring at Patrice.

"Leona," Patrice said, flushing with shame. "'Tis no' what ye think."

"I said, remove yer person from me husband's lap."

Patrice tried to wriggle free, but Alec would have none of it. Still filled with self-loathing and anger over his failure to sell their crops, he refused to let Patrice go. Staring into his wife's eyes, he said, "She'll no' move until I say so. I am the laird of this keep."

'Twas a full-on challenge. The gauntlet was thrown, the lines in the sand drawn.

Leona would not back down. She was too hurt, too angry to think logically. She leaned in a bit closer. "Ye promised me, Alec."

"I promised ye what?" he demanded in a low tone.

She swallowed back the tears. Nay, she would not let him see her pain, not right now. "Ye promised me that if ever ye took a mistress ye would no' flaunt her in front of me."

"Och! Leona, I be no'—"

"Patrice, I suggest ye be quiet, fer I will no' be responsible for me own actions should ye keep talkin'." 'Twas the most powerful wound to her pride and her heart that Leona had ever felt.

"What are ye goin' on about?" he asked, his words were slurred and filled with malice.

"'Tis as plain as the whore sittin' on yer lap," Leona replied.

Alec stayed Patrice's retort by squeezing her waist. Leona's accusations only added fuel to Alec's burning fury. "I am the bloody laird of this keep! I am the bloody chief! I shall do what I want, when I want, and ye will no' stop me!"

Leona slammed the pot of jam onto the table. "Then fix yer own bloody meals from now on!" She cared not now who heard them or who witnessed the display.

Alec all but tossed Patrice from his lap. Thankfully, Willem was there to catch her before she fell to the floor.

Alec was towering over Leona, but she did not cower, did not back down. Why that infuriated him, he was too drunk to figure out. Leona did something unexpected then. She took a few steps forward, leaned her head back and looked him directly in the eye. He found her behavior distinctly unnerving, but was not about to admit it.

"Ye've lost yer mind, woman! Orderin' a man about in his own keep!"

"Might I remind ye that this is *my* home as well?" she asked him through gritted teeth.

"Bah!" he exclaimed as he threw his hands in the air and stepped away. "Ye and yer bloody home!" His head was beginning to pound. "'Tis a keep, nay a wee cottage. I keep tellin' ye such, but ye will no' listen!"

Leona glowered at him, waiting patiently for him to end his tirade so that she might have a word or two of her own.

The tapestries by the hearth caught his attention. He thundered angrily across the floor and yanked one of them from the wall. Leona was appalled at his behavior.

"Ye think I have no' noticed all the brick-a-brack, wife? Think ye I have no' noticed what ye've done to this keep? Turnin' it into yer version of a warm and happy home. Bah!"

"Think ye a few tapestries or curtains make a warm and happy home?" she yelled back at him.

"Bloody hell! Ye make no sense, woman!" He tossed the tapestry to the floor and went to the next and tore it down. "I never wanted this! I never wanted any of this! If I could have one wish, 'twould be fer everythin' to go back to the way it was before ye ever arrived!"

His words hurt more than fists or belts or even a sword to her heart ever could. Mustering all the dignity she could imagine, she grabbed a fist full of skirt. "Verra well, Alec Bowie," she began. Her tone was even, yet firm. "Yer wish is my command." She offered him her most elegant curtsy before quitting the gathering room and heading for the stairs.

Her guests had witnessed the entire spectacle through stunned and perplexed eyes. They sat now in stone silence, uncertain what they should do or say. Alec, who was swaying to and fro, looked out at the silent onlookers. "Bah!" he yelled as he waved his arms. "Leave us!"

They scurried like leaves in an autumn wind.

GYLYS AND KYTH HAD FOLLOWED THEIR MISTRESS ABOVE STAIRS. NOT because they worried for her safety, but because they were appalled by their laird's behavior and wanted to make certain she was all right.

Leona threw open the door to her room and immediately headed for her trunk. She tossed open the lid and began shoving her belongings into it.

"What are ye doin', mistress?" Gylys asked with a good measure of uncertainty.

"Granting me husband's wish," she said. Her voice cracked, but she fought hard to keep those injured tears away.

The two men stood at the doorway, neither knowing what they should do. Or if anything they could say would help soothe her injured feelings. "Mistress," Kyth said as he took a step inside. "Alec did no' mean what he said. He be drunk."

Leona grunted as she grabbed her cloak from the peg. "I care no' what his reasons," she told them. "I can no' help but feel he meant all that he said. Now please, take me trunk below stairs. And get me a horse. I wish to away this place tonight."

Now, both Kyth and Gylys knew unequivocally that there was no way in hell Alec was going to allow her to leave. Drunk or sober. "'Tis no' less than what he deserves," Kyth muttered to Gylys.

Gylys was of the same mindset. While Kyth hefted the heavy trunk, Gylys led the way out of the bedchamber and down the stairs.

ALEC KNEW HE HAD HURT HIS WIFE. DEEPLY AND MOST PROFOUNDLY. But what could he do about it now? He raked a hand through his hair and headed toward the stairs. Mayhap a good night's sleep would do them both good. In the morn, when he was sober, when his head was clearer, he would apologize and beg her forgiveness.

He had just reached the bottom of the stairs when she began her descent. Even in his current state of inebriation, he knew she was as enraged as she was hurt. But what confused him was that she was wearing her cloak. And what the bloody hell was Kyth doing carrying her trunk?

He blocked her path by spreading his arms out. "What do ye think ye be doin'?" he asked.

She quirked a brow. "Givin' ye yer wish, m'laird. I will be leavin' now."

"The bloody hell ye will!" he said through gritted teeth. "Kyth! Take that trunk back above stairs." Kyth shook his head and turned to do his laird's bidding.

Unbothered by his harsh tone, she said, "Kyth? Do no' dare to take it back."

Alec's eyes grew wide, astonished his wife would defy him or that she would give *his* warrior an order. He was even more astonished when Kyth paused and turned back toward Leona.

"Kyth? Have ye a death wish?" Alec asked. "Take it back. Now."

"Do no' dare, Kyth," Leona countered.

Alec grew livid. "Ye are no' goin' anywhere," he told her.

"I am," she politely informed him. "I am goin' home."

She was, of course, referring to Macktinosh lands. Home to Ian and Rose. Home to a place where she would not have to be ashamed to hold her head high.

"Nay, I think no'," Alec said. He crossed his arms over his wide chest, his feet planted firmly apart.

"Need I remind ye, Laird Bowie, that ye signed an agreement the day we were married. In it, ye agreed to allow me to go back to my family at least twice a year. I wish to go now."

Alec grunted, then growled. "They be no' yer family. And ye're no' goin'." He glared at Gylys. "And why the bloody hell are ye no' takin' her trunk back to our bedchamber?"

Gylys smiled wryly. "I be waitin' to see who wins."

Alec's eyes all but sprang from their sockets. "Are ye daft? Take it back. Now!"

Gylys gave up. With a shrug of his shoulders and a disappointed shake of his head, he turned around and headed back up the stairs. Kyth remained on the landing to observe.

Leona realized that her husband was not going to allow her to leave. Too hurt and humiliated to care what he wanted, she lowered her voice. "But Alec, ye promised. Ye signed the contract."

He said the first thing that came to his mind. "I lied."

He lied? Nay, he could not have lied.

Leona studied him closely, waiting for a sign that he was not serious. He was glowering at her with bloodshot eyes as he worked his jaw back and forth. "Ye jest," she stuttered.

"'Twas the only way to get ye to marry me!" His voice boomed and echoed off the empty walls.

The pain was too great. He had only signed her contract in order to get her to marry him. This was worse than discovering Patrice was his mistress. Far worse. That he had no intentions of keeping to the contract felt like a kick in the stomach. She would have preferred a beating over this.

Leona would rather die than let him see her cry, to allow him to know she was affected by this new revelation. She was done. Without uttering another word, she turned away from Alec and went back to her room.

Gylys and Mairi were in the hallway, just outside Slaien and Fionn's room. Leona ignored both of them, stepped into her own quarters and softly shut the door behind her.

In a daze, she sat by the hearth and stared into the flames. *He lied to me.* Like a tiny stream winding down her cheeks, the tears fell.

All this time I thought he truly cared. But he didn't. At least no' about me.

Working out the reasons for such a betrayal was easy. *Peace.* Peace for his clan had been his sole motivation for marrying her. But she had known that from the beginning.

But after? When she thought they were growing close, when she believed with all her heart he truly cared for her? Nay, 'twas nothing more than her vivid imagination wanting something she could never have. He needed to keep her happy in order to keep Ian Macktinosh from burning down this keep. These past few months had nothing to do with Leona the woman, but everything to do with his clan.

And Patrice? 'Twas one betrayal atop another. How could she not have seen it before? Effie had warned her more than once, that Patrice could not be trusted. *'She'll pretend to be yer friend, all the while she be plottin' how she can put the knife in yer back,'* Effie had said numerous times. What she had previously thought was nothing more than a rift betwixt sisters, turned out to be true. Patrice could not be trusted.

He will never love ye, no' as a woman, no' for the person ye are. No matter how clean ye maintain his keep. No matter how many meals ye prepare. No matter how good and decent ye are. And no matter how many bairns ye give him. Alec will never love ye.

Thinking of the babe within, she placed her palms on her stomach. With her world shattering around her, the babe was the only thing she had to hold on to. A chill settled over her shoulders as she wept for the life she had imagined with Alec. 'Twould never happen now. That sweet life filled with love and laughter and tender moments with family and friends that she had somehow allowed her heart to imagine could happen.

"I can no' stay here, no' like this," she murmured. Taking a deep breath, she stood and went to the little table near the window. Pulling out parchment and quill, she wrote a letter to the one person left in this world she believed she could trust: Rose Mackintosh.

EVEN AFTER LEONA HAD DISAPPEARED AROUND THE CORNER, ALEC stayed at the bottom of the stairs. He knew he should go after her and confess he had lied about lying. But even in his current state of inebriation, he knew he would muck it all up. The kind of apology his wife deserved needed to be done when he was sober. Not now when he reeked of whisky, when he could not stand without swaying, when his words were not slurred.

His head began to throb and exhaustion began to settle in. He needed to sleep but knew he could not go to their bedchamber. Not now, not when his wife was so upset.

Deciding the best course of action he could take tonight, was to keep away from Leona lest he say something else he would regret. Tonight, he would sleep in his study. On the morrow, when clearer heads prevailed, he would go to her and tell her the truth.

CHAPTER 30

*A*lec had spent a fitful night sleeping on the cold hard floor of his study, where he had passed out from too much drink. When he woke the next day, his brain pounded mercilessly inside his skull. His mouth was as dry as the ashes of a cold fire.

It took a moment before the fog of a whisky-induced, unsettled sleep to lift. When he remembered where he was and why he was here, his head spun. Sitting up, he rubbed a hand across his stubbled jaw. "Ye're a complete arse," he mumbled to the cold, stark room.

The first order of business would be to wash off the stench of last night's drunk. He did not want to go to Leona on bended knee smelling like an alehouse. Doubtful as he was that his wife would manage a hot bath for her cur of a husband, he decided the loch was the best place to go.

Somehow, he managed to get to his feet without spilling the contents of his stomach. His head swam for a moment or two before he could manage a few slow, cautious steps.

Leaving his study, he walked down the long corridor. The keep felt and sounded eerily quiet. He entered the gathering room and paused. 'Twas empty.

The tables were still filled with the dishes from last night's uneaten feast. The benches and chairs sat haphazardly around those tables, as if their guests had left in a great hurry. Of course they had, because Alec had seen to it.

Passing by the hearth, he saw the tapestries still lying in heaps on the floor. Tapestries his wife had hung with loving care. The same ones he had torn down like a madman.

Guilt assaulted him, increasing the churning sensation in his stomach. With a heavy, guilt-ridden heart, he left the keep.

BATHING IN THE FRIGID LOCH MADE HIM FEEL NO BETTER, BUT IT DID allow him some time to gather his thoughts, to find the right words he would need to apologize to Leona.

The mess was still present in the gathering room when he made his way back inside. Half-tempted to clean it himself, he realized he was trying to avoid the inevitable. With a heavy sigh of resignation, he went above stairs to his room.

Although 'twas his bedchamber door, he still knocked. Either out of respect for his wife or to warn her, he couldn't say.

No answer came from within, so he knocked once more before pushing the door open.

The room was as empty as the gathering room. A quick glance around told him her trunk was missing. Had she waited until he passed out before she left? Panic settled in as he left the room in a hurry and went in search of Leona.

Below stairs, he found Adhaira just entering the gathering room. In her hands she carried a large tray, no doubt to begin cleaning up. "Where is me wife," he asked her. His tone was firm, his words clipped.

Adhaira stared at him with wide eyes and open mouth.

"I asked ye where is me wife," he repeated.

"In her room," the girl replied. She sounded frightened and uneasy.

"I was just in my room, lass, and she was no' there. Her trunk is gone." He was doing his best not to sound as panicked as he felt.

Adhaira stammered her reply. "Nay, no' *yer* room, but *hers*."

Mayhap he wasn't as sober as he thought, for the girl wasn't making any sense. "What do ye mean, *hers?*"

"She came to us last night and asked us to move her out of the laird's chambers. We moved her into an empty room down the other corridor, m'laird."

He didn't know if he should feel relieved that she had not left him altogether, or if he should be upset that she had procured her own sleeping chamber. "Which one?"

"The last one on the right, m'laird," Adhaira replied.

Alec spun on his heel and took the stairs two at a time.

He paused outside his wife's new quarters, doing his best to settle his nerves and burgeoning anger. More angry with himself than with Leona, he took several deep breaths before he opened the door.

He found her asleep, lying in a small bed in a little ball with furs drawn up around her neck. There was no fire burning in the brazier, no sunlight streaming in through the fur-covered windows. 'Twas cold and stark, just like the keep had been before she arrived.

She must have sensed his presence, for her eyes fluttered open. A few rapid heartbeats later, she sat up in the bed. She covered herself with the furs, and looked at him as if he were the devil himself.

'Twas that look of fear, of uncertainty, that nearly sent him over the edge. "Why?" he somehow managed to ask without yelling.

"Why, what?" she murmured softly.

"Why did ye move out of our bedchamber?" he asked through gritted teeth. 'Twas difficult to keep his anger with himself at bay.

She swallowed back tears before she responded. "The truth?"

"Aye," he said with a nod.

"I can no' trust ye anymore, Alec."

The words, though spoken softly and without malice, pierced his heart.

"Ye betrayed my trust by lyin' to me."

Aye, he had lied, but not in the way she believed he had. Angrily, he raked a hand through his still damp hair. If he had possessed an ounce of common sense, he would have explained it to her then and there. Instead, his outrage that she no longer trusted him took over. He was prepared to lift her up into his arms and carry her back to their bedchamber.

But when he stepped forward, her eyes widened with fear and she shied away, as if he were going to harm her physically. Her expression, her fear, stopped him in his tracks.

"Ye said ye would never flaunt yer mistress in front of me! Ye said ye'd allow me to go back to Rose to visit, but ye lied! What will ye do now, Alec? Beat me? Take me against my will?"

Staggered by her accusations, he took a step back. "I would never beat ye! I would never take ye against yer will!" he shouted.

"And I am to believe ye? After last night? Nay, Alec. Ye betrayed me. Ye took everything I believed in and ground it to dust."

Tears pooled in her eyes. Tears that were there because he had been such a fool.

He could rail and rage on. He could pick her up and carry her back to their room, all the while hollering like an idiot as he tried to explain his actions of the night before.

But 'twould do him no good. She was too hurt, to distressed right now to listen.

Without another word, he hung his head in shame and left his wife alone.

"Ye need to eat somethin'," Mairi told Leona. They were in Leona's new bedchamber one late afternoon. It had been three days since that awful night, that awful argument with Alec. He had stayed away from her, locked in his study, avoiding her at any cost.

Leona dabbed at her eyes with a bit of linen. "I ken, but I fear it all comes back up when I do."

"That be perfectly normal," Mairi said as she offered her a hunk of bread from the tray Adhaira had brought up earlier. "But ye must keep up yer strength fer yer babe."

The babe she carried was the only thing that kept her from falling completely apart. 'Twas the only thing that kept her from curling into a little ball and dying from her broken heart.

She tore off a small piece and placed it in her mouth. Bread was one of the few things that did not upset her stomach.

"Have ye tried speakin' to Alec?" Mairi asked.

"Nay." She truly did not wish to speak about her husband right now. "How fairs Slaien and Fionn?"

"'Tis a miracle, it is," Mairi said with a bright smile. "Slaien has finally awoken. Her fever broke late last night. She even managed a bit of broth."

"And Fionn?"

"He is perfectly fine. Gainin' weight he is. Eatin' as much as five of Alec's warriors."

Leona managed a wan smile. *Fionn*. Alec had been perfectly willing to take these two people in. And even more willing to give the boy a home in the event his mother had not survived. How could a man such as that, end up being nothing more than a liar?

"Slaien has asked to see ye," Mairi told her. "She wants to thank ye and Alec fer what ye have done fer her and her son."

Leona was in no state of mind to see anyone, least of all their new charges. "Mayhap on the morrow," she said.

"Leona, I do no' want to have to do this," Mairi said as she stood up. With hands on her hips, and a fierce disposition, she said, "If ye do no' snap out of this, ye're going to end up losin' yer mind or yer babe. Now come, up with ye!"

Leona sat, nonplussed, looking up at Mairi. "Where are we goin'?"

"Fer a wee walk. The fresh air will do ye good. Mayhap, while we be walkin', ye'll come to realize ye have been just a tad foolish."

"Me?" she exclaimed. "How have *I* been foolish?" She stood up and face Mairi head on. "'Twas no' I who took a lover! 'Twas no' I who lied to Alec and broke my word!"

Mairi smiled. "'Tis good to see some fire in ye!"

Leona was not amused. "Ye called me foolish in order to see me angry?"

"Aye, I did. But I spoke only the truth. Now, let us walk and I will explain meself."

~

"Now, I no' be sayin' what Alec did was right," Mairi said as she draped an arm through Leona's. "He was a bloody fool fer gettin' drunk and sayin' what he said."

"He was," Leona agreed wholeheartedly.

"But the way ye reacted to it? 'Twas no' better than what he did."

Leona raised a confused brow. "What do ye mean?" she asked as they walked across the drawbridge. "I do no' think 'twas unreasonable to get angry. And how else was I to respond when I saw his mistress — who was supposed to have been me friend — sittin' on his lap, all a giggle. And he admitted to me that he lied about the contract, Mairi. He only signed it in order for me to agree to marry him."

"Are ye so certain of these things?" Mairi asked.

"Of course I be certain!" Leona exclaimed. She was growing weary of the conversation.

"How many times have ye caught Alec alone with Patrice?"

She searched for an answer. "In truth? Never. Not until the other night when she was on his lap."

"I see," Mairi said with a nod. "And did ye think to ask anyone else in attendance what had happened?"

Leona snorted. "Me eyes might be odd, but they work perfectly well."

Mairi looked momentarily appalled with her mistress. "And *ye* called yerself Patrice's friend?"

Confused, Leona said, "I was no' the one sittin' on *her* husband's lap!"

They had just stepped onto the path that lead to the cottages. Mairi came to an abrupt stop. "Certainly, ye can no' be as daft as that."

"Daft? Me?" Leona struggled to find the right words.

"Aye. *Ye*," Mairi said with frown. "I be here, tryin' to get ye to see reason. And again, I ask ye, did ye ever stop to think to ask those of us who were there what had truly happened *before* ye walked into the room?"

No, no she hadn't. She didn't see a reason to make such inquiries. An uneasiness began to settle in as awareness developed. "What are ye tryin' to tell me?" Leona asked.

"I be sayin' that Patrice is no more Alec's mistress than Gylys or Kyth are."

Mairi looped her arm through Leona's and once again, they began walking down the path.

Leona's mind raced to make sense of what Mairi was telling her. Was it the truth? Was it possible that she had jumped to a conclusion she shouldn't have?

Mairi went on to explain everything that had happened that night. The cold hard truth was that her husband had been the one to grab Patrice after she had tried to convince him to switch to the cider. Patrice had tried to explain how important the night was to Leona. Her *friend*.

Leona wanted to cry, but fought the tears back. She would have to make it up to Patrice, but how? It made her heart hurt to think how cruel she had been. She'd even called her a whore!

But why hadn't Alec denied it? And what of what he said about their marriage contract? He had refused to allow her to leave and admitted to lying about it. Regret began to ensnare her heart. The things she had said to him! *Ye betrayed me trust.*

"But what of his lie? About no' allowin' me to leave?"

Mairi gave a slight shrug of uncertainty. "Have ye ever said somethin' in anger that ye did no' mean and later regretted?

Aye, she had. There was no denying it.

Leona was paying no attention to where they were going. When Mairi stopped at the door of a tiny cottage, Leona scrunched her brow. "Who lives here?"

"Patrice," Mairi informed her. "I think ye should make amends with her."

∿

PATRICE SAT NEXT TO DOUGALL'S BED AND PLACED HIS COLD HAND IN hers. The action brought back a flood of memories. Memories she had tried for years to set aside and ignore.

Once, long ago, they had been betrothed and did far more together than just hold hands. God, how she had loved this man! Then something had happened. Something that had very nearly destroyed her tender, young heart.

Dougall ended up breaking that heart. He married Effie. Six months later, Effie gave birth to Wills. Dougall had betrayed her by sleeping with her sister and subsequently getting her with child. Though he had adamantly denied it, the evidence was as plain as the nose on her face. No one gives birth that early to a child as big as Wills had been. Any baby born that early died within hours of birth. Nay, Dougall had lied. He had betrayed her in the worst possible way.

As had Effie.

Dougall opened his eyes slowly. Surprise settled in when he saw 'twas Patrice holding his hand. He gave a quick glance around the room. "Where be Effie?"

"I do no' ken," she answered. "She was gone when I got here." It stung that his first thoughts were of his ungrateful wife. Oh, if he only knew the truth about her.

But to this day, she loved him too much to tell him just how wicked a woman she was.

"How do ye fare?" she asked him.

He smacked his dry lips together. "I be thirsty," he answered. "Effie has a tisane fer me, on the table."

Something began to niggle in the back of her mind. Dougall looked exactly as her father had right before he died. Cracked, bloody lips, yellow eyes, cold and clammy skin.

She went to the table and grabbed the cup. "This?" she asked him.

"Aye, that be it," he said as he wiped his mouth with a drying cloth. "'Tis supposed to help me feel better. But at this juncture, I fear only death will bring relief."

She gave the mug a cursory sniff, only to test for freshness. Her face twisted in a grimace at the foul stench.

"Aye, it tastes just as bad as it smells," he told her.

Believing the healer knew more than she, Patrice went back to Dougall. She lifted his head with one hand while holding the mug to his lips with the other. He took only a few sips before pushing the mug away.

When she pulled her hand away from his head, she noticed she was holding clumps of his dark hair in her hand. *Just like Da.*

But her da had died of a heart ailment, or so she had been told. She stood there, thoroughly perplexed. Although she was no healer, she had seen enough in her life to know that each illness or disease had its own unique set of symptoms.

Could Mairi have misdiagnosed Father all those years ago? Or had she made a mistake with Dougall? Something was wrong, but she could not quite put her finger on it.

For days she had worked beside Mairi, had seen her mixing potions and concoctions together to help Slaien and Fionn. "Dougall, did Mairi tell ye what was in the tisane?"

His eyes were closed, his breathing labored. He shook his head slightly. "I do no' ken," he replied. "Ye should ask Effie. Mairi gave it to her to give to me."

Her heart dropped to her toes and bounced back up again. Reluctantly, she asked another question. "Dougall? When was the last time ye saw Mairi?"

Another slow, laborious shake of his head before he fell asleep.

Patrice hated the little voice that began to scream in the back of her mind. How could her father and now Dougall be dying from two entirely different diseases but suffer the same way? Nay, this made no sense!

Was Mairi poisoning Dougall?

She didn't know, but there was only one way to find out. She took the mug of tisane and dumped it into the chamber pot. "Dougall?" She had to shake his shoulder in order to rouse him. "Dougall, please listen to me. Do no' drink any more tisanes."

"What?" he asked through groggy eyes.

Not wanting to upset him or otherwise cause him any more distress, she lied to him. "I think the tisane went bad. That happens sometimes, ye ken. So please, do no' drink or eat anythin', no' even a sip of water, until I return. Can ye do that fer me?"

He was trying hard to focus on what she was saying. "Aye, I can," he replied.

If she was correct, Dougall wasn't dying of the wasting disease. He was being poisoned. And by the same person who had poisoned her father.

She left the tiny cottage in a rush and went in search of Mairi Bowie.

ALEC HAD SPENT THREE DAYS SULKING LIKE A COWARD, HIDDEN AWAY IN his private study. How could Leona believe such things about him? How could she assume, after all they had been through, that one) he had taken a mistress, and two) that he was no better than a flea-ridden rat!

How? Because ye are no better than a flea-ridden rat!

For the better part of the first day of his self-imposed exile, Alec tried blaming the whisky for his actions his first night home. *If I had no' been so into me cups...*

Nay, 'twas not the whisky's fault. He had no one but himself to blame. His pride was powerfully wounded. He kept coming back to the question of how Leona could believe such horrible things about him. How could she believe that he had taken Patrice for his mistress?

Finding the woman on his lap did not help his argument.

Telling her he had lied about the contract, about signing it under false pretenses certainly did not help his argument. Coming home from his trip in a foul mood hadn't helped any either. Not telling Leona how much he had missed her. Not taking her above stairs the moment he arrived to *show* her the intensity with which he had missed her was yet another mistake among many.

Now, his sweet wife had moved out of their bedchamber. Convinced she was that he would beat her, or take her against her will, or do any of the other things in that blasted contract of hers.

Back and forth his heart went. One moment, he was filled with self-hate, the next he was angry at Leona. The longer he sat alone in this stark, empty room, the worse he felt.

A knock at his door drew him out of his reverie. "Come!" he yelled, perturbed he was being disturbed. He still had gallons and gallons of self-pity in which to wallow.

'Twas Adhaira who opened the door and entered. In her arms was a tray with a bowl of stew, fresh bread, and a mug of what he hoped was good ale. "M'laird," she said as she bobbed a curtsy. "I thought ye might be hungry."

"Put it on the table," he said from his seat in front of the fire.

Adhaira did as he asked. She started to leave, but paused at the doorway. "M'laird, I ken ye might no' want to hear this, especially from me, but yer wife, she be hurtin' something fierce."

He drew his gaze away from the flames and stared at her.

"She has been cryin' almost nonstop for days now," she added.

Alec grunted. "Have ye ever been married?"

"Nay, m'laird, I have no'."

"Then ye be the smartest person I ken at the moment. Marriage, it can be hell on earth, lass. Avoid it like ye would the devil."

The last person he needed advice from was a young scullery maid. Adhaira smiled. "Me da used to say the same to me."

Alec quirked a brow. "Smart man."

"He died of a broken heart just two months after me mum passed from the ague," she told him. She bobbed another curtsy before quitting the room.

Alec was still contemplating her words long after she left.

He thought back to the time Leona'd been locked in the north tower. Then to a few weeks ago when she'd very nearly killed herself cleaning the gathering room. He remembered, then, how distraught he'd been.

'Twas like being hit in the head with a mace. The overpowering realization that he loved his wife. He not only adored her and cared for her, he loved her. Like the fool that he was. Like the fool his father had always warned him *not* to be.

"I love me wife," he told the fire in the hearth.

Bloody hell.

CHAPTER 31

Once Alec realized the depths to which he loved Leona, he swallowed back his pride, splashed cold water on his face, and went above stairs to tell her. Her new quarters were empty. Thinking nothing of her absence, he went around the corner to see if by chance, she was tending to Slaien and Fionn.

He knocked and waited for permission from within before he entered. Little Fionn was sitting on the bed, next to his mother. He was showing her a little wooden dirk. "Gylys carved it fer me," he told her proudly.

"That was verra nice of him," Slaien said, managing a weak smile.

Slaien pulled her eyes away from her son to look at the stranger who had entered. "May I help ye?"

"That be Alec, the chief of clan Bowie," Fionn told her. "He be the one who pulled me from the ocean. I told you about that, remember, Mamma?"

"Aye, ye did tell me," she answered. "I have much to thank ye fer, m'laird." Her voice was breathy, undoubtedly from being so ill for such a long time.

"Think naught of it, lass," Alec said.

"As soon as I am better, me son and I will be out of yer hair, I promise."

Alec studied her closely for a long moment. He detected an Irish lilt in her voice. "Ye need no' worry over it. Ye have a home here fer as long as ye like."

Fionn flashed his mother a beaming smile. "I told ye, Mamma! But ye did no' believe me."

With a weak hand, she patted his leg. "Shush, now, lad."

"I was wondering if ye have seen me wife this day?" Alec asked.

Slaien gave a slight shake of her head. "Nay, m'laird. Mairi went to see her earlier, but I've no' seen yer wife today."

Alec thought that odd, but assumed that with Slaien on the mend, Mairi felt comfortable leaving her for a short while. "Thank ye," he said, offering a bow at the waist. "I shall send Adhaira up to ye, to sit with ye until Mairi returns."

"That might be a long time," Fionn told him as he studied his wooden dirk. "She went to help someone have a baby."

Now, he tells me. Alec chuckled at the boy. "And was me wife with her?"

The lad scrunched his face as he thought on it for a moment. "Nay, I do no' think so. 'Twas Gylys who told me."

Alec gave them each a nod, bid them a good day, and quit the room.

Neither his wife, nor Mairi, nor Patrice, were anywhere to be found. As far as Alec could ascertain, the women were not together. Mairi was miles and miles away, acting as midwife. But no one had seen Patrice or Leona for hours.

Worry gnawed at Alec's gut. Night would soon fall, the air cold and damp. The skies held the promise of rain.

His first inclination was to search the north tower, which he did. Then the remaining towers and rooms of the keep. His search revealed nothing. As one hour turned into another, his worry and dread for his wife increased a hundred fold.

And when he learned that Leona had left *without* the ordered guards, he became incensed and outraged. In the barracks, he was giving his men a thorough dressing down. "I told ye she was to be watched at all times!" he yelled at them.

"She was with Mairi, m'laird," one of the younger men said, his voice shaking with fear. "I be terribly sorry, but I thought she would be safe with Mairi."

Alec towered over the young man, his face purple with rage. "Ye thought? *Ye* thought? I did no' ask ye to think! I ordered ye to stay with me wife at all times!"

The young man looked ready to pass out. His face went pale and his hands trembled.

Alec shook his head in disgust. He turned away from him and addressed the rest of his warriors. "I want search parties formed immediately. Ye will turn this keep, every building, and every cottage upside down until she is found!"

Not one man questioned his order. Like rats fleeing a sinking ship, they hurried to do his bidding.

"The last time I saw her, Alec, she was with Patrice."

Alec was standing at the foot of Dougall's bed, hoping against hope that either Dougall or Effie would know something, anything that would lead him to his wife. Archibald was sleeping in a little cradle near the hearth. The older boys were out of doors pretending to be the King's guards. Alec and his men had questioned everyone from the stable master to auld Melvin. The results were the same no matter who they spoke with. It had been hours since anyone had seen Leona or Patrice. Nightfall would soon be upon them. He could only pray the women were together, safe and sound.

Dougall looked like death and was of very little use. Effie put a warm hand on Alec's arm. "Are ye certain she was with Patrice?" Alec asked her.

"Aye," Effie told him. "They were on the path by Patrice's cottage. They were walking north and west. I thought mayhap they were goin' to visit our mum. She lives up that way, ye ken."

Aye, he knew where Alyce lived. Several miles away, across rocky terrain. For the life of him, he could not figure out why the woman refused to leave that desolate place and move closer to the keep.

"I fear I have no' been able to visit mum of late, what with the new babe and all. And we all ken how mum's health be. One day she is as right as rain, the next, ye'd swear she was at death's door." Effie looked genuinely concerned.

"Thank ye, Effie," Alec told her as he turned to leave.

"Alec," Effie called to his back as she approached. Alec turned to face her. "I do no' want to worry ye, but," her voice trailed away.

"But what?"

She lowered her voice and leaned in, he supposed so she would not wake Dougall. "Mayhap it be naught a thing, but Patrice. She has no' been *right* since she lost Rutger."

Alec's brow drew into a thin, hard line. "What do ye mean?" The fretfulness in her eyes was bothersome.

"'Tis no' just one thing that bothers me, but many. Sometimes, I catch her cryin' as she talks to herself. Which, I admit, even I have done a time or two. She talks about Rutger all the time, and how much she loved him. On and on she goes about him. Sometimes, I think it be too much."

'Twas unusual that anyone could have loved his brother, at least the last months he was alive.

"But after the other night, when Leona accused her of bein' yer mistress, and then callin' her a whore, well, 'twas like somethin' inside Patrice snapped. She had this odd look in her eyes. She told me she would get even with Leona, if 'twas the last thing she ever did."

Alec's chest tightened. "Why did ye no' tell me this sooner?" he ground out, his voice rising.

"Wheest," Effie told him as she glanced back at Dougall. "I did no' think 'twas anythin' to worry over. I thought she was just angry and rantin' like we all sometimes do."

Alec's clenched his jaw as he tamped down his anger, studying Effie closely. "What is it ye are tryin' so hard no' to say?"

Effie took in a deep breath before answering. "I do no' want to speak ill of me sister, Alec, fer I do love her. But I worry that maybe she be no' in her right mind. Her grief over losin' Rutger and then with ye marryin' Leona instead of her—"

"Are ye tellin' me that Patrice thought I was goin' to marry her? I never gave her any indication of such a thing!"

"I ken that," Effie said as she placed a hand on his forearm. "But Patrice thought ye should. She told me so many times. She felt 'twas yer duty to step in and marry her, what with ye being chief and Rutger's promises."

Was it possible that it had been Patrice who had turned the clanswomen against his wife? How had he not seen it?

"I love me sister," Effie said again. "But I fear... I do no' think she can be trusted."

The dread he had been trying to avoid came crashing into his heart. If what Effie was telling him was true — and he had no reason to doubt it — then his wife was in grave danger.

Kyth and five other men were waiting for Alec outside of the cottage. He was as furious as a rabid bear. "We need horses," Alec told Kyth. "Send someone ahead to gather as many men as ye can. We leave *now*."

Kyth grabbed one of the men and gave Alec's order as they hurried down the path. "What happened?" Kyth asked.

Alec told him all that he had learned from Effie. By the time he finished explaining, they were almost to the drawbridge.

"Patrice?" Kyth asked disbelievingly.

"Ye do no' believe she is capable of such a thing?" Alec asked, his voice laced with anger.

Kyth gave a slow nod of his head. "Aye, in truth, I do no'."

"And who would know better than one's own sister what a body is capable of?" Alec asked as they thundered over the drawbridge. He drew upon his experience with Rutger. He'd been a good man once. But greed changed him. 'Twas just as likely that a broken heart had changed Patrice.

WHEN ALEC AND HIS MEN CRASHED INTO ALYCE BOWIE'S WEE COTTAGE, the poor woman was given the fright of her life! She screamed as she grabbed her broom, holding it out as if it were a broadsword.

"Get out o' me house, ye heathens!" she yelled, though weakly and with a good deal of fear.

"Where is Patrice?" Alec shouted at her. He didn't give a wit if the woman was afraid or not. "Where is me wife?"

He knew at once, from her confused expression, that she had not an inkling what he was talking about. "Patrice? Yer wife?" she stuttered with fear. "I have no' seen Patrice in days. And as fer yer wife, I have ne'er met her!"

Kyth stepped forward, a dirk in his hand and a scowl upon his face capable of making a grown man shake. "Do no' lie to us, woman! We ken they came here!"

"The bloody hell they did!" she shouted back. "I tell ye, I have no' seen Patrice in days. She has been up at the keep, takin' care o' some woman and her son."

Alec studied her closely for a brief moment. Though he did not know Alyce well at all, his gut told him she was telling the truth. "Ye have no' seen Patrice, but have ye received word from or of her?"

"Nay, m'laird, I have no'!" she shook her head so rapidly, her graying hair fell loose from her braid. "Now, what in the bloody hell be goin' on? Ye come crashin' in here in the dead of night and scared ten years off me! And I do no' have ten years to spare!"

Alec was not about to share his suspicions with her. "Me wife has gone missin'," he said. "We think she be with Patrice. If ye see either of them, please, send word."

"Now how am I to send word, m'laird?" she asked, her tone saying she suspected his level of intelligence was that of a piece of wood. "I be here all alone. Do ye wish me to walk all the way to yer keep?"

Alec rolled his eyes. "Alyce, if ye see them, tell them they need to return to the keep at once."

"Verra well," she said, as she finally lowered her broom. "And the next time ye come here, ye better wipe yer feet before ye enter! I'll be wearin' me sword from now on."

Alec took her warning to heart. He could not help but think Effie had gained her fierceness from her mother. With a nod of his head, he led his men out of the cottage.

They had thundered across the countryside to get here, only to come up empty-handed. There had been no sign of either woman along the way. *Where in the bloody hell has Patrice taken Leona?*

"What now, Alec?" Kyth asked as they took to their horses.

Alec pulled on Ares's reins as he answered. "We spread out. Mayhap they turned somewhere along the way."

Kyth looked up at the moonlit sky. Thankfully, the dark rainclouds that had passed overhead an hour before moved on without leaving more than a mist in their wake. "I have a better idea," he said as they headed back the way they'd come.

"At this point, I be willin' to listen to anything," Alec ground out as his stomach churned with worry.

"Instead of traipsing across the world lookin' fer them, I say we go back to the keep and release Patches."

Alec pulled rein, feeling as though he'd just been hit in the head with a tree trunk. *Why had he not thought of that before?*

"It worked once," Kyth reminded him. "And we all ken that Patches has a keen fondness fer yer wife."

"The dog's name is *Satan*," Alec reminded him. *But if he can find me wife, she can name him whatever the hell she wants to!*

⁓

ALEC HAD SENT WORD AHEAD OF THEM TO WARN SEAMUS AND HAVE him prepare Satan to search for Leona and Patrice. Alec could only pray that Satan would be able to track down his wife. It had rained earlier, but he hoped it had not been enough to wash the scent away.

He kept thinking the events of the past few months. First the salt, then Leona locked in the tower. Had it been Patrice all along? Had she been the one to turn the clanswomen against his wife?

Anger boiled in his gut, along with the turmoil of not knowing where Leona was, until his stomach was nothing more than a cauldron of fire.

She could be anywhere, lost, alone, injured.

She could be dead.

Nay! He told his heart. He could not, would not allow his thoughts to turn in that direction. She had to be alive. He needed her.

He loved her.

As they tore across the drawbridge, one of his men came rushing up to meet him. "Alec! We found Patrice!"

Alec pulled Ares to a halt and slid from his back. "And Leona?" he asked, holding his breath as he waited for the answer.

"Nay," he replied solemnly. "She swears she does no' ken where she be."

Furious, he demanded to know where Patrice was.

"She be in the gatherin' room," he replied. "I have five men watchin' over her."

Alec handed the reins off to him as he stormed across the courtyard and into the keep.

Patrice had been sitting in a chair by the hearth. As soon as she saw Alec, she leapt to her feet and started toward him. "Alec! Thank God ye are here!"

He stopped just inches away from her. Her relief at seeing him changed to confusion when she saw the anger in his eyes.

"Where. Is. Leona?"

"That is what I have been tryin' to tell everyone," she said. "I do no' ken!"

"Ye were the last person she was seen with, Patrice," Alec said through gritted teeth. "Do no' lie to me."

Stunned, she took a step back. "I have no' seen Leona since the night the two of ye fought!"

"Mairi dropped her off at yer cottage door this afternoon," Alec told her. "I have witnesses who say they saw the two of ye together." 'Twas a partial lie. Thus far, there was only one.

"That be no' true!" she cried. "I was no' home, I was at Dougall's. Alec, ye must listen to me. I think Mairi has been poisonin' Dougall."

Aye, she was completely mad. Why else would she accuse Mairi of such a thing? "Patrice, please, ye must tell me where Leona is."

"I do no' ken!" Her eyes were filled with tears. "Please, listen to me. Ye must get to Dougall straight away! I tried to find Mairi, to confront her, I even walked all the way to Almot and Deena Bowie's cottage. But I could no' find her. I think she be poisonin' Dougall, just as she poisoned me da!"

Alec was convinced then, that she had lost her grasp on reality. He had no time to feel pity or remorse for Patrice. Now, more than ever, he was certain 'twas Patrice to blame for Leona's disappearance. Leona was now his sole focus. He would find her. He had to.

"Put her in the dungeon, under heavy guard," he ordered as he spun on his heels.

"Nay!" she cried out! "Alec, please, I beg ye! Ye must listen to me."

Ignoring her cries, he left her to go in search of his wife.

Seamus was waiting in the courtyard, with Satan barking, howling, and ready to run. Alec bent down to speak with his bandogge, much like his wife would have done. "There, now, ye beastie," he said. "We have important work to do. Are ye ready lad?"

The dog was eager. He pulled, stretching tight the heavy leather tether lashed to his collar, the end of which was in Seamus's hands. Drool fell from his mouth in long tendrils as the dog barked and howled, signaling he was ready to run.

Alec petted the dog's head once and took to Ares before giving the order to let loose the dog. Satan took off like an arrow from a bow. Out of the courtyard and across the drawbridge. Alec and his men were fast on his heels.

Down the path, with many men on horse and even more on foot, carrying lighted torches, the large army went. Around the path, this way and that, with his nose to the cool, damp earth, they followed the bandogge. Satan picked up speed, taking them straight to the door of Patrice's cottage.

Alec sat atop his steed as his stomach tightened. *So she had been here!* People, upon hearing the sound of horses and men, began to poke their head's out of cottage doors or step into the cool night. Alec ignored them, his focus completely and solely on his bandogge.

Torchlight flickered in the cool night air. The waxing, gibbous moon offered them even more light. Still, 'twas not enough to bring any ease to Alec's agitated heart.

Satan sniffed the ground in circles before picking up the scent once again. No longer at a full run, rather a fast trot, the dog next led them to a spot not far from Dougall's front door. For a long moment, he sniffed the ground in circles, before he approached the door and came back again.

Alec waited, growing disconcerted. Satan sniffed the ground, going around in circles. He sat down and whimpered, looking up at Alec.

Seamus, who had been following on foot, came up to the dog and held Leona's nightdress in front of his snout. Satan stood up, sniffed, licked it once, and whimpered. A moment later, he was off again, this time going in a northeasterly direction. Seamus tucked the nightdress into his belt, picked up his torch, and followed after the dog. They were going *away* from the direction Effie had said she'd last seen Leona and Patrice. That was not entirely odd, especially if Patrice and his wife had backtracked, deciding at the last minute to go in a different direction.

Satan led them through thick bracken and brambles, a small, dense pocket of trees. Soon, Alec realized they were heading to the auld keep. Never would he have thought to look here! The place had been abandoned for decades and most were convinced 'twas haunted.

The dog took off again, once he got through the dense, tangled knot of brambles. As Alec and his men dismounted in order to hack their way through, they suddenly heard Satan's plaintive wail.

A distinct, guttural wail that indicated he had found his prey.

WITH HIS HEART THREATENING TO BATTER ITS WAY OUT OF HIS CHEST, Alec ran on foot across the small open space. Kyth was right beside him, with a lighted torch in one hand. Through the opening in the old wooden wall, they went. A few feet later, Alec stopped dead in his tracks.

Satan was encircling something on the ground, wailing, barking, clearly distressed. From where Alec stood, he could not see what exactly the dog was barking at.

Although he was moving as quickly as he could, life seemed to slow down all around him. He stopped, a step or two from where Satan now sat. Kyth held out the torch to gain a better perspective.

There, in the ground, was an opening to an old well.

Alec's heart shattered into inestimable pieces when he realized he had just found his wife. Or at least, her final resting place.

KYTH HAD LOWERED THE TORCH AS FAR AS HE COULD, BUT 'TWAS NO' enough to see anything but endless black.

From somewhere behind him — Alec couldn't be sure who had done it — appeared long lengths of rope that had been tied together. He heard voices, muffled and discombobulated, like haunting apparitions.

His men moved swiftly, quickly, while he sat on his knees, staring down into blackness. *She be gone.*

"Alec!" 'Twas Kyth shouting at him. "Alec!"

Slowly, Alec turned to face his friend. "Do ye wish me to go down?" he asked, a look of desperation on his face.

"Nay," he said. If anyone was going to bring up his wife's lifeless body, 'twould be him. He gave a hard shake of his head, to push away the sorrow and grief. A loop had been tied to one end, and tossed over the opening of the well. Alec took up enough of the rope to wrap around his waist. Lying on his belly, he wriggled his foot until he found the loop. Once he found his footing, the rest of the rope was tied off onto the saddle of one of the horses. After he was completely over the edge of the well, Kyth handed him a torch.

Slowly, they began lowering Alec into that eery black void.

CAREFULLY, SLOWLY, ALEC WAS LOWERED INTO THE AGES OLD WELL. ON his way down, the space narrowed significantly. Decades old tree roots and vines sprouted and poked out from the sides like long, grotesque fingers reaching up from hell. If he were not a full grown man, he would have sworn they were alive, trying to keep him from gathering up whatever lay at the bottom.

Soon, his sword got tangled up in one of those thick, gnarling vines. It took a long moment, a bit of struggling and a few choice curses before he was able to untangle himself.

"Can ye see anythin' yet?" Kyth called out from above.

"Nay!" Alec said as they continued to lower him down. He could feel beads of perspiration breaking across his forehead, more from desolate heartache than physical exertion.

More long moments passed before his torch lit upon something below. A few more inches down, he began to see more clearly.

In that tiny moment, he felt as though his heart had been ripped from his chest. There, on the bottom of the well, was his wife's cold, dead body. Ghostly, her body seemed, as the torchlight flickered in the dank air, casting her in unworldly, hideous light.

His feet soon hit bottom, splashing in inches of frigid, dank water. He kicked his foot from the loop and crouched down beside her. She was lying on her side, against the muddy wall, in a mangled mess of skirts and mud.

Tendrils from the gnarling vines above had almost reached the floor of the well. They hung now, like otherworldly curtains, just a hair's breadth from her face.

He could hear nothing but the blood rushing in his ears. He jabbed the torch into the wall so he could have both hands free. For a long moment, all he could do was stare at her. Finally, he gained the courage to reach out and touch her face. "Och!" he cried softly. "Leona, please fergive me."

LEONA HAD NEVER GIVEN HIM THE FULL REASON AS TO WHY SHE HATED the dark. He'd always meant to ask her, but for whatever reasons, he had never gotten around to it. Now, he would never know.

For the first time in his adult life, Alec Bowie wept. Tears fell from his eyes as his shoulders wracked with intense guilt and grief. She died alone, in the coldest, darkest of places. All alone, without anyone there to say goodbye.

He had to get her out of here. He would take her back to the keep and prepare her himself for a proper burial.

Then he would have Patrice Bowie hanged.

Grief and fury enveloped him, coming out in great waves of quiet tears.

"Alec?" Kyth called out from above. "Are ye all right?"

All right? Nay, I will never again be all right.

"Have ye found the bottom yet?"

Alec swallowed back his tears, took in a deep breath and called up to Kyth. "I found her."

"Be she all right?" he yelled down, his voice filled with hope.

Alec didn't have the strength to answer. He shook his head, and took in another cleansing breath. When he felt he had gained enough strength and courage to touch her, with great care and tenderness, he began to lift her into his arms.

For a long moment, he could have sworn he heard her mumble.

"Leona?" he whispered her name.

"I hurt," came her weak reply.

NEVER HAD HE FELT SUCH A STRONG SENSE OF RELIEF. HE FELL BACK onto his rump against the wall, with Leona in his arms. Tears fell again, but this time for entirely different reasons.

"Lass!" he cried. "Talk to me, please!"

"I hurt," she repeated, her voice weak and strained.

Slowly, he breathed in and out, as he tried to settle his nerves. Elation, sheer, unadulterated elation exploded from his stomach to his fingers. "Thank God!" he whispered repeatedly. "Thank God!"

The tight confines of the well made it difficult to move. Using the wall for support, he hugged her close and stood. "I am goin' to get ye out of here lass!" he told her. "I am going to tie this rope around yer waist, aye? I need ye to hang on."

"Help Dougall first," she said.

Assuming she must be delirious from having been in the water and dark for so long, he kissed the top of her head before speaking louder. "Leona!" he said as he gave her a little shake. "I need ye to wake up." Again, he told her he was going to tie the rope around her waist. "I need ye to stand up," he said. "Stand up, Leona!"

She grumbled and winced when he tried to set her on her feet, and collapsed against him. "Nay!" she cried out. "Me arm be broken."

He set her back down against the wall, using great care. He removed the dirk from his boot and cut away the sleeves of her dress. Her right arm had naught but a few nasty scratches and cuts. Her left, however, proved her correct.

Her forearm was bent, twisted, the bone not quite poking through the skin. God only knew if her legs were similarly damaged. Lifting her skirts, he checked as best he could. Both ankles were swollen, but nothing appeared to be broken. *How on earth had she survived such a fall without breakin' her legs?*

He would have to hold her while his men pulled them both up at the same time. But he was not certain they would both fit through the thick vines above. *Bloody hell!*

Knowing he risked damaging her arm even further should it become tangled in the vines, he had to make a decision.

"Kyth!" he shouted. "She be alive!"

A great cheer erupted from above. He had to call Kyth's name three times before he could hear him over the happy men. "Her arm be broken! Send down something to make a splint!"

He was going to have to set her arm before he could get her out of the well. Lord above, he did not want to have to do it, but he had no other choice.

Moments passed by before Kyth called down to him. "Heads up, Alec!" A moment later, he tossed a bundle down. Alec caught it before it could splash into the murky water.

The fabric, he was certain, had once been someone's tunic. Probably Kyth's. Wrapped around it were several long sticks, straight as they could find. He unravelled the bundle and carefully set everything on the vines.

Taking several deep steadying breaths, he studied his wife's arm and the best manner in which to proceed.

"Leona, this is goin' to hurt like the devil," he whispered. "Fergive me."

The pain was so intense, Alec imagined she could feel it to her toes. She screamed, a God-awful scream. With glassy eyes she stared at him for the briefest moment, before she passed out.

With the bone set, he quickly set about making the splint. He dropped one of the sticks twice, both times into the murky water. The entire process took longer than he would have liked, for his hands trembled.

Calling up to his men, he said, "She's ill and weak! She cannot make the climb. I have to bring her up with me!"

"We be ready when ye are!" Kyth called down.

Alec found the slip-knot and put his foot into it. After wrapping the rope around his own waist a few times, he lifted his wife into his arms. He gave a yank on the rope, and was soon being lifted into the air.

He left the torch behind, for there was no way to carry it and hold onto his wife.

Into blackness they ascended, all the while he whispered words of encouragement to Leona. "Soon, we shall have ye back at the keep, love."

CHAPTER 32

*W*ith Leona wrapped in his arms, covered with plaids his men had given him, they rode like lightning back to the keep. Down the paths, across the drawbridge, and into the courtyard.

Pulling Ares to a stop, Alec swung a leg over and jumped to his feet. He refused to hand Leona off to anyone. "Where is the healer?" he yelled into the semi-darkness. Without waiting for a response, he bounded up the stairs and into the keep.

Adhaira was waiting for him near the stairs. "Och!" she exclaimed when she saw Leona. "I have a tub of hot water waitin' above stairs, m'laird." She rushed ahead of the others.

As Adhaira lit more candles, Alec laid Leona on the bed and began to check for further injuries. Abrasions and scratches, nothing so deep to require stitches, were scattered across her face and neck.

"Ye must get her out of those wet clothes," Adhaira said. She ushered the men out of the room.

"Where be Mairi?" Alec asked as he began to cut away the already torn and tattered gown.

"We sent word to find her, m'laird," Adhaira replied.

As he carefully sat his wife up, Adhaira gently tugged away the dress. "They said she was at the bottom of an old well?"

Alec gave a quick nod of affirmation. "Her arm was broken. I had to set it," he replied as they got her out of the chemise. Adhaira pulled off Leona's slippers and woolens.

As far as Alec could tell, there were no other broken bones. Although her ankles were swollen, he believed they were only sprained.

Leona started to shiver then, violently. "Get her in the tub," Adhaira told him.

With great care, Alec scooped Leona up and set her in the warm tub. "I can no' tell if she has a fever. Her skin be too cold."

She stank to the high heavens, from being in the dank water for God only knew how long. The dress had been soaked up to her waist. With a broken arm and those conditions, 'twas no wonder she was so cold.

Using a clay pitcher, Adhaira poured warm water over Leona's head. Alec held her up, making sure to keep her broken arm out of the water.

The shivering soon subsided and Leona began to mumble once again about Dougall. "Dougall," she whispered. "Ye must help him first."

"Aye, lass, we will help him," Alec replied, though he could not begin to guess as to why she was thinking of Dougall.

"Poison," Leona stammered. "He's bein' poisoned."

Alec very nearly let go, so stunned he was to hear his wife mention the same thing Patrice had: that Dougall was being poisoned.

As soon as they were done bathing her, Alec lifted her up into his arms again. Adhaira wrapped a drying cloth around her as best she could. While Alec sat next to the hearth with Leona on his lap, Adhaira dried her hair.

"Leona, who told ye Dougall was bein' poisoned?" Alec asked as he rubbed her cold skin with the palm of his hand. Her head lolled from side to side. "Leona? Please, lass, I need ye to wake up. Did Patrice tell ye she had poisoned him?"

"Nay," she replied as she fought to open her eyes. "No' Patrice."

His stomach tightened. Had Patrice been telling the truth? "Are ye certain, Leona?" he asked, as he gave a gentle shake to her leg. "Did Patrice put ye in the well?"

Leona shook her head and tried once again to open her eyes. "Nay, no' Patrice."

He swallowed hard before he asked his next question. "Was it Mairi, then? Was Mairi the one who put ye in the well?"

Fighting hard to wake, to focus on her husband, she said, "Nay, no' Mairi or Patrice. Please, Alec, help Dougall."

Cold, exhausted, and in pain, she fell back to sleep, with her head resting against Alec's shoulder.

If 'twas no' Mairi or Patrice, then who the hell was it?

Adhaira slipped a heavy sleeping gown over Leona's head. She'd cut the right sleeve off so they would not have to disturb the broken arm any more than they already had.

Alec put her into the bed and pulled the furs up around her neck. He sat next to her, dumbfounded, wondering who on earth would have poisoned Dougall and for what purpose? And who in the name of God had tried to kill his wife?

"Alec," Leona whispered his name. "Please help Dougall."

Alec leaned over and laid down beside her. "Leona, who did this? Who hurt ye? Who hurt Dougall?"

She whispered her reply so softly that he had to ask her to repeat it.

Hurt and anger churned in his gut when she repeated the name.

A DENSE, HEAVY FOG BLANKETED THE LAND, ENCASING THE KEEP IN A cocoon of stillness. Lit torches burned along the upper wall. They did nothing more than act as tiny, ghost-like beacons. If one could see through the leaden fog, they would see a ghost-like figure all but float across the stone courtyard.

Inside the keep, a tranquil peace filled the grand place. It sat as still as a frozen stream in winter time. Dark, calm, and seemingly at sleep. The only identifiable sound below stairs was the soft crackle of a low-burning fire.

A few torches, burning softly, cast the stairway in soft shades of gold and saffron. Otherwise, the space was dark.

The lone figure, cloaked in wool, a cowl covering its head, crept up the stairs. Soft footfalls against the stone steps barely discernible in the sleepy, calm keep. It moved effortlessly and was unaware of other cloaked figures hiding in the darkness. One stone stair step at a time, it moved unchallenged but not unseen.

The corridors above were darker. No torches lighting the way. But the ghostly figure knew this keep well. Every nook, every cranny, almost as well as the back of its own hand.

Noiselessly, the door to the laird's chambers was pushed open, a hairsbreadth at a time. Peering inside, it could see the object of all its hate, lying in the laird's bed. *Leona.*

A single lit candle sat on a small table in a corner of the room. It flickered and danced slowly, along with the low-burning flames in the hearth.

Heedful of the danger it was taking, it stepped cautiously inside. A quick glance about the room said it was alone once again.

A sense of calm fell over the figure as it stepped soundlessly toward the bed. *I have tried to kill ye twice before, Leona, but I failed. I shall no' fail again.*

Long, slender fingers reached out from under the cloak. Moving slowly so as not to wake its prey, it reached for a pillow. *'Twas no' the way I wanted to kill ye. But ye will be dead all the same.*

Holding the pillow with both hands, it slowly lowered it over Leona's face.

～

ALEC HAD LET IT BE KNOWN THAT HE WOULD BE IN THE BARRACKS WITH his men that night, working on a plan to find the person responsible for putting Leona in the well. Intentionally, they had spread the word far and wide, that Leona had not wakened yet, her prognosis grim. Adding to the rumor, 'twas told Leona had hit her head during her fall to the bottom of that well. No one knew if she would live through the night, let alone wake from that deep sleep and name her attacker.

He had watched from the dark shadowy spaces of the gathering room, as the cloaked figure ascended the stairs. With nerves of steel and a fierce determination to seek justice, he waited until the figure was out of sight before making his move.

Well trained as both a thief and a warrior, Alec moved stealthily, noiselessly up the stairs. He watched from the shadows once again, as the figure stepped into his bedchamber.

Inside the doorway, he stood and watched as that cloaked figure lifted a pillow and placed it over Leona's head. He was on it in a few quick strides, lifting it up and away from his wife. Immediately, his men swarmed the room.

"Och! Alec! I be so glad ye're here! I came to check on Leona, and saw someone had placed a pillow over her head!"

With his jaw clenched, Alec dragged the figure below stairs, against noisy claims of innocence. "I was tryin' to help her, Alec!"

He shoved her into a chair by the fire. Kyth and Gylys stood behind her and held her in place with their hands on her shoulders.

"Alec, ye must believe me!"

"Effie, stop!" he yelled. His booming voice bounced off the walls. "I ken 'twas ye!"

"Nay, Alec, I swear it! Leona be me friend!" She feigned ignorance, feigned true concern. Her brown eyes filled with tears as she pleaded with him to believe her.

But Alec knew better. Leona, though quite ill, was awake long enough to tell him 'twas Effie who was poisoning Dougall. 'Twas also Effie who had thrown her into the well.

"Silence!" he shouted as he took a step away. Shaking his head in disgust, and aye, disbelief. He paced in front of her for a few moments, gathering his thoughts, as he tried to quash the near-ferrel need to strangle her with his bare hands.

When he was able to look at her again, he studied her closely. She was still lying, with her eyes, the false tears, and pained expression.

Leona had been unable to tell him much of anything, other than identifying Effie as her attacker. *She told me she was poisonin' Dougall with a tisane. She killed her own da as well.*

Those facts were soon confirmed by Mairi, just a few short hours ago. *"When I first saw Dougall, I thought 'twas something he'd eaten. I never said he had the wastin' disease."*

Lies upon lies. Rumors, secrets and more lies. All from the lips of a woman he had known the whole of his life. "Why, Effie?" he asked. "Why did ye do it?"

The look of stunned surprise faded slowly. Soon, 'twas replaced with indignant indifference. She refused to answer.

"Take her to the dungeon," Alec ordered. "I want at least two men watching her at all times."

As Kyth and Gylys dragged her away, she kicked and screamed. "Ye will regret this, Alec Bowie! I will make certain of it!"

He might have many regrets, and would undoubtedly accumulate more over the course of his lifetime. But capturing Effie Bowie and sentencing her to death would not be one of them.

CHAPTER 33

*A*fter seeing to it that Effie had been caught and locked away, Alec immediately returned to his wife. From their bedchamber, he gave the order to have Dougall and his sons brought to the keep, and given quarters across the hall, beside Slaien and Fionn. 'Twould make it far easier for Mairi to tend to them.

He'd ordered that not a word be spoken about Effie in front of her sons. If, by some miracle, Dougall lived, 'twould be best the news came from him. The younger boys kept asking after Effie. "Where be our mum?" Alec told them that she too, was quite ill and left it at that.

Dougall was far too ill to speak, let alone able to make any sense of the events. Later, if and when he got better, Alec would tell him. Patrice thanked him for the noble effort, and asked permission to take care of him. Alec agreed.

One of the womenfolk volunteered to act as wet nurse to Archibald. Poor Adhaira was run ragged with fetching water, bandages, and whatever else was called for. Kyth was all too willing to help her. Alec could not help but wonder if there wasn't a romance budding betwixt the two.

Gylys was all too happy to continue helping with Fionn and Slaien.

Leona's fevers came and went for the remainder of the night. Alec never left her side once he returned to it. Occasionally, he would doze off as he lay beside her, holding her hand, but otherwise did not speak. There were too many emotions running rampant through his heart. He would not speak them aloud until she was awake and could hear.

'Twas late the following night when Alec left the chamber. Though there was no longer a clear danger to his wife, his men still kept watch below stairs. He had to admire their dedication and loyalty.

Curiosity had taken a strong foothold in his mind. He had to know the *why* of it all. He passed through the gathering room where his men asked after Leona. There had been very little change since the night before. The fevers still came and went, he informed them before thanking them for their concern and diligence.

THROUGH THE GATHERING ROOM, AND DOWN THE CORRIDOR, HE WENT to the dungeons. One of his men was sitting in a chair at a small table, the other in a chair leaning against the wall next to Effie's cell.

When he'd been made chief, one of the first orders he'd given was to have all the torture devices and implements of death removed. Everything had been set afire in an open field not far from the keep.

For a brief moment - with his grief and rage so profound — he almost wished now that he hadn't given that order.

Effie was lying on a cot, facing the wall. Alec took a slow, steadying breath before speaking to her. "Effie," he said. "I should like to talk to ye."

She was still and quiet for so long that he wondered if she wasn't dead.

"And if I should *no'* like to talk to ye?" she finally replied.

"I want to know the *why* of it, Effie."

"What benefit is it to me, if I tell ye?" she countered.

If she thought to negotiate her way into a lenient sentence, she was sadly mistaken.

"Help me understand, Effie. I can no' pass sentence on ye unless I ken the why of it." 'Twas a full-out lie, but one he was willing to speak in order to gain answers.

A bit of time passed before she let out a heavy sigh and sat up to face him.

"Did ye know that I was once betrothed to Eduard?" she asked as she slowly got to her feet.

Nay, he had never heard that bit of news.

"I was all of seven and ten, ye ken. Och, how I loved that man!" She began to pace, slowly, back and forth, as she told her tale.

"I was to be the chief's wife, ye ken. The chatelaine of the keep. People would adore me. They would bow at me feet. Eduard would adorn me in fine jewels, silk dresses, and treat me as if I were a queen."

Alec hadn't lived here at that time. He was in Italy, gaining his education. Would he not have heard some rumor upon his return?

"I got with his child," she went on to tell him. "Wills, he be no' Dougall's, but Eduard's."

'Twas something else he was not aware of, but made no comment on the matter. Later, he would ask Dougall for verification.

"Me dear da, he did no' care at all for Eduard. He thought him too pompous and said he had a black heart. He talked Eduard in to settin' me aside, Da did. I hated him fer it. But since I was with child, I needed a husband. Da somehow persuaded Dougall to marry me. At the time, I was so angry, I did no' care. I hated Patrice as much as I hated me da. So marryin' Dougall? 'Twas one way I could make her hurt. I was Da's favorite until she came along and ruined everythin'."

She paused at the wall, using her fingernail to scrape at one of the stones. Alec knew that Dougall had always held Effie's father in high regard. He was the father Dougall never had.

"It hurt Patrice, it surely did, when 'twas announced I'd be marryin' Dougall. 'Twas no less than what the conniving wench deserved."

"Dougall never said a word of this to me," Alec said.

"Of course no'!" Effie laughed. "He be too *honorable*, too much of a good man! He is as big a weak-minded, insipid fool as me da was!"

Her tone of voice, the malice sickened him. Still, he listened patiently, hoping she would eventually begin to make some sense.

"For years, I resigned meself to the fact that I would never be chatelaine," Effie told him as she leaned her head against the stone wall. "For years, I pretended to be happy. Pretended to love Dougall." She snorted derisively. "I hate him as much as I hated me da." Turning again to pace, she said, "But what was I to do? I had no other choice. Then, one day me prayers were answered when Aggie Mackintosh killed Eduard." She paused and looked at Alec once again. "I mourned his loss, I truly did. Even after all those years, I still loved him, even though he was black-hearted and selfish." She smiled fondly at memories she was not about to share. She was lost in a quiet reverie; 'twas the sound of a chair scraping against stone that brought her out of it.

"But then Rutger became chief and my hope was renewed." she exclaimed. "I seduced him - yer fool of a brother. I did no' love him. He was an eejit, ye ken. But if I wanted to be chatelaine, lettin' him crawl on top of me was worth it."

Although a knot had formed deep in the pit of his stomach, Alec kept a calm facade.

"I started to poison Dougall back then. Slowly, this time, so as no' to draw too much suspicion. But then Rutger set his eye on Patrice. Bah! Why do all the men want her? When she is weak? What is wrong with strong women who can see the truth more clearly than anyone else?"

Alec would make no attempt to answer.

"When I told yer brother I was with child, that 'twas his, he denied it. Refused to claim him. But he was dead before I could do anythin' about it. Archibald be Rutger's."

Somehow, that did not surprise him.

"Then came *ye*," she said, taking a few steps toward him. "The great and powerful Alec Bowie!" She shook her head in disgust before spitting on the floor. "The bringer of peace! I would have married ye, Alec! I would have! But ye went off and married yer witch. Yer odd-eyed, tetched-in-the-head, witch!"

438

"Did ye truly think I would marry ye?" he asked, appalled at the notion.

"Ye would have," she said. "I would have seduced ye one way or another. Everyone kens I can get with child easily. And with Dougall dead, ye'd have married me out of yer strong sense of honor and duty! But ye married Leona instead!"

His level of disgust was undeniable. "Ye're mad!" he said. "Ye tried to kill Dougall and Leona, all so that ye might be the chatelaine?"

"Och! Alec, aye! I have killed before, ye ken. I killed me da. Everyone thought 'twas a heart ailment, because that is what they wanted to believe."

Patrice had been half right. Her father had been poisoned, but not by Mairi's hand.

Disgusted, he started to step away. Effie stopped him by reaching through the black, steel bars. "Alec, wait!" she cried out. "We can still be together! Leona will no' live much longer. Ye could challenge Dougall and kill him. We could be together, Alec! We can put these crazy ideas of yers fer peace aside. We can build this clan back to what it once was! Do you no' see?"

He yanked his arm from her grasp. "See?" he asked, appalled. "All I see is a woman so filled with greed and hate that she would kill innocent people just to get what she wants."

As he walked away, she continued her tirade. "Alec! I can give ye more than Leona ever will! Alec! Do no' walk away from me!"

Even if Effie were not deranged, she could never have given him what Leona had: a peaceful, loving home.

ALEC STAYED BY LEONA'S SIDE FOR ANOTHER TWO DAYS. STILL, SHE HAD yet to waken from her fever-induced sleep. Betimes, she would whimper and cry out in her sleep. Others, she lay so still and quiet he thought she had passed away.

He rarely slept, refused to eat or to leave her side. When she woke, he wanted his face to be the first thing she saw. His voice, giving her the words he wanted her to have.

'Twas late on the evening of the third day after her rescue that things took a turn for the worse. Mairi and Adhaira had come to check on her and to change her sweat-soaked sheets. 'Twas then they saw the blood. They had to call for Kyth and Gylys to physically remove him from the room.

An hour later, Mairi was telling him that Leona had lost her babe.

A babe he had no idea even existed until 'twas too late.

"She swore me to secrecy, Alec," Mairi explained as they stood in the hallway outside his bedchamber. "She wanted to be the one to tell ye."

Alec stood as still as stone as his eyes bored holes in the floor at his feet. Working his jaw back and forth, clenching and unclenching his teeth, he seethed with fury. "Ye should have told me," he said, his voice low and scratchy.

"Alec, I could no' break a confidence," Mairi replied. "Why are ye so angry?"

He raised his head to look her in the eye and realized, she thought he was angry with her. "I be angry with Effie," he told her. "'Tis all her fault!"

'Twas a point that Mairi could no' argue.

"What be Effie's fault?" 'Twas Dougall's voice coming from behind Alec's shoulder. For the first time in days, the man was out of bed. Alec thought he still looked like death. Patrice stepped out of the room and placed a comforting hand on Dougall's side. "Come, Dougall, we need to talk."

Dougall bore the most confused expression on his face. Too weak to argue, he allowed Patrice to see him back to bed.

Alec was not yet ready to have a meaningful discussion with Dougall. Nay, he placed no blame at Dougall's feet. It all belonged to Effie.

'Twas only out of respect for her children as well as Dougall, that Alec hadn't already ordered her hanging. But Effie was the last person he wanted to be thinking about now. He had to focus on Leona.

His voice caught on the lump in his throat when he asked Mairi his next question. "Be she all right? Can she—"

Mairi knew exactly what he was going to ask. "Aye, Alec. She can have more children."

His shoulders sagged with much relief. Not for his own needs, but for love of his wife. Above all else, she wanted to fill this cursed keep with as many children as she could manage to bear.

He raked a hand through his hair as he let loose a heavy breath, his mind reeling, his heart breaking for the loss of the babe.

"Alec," Mairi spoke in hushed tones. "Ye have sat by yer wife fer days now. But ye do no' speak a word to her. Why is that?"

"She can no' hear me," he replied.

"Of course she can hear ye. She might no' be able to understand all of what ye're saying, but she can hear ye. Though, she might no' remember any of it when she wakes."

He gave a dismissive shake of his head. "Do ye think she will live?" 'Twas the one question he had refused to ask until now. His worry was so intense, he did not know how much more he could bear.

Mairi was not going to lie to him. "Alec, I honestly do no' ken. A few weeks ago, I would have sworn to ye that Slaien would no' make it through the night. And now look at her. Sitting up in the bed, able to eat broth and bread. 'Tis a miracle if ever I saw one."

"Do ye think God will grant us another miracle?"

Mairi shrugged a shoulder. "I do no' ken. But I reckon ye should ask Him."

Alec rolled his eyes heavenward. 'Twas not that he did not believe in God or the power of prayer. But certainly God would have turned his back on this motley band of thieves, traitors, and ne'er-do-wells long ago.

"Alec, I will tell ye somethin' that I *do* know."

He cast her a suspicious look before bidding her continue.

"Ye need to give Leona the words. The words to either leave God's earth in peace, or to stay. The choice be yers." With that, she left him to go back to Leona.

~

GIVE HER THE WORDS. TO LEAVE GOD'S EARTH IN PEACE, OR TO STAY. ALEC played Mairi's words over and over in his mind as he paced the hallway. What if Mairi was wrong and Leona could not hear him? Worse yet, what if she was right and Leona misunderstood?

When Mairi stepped out of the room, she had taken with her a bundle of blood-soaked bedsheets. The lump in his throat seemed to have taken up permanent residence, for it prohibited him from articulating even a slight whisper.

Alec stood for a long while, working up the courage to speak. He'd forgottten to ask if Leona knew she had lost the babe, or even if she was still feverish. Taking a deep breath, he moved toward her.

She appeared at rest, peaceful and serene as she slept. That answered his first question. Nay, she did not know.

Heedful of her broken arm, he climbed into the bed beside her. Fully clothed and atop the covers, he lay on his side and watched her. As she slept, he twined a lock of her hair around his finger, as he had done countless times before. In the quiet stillness of the night, he gave the words to his wife.

"Leona," he whispered softly. "I do no' ken if ye can hear me or no', but there be things I need to tell ye, lass. Important things." He took a deep breath as he thought on the best place to start. "Dougall be safe, as are his sons. They be in the room right across the hall. He be doin' much better, thanks to ye. I saw him standin' up without help not long ago." He paused, fighting back his anger toward Effie before he mentioned her name. "Effie be in the dungeons. Nay, I've no' given sentence yet. I wanted to hear yer thoughts on the matter first."

Leona did not stir, or give any other indication that she heard him. Still, he needed to keep talking to her. "There be a good deal of people prayin' fer ye, lass. No' just the men either. The womenfolk too. Once they realized what Effie had done, the lies she had told and rumors she had spread, they finally came to their good senses." 'Twas all true. Over the last two days, the womenfolk had been dropping by the keep to see if there had been any change in Leona's condition. Many brought food, stews, meat pies, and sweets. With his men still standing watch below stairs, the food was much welcomed. As were the kind words and apologies.

"There be somethin' else I need ye to ken lass," he took a deep breath before going on. "Leona, 'tis true me life has no' been the same since ye arrived. And fer that, I be forever grateful to ye. For the whole of me life, until I met ye, I never wanted a happy home. I think it was because my mother always bragged about what a happy home she provided to her husband and sons. But ye see, 'twas anythin' *but* that. 'Twas filled with hate and malice, harsh, ugly words, and aye, a few chamber pots crashin' against the walls. Me mum, she claimed she loved me da. He claimed she loved his coin and drivin' him to madness. He taught me from an early age, never to give me heart to a woman. *'She will use it as a weapon against ye!'* he would claim. I looked up to me da, fer he was such a strong, big man and people thought him important. In truth, I was just a little boy vyin' fer his love. Love he never gave."

Alec was admitting things aloud for the first time in his life. 'Twas cathartic and after a while, he began to feel as though a heavy weight had been lifted from his shoulders. He hadn't realized until then that he had been carrying that anvil of hurt around all of his life.

"I owe ye so much, Leona, I truly do. Ye showed me that a man can give his heart to a woman without fear. I realized, too late now, it appears, that I am no' me father and ye are no' me mother. There be no' a malicious bone in yer body. Ye be nothin' but all that is good and right in this world."

He pressed a tender kiss to her forehead as his eyes grew damp. "I love ye, Leona. I think I always have. But I was too afraid to admit it. Please, Leona, do no' leave me. I need ye, lass. I love ye."

FOR HOURS ALEC SPOKE TO LEONA, THOUGH SHE NEVER GAVE ANY SIGN that she heard him. He told her of his childhood, of the kind of brother Rutger had been *before* greed and avarice took over his heart.

He told her stories of when he fostered with the MacGregors and the fallout that happened when they learned the truth about who he was. He spoke of his time in Italy, France, and Germania, and how he hoped he could someday show her all of the world that he had seen.

He shared his fears and worries, the truth about what had transpired during his visits — or lack thereof — with their neighboring clans. Any thought that entered his mind or heart, he shared with his sleeping wife.

At some point in the night, he must have finally succumbed to exhaustion and fell asleep beside her. When he woke next, Leona was still fast asleep beside him. With the furs drawn to keep out any chill, 'twas nearly impossible to tell whether 'twas day or night.

Quietly, he left the bed to relieve his bladder. He splashed cold water over his face and neck. Drying his face and hands against the linen cloth, he was heading across the floor to add more kindling and wood to the fire.

He cast a glance at his wife. One hand lay on her stomach while tears streamed down her face.

"I lost me babe."

FROM THE MOMENT SHE AWAKENED, LEONA KNEW SOMETHING WAS wrong. Her stomach felt odd. Cold and empty. No one needed to tell her what she already knew. She had lost her babe. She could feel it even before she placed her hand on her abdomen.

Weak from lying abed for God only knew how long, she was unable to keep the tears at bay. At once, she was consumed with grief and agony. Bitter tears of remorse fell from her eyes.

She cried openly and without restraint, repeating the same phrase, *I lost me babe! I lost me babe!* She cared not who heard her plaintive wails of grief, cared not who might be witnessing the single most difficult moment of her life. Alone, or in front of a thousand eyes, it mattered not.

She'd lost her babe.

The one thing that she would ever be able to call her own. The only person who would love her without condition. The one life that would matter more than her own. The one person with whom she could shower all the love in her heart and no one would judge her for it.

God! Where was Alec? Why was he not here? Did he know? Did he care? Leona slipped into an abyss of torment and bereavement, a dark, empty place.

MAIRI, PATRICE, AND ADHAIRA HAD HEARD LEONA'S CRIES ECHOING OFF the walls of the keep. They came running, from different directions, and raced to her room.

Alec was beside her, doing his best to comfort her, but to no avail. She screamed and cried out, banging her hands against his chest, begging for someone to take her own life, for now, she was completely and truly alone.

Mairi was quite certain Leona knew not what she was saying. Still, her sorrow was as real as the sun rising and setting each day. During those times of severe loss and sadness, a body sometimes said things they did not mean. Leona did not want to die any more than Mairi wanted to grow a beard.

They had pushed Alec away, off to the side, while they did their best to console their friend.

When Mairi realized their attempts were failing, she sent Adhaira below stairs for hot water, and Patrice across the hall for her bag of herbs. While she ground the herbs in her mortise, Adhaira brought a mug of hot water. It took time to properly steep the herbs, all the while, Leona wept against Patrice's chest. Great, wracking sobs, as her shoulders shook and hands trembled.

There was not a woman in the keep who could not sympathize with her pain and suffering. Though Mairi had never married, had never been with child, she could well imagine how badly Leona hurt.

Once they were able to get enough of the potion inside her, she began to calm. A little while later, she was once again fast asleep.

Mairi wiped the sweat from her own brow with her apron and let out a slow, steady breath. 'Twas then she realized Alec had left.

"She has a long path ahead of her," Mairi told Patrice. "I only hope Alec be strong enough to help her down it."

DOUGALL HAD SENT WORD THAT HE WANTED TO TALK TO ALEC. Reluctantly, and only because the last thing he wanted was to bring his friend more pain, Alec went to see him after the noonin' meal.

Patrice had taken the boys outside for some much needed exercise and fresh air. So Alec and Dougall sat alone in the quarters Dougall was sharing with his sons.

Dougall took one look at Alec and declared, "Ye look worse than I do."

Alec could not argue the point, even though he hadn't seen his own reflection in days. He grabbed a chair and sat next to Dougall, who was resting in the big feather bed. His color had much improved over the past days. His skin no longer held the pallor of death. His lips were no longer red and cracked and his breathing sounded stronger. But his eyes bespoke more than anything that he was far from fine. There was a deep sadness in them.

"Alec, ye must know I had no idea what Effie was doin'," he told him.

Alec raised a palm to halt his apology. "Dougall, I ken that. I do no' hold ye to blame fer anything that has transpired."

He look much relieved at hearing that.

"Have ye told yer boys yet?" Alec asked. God, he did not envy this man right now.

"Nay, I have no'," he admitted. "I fear I do no' ken what to tell them. 'Tis the truth that I am lost."

"I have only told them that their mum is quite ill," Alec said. "Fer that is the truth. She be sick in her mind, Dougall."

"And her heart," he replied with a good deal of sadness. "I never saw it, Alec. I never once saw her as anythin' but me kind, sweet wife."

Alec thought on that for a long moment. "Mayhap, because that was what ye *wanted* to see. Ye knew, did ye no', that Eduard was Wills' father?"

"Aye, I did," he said sadly. "I only married her because Effie's da, Edgar, begged me to. Had I ken then, what I ken now …"

"'Tis always easier to see things clearly *after* the fact," Alec told him.

"I feel like a fool, Alec. I was married to her for more than eleven years. I fathered at least five of her children. Or at least I believed I had. Now, now I can no' be certain of anythin'. Me entire world has fallen apart."

Alec rubbed the back of his neck for a moment. "I ken verra well how that feels, Dougall. But no matter whose blood runs through the veins of the boys who call ye da, ye are their father. They need no' ever ken the truth of it."

"Nay, I need to ken, Alec. What if someday they fall in love with a lass and she turns out to be their half-sister? Nay, I could no' do that to them."

"Mayhap ye should ask Alyce first. Think ye she would know?"

"Aye, she might. Effie was always her favorite. Thick as thieves they were, though 'twas always Patrice that Alyce turned to whenever she wanted fer somethin'."

'Twas an odd family, that branch of the Bowie tree.

"Have ye decided what ye will do with Effie?" Dougall asked.

Alec gave a slow shake of his head. "Nay, I have no'. I wanted to speak to ye first, and to Leona. The two of ye were most hurt by her actions."

"God, Alec!" Dougall exclaimed. "Do no' ask me to pass judgment on the woman! I have her sons to think of!"

"I only meant, that if ye wished to speak to spare her life, I would listen."

Dougall let out a relieved, heavy breath. "'Tis the truth I ken no' what to do, or to think, or even to feel."

"Then we shall wait on it, cousin. We need not move quickly, fer she is safely locked away. We can wait to make our decision."

Little did either of them know that Effie Bowie had already made the decision for them. Less than two hours later, they would receive word that she had taken her own life. Apparently, the necklace she was wearing at the time of her capture, contained a fatal poison.

THE FOLLOWING FEW DAYS WERE THE WORST OF HIS LIFE. LEONA SEEMED to have withdrawn from the world around her. He knew not what to say or how to console her, to help her with her grief.

Although her fevers had subsided, she was far from healed.

Alec would enter their chamber, feeling rather like a child who knew not what he should do. He wanted to help, wanted to comfort her, to tell her all would be well. But the fear he would make matters worse usually overruled those thoughts. And those few times he did manage the courage to speak, she would turn away and stare at the wall.

For hours, he would sit by the fire with a blank expression, while Leona would cry softly into her pillow. Each of them were suffering, but neither knew what to do about it.

Alec, out of fear and respect, slept on a palette in his office. He had tried, that first night, to sleep next to Leona. But 'twas impossible, for she slept so fitfully. Tossing and turning, mumbling things he couldn't understand. So he left the bed to her in the hopes she would be more comfortable.

An unseen chasm of torment and sorrow now separated the two of them. *Give her time,* Mairi would tell him. *She needs to work through this on her own.*

Believing he knew very little about such things, he took Mairi's advice.

On a dark, dreary day less than a sennight after Leona had learned she had lost the babe, one of Alec's guards came rushing into the keep. Alec was in the gathering room, looking absentmindedly into the roaring flames of the hearth. "M'laird," he said excitedly. "We have visitors! They be waitin' fer permission to enter."

They never had visitors. 'Twas the cold hard truth. With a curious brow, Alec stood and asked, "Who is it?"

"Ian Mackintosh and his wife. And some one hundred of their men."

Why a cold shiver raked up and down his spine, he could not rightly say. "Have they said why they are here?"

The young man hemmed and hawed for a long moment before answering. "They say they've come to take Leona back."

WITHIN A QUARTER OF AN HOUR, ALEC BOWIE WAS STANDING IN HIS study listening to Ian Mackintosh explain the way of things.

"Me wife and I were quite confused when we received Leona's letter," Ian said as he sat next to the fire, sipping on a mug of ale. "Though she did no' go into details as to the *why* of things, she made it perfectly clear she wishes to leave. She no longer feels safe here, or even wanted."

Alec worked his jaw back and forth as he listened intently. More than a week's beard covered his face. He had not bathed in days, nor had he eaten much of anything. Before he'd received news of Mackintosh's arrival, he'd felt as strong as a dying moth. But now? With the news that Ian was here to take Leona back? He was mad enough to bite through steel.

"Now, I am of a mind that ye and Leona should work this out betwixt ye," Ian said.

'Tis the first intelligent thing ye've said since ye entered me keep.

"But me wife? Well, Rose be of an entirely different mindset."

With a facade of stone cold indifference, Alec waited for Ian to explain.

"Rose believes we should have ye drawn and quartered for injuring her dearest friend's tender feelings."

449

Alec was not amused. Though he did think rather highly of Rose Mackintosh, he did not think he or Leona needed her interference.

"Rose also believes that if I do no' do what I can to take Leona back into the lovin' fold of the Mackintosh and McLaren clan, then she will make me life a livin' nightmare."

Alec raised one curious brow.

"Alec, tell me what happened," Ian said as he leaned forward in his seat. "I will never hear the end of it if I do no' hear from yer own lips how ye see things."

"How *I* see things?" Alec asked drolly. "How I see things is that a man I once considered my friend is here, in me own home, drinkin' my ale, and informin' me that he is takin' me wife."

Ian chuckled and shook his head. "Nay, that be no' my intent, Alec. I want to ken what truly happened. Why would Leona have written such a letter, beggin' fer us to come to her aid? To take her back home."

"*This* is her home," Alec reminded him.

"Be that as it may, I need to know. All of it. Else, I will be forced to see me wife's wishes come true."

ROSE BARELY RECOGNIZED HER FRIEND. LEONA WAS PALE AND GAUNT. Dark circles lined her red-rimmed eyes. In a swish of pale blue wool and silk chemise, Rose crossed the floor, sat on the bed and pulled her into her arms.

"Leona!" she exclaimed. "We came as soon as we could." She set Leona back to gain a better look at her. "What in the name of God has happened to ye?"

"I lost me babe," Leona whispered. Just when she thought she could shed not another tear, more filled her eyes.

Rose was glad now that she had left her son with one of the Mackintosh women. Seeing the wee babe now might have been too much for Leona. Rose pulled her in for another embrace. As she patted her back, she whispered words of encouragement. "We shall get ye through this," Rose told her. "Is that why ye wrote to us? Is that why ye want to come back?"

Leona sniffed as she fought to remember when she had sent the letter. That was more than a sennight ago, closer to two. She'd sent it right after she and Alec had fought that night. That night that had changed everything between them.

"Why do ye no' tell me what happened. I will do me best to help."

Leona took a deep breath, wiped her tears away, and began to tell her everything that had transpired since she'd married Alec Bowie.

"My, God!" Ian exclaimed when Alec finished recounting the tale. "She really poisoned her own husband? And tried to kill Leona, just to be chatelaine?" He let out a low whistle.

"Aye, she did," Alec replied.

"Where is she now?" Ian asked.

"Dead," Alec said. "She took her own life."

Ian sat his mug of ale on the floor at his feet before rubbing his hands across his face. "I fear I know not what to say or do, Alec."

"There is nothing fer ye to say or do."

Ian chuckled half-heartedly. "I fear me wife will no' agree."

As far as Alec was concerned, he did not care what Rose Mackintosh had to say on the matter of his wife.

The following morn, Alec sat in dumbfounded silence in front of the hearth in his bedchamber. His back was to Leona, for he didn't have the strength to look at her.

With Rose's help, Leona had packed her belongings, dressed in her old blue gown, and informed him she was leaving. That very afternoon. She was going back to Mackintosh lands. She hadn't provided him with any other information. Just a simple, "Alec, I be leavin' with Ian and Rose today."

He had been too stunned to speak, to argue or rail against it.

She was leaving him.

The last time she had told him such, they'd fought horribly. He had said things he would regret until the day he died. He had behaved abhorrently, which in turn, led to her nearly being killed by Effie. And that had led to her losing their babe.

Everything he never knew he wanted or needed was standing in the doorway. His entire world. His heart.

Silence filled that chasm of pain and sorrow that had formed between them. He could not look at her, for he knew he would fall apart. Or worse yet, his anger and hurt would get the better of him.

Once, he had refused to let her go. If he did so again, he would destroy her. And he could not do that. He loved her far too much.

"Alec," Leona said, her voice soft and low, "may I ask ye one thing before I go?"

With his heart shattering once again, this time for entirely different reasons, he gave a slow nod.

"Did I ever once, in all the time we were together, make ye happy?"

Happy? His heart fell, lodged itself firmly in his already churning gut. He sat for a while, searching for the right words, for a way to answer that would make sense.

"Aye, lass, ye did. I was never truly happy until ye, Leona," he said, his voice low and filled with sorrow. She was leaving him, and there was naught he could do but speak from his heart. "I never knew what a happy home was, until ye. I never knew I could find joy in somethin' as simple as the sunset. I never knew what true love was, until ye came into me life. So yes, lass," he stood to face her.

But she was already gone.

CHAPTER 34

Because of her injuries, Leona was unable to ride atop a horse. Someone had found a cart in which she could return in more comfort on that long, depressing route back to Mackintosh lands.

She sat in the back, atop fresh straw and pillows, next to Rose. A cool mist filled the morning air, chilling her to her marrow. The furs did nothing to keep the cold from settling deep into her bones.

He didn't try to stop me, she wept silently as they rode over the drawbridge. *He didn't rave and rant and tell me he wasn't going to allow me to leave.*

Alec no longer wanted her. Somehow, she assumed 'twas because she had lost their babe; she had let him down. Disappointed him. Disappointed him so much that he could no longer look her in the eyes.

Her heart ached, her world torn asunder with the loss of her babe, and now, the loss of her husband.

Alec may have cared for her at one time. But now? Now he didn't care enough to face her when she told him she was leaving. He didn't care enough to answer the last question she had ever put to him.

"We will have ye right as rain verra soon," Rose said as she drew the furs up around Leona's shoulders.

"I will never be right again," Leona murmured.

Rose, always kindhearted, patted her hand but offered no other encouragement.

They were being jostled about in the back of the cart as it rattled over the bumpy road. Leona watched as the large stone walls, the keep, and cottages grew smaller and smaller. Oh, what hopes and dreams this place once held for her. Now, they were ground into dust.

"Rose, I do no' wish to go back to Mackintosh lands," Leona told her.

"Ye wish to go back to yer husband?" she asked with a raised brow.

Leona shook her head. "Nay. Take me to St. Agnes's."

"The convent?" Rose exclaimed. She'd have been less surprised had Leona sprouted horns. "Ye can no' be serious!"

But she was. "I can no' go back to yer clan. I can no' face me father, or the people there. The whispers, the looks of reproach. I would be goin' back an even bigger failure than when I left."

Rose could not argue the point. Though many of her people were good, kind, and decent, there were still many who believed the lies Ingerame told of his only daughter. They believed, all because of her odd eyes, that she was a witch. 'Twould be next to impossible to change their minds.

"Ye loved him deeply, aye?" Rose asked as she too watched the buildings getting smaller.

"Aye, I did, Rose. But he could no' love me back."

Rose turned to look at her. "Are ye certain?"

All she could manage was a nod and a sniffle in reply.

"Ian seems to think Alec cares for ye a great deal."

"Carin' and lovin' are two different things," she told her. "He also cares fer his men, his bandogge, and his horse. It means naught."

Rose gave a nod of understanding. "So no' once, in the time ye were married, did ye feel safe? Cared for? Or even adored?"

"I did," Leona told her. "But I can no' stay with him, knowing me heart belongs to him, but his will never be mine. It hurts too much."

They sat in quiet reverie for some time. The sun broke through the morning mist, the Bowie keep now nothing more than a tiny dot on the horizon.

"Do ye no' think a husband should love his wife?" Leona asked.

"Well, it certainly helps," she replied. "But love will take its own sweet time."

Leona wasn't certain she understood Rose's meaning, but left it alone. "I have gone the whole of me life without bein' loved by those people who should have. Me da did no' love me; that, no one can deny."

Rose agreed with that assessment.

"And me husband, he should have loved me as well. Do ye no' see? I be no' the kind of woman any man can love. No' me da, no' Alec. No one."

"Do ye think it be possible that he *did* love ye? Alec I mean? But mayhap he was too afraid to give ye the words."

Nay, she did not think such a thing possible. "Then why did he no' stop me from leavin'? He did no' even say goodbye or fare thee well."

SHE WAS GONE.

She had left him.

Left him in this dark, empty keep, with its cold and drafty winds, its dark walls, and empty rooms. He could have lit a thousand candles and a thousand more fires, and none would have warmed the place or made it as bright as she had.

Alec stood at the window and watched as the cart made its way across the drawbridge and down the path. He continued to stare out the window, long after the cart, and the very last of the Mackintosh warriors were out of sight.

Never had he felt so utterly and profoundly empty.

He began to wander aimlessly through the keep. Touching things she had touched. The tapestries, the candlesticks, and sideboard, the pillows and rugs. Anything, just to feel a part of her again.

When he went to the kitchen, 'twas empty. He did not know, nor did he care where Adhaira was. He needed the quiet and emptiness.

Everything was just as she had made it to be. Homey, warm, and inviting, and well organized. Each of these things were *hers*. At one time, this had been her favorite place. She took great joy in cooking for him, for his men, for anyone.

He heard a scratch at the back door, then a whimper. He knew it was Satan before he opened the door. The black bandogge came inside, sniffing the floor, looking for his mistress. "She be gone," Alec told him. "She has left us both."

The dog whimpered, licked his drool laden chops once, before taking a spot by the cold hearth.

Feeling exhausted and numb, Alec sat on a stool next to his dog. He stroked the animal's back as he continued to look about the space. Something on the shelf, under the center table caught his eye. 'Twas a small package, wrapped in linen, with a string tied around it and a little bit of parchment. Curiosity won out, so he grabbed it and read the tiny note.

For Alec, was all it said.

Seeing no harm in opening it — for she was never coming back — he carefully untied the string. Carefully, he lifted away the corners and dumped the contents into the palm of his hand.

'Twas a plaid brooch. Beautifully crafted, carved in pewter. 'Twas the raven from the Bowie crest. Intricate and fine, with ruby red eyes.

Alec closed his eyes and pressed the brooch to his lips as he fought back the tears. This had to have been the gift she had spoken of weeks ago, but refused to tell him about. *I must do this one thing on me own, Alec, with me own coin.*

Everything she had done for him had been done because she loved him.

And he loved her.

Why wasn't it enough?

Gently, he re-wrapped the brooch and put it back where he had found it. When he removed his hand, he knocked a bowl from the shelf, startling Satan. The dog lifted his head, looked up at Alec with sad eyes, before returning to his nap.

Alec stood, retrieved the bowl and returned it to the shelf. He debated on whether or not he should return the bandogge to his kennel, or allow him free reign of the keep. He chose the latter.

"Come, Satan," he said as he stood at the door. The dog looked up, yawned a wide, drooling yawn, and laid his head back down. "Satan!" Alec said, more forcefully this time. Still, the dog ignored him. He hated doing it, truly he did. But he'd prefer the dog's company over his own, so he relented. "Patches! Come!"

The dog thumped his tail once before he stretched and stood up to follow his master.

WITH PATCHES NOW DUTIFULLY FOLLOWING HIM, THEY ASCENDED THE stairs and returned to Alec's bedchamber. Why he felt drawn to return to this place, he did not know. 'Twas filled with many happy memories, as well as several that bordered on ugly.

With a heavy heart, he wandered about the room without a clear reason or destination. He stopped at the little table where he had on occasion found his wife writing in one of her handmade journals. 'Twasn't until he lit the candle that he saw something she had forgotten. The leather pouch she often wore on the belt at her waist. He sat in the small chair, it creaked and groaned in protest, used to, he supposed, his wife's wee body.

Carefully, he withdrew the contents, one item at a time.

At first, 'twas a tiny bundle of dried heather. He pressed it to his nose and breathed in deeply. It reminded him of the soap she often used.

Next, he found a leather necklace with a round piece of pewter dangling from it. In its center was carved the letter R. He had no idea what or who the letter stood for. Carefully, he set it aside, next to the flowers.

Finally, he pulled out her small, leather bound journal. He flipped through the pages, thinking it was nothing more than a record of the goings on and daily life of the keep. Women, he knew, often kept their own records of such things.

But he was wrong. He found sonnets and poems, all on separate pieces of parchment, carefully folded and tucked inside. A date caught his eye. 'Twas from May of that year. He knew he probably should not read it, but he did.

I never thought this day would come, she had written. *But it has. I will be married in three weeks time!*

Me heart is filled with so much joy and surprise. I never thought I would marry, or have bairns of me own. I had resigned myself to dyin' an auld maid, untouched and unloved.

But Alec Bowie needs a wife, and I volunteered. He accepted!

He be a handsome man, tall and braw and a voice, deep and warm that makes me stomach feel as though I have swallowed a bird who wants to take flight. I hope I do no' disappoint him. I want to be a good wife and give him many bairns.

His chest felt tight, restricted, as if it were banded with iron as he read. Disappoint him? Nay, not once had she ever disappointed him. If anything, he had been in awe of her.

Before he realized it, he was reading every word of every page. The journal was filled with her fears, her worries, as well as her happiness. Page after page extolling his virtues as well as pointing out his flaws. These were her deepest, most private thoughts.

'Twas the last few pages that nearly sent him to his knees.

I love him. I love him more than I ever thought possible. But I have sorely disappointed him, for I lost the babe.

Alec can no' look at me. He refuses to speak. He does not offer me any comfort. I can only think it is because I lost our babe, for I can think of no other reason for him to turn away, to stare at his feet all the while he sits in our room.

I want so desperately to tell him how I feel. That I love him with all of my heart, to tell him how much it hurts to lose our babe, to tell him I am sorry for lettin' him down.

I wanted this babe more than I have ever wanted anythin' in my life. The babe would love me without condition. I would be able to shower all my love on him or her, and no one would think me daft, for that is what good mothers do. They love their children. They protect them, teach them right from wrong, and give them all the love in their hearts.

I ken Alec can no' love me, for I be one of those poor, wretched creatures that God puts on this earth, for whatever reason, to go the entirety of their lives without knowin' deep down and without question, what it is like to be loved. Aye, we can love, but there be no one to love us back.

I can no' stay here, knowin' that Alec is unable to love me at all. Knowin' that my heart will always be his. 'Twould be too painful to keep these words to myself. I can no' tell him, fer I ken he would no' like it. We made a pact on the day I agreed to marry him, that this would never be a love match. He does no' want that. He does no' want a warm, happy home. He does no' want me to love him. I can only love him the one way I know how – with all that I am. I have tried showin' him, with all the cookin' and cleanin', washin' his clothes, keepin' a warm fire burnin', and with all the lovin' in our marital bed. Still, it be no' enough. 'Twill never be enough to earn his love.

Tears fell from his eyes. Slowly, he shut the journal and returned it to her pouch. He knew then what he must do.

"Patches! Come!" he said as he leapt to his feet. He grabbed his cloak from the peg and bounded down the stairs, calling for his horse.

THE JOURNEY WAS NOT EASY, WHAT WITH BEING TOSSED ABOUT IN THE back of the cart like leeks in a sack. They had been gone from the keep for several hours. Leona doubted they had made much progress. At this rate, it would take a fortnight to make it to St. Agnes's convent.

They had stopped twice, once to answer nature's call and once to eat. Leona could not help but think back to when Alec had brought her here, after they had married.

She felt ill at heart, exhausted, and bereft. She wondered if she would ever feel whole again. 'Twas highly doubtful.

Rose, to her credit, had remained quiet for most of the day. She offered no false words of hope for a good and happy future. Leona was thankful for that.

They were making their way over a small hill, when the men following behind them turned their horses around. Something had drawn their attention. Ian ran past the cart and past the men.

"What is happenin'?" Leona asked Rose.

"I do no' ken," she answered.

Long moments passed before she heard Ian shouting. Then came a familiar voice.

"If ye do no' let me pass, I shall gut every one of ye!"

'Twas Alec!

She refused to let her heart run away with her mind. Nay, 'twas too much to hope for.

The horsemen soon parted, giving wide berth to Alec.

Och! He looked fit to be tied "Wife!" he called out to her from atop Ares.

Leona did not know what she should say or do. Rose gave her hand a gentle squeeze and whispered in her ear. "Pretend indifference," she advised.

Indifference? Nay that is no' possible, fer he looks ready to kill.

"Aye?" she managed to whimper.

"What are ye doin' in the back of that cart?" he asked, drawing nearer and nearer the cart.

"He's gone mad," she whispered to Rose. "He is goin' to kill me."

Rose giggled. "Nay lass, that is no' a man about to kill. That be a man in love."

"Wife! Have ye lost yer hearin'?"

Leona shook her head rapidly.

"I have changed me mind," he called to her as he inched his way toward the cart. "Ye can no' leave."

"I can't?" she asked with a shaking voice.

Rose jabbed her in the ribs. "Ye do no' ken it, but ye have the upper hand right now, Leona. If ye let him order ye about now, he will think he can order ye about all the rest of yer days."

Leona glanced at Rose and finally began to understand. If Alec Bowie wanted her, he was going to have to fight for her. Taking a deep breath, she mustered every ounce of courage left in her bones. "Ye will no' order me about, Alec Bowie. I be no' one of yer warriors!"

"Leona, come here," he said, still inching Ares closer and closer to the cart.

"I will no'!" she yelled back. "'Tis apparent ye do no' want me!"

"Och! But I do. I have no' had a decent meal in days. And me shirts need washin'. And I have a pair of trews that need mendin'. And a keep that needs cleanin'."

To say she was appalled would have been a tremendous under-statement of fact. Nay, she was livid. Furious!

She scooted to the edge of the cart. "Ye can go to the devil, Alec Bowie!" she shouted at him. "Ye are the most ungrateful, ignorant, low-born, bloody son-of-a-whore that ever graced God's earth! I would rather die than take ye back!"

His ploy was working. 'Twas the first time in far too long that he saw a spark of life in those beguiling eyes. And she was making her way to the front of the cart, right where he wanted her.

"Och! Do no' try to flatter me lass, fer it will no' work."

"Flatter ye? Ye think I am tryin' to flatter ye?" She asked, aghast at the notion. "Ye're daft!"

They were inches apart now, with Alec atop his steed and Leona on her knees, fighting mad.

"Daft?" he asked, as if he were giving a measure of thought to it. "I suppose I am."

She paused in mid insult, wholly surprised that he had agreed.

"I am daft. Hopelessly and forever daft. And it be all yer fault."

"My fault?" she asked.

"Aye, lass. I blame ye."

"Blame me fer what?"

"Fer comin' into me life and turnin' it upside down and sideways.

Fer showin' me what a good and happy home can be. Fer makin' me see what a man can have in his life."

Uncertainty and doubt reigned.

"Ye see, I came to a profound realization lately," he told her.

"Ye have?" she asked, by now, thoroughly confused.

"Aye. It seems I can no' live without ye."

She blinked twice and swallowed hard. "Ye can no'?"

He gave a slow shake of his head before flashing that smile she found so endearing. "I can no'," he said. "Fer I love ye far too much to ever let ye go."

Her heart all but leapt from her chest. "Ye do?" she asked, uncertain she had heard him correctly.

Alec pulled Ares closer, grabbed her about the waist and pulled her up to his lap. "Aye, I do. With every beat of me heart, I love ye more."

Tears fell and she cared not who saw them. She had no doubt that he meant the words he spoke so sweetly to her. "I love ye, too, Alec," she said as she laid her head against his chest.

Alec turned his horse around and headed toward their keep. Nay, their *home.*

"I be thinkin', mayhap we should draw up a new contract," Leona told her husband.

"And what will this new contract entail?" he dared ask.

"The same as the original, but with a few additions," she said as she rested her head against his chest again. "I should like to add that we will always be honest with one another. And when we are filled with grief and sorrow, no matter the cause, we will talk to each other, openly and without worry. No more turnin' away from one another, aye?"

He could live with that.

"I will also add that ye're never again to use yer sleeves to wipe yer mouth at me table. 'Tis disgustin'."

That, he could also live with.

"And whenever we are together and ye need to leave the room or the keep, ye shall bid me a polite goodbye with a kiss. No more just walkin' away."

Alec chuckled softly. "That should no' be a problem," he said before pressing a kiss to the top of her head.

"No matter who might be around us, ye shall kiss me and bid me a good day. I mean it."

"I will," he agreed once again.

"And for all the rest of our days, ye shall love me, and tell me so at least once a day. No matter if me hair turns gray and I get wrinkled."

"Lass, 'twill be me great honor and privilege to grow auld with ye. And aye, I shall tell ye every day how much I love ye." *But he would tell her at least a dozen times.*

Alec kept the horse at a slow pace, so as not to bother Leona's broken arm. Carefully, he wrapped his plaid around her, and hugged her gently.

"I love ye, Leona," he whispered as he lay his head against hers.

"And I love ye, Alec Bowie."

EPILOGUE

"Well, it be about time," Rose declared as she climbed down from the cart. She smiled, a bright smile as she watched her friend ride away.

Ian had pulled his horse alongside the cart. He'd seen and heard every word spoken between Leona and Alec. He cast a curious glance at his wife before pulling her up to ride with him. "What are ye goin' on about?" he asked. "Ye told me Alec Bowie was no better than a flea infested cur."

"Oh, that still holds true," she told him. "But he be *Leona's* flea infested cur. She loves him. And I knew he loved her."

"Ye never cease to amaze me," Ian said. "Ye knew he would come fer her?"

Rose smiled up at her husband. "Of course. He loves her. Though, I dare say I thought he'd no' let her more than a few hundred feet from the walls. Fer a little while, I thought we'd actually have to take her to St. Agnes's."

Ian gave the command to a handful of his men, to take the cart and Leona's belongings back to the Bowie keep.

"Pray tell me, how did ye ken he loved her?"

"Because he looks at Leona the same way ye look at me."

"With a bewildered and dumbfounded expression because ye vex me?" he asked playfully.

"Aye, that as well," she replied drolly.

They rode in silence for a long while before Rose spoke again. "Now that we have Leona married, settled, and hopelessly in love, what are we to do about Brogan?"

"Me brother?" he asked, his voice filled with surprise and just a touch of trepidation.

"Aye, yer brother."

Ian swallowed hard, trying to decide the best way to tell his wife she should not interfere where it pertained to Brogan.

"Well?" she asked when he'd been quiet for far too long.

"I be thinkin'!" he told her gruffly.

"Ye be thinkin' I should no' interfere," she told him.

He let out a frustrated breath.

"It has been four years now, since he lost his wife. Do ye no' think it be time he took another?"

"A wife fer Brogan?" he asked with the same level of surprise as before, but with far more than just a touch of trepidation. It bordered on horror.

"Aye, a wife fer Brogan. I do no' ken why ye sound so horrified by the idea. He be a good man. He should no' spend the whole of his life alone. He *needs* a wife. Ian, do no' roll yer eyes at me. I have no' lost me mind."

Brogan would beg to differ.

"Let me guess," Ian said. "Ye already have someone in mind."

Rose gave a shrug. "Mayhap I have, and mayhap I have no'."

Ian sighed once again. "I ken what that means. It means ye already have and ye're no' about to tell me yet because ye think I would disagree."

"Mayhap," she replied.

"Ye're no' goin' to tell me, are ye?"

Rose shook her head slowly. "Nay, nay I will no'."

"Why no'?" he exclaimed.

"Because ye will warn Brogan of me plan, and before I can do anythin' about it, he will be back at yer father's keep."

Ian knew 'twould do him no good to argue. He also knew 'twould do no good to warn Brogan. For it he knew his wife at all, she had already set her plan in motion.

He sent a silent prayer heavenward, on behalf of his brother.

God, help us all.

A SNEAK PEEK AT BROGAN'S PROMISE

PROLOGUE

*N*o one understood the depths of her grief. Despair and sorrow clung to her heart, weighing it down to the point Mairghread was no longer certain it even beat any more. Her soul was empty. Void of any good feelings. Only the pain, the sorrow and heartache remained.

Even now, three long years after the deaths of her husband and only child, the pain was as real and as intense as if it had only happened moments ago.

In order to help pass the time, until she could once again be reunited with them in heaven, she drank. Aye, there were many a late night when she contemplated taking her own life only in order to escape the deep suffering in her heart. The only thing that kept her from slicing through the tender flesh of her wrists, or wrapping a rope around her neck, or throwing herself off the parapet, was knowing if she acted on those thoughts, she would never see either of them again. God would not allow her entry to heaven.

As it stood, there was a good chance He would not allow her entry any way. Not if the rumors whispered behind her back were true. Not if what her Uncle hinted to but never really said was actually true.

There was a time when she would have demanded to know the

whole ugly, sordid truth of what truly happened that awful night when her world fell apart. Her memories were nothing more than fragments, hazy bits and pieces so tiny she could not put them all together to form a complete memory. She herself nearly died that night. Forced now, she was, to rely on what was told to her by her uncle, and her maids. And rarely did any of their stories match up.

So horrific was that night, so horrible was her loss, she took up the flagon not long after.

After countless nights of drinking to the point she could not have found her own hands with the help of guide and map, drinking was as common and natural as breathing. Now, after three long years of self abuse, she doubted she *could* breathe or think without the aid of drink.

She cared not anymore what people thought of her. Cared not a whit about the whispers behind her back. Cared not of anything or anyone.

Were it not for her maid, Gertie -- who had taken care of Mairghread from the day she came into this world -- 'twas highly unlikely the young woman would still be walking amongst the living. If one could even count Mairghread amongst the living.

Once, before that dark, pitiful night, Mairghread Mactavish had been a beautiful, vibrant woman who put the needs of her family and people ahead of her own. Aye, she had turned more than a few heads in her youth, what with her long, thick, auburn hair and dark, emerald green eyes. Mairghread was more than just a beautiful woman, however. She was a beautiful soul. The kind of giving, loving woman that the world definitely needed more of. Or so her maid Gertie would declare to anyone who would listen.

But now? Now, when Gertie would look upon her lady, she felt a profound sense of loss. Not just for the man and babe killed that dark day. Nay, they also lost Mairghread.

As far as Gertie was concerned, the world lost more than two souls that ugly day. They lost her sweet lady.

An empty a shell if ever there was one, was Mairghread Mactavish. And that was the saddest part of all.

BROGAN'S PROMISE CHAPTER ONE

*B*rogan Mackintosh was a sensible, logical thinking man. Whenever possible, he tried to see the good in people and all situations. It could also be said he was as honorable as he was generous. The kind of man who would give you the tunic off his back if you needed it. There was naught he wouldn't do for the down-trodden or poor creatures of this earth.

Never, in the whole of his adult life, did he ever regret being such a man.

Until now.

"Ye want me to do *what?*" He could not have been more surprised had the sun risen in the west that morn.

He sat at a long trestle table in the newly finished tower -- a tower he had helped build with his own two hands. Across from him sat his sister-by-law, Rose Mackintosh, and two auld women he had met less than a quarter of an hour ago. Rose was a pretty, wee woman, whom he had always admired, adored, and respected.

Until now.

"Ye act as if I just asked ye to kill the King," Rose replied.

To his way of thinking, the request was just as difficult, just as insane as killing the King. Nay, killing the King would have been easier.

He sat in dumbfounded silence as he tried to wrap his head around her entreaty.

"She be a fine woman, m'laird," the old woman named Gertie said. She was seventy if she was a day. A short, round woman, with light blue eyes and hair the color of the blade of his sword.

"I do no' doubt that she is," Brogan said.

He was cut off from saying more by the one named Tilda. The mirror image of Gertie, save for her dark blue eyes and missing upper teeth. "Ye will ne'er find a lass more beautiful." With the missing teeth, she had a very distinct lisp.

"Aye, as beautiful as the Highlands in springtime, I says," said Gertie as she looked at her friend.

"Aye, as beautiful as that. And kind! Och, m'laird, ye'll ne'er meet one as kind!"

"Or as givin'," added Gertie.

"Or as givin'," agreed Tilda, adding a nod of her silver-gray noggin.

At a loss for words, Brogan could only stare at the three women. Not a one of them understood the severity of their request.

Rose was studying him closely, undoubtedly looking for signs his resolve was waning. "Brogan, ye have been alone for far too long," she said. Her tone was soft and filled with warmth.

Brogan knew her intentions were sincere, born out of a sense of familial devotion. But really! Marriage? To a woman he'd never once laid eyes on? His brother Ian was right; while Rose was a bonny and kind woman, she was, betimes, a bit tetched.

"M'laird," Gertie said, drawing his attention away from Rose. "We ken we be askin' much of ye, me and Tilda. But we ask because we love our lady verra much."

"Aye, we do," Tilda agreed.

"If she be forced to marry that foul Frenchman, well, 'twill mean the end of our clan and the end of our lady," Gertie said. Her tone was forlorn, sorrowful and matched the sadness he saw in her eyes.

"Aye," Tilda said. "He beat his last wife to death, ye ken."

Gertie looked at her friend. "All because she gave him a daughter and no' a son."

"He be a bloody son-of-a-whore if e'er there was one," Tilda said.

Brogan had heard enough. "Certainly, there be someone in yer clan who would be willin' to marry yer lady."

Gertie and Tilda exchanged conspiratorial glances with Rose before Gertie responded. "Well, ye see, there might be a man or two willin' to do such ..."

He sensed a *but* coming.

"Ye see, she needs a strong man, m'laird," Tilda offered.

"Aye, a strong man," Gertie said.

"Are ye sayin' the men of yer clan are weak?"

Both women shook their heads, aghast at the notion. "Nay, m'laird!"

Brogan had had enough. Pushing away from the table, he glowered at Rose. "I shall have to politely decline," he said. Bowing to the three women, he bid them all a gruff fine good day, and quit the tower.

"Och!" cried Tilda. "Our poor lady! Now, she will be forced to marry the Frenchman!"

Gertie, the more devious minded of the two, looked at Rose.

"Nay, all be no' lost yet," Rose said with a smile.

"What do ye mean, m'lady?" Tilda asked.

Gertie gave her friend a warm, yet slightly devious, smile. "We need to introduce them."

ROSE KNEW HER HUSBAND HATED LEAVING THEIR KEEP – WHAT THERE was of it. 'Twas a work in progress with only one tower completely finished. The main keep, which would house a gathering room, a study for Ian, and fifteen bedchambers, was only partially built. This fine spring day, Ian and his men were working feverishly to finish enclosing the outside of their future home. If it were finished by winter, 'twould be a miracle.

Knowing her husband as she did – his penchant for working from dawn to dusk and his strong dislike of shopping – played to Rose's advantage this day. 'Twas less than a sennight since Brogan had *politely* refused to marry a woman desperately in need of a good, strong husband.

Knowing men as she did, she had to believe that Brogan was no different than all the rest. Physical desire could be a grand motivator.

Thus, when there was a mysterious and sudden need for flour and other sundries, which required an immediate trip to *Camhanaich* – a small village a few hours north and east of their lands. Ian all too happily volunteered his unwitting brother to go in his stead. Brogan had as much of a liking for shopping as his brother, which was to say, he detested it. But adoring his sister-by-law, and being the kind, generous man that he was, he agreed to act as her escort.

They took ten Mackintosh men with them, all well-trained and armed to the teeth. After the events of more than a year ago, when Rose had been kidnapped and held for ransom by Rutger Bowie – may he continue to burn in hell – Ian spared no expense for keeping the love of his life safe.

Brogan was completely oblivious, as most men were, and had not an inkling of what lay ahead for him.

They left before Brogan had a chance to break his fast, for Rose insisted they must get there before all the 'good flour' was gone. Brogan's knowledge of such things was nonexistent; therefore, he was forced to believe her.

With her son, John, a sweet boy of nearly one, in the good and capable hands of two Mackintosh women, they set off for *Camhanaich* just after dawn. Intentionally, she nearly talked Brogan's ears off on the two-hour journey west. 'Twas a purposeful ploy to frustrate and annoy so that by the time they reached the town, he would be all to eager to leave her to her shopping.

Unfortunately, being the honorable man that he was, he refused to leave her side. "If anythin' happened to ye, Ian would kill me."

Onto a different plan, she decided. She deliberately took her time, lingering at each merchant stall. Just enough to annoy her brother-by-law.

"Brogan," she said as she was shifting through fabrics at the wooler's stall, "I may be a while. If ye would like to go on ahead, mayhap get a meat pie? I be certain I shall be safe with the rest of Ian's guards," she said with a nod in their direction.

'Twas after noontime and Brogan had not eaten so much as a crumb of bread since last eve. Starved, tired of his sister-by-law's incessant chatting and need to look at every item at every stall – none of which had yet to contain an ounce of the desperately needed flour – he could not wait to be away from her. He gave a few quick instructions to the men before leaving Rose in their capable hands.

Rose smiled an all-knowing smile as she watched her brother-by-law all but run away.

∾

LORD, HOW HE HATED LARGE CROWDS.

Were he not so hungry, Brogan would have declined Rose's suggestion that he get himself something to eat. Instead, he would have politely insisted they hurry on with purchasing the 'good flour' and get back to their keep. He knew his pleas would fall on stubborn, deaf ears.

Making his way through the crowded street, he caught the scent of meat pies and freshly baked bread wafting in the air. His stomach growled and his mouth watered as he politely pushed his way through, motivated solely by hunger. With gratitude, he found the meat pie maker, made his purchase, and stepped away. The second pie was just as delicious as the first, both eaten in quick succession as he stood next to the stone wall of the ale house.

Though he was quite thirsty – the temptation to step inside and purchase just one ale quite strong – he knew he could not. *Just one* would lead to *a second will not hurt,* which in turn would lead him to drinking an entire barrel. He had fought too hard and too long three years ago to become the sober man he was today. After the death of his wife, he had fallen so far into the abyss of drunkenness he nearly died. Had it not been for his parents, more specifically his father, chances were he would be rotting in the earth at this very moment.

Now, he could have gone into the alehouse and purchased a cider. But experience taught him that a man of his size and stature going into an ale house and ordering cider, led to being taunted and ridiculed. The taunts and ridicule he could deal with. But eventually, and nearly always, someone would challenge his manhood or call him a coward. It never ended well for the drunkard. A brawl would always ensue. And Brogan, being the sober man he was, would always win.

So thirsty as he was, he decided to forgo entering. Instead he decided to take his time returning to Rose. She was probably *still* looking at silks and wools. 'Twould be hours before they left this awful place overrun with people.

He decided, instead, to walk along the street, alone with his thoughts. 'Twas not often he had time to himself, so busy they were with building the keep and ensuring the clan was safe. Mayhap, he would find a quiet spot, somewhere in this town, where he could sit and think without being interrupted. He had been here only once before, last autumn, and again, with Rose.

Rose.

She *was* a good woman, with a good heart. His brother Ian loved her with all that he was. There were times when Brogan envied him. Ian had everything Brogan had at one time wanted. A wife, a child, a loving home. But fate intervened and took his sweet wife before he even had time to get her with child.

God, how he had loved Anna. She was much like Rose in many respects. Good and generous she had been. Not a day had gone by that she had not made him laugh, usually over something innocuous, and betimes, off-color.

He knew Rose had only good intentions in her heart when she had suggested he marry the Mactavish woman. But four years ago, he swore he would never marry again – even though he had promised his sweet Anna he would. The pain he had endured at loosing Anna had nearly killed him. He refused to tempt fate a second time.

So he remained single. And alone.

Brogan refused even to seek the comfort of bar wenches or whores. Not because he did not have any physical needs or desires. On the contrary, he did have desires. However, he refused the comfort of women because he felt he would be dishonoring the memory of his wife.

Down the street he went, passing by one merchant stall after another. 'Twas a nice spring day, with the sun shining brightly and just enough of a breeze to help take away some of the more foul smells lingering in the street.

He was just passing by an alehouse, when someone stumbled and fell into him. Startled, he caught her before she could fall to the ground.

"Och!" she exclaimed as he was righting her onto her feet. "I be terribly sorry!"

'Tis odd, at times, how God works. Or mayhap 'twas fate, or the stars had aligned perfectly. No matter what had caused the woman to stumble into him, Brogan would never be the same man after. He just didn't know it yet.

She was one of the most magnificent women he'd ever laid eyes on. Gloriously rich, auburn hair hung in riotous waves across her shoulders. A perfectly oval face framed big, green eyes, the color of emeralds. Auburn lashes, a straight nose, and full, pink lips; God's teeth, she was beautiful. A long moment passed before he realized she had stolen his breath away.

Someone bumped into her again, causing her to let out a yelp of surprise and cling to him even tighter.

They stood, these two oblivious souls, staring into one another's eyes while the rest of the world passed by. Brogan found it next to impossible to tear his eyes away from hers.

Another bump against her back, jostled him out of his current state of awe. Had he not been as tall and strong as he was, they would both have fallen to the ground.

"Gertie!" the auburn haired woman exclaimed as she turned away from Brogan. "Stop that!"

Brogan blinked. His brow furrowed at the recognition of the name

Gertie.

"Sorry, m'lady," came the scratchy voice he recognized from a sennight ago. "It be awful crowded here today."

Brogan finally tore his eyes away from the stunning woman in his arms. Standing next to her, were Gertie and Tilda. Though they feigned innocence and refused to look at him, he knew better. Gertie was rocking back and forth on her heels, whistling as if she were as innocent as a newly born babe. Tilda was picking imaginary lint from her dark green shawl.

Stunned, he stood like a fool, looking at the old women and back to the woman he was still clinging to, and back again.

"Och!" Gertie finally exclaimed, as if she had only just now realized 'twas *he* who had saved her lady from falling flat on her face. "'Tis ye! How be ye this fine day, Brogan Mackintosh?"

His stunned expression evaporated in the blink of an eye as he replaced it with a cold, hard stare. A stare that would have sent a grown man to quaking in his boots.

"Och! Ye be right," Tilda exclaimed as if she were only now realizing who he was.

Brogan glowered at her as a tic began to form in his lower jaw.

"What a surprise it is to be seein' ye here today!" Tilda said with a wide, happy smile.

If he spoke a word now, he knew he would say something he might later – decades later – regret.

"Ye know him?" Mairghread asked, rather perplexed.

"We have met, aye," Gertie replied. "When he came to the keep last year to purchase horses."

She lied.

Right to her lady's face.

Mairghread turned her attention back to Brogan. "I fear I do no' remember ye," she said, her voice but a whisper and her eyes filled with something akin to regret. Brogan found her response odd, if not a bit intriguing.

I would have remembered ye, he thought to himself.

"Come along, m'lady," Gertie said as she pulled on Mairghread's arm. "We still need to purchase flour, remember?"

Brogan's jaw dropped. *Flour?*

Aye, he knew then he'd been set up to meet Mairghread Mactavish. And there wasn't a doubt in his mind that Rose was involved. Up to her pretty little neck!

FOR THE REMAINDER OF THE DAY, BROGAN REMAINED SILENT, REFUSING to speak to Rose. He met every one of her questions and all her chatting with a cold-as-ice glower and even colder silence. After some time, she realized she was going to get nowhere with her brother-by-law and gave up trying. Even the men who travelled with them could tell he was in a black mood. Unlike Rose, they left him alone.

'Twas nearing the evening meal by the time they returned to the keep. Not quite ready yet to give up his frustration, he saw to it that Rose and the other guards were well within the walls of the keep, then left. One of the warriors had the audacity to ask where Brogan was off to. His reply was nothing more than a clenched jaw and a near murderous glare.

He had no real destination in mind. He simply needed to be away and alone. 'Twas doubtful he would be able to make it through the evening meal without saying something to his sister-by-law that wouldn't injure her tender feelings. Even if it was well-deserved.

Though he'd already ridden his mount to *Comhanaich* and back, they hadn't ridden fast or hard. Still, he was never a man to be cruel to anything, least of all a horse. So he kept a slow, unhurried pace.

Brogan took his mount south of the keep, along the little stream that ran through their lands. It led him away from all the construction and daily chaos that was the Mackintosh and McLaren clan.

The further away he rode, the more at peace he began to feel. The sun still shone brightly against the pale blue sky. The spring grass danced in the cool breeze as birds flew noiselessly high above. The gentle sound of water rippling across stones and pebbles was just what he needed to calm his frayed nerves.

Then he thought of Mairghread.

The woman was beautiful. Damned beautiful.

He hadn't been so physically drawn to a woman since his sweet Anna had died.

But Mairghread? The moment he looked into those emerald green eyes, he felt an instant, visceral reaction. A need, a deep-seeded need to keep touching her, to press his lips against the tender flesh at her neck, and not stop. 'Twas as profound as a kick in his gut and nearly as painful.

Aye, Brogan had much to think about and he crossed the little stream.

What would his sweet Anna say to him? He shrugged for he already knew the answer. *"Do no' leave yerself alone in this world, Brogan Mackintosh. Do no' keep yer heart or yer life fer a dead woman."*

Those had been her exact words less than a sennight before she died.

That was four years ago.

Aye, he had promised her he would not mourn her all the rest of his days, but the promise had been a lie. Anna was everything good and right in his world. She was everything to him. Without her, he felt *less*. Less a man. Less alive. Less of everything.

Losing her had left a tremendous, yawning wound to the very marrow of his soul. Brogan started drinking the day she died and did not put the bottle down for more than a full year. No matter how much he drank, he could not rid himself of the pain and loneliness he felt at her loss.

A dull throb began to pulse at the base of his neck. He pulled his horse to a stop and dismounted. Stretching his arms wide, he turned his head from side to side, his bones cracking loudly with the motion.

"Ye be an auld man, ye fool," he said aloud. Only his horse had heard him. "Yer bones crack and groan far too much." The horse had no opinion. Instead, he chose to lower his head and nibble at the grass.

"So what am I to do?" he asked God as he looked up at the clear sky.

It appeared God was no more interested in having a discussion with him than his horse was. Puffing out his cheeks, he let out a quick breath and gave a tug on the reins. The horse snickered once before complying.

Together, they walked leisurely across the open field. His thoughts kept turning back to Mairghread Mactavish. Their meeting had lasted only a few moments, but 'twas still far too long to suit him. He blamed the three she-devils; Rose, Gertie, and Tilda.

Had they not interfered with this ridiculous notion that *he* of all people marry the fair Mairghread, he wouldn't be feeling as low as horse dung on the bottom of a poor man's boot. He would not now be wandering aimlessly along the countryside, tired and hungry and confused. Nor would he be struggling with thoughts and memories that were best left in the past.

But alas, they had. The she-devils.

"Even if Rose be right, and I am no' admittin' to anythin', it still be no' her place to interfere," he spoke to his horse as if he were an auld friend. "'Tis *my* life we be speakin' of, ye ken? No' hers."

Mayhap he *had* been living in the past for too long. Mayhap it *was* time to start thinking about his future. "It still does no' give her the right to do what she did," he said.

"Even if it be the right time, it should be left to me to decide who my bride should be, aye?"

The horse snickered once and gave a great shake of his head, as if to disagree.

"What do ye ken?" Brogan said dismissively.

Across the glen was a small thicket of trees. Brogan tossed the reins over the neck of his horse to allow the animal a little freedom to roam and graze. While the animal ignored him, Brogan picked a tree to lean against. Sliding down the trunk until he was seated comfortably on the grass, he stretched one long leg out and tossed his wrist over a raised knee.

He sat for a long while, struggling with his thoughts and feelings. 'Twas a heated debate betwixt heart and mind.

While he understood 'twas high time he left the past behind him, his heart was not quite as ready to give it up. His chest tightened when he thought of his sweet Anna. To this very day, it did not seem fair nor right that such a sweet, giving lass had died so young. As far as he was concerned, the world would have been much better off with a woman like her in it instead of a man such as he.

Or the kind of man he *had* been before he met Anna.

Nay, he was not the same man he had once been. Just as he was not the same after meeting her, after falling so hopelessly in love with her, he was also not the same since losing her. Some might believe a man incapable of change, but Brogan knew better.

Was he ready to move on? Was he ready to take another wife, to start a new life, mayhap be blessed with a bairn or two? Could he leave the memory of Anna behind and begin anew?

His heart ached still with missing her. He was not quite ready yet to let go. But now he was, at the very least, willing to *think* about it. 'Twas a step in the right direction.

BROGAN HAD SLEPT OUT OF DOORS UNDER A CANOPY OF SPARKLING stars with only his horse and his confused heart for company. Although he had come to the conclusion it might be time for him to move on with his life, he felt no better for it.

He walked his horse, rather than rode it, back to the keep, just after the break of dawn. Morning dew clung to everything around him. By the time he walked through the gate, his boots and trews were damp with it.

As was typical, everyone was already up and about. Several women were cooking over open fires whilst others were readying the long trestle tables inside the large gathering tent for the morning meal. He passed by a small group of men who were readying teams of horses to be used in the quarry. Other men were lined up to take bannocks and sausage with them, to eat as they headed either to fell trees in the forest or to work in the deep pits of the rock quarry. Children giggled happily as they chased one another around the encampment. All in all, 'twas as fine a morning as any.

So why did he feel such a strong sense of mourning?

He led his horse to the stables. The stable master, an older man named Ennis, volunteered to tend to his mount. Brogan politely declined his offer and tended to the animal himself.

He took his time rubbing the horse down, making sure he had plenty of food and water. He ignored his own growling belly to take the time to clean the bridle and bit. Aye, he knew he was delaying the inevitable, like a child finds every conceivable dawdle when it is time to bathe or sleep.

Finally, his need to eat outweighed his desire to avoid Rose and his brother, Ian. He rubbed the back of his neck with his hand, took a deep breath, and left the stables.

He let out a relieved breath when he did not see Ian or Rose about. With a thankful heart, he happily took a trencher of food from one of the cooks and headed into the large tent. The tent was used as the clan's gathering room, until the rest of the keep could be built. Upon entering, he quickly perused the tables. No sign of Rose or Ian, which induced him to sigh in relief once more.

Mayhap this eve, he told himself as he took a seat at one of the tables. Mayhap later, he would sit down with his brother and seek his good counsel. Purposefully, he sat in the darkest corner with his back to the entrance. He hadn't taken his first bite yet when Rose sat down beside him.

"Are ye through bein' angry with me?" she asked with a quirked brow.

"That depends," he answered drolly as he pulled off a hunk of brown bread. "Are ye done interferin' in me love life?" He popped the bread into his mouth.

Rose gave him a glance that said she thought him addlepated. "I do no' ken why ye were so upset."

He chewed and swallowed before answering. "Because my life is my own, Rose."

Anger flared behind her bright eyes as she stood up from the table. "Then ye best start livin' it, Brogan Mackintosh. Else ye'll wake up some day and find out ye're an auld man who is all alone in this world. And ye'll have no one to blame but yerself."

With grace reminiscent of a queen, Rose left Brogan alone to simmer and think.

FOR REASONS HE COULD NOT BEGIN TO UNDERSTAND, LET ALONE explain to anyone, Brogan became angry. Mayhap 'twas the fact he hadn't had a decent meal in two days. Mayhap 'twas because he had slept out of doors the night before.

Or mayhap, just mayhap, 'twas Rose's *I know what is best for you* attitude. Or, more likely than not, 'twas that she was right that he found so irksome. Either way, he pushed his trencher away, jumped to his feet and went in search of his sister-by-law.

He was fully prepared to give the woman a piece of his mind. *I will marry when I decide the time is right! I will choose me own wife, thank ye verra kindly!*

How on earth did his brother stand being married to such a meddlesome woman?

It took a bit of searching and asking around before he learned that Rose was in her cottage, tending to her son. He knocked once, rather harshly, upon the door. She had barely gotten out the words, "come in" before he shoved the door open.

He took only one step inside, seething mad. "'Tis *my* decision to make, Rose."

Pretending she hadn't a clue to what he was referring, she lifted one fine brow. "And what decision be that?" she asked before turning her attention back to her son.

Brogan growled deep in his throat. Aye, she was a meddlesome pain in his arse. But she was still his brother's wife. Without uttering a word, he turned around and slammed the door behind him.

He stood just a few steps away from the door, his frustration building. Later, with a good deal of hindsight, he would realize he should have walked away. But he didn't. Instead, he turned around and threw open the door again. "Ye may be me brother's wife, but that does no' give ye the right to interfere in my life, Rose."

He gave her no opportunity to respond. Once again, he spun around abruptly and slammed the door behind him.

'Twas all he could do to keep from yelling at the top of his lungs. His hands, clenched tightly into fists, fair shook with his anger. He thought back to the day before when he had first met Mairghread. Aye, she was a beautiful woman. But to have the three she-devils lie to his face and force a meeting betwixt them? Nay, 'twas as wrong a thing as any.

Once again, he spun around and went back into the cottage. Rose was now sitting in a chair by the fire, nursing her son. Brogan did not care about the impropriety. "Ye lied to me and ye lied to Ian. 'Twas deceit and trickery ye used to get me to meet Mairghread Mactavish! Did ye think I would take one look at her and change me mind?"

Rose rolled her eyes and gave him a look that suggested he was insane. "Would ye have agreed to a meetin' with her had I asked nicely?"

Realizing he was on the precipice of losing his temper completely, he left again.

Lingering outside the door of his brother's cottage, Brogan fumed. His sister-by-law was tetched. 'Twas the only plausible explanation. *"Would ye have agreed to a meetin' with her had I asked nicely?"* Of course he wouldn't have! But that did not make her actions right or just.

And what of Mairghread? He could not be married to a woman who would be party to such a scheme, no matter how beautiful he found her to be. Was she in on the deception? 'Twas a good question, he supposed. So he marched back into the cottage. "Did Mairghread know about yer game?" he asked. His tone was harsh, his words clipped.

"Nay, she did no'," Rose replied. Her tone and expression were such that he had to believe her.

Some of his anger began to ease away. There was, he reckoned, no use in being so bloody angry he could bite his own sword in two. He offered Rose a curt nod before leaving. This time, he didn't slam the door behind him, nor did he thunder away only to return a moment later.

What truly has ye so angry? He asked himself as he stood in front of the cottage. Mayhap the number of things that were angering him at the moment were too long to list. He hung his head, rested his fingertips on his hips and thought long and hard about his current situation.

What of Mairghread? If she did not know about the deception of yesterday, he had to wonder if she had any knowledge at all of the plans the three she-devils had in store for them. What if he *did* agree to such a union only to find out Mairghread had no interest in marrying him? What then?

If he conceded – and he was not quite ready yet to do so – and she turned him down, why the ramifications would be significant. Rose would not rest until she had him well and duly wed.

He blew out a heavy breath and went back into the cottage. Rose was still sitting in her chair, still nursing her babe. 'Twas in that moment he realized *this* was what he wanted. A home, a wife, and bairns. The realization left him breathless and feeling as though he'd just been kicked by a horse.

"Is Mairghread for or against this union?" he asked, grinding his teeth together.

Rose looked at him for a long moment. He could not help but wonder what nefarious deed she was plotting now.

After a long moment, she blew out a breath and said, "I do no' ken. But ye may ask her this night."

He could feel the anger burning in his neck. "What do ye mean?" he asked. His words were clipped, his tone low.

"She will be here later. Ian has invited several of our neighborin' clans to sup with us."

Brogan's gut tightened. "When were ye plannin' on tellin' me?"

Rose shrugged one shoulder. "Mayhap when I introduced ye to her when we sit down to sup."

He gave a long, slow shake of his head. "Ye are tetched," he whispered incredulously.

"I did no' tell ye because I was worried ye'd hie off. Ye can no' blame me."

I can no' blame ye? "Aye, I blame ye, Rose. I blame ye—"

Rose did not give him time to finish his tirade. Waving her hand at him dismissively, she said, "Aye, ye can blame me all ye wish, Brogan. I give up. I was wrong to think ye were ready to start livin' yer life again. I was wrong to think ye'd be willin' to save a young woman's life." She looked disgusted with him.

Certain he was that she was being over dramatic, he rolled his eyes. "Save her life?" he exclaimed. "From what, pray tell?"

"From having to marry Pierre Claude Courtemanche."

His eyes widened in horrified surprise as his heart seized. "The Frenchman."

ALSO BY SUZAN TISDALE

The Clan MacDougall Series

Laiden's Daughter

Findley's Lass

Wee William's Woman

McKenna's Honor

The Clan Graham Series

Rowan's Lady

Frederick's Queen

The Mackintoshes and McLarens Series

Ian's Rose

The Bowie Bride

Brogan's Promise - June 27, 2017

The Clan McDunnah Series

A Murmor of Providence

A Whisper of Fate

A Breath of Promise

Moirra's Heart SeriesThe Clan MacDougall Series

Laiden's Daughter

Findley's Lass

Wee William's Woman

McKenna's Honor

The Clan Graham Series

Rowan's Lady

Frederick's Queen

The Mackintoshes and McLarens Series

Ian's Rose

The Bowie Bride

Rodrick the Bold

Brogan's Promise

The Clan McDunnah Series

A Murmur of Providence

A Whisper of Fate

A Breath of Promise

Moirra's Heart Series

Stealing Moirra's Heart

Saving Moirra's Heart

Stand Alone Novels

Isle of the Blessed

Forever Her Champion

The Edge of Forever

Arriving in 2018:

Black Richard's Heart

The Brides of the Clan MacDougall

(A Sweet Series)

Aishlinn

Maggy (arriving 2018)

Nora (arriving 2018)

<u>Coming Soon:</u>

The MacAllens and Randalls

Stealing Moirra's Heart

Saving Moirra's Heart

<u>Stand Alone Novels</u>

<u>*Isle of the Blessed*</u>

<u>*Forever Her Champion*</u>

<u>*The Edge of Forever*</u>

<u>The Brides of the Clan MacDougall</u>

(A Sweet Series)

Aishlinn

Maggy (arriving 2017)

Nora (arriving 2017)

<u>Coming Soon:</u>

The MacAllens and Randalls

ABOUT THE AUTHOR

USA Today Bestselling Author, storyteller and cheeky wench, SUZAN TISDALE lives in the Midwest with her verra handsome carpenter husband. All but one of her children have left the nest. Her pets consist of dust bunnies and a dozen poodle-sized, backyard-dwelling groundhogs – all of which run as free and unrestrained as the voices in her head. And she doesn't own a single pair of yoga pants, much to the shock and horror of her fellow authors. She prefers to write in her pajamas.

Suzan writes Scottish historical romance/fiction, with honorable and perfectly imperfect heroes and strong, feisty heroines. And bad guys she kills off in delightfully wicked ways.

She published her first novel, Laiden's Daughter, in December, 2011, as a gift for her mother. That one book started a journey which has led to fifteen published titles, with two more being released in the spring of 2017. To date, she has sold more than 350,000 copies of her books around the world. They have been translated into four foreign languages (Italian, French, German, and Spanish.)

You will find her books in digital, paperback, and audiobook formats.

Stay up to date with Suzan's App for Readers! Available for iOS, Android, and other smart devices.

Apple Store
GooglePlay

www.suzantisdale.com
Email: suzan@suzantisdale.com
Tap any of the icons below to follow me at Facebook, BookBub, Instagram, Twitter, Goodreads, and Amazon.

FOLLOW SUZAN ON BOOK BUB

If you would like to receive alerts whenever I have an upcoming or new release, you can follow me on BookBub! It's also a great way to find out about deals on other books by other authors.

Book Bub is FREE and super easy to use.

If you'd like to follow me Just Tap Here.

85803198R00300

Made in the USA
Middletown, DE
27 August 2018